FOULSHOT

A FRANK RENZI CRIME THRILLER

"Why is gambling worse than any other method of acquiring money? True, out of a hundred persons, only one can win; yet what business is that of yours or of mine?" — Fyodor Dostoyevsky, *The Gambler*

"Gambling: The sure way of getting nothing from something."
– Gamblers Anonymous

SUSAN FLEET

Music & Mayhem Press

Foulshot is a work of fiction. All characters are the product of the author's imagination. Any resemblance to actual persons living or dead is entirely coincidental. Names of any public figures are used fictionally for dramatic purposes. Events that take place in actual locations are the products of the author's imagination.

Published by Music & Mayhem Press

ISBN-13   978-1-7321301-2-8

Front cover photograph: basketball and basketball hoop with metal support, courtesy of Marcel Schreiber on Unsplash

Back cover author photo by Pete Wolbrette

Praise for Susan Fleet's Frank Renzi crime thrillers

ABSOLUTION

Best Mystery-Suspense-Thriller of 2009 — Premier Book Awards
"Relentless tempo . . . sharp writing." — Kirkus Reviews
"Creole-flavored suspense." — Attleboro Sun Chronicle

DIVA

"Fleet subtitles *Diva* a novel of psychological suspense. That's an understatement. A killer thriller!" — Arts Journal
"Creepy villain, but I couldn't put it down. Fleet's stories are riveting. As soon as I finish one, I want to read the next!" – Amazon reader.

NATALIE'S REVENGE

Best Mystery-Thriller of 2014 – Feathered Quill Book Awards
"An amazingly great read! Fast paced and extremely challenging to put down." — Rebecca's Reads
"Frank Renzi has a new crime to solve. Natalie is a truly intelligent and seductive character." – Feathered Quill Book Reviews

JACKPOT

"Thrilling and gripping. Builds to a tense climax." — Readers' Favorite
"A serial killer murders lottery winners. How scary is that? Winning the lottery can kill you! I highly recommend to those who love the thrill of a twisted web of deceit." – Amazon reader

NATALIE'S ART

"Non-stop twists begin on page one. A fast-paced, action-packed read!"
– Feathered Quill Book Reviews
"Compelling characterization, unpredictable twists and a logical, yet surprising conclusion. That's fine art, indeed." — Midwest Book Reviews

MISSING

"Fleet opens with a bang. A fast-paced, hard-hitting emotional roller-coaster ride far above the usual whodunit." — Midwest Book Reviews
"[The] action never stops and the suspense is palpable." — Feathered Quill Book Reviews

NATALIE'S DILEMMA

"There is no better place to begin a suspense thriller than on the gritty streets of New Orleans with Homicide Detective Frank Renzi. You will not see the end coming." – Feathered Quill Book Reviews

"The gritty atmosphere comes vividly to life. An especially well-done story, and characters who face difficult choices, will delight fans of intrigue who seek ethical dilemmas in their crime read."– Midwest Book Reviews

SNIPER

"The Frank Renzi series is among the best in the crime fiction realm. Action at its finest, plot turns faster than the sniper's bullet. Fleet [is] a master at writing crime fiction." – Feathered Quill Book Reviews

"*Sniper* is delightfully unpredictable. A thriller that turns expectations upside down and weaves a far more sinister tale than that of a lone random sniper."

– Midwest Book Reviews

"A fast paced thriller strewn with international intrigue and a veritable gumbo of characters. It plays like a jazz combo trading eights in a dark sweaty French Quarter nightclub. Detective Frank Renzi races to see the big picture before it's too late." – Amazon reader

PAYBACK

"*Payback* is the perfect title for a story that takes the premise of "Payback" to a heightened level and then some. [From] New Orleans to Boston, Fleet nails each character, terrific scenes with that cheeky dialogue that is her signature style. Fleet is a master with her Frank Renzi series. With *Payback* she has hit it out of the park!" – Feathered Quill Book Reviews

"Mobster Brian Devlin, a man Renzi put in jail fifteen years ago, is out of prison and seeking revenge. He intends to destroy everything Renzi holds dear. But Renzi is capable of exacting his own payback. A hard to put down thriller, riveting to its unpredictable conclusion." – Midwest Book Reviews

"The story begins in New Orleans with the spray of gunfire and the senseless death of a ten year old boy—the unintended victim of a gangbanger drive-by. A harbinger of fateful events about to befall Detective Frank Renzi. Loyalty and betrayal are prominent themes as Renzi faces the challenge of his life."

– Amazon reader

Dedicated to my son and daughter
Jim and Deb
Always there when I need them.

CHAPTER 1

FRIDAY OCTOBER 10, 2014 – 1:15 PM – New Orleans

Jittery as a junkie waiting for a fix, Richie focused on one of the big-screen TVs above the High Roller Club bar. Two men were sitting in the booth with him. Benny, his best friend from Atlantic City, and the Macaroni Man, a guy some people feared more than death.

Ignoring them, he watched the highlights from last night's game, the San Antonio Spurs playing the Lakers in Los Angeles.

He wished he was there. Anyplace but here.

Last week, Jackie had dropped a bomb on him. Screaming at him, saying she knew he was having an affair and he spent all his money on his fucking girlfriend, barely gave her enough to buy groceries. She didn't know his bank account had hit bottom. As if that wasn't enough to worry about, three days ago Benny had called, saying the feds had questioned him.

Nudging his arm now, Benny said, "Did you see Kobe stuff that breakaway layup?"

Faking enthusiasm, he said, "Fantastic move! He's a great player."

"The Lakers might make the playoffs this year," Benny said, running his mouth as usual.

On their table The Daily Double Appetizer featured a platter of fried oysters and pink jumbo shrimp piled on a bed of ice. But Benny—his overweight out-of-shape friend—wasn't eating any. Why not?

He conjured various scenarios, none of them good.

The smell of fried oysters made him want to puke. So did the Macaroni man, sitting across the table, stuffing shrimp down his gullet. Staring at him, his dark predatory eyes flat and expressionless.

Richie wiped sweaty hands on his pants. He suspected Benny hadn't told him everything on the phone. That's why they were here. To talk privately. But the Macaroni Man had jumped them in the foyer, smiling at him like they were buddies. Bullshit.

Benny gestured at the TV screens. "Who do you like this weekend, Richie?"

To compose his answer, he took a long swallow of beer. "My wife. I'm not working this weekend so we're taking the kids to Disney World."

Like hell they were. He and Jackie were going nowhere this weekend. He'd be lucky if she let him take the kids to the French Quarter for beignets and hot chocolate.

"That's nice, Richie, but there's a lotta games this weekend—"

"Benny," the Macaroni man said sharply. "You talk too much."

Dead silence. Silence riddled with tension like the last minute of a crucial NBA game. Tempers flare, two sweaty bruisers go at each other, the benches clear and there's a brawl.

Raucous laughter erupted in the booth beyond them, a well-dressed young couple with plenty of bucks, not a care in the world, no worries this Friday afternoon. Unlike Richie.

He glanced at Benny who wouldn't look at him, gazing at the fried oysters but not eating any.

The Macaroni man put down his fork and iced him with a look. "We got a shitload of Snickers in the warehouse. Our friends wanna know where to send them."

Our friends. Rickie clenched his hands in his lap. *It all seemed so easy at first.* Too bad he couldn't rewind the tape like they did with a flagrant foul. Turn back the clock to the days when he and Jackie were madly in love, happy young newly-weds with their whole lives ahead of them.

He heard a disturbance up front near the door. Someone trying to crash the gate maybe. That happened a lot here. The High Roller was a members-only club.

Then he saw a man in a running suit stride down the aisle between the booths and the bar, like he knew exactly where he was going. And what he'd do when he got there.

Three booths away but closing fast, a black-and-gold Saints cap tugged down to hide his face. Richie felt a sudden flash of fear.

"I gotta hit the men's room," he said.

The man raised his right arm.

Jesus, he had a gun. His heart pounded, a frenzy of terror.

Beside him, Benny uttered a low moan. He'd seen the gun too.

Desperate to save himself, Richie leaned sideways, trying to get out of the booth. But it was too late. Pain stabbed his forehead like a bolt of lightning.

Another *pop*, his chest pulsing with agony.

He tried to get his breath. Opened his mouth, gasping for air. An acrid smell burned his nose, like smoke from a raging wildfire.

Screams erupted, then silence, like someone had muted the TV.

His eyes closed and blackness engulfed him.

No! He had to keep his eyes open or he would die.

But he couldn't. His body went into spasms and blackness descended.

His last conscious thought: *Would Jackie find the note he'd left for her?*

———

Buzzed on adrenaline, Homicide Detective Frank Renzi parked his unmarked Dodge behind the NOPD cruisers scattered along the street. Fifteen minutes ago a deluge of calls had swamped the 9-11 emergency line, agitated voices screaming about a man shooting people inside the High Roller Club.

Twenty years as a homicide detective, Frank had investigated countless murders, deadly stalkings and bloody domestic disputes, but never a mass shooting.

Patrol officers had already secured the scene. Now several of them kept out the looky-loos, drawn like flies to horrendous crimes. Others stood outside yellow police tape stretched across an alley. Any minute now the media would arrive, swarms of reporters, shouting questions.

He slung a canvas bag over his shoulder that held his crime scene kit: latex gloves, plastic booties, and paper evidence bags. His friend Tony Coppola stood outside the front entrance, an older cop who'd helped him with a few cases. They were the same height, six-one, but Tony outweighed him by thirty pounds. In his mid-fifties, Tony was hip to the fallout from high-profile murders.

"Hey Tony, what have we got?"

"What we got is a bloodbath," Tony said. "Three dead guys in a booth. Bad-da-bing. Looks like those pictures of old time Mafia hits in New York. Plus a couple of workers who got in the way."

Tony was a walking encyclopedia of Mafia lore, owned a slew of books and films about them. His grandparents had come to America from northern Italy. Frank's paternal grandparents had arrived from Sicily. He had inherited his volatile temper from his Irish grandmother.

"The shooter's in the kitchen," Tony said. "Two workers grabbed him, you believe it?"

Frank shrugged. "Hey, good for us, bad for him."

"After we cleared the joint, the EMTs went in to check for signs of life, got nothing other than the owner, hiding in his office. A patrol cop is holding him there to make sure he don't split."

"I better get inside before anyone else shows up." He wanted to view the scene before the coroner and the crime scene techs cluttered it with evidence markers and fingerprint powder.

"I hear ya," Tony said. "Better hurry though. The coroner's on his way."

Frank pulled plastic booties over his shoes and stepped into the foyer. A husky black man lay on the floor, a Taser clipped to his belt, shot dead before he had time to use it. Bloody shoe prints dotted the tile floor, the first officers on the scene charging inside, not knowing what they'd find.

He'd been to the High Roller Club before, a private club with a hefty initiation fee and monthly dues. Most of the members were well-heeled sports fans. Or compulsive gamblers.

Beyond the foyer, the main room was a wreck. Overturned chairs, broken wineglasses, smashed plates, glass everywhere. Along the left wall, a dozen stools lined a well-stocked bar. On the right, a line of booths extended toward the back. All vacant, except the one nearest the kitchen.

The room was eerily silent. Muted television screens above the bar continued to show various horse races and highlights of NBA games, casting garish light over the chaos.

Frank strode past booths with half-eaten food, beer bottles and women's handbags. He stopped at the last booth and studied the victims. Three deceased white males, two on the left side of the booth, facing the foyer, a third on the opposite side. Topped with a white tablecloth, the table held platters of appetizers, beer bottles, soiled plates and silverware. And copious splatters of blood.

The two men nearest the wall had slumped over the table. The one on the left had been shot once in the forehead. A well-placed killshot. The other man's head faced the wall, no telling where he'd been shot, blood pooling under his torso.

The body of the man seated on the aisle was half out of the booth, his head and his right arm dangling, dripping blood on the carpet.

Two killshots. One in the forehead, another in the chest.

Did he know the shooter? Did he see him coming? Or did he spot the gun as the shooter approached the booth and try to escape?

Beyond the booth, a waitress lay on the floor, her metal serving tray two feet away. He imagined her standing there, paralyzed with fear as the gunman approached. The killer had shot her in the chest. Because she was in the way? Or because she might be able to ID him?

A cold act by a callous killer. But when he tried to escape through the kitchen, two workers had captured him and held him until police arrived. Patrol officers were guarding him in the kitchen.

Frank checked the ceiling and upper corners of the room. Security video from inside the club would be helpful to the investigation. Unfortunately, he saw no cameras. But it wasn't hard to figure out what happened.

The shooter had entered through the front door, shot the doorman in the foyer and passed up other targets to shoot the men in the last booth. This was no random spree-kill by a crazed gunman. This was a planned hit.

To send a message to someone? Maybe, but who?

And why these three men in particular? The answer would likely depend on who they were. And who wanted them dead.

In any homicide investigation, the first forty-eight hours were crucial. He wanted to interview the victims' families, friends and co-workers. But victims don't wear name tags. NOPD protocol said he should wait for the coroner and let him identify the victims, likely from their driver's licenses.

But that might take hours and this was no ordinary shooting. Five people massacred in a club near the French Quarter, this was a shitstorm waiting to happen. Hyped by the media, the case would bring heavy duty pressure from politicians and the NOPD top brass.

He took out his Smart phone, stepped back and snapped a photo of the three men in the booth, pulled on latex gloves and studied the man leaning out of the booth. His sports jacket had fallen open and Frank could see something in the inside pocket. Careful not to disturb the body, he eased his fingers into the pocket and pulled out a leather wallet. Inside he found a driver's license.

Richard Bauer. The name didn't ring a bell. Age forty-nine, according to his DOB. Bauer lived in Ponchatoula, north of the lake, no way to tell if he was married or not.

Frank sidestepped to the adjacent booth, put the DL on the table and took a closeup of it. He took a paper evidence bag from his crime kit, dropped in the wallet and the DL and sealed it.

Conscious of the passing minutes, he returned to the murder booth.

The vic beside Bauer had on a sweatshirt, no pockets visible, but below the table, one pocket of his trousers had gaped open. Frank planted his gloved right hand on the table and leaned forward, sickened by the coppery odor of blood and fried oysters. Extending his left hand, he stuck his fingers in the pocket and pulled out a black billfold. Thumbed out a New Jersey driver's license.

Benny Green lived in Atlantic City, no telling who he was or why he was here. And no time to waste. He set the DL on the adjacent table, took a closeup and sealed the DL and the wallet inside another evidence bag.

Any attempt to identify the third victim would disrupt the body, which Frank didn't want to do. He had a good working relationship with the coroner and he wanted to keep it that way.

Besides, he wanted to talk to the shooter.

CHAPTER 2

FRIDAY OCTOBER 10, 2014 – 2:20 PM

Frank pushed through the double doors and hot air hit him like a bomb. The kitchen stank of cooking oil, onions and fried fish. Directly ahead of him, beyond a metal prep table strewn with chopped onions, two Asian men in muscle T-shirts stood near a patrol cop.

The men who'd captured the shooter, Frank presumed.

Far off to his right, orange evidence markers sat beside a snub-nosed revolver and a Saint's ball cap. Twenty yards beyond them, an open door led to an alley. The shooter's likely escape route.

Along the right-hand wall between the alley and the prep table, two uniforms guarded a man in shackles. The man who'd just murdered five people didn't look like a hired gun, five-foot-nine or so, weighed 150 tops.

It wasn't hard to imagine the workers taking him down. Except for the fact that he had a gun.

Captain Zeke Harris, a heavy-set black man with receding gray hair, approached him. The District-8 patrol supervisor went by the book, clean shaven, wearing his dress uniform. No flies on Zeke. When he went outside, the TV cameras would zoom in and reporters would shout his name, asking for a comment. Viewers at home would see him and so would the NOPD top brass.

Frank had on his usual work outfit, a sports jacket and slacks, not that this would let him avoid the media. All the local reporters knew him.

"Glad to see you," Zeke said. "I stayed with the shooter till you got here."

"Thanks, I appreciate it. You get anything?"

"Won't say boo. No ID on him. I had a medic check him out, read him his Miranda rights." Zeke leaned closer. "Had my guys hold the owner in his office, too. He's a snake, that one. You talk to him yet?"

"No, but I will."

Zeke gestured at the Asian workers. "The muscle guys are his sons. We left the weapon on the floor, didn't touch it. A peashooter .22."

"Get close enough, a .22 can put anyone down."

"You got that right, but you might not get any prints. The guy wore gloves. I better go outside and calm the public. By now the reporters are probably saying he's Charles Manson, got a posse of shooters with him."

Frank laughed. "Go get 'em, Zeke. Take the heat off me."

Zeke rumbled a laugh. "Talk to the shooter, Frank. Be nice if you got a signed confession. The Super wants to do a press conference before the early news. "

Frank approached the killer, leaning against the wall with his eyes closed. He motioned to the older patrol cop and they stepped away from the shooter.

"Did he say anything when you got here?" Frank asked.

"Not a word. We searched him, nothing in his pockets, so we cuffed him and stood him up against the wall. The men that caught him said they whacked his arm with a cutting board to make him drop the gun. But even then he didn't say anything, not a peep."

"Okay, thanks." He returned to the shooter. A gaunt face, shaggy black hair drooping over his forehead. Up close, he looked young, mid-twenties, olive complexion, clean shaven but for the dark stubble on his chin and upper lip.

Frank squeezed his shoulder and the man's eyes opened.

"I'm NOPD Homicide Detective Frank Renzi. What's your name?"

Got back a dead stare.

"We'll get it sooner or later. Better you tell me now. Otherwise we take you to the station, print you, take a mugshot and book you for murder as John Doe."

The shooter said nothing, staring at the floor.

Frank had seen plenty of foreigners pass through New Orleans: Asian, Hispanic, European, Russian. The shooter had a Slavic look about him, sharp cheekbones, angular features. "You speak English?"

A flicker of interest in his eyes. Still, he said nothing.

Frank fought down his irritation. Play good cop, maybe he'd get something.

"You just killed five people so you're looking at Murder-One. I can help you. Maybe someone made you do it. Maybe that someone warned you not to talk if you got caught. Is that it?"

The man stared at the floor, mute.

This was a waste of time. And time was precious. The coroner would be here any minute and he wanted to talk to Johnny Wu first. He'd grill the shooter later. He told the patrol cops to take him to the station. "One sits in back with him so he doesn't do anything stupid, the other drives."

"What about the workers?"

"We know where they live. Tell them we'll take their statements later. I need to talk to their father." Jian Wu, boss of the New Orleans branch of the TRG triad, a Chinese tong known for loan sharking, drug trafficking and illegal betting operations.

He left the kitchen and his cellphone buzzed. He checked the ID. His long-time partner, Homicide Detective Kenyon Miller. "Kenyon, where y'at?"

In a deep rumbling bass, Kenyon said, "Just left the courthouse on the West Bank. Been out of the loop, you know, testifying on that double murder last year. Come out the courtroom, turn on my phone and get all kinds of messages about a massacre. Whadda we got?"

"A bloodbath at the High Roller Club, five dead. I'm about to talk to the owner."

Kenyon chuckled. "Our favorite Chinese gangster, Johnny Wu?"

"Exactly and I've gotta hurry. The coroner's not here yet and I need to talk to him, too. We got the shooter."

"Great! Who is he?"

"I got no clue. He's not talking. Meet me at the station and we'll grill him."

"Okay, Frank. Be there as soon as I can."

He put away his phone and hurried to the foyer. Beyond the blood-spattered foyer, a female officer stood outside a door. "The owner's inside," she said. "Not happy about it."

"Lots of people not happy today," Frank said. "Five of them will never be happy again."

The woman nodded, her eyes somber. "Family and friends be in a world of hurt tomorrow."

When Frank entered the office, Johnny Wu sat at his desk. Sixty-two years old, jet black hair, large black eyes and a blank expression. "Detective Renzi," Wu said. "What can I do for you?"

"Got a few questions for you." Many questions, but he'd prioritized them. Softballs first, fastballs later. "Are there security cameras in the club?"

"No. Members not want cameras in club. They come, bring guest here, maybe not want someone else to see."

"Like who?"

"Like wife, maybe. Come here to relax, have good time, eat tasty food, watch sports on TV."

Frank figured Wu was right. Certain clientele, big money types and well-known celebrities didn't want their pictures showing up on social media.

"Do they bet on games?"

Feigning shock, Wu spread his hands, his eyes wide. "Not here, no."

Frank didn't believe it, but let it go. "Two of your workers are dead. I need ID for them."

Wu spun his chair, opened a file cabinet and pawed through some papers. Pulled out a slip of paper. Pawed through more papers, pulled out another slip of paper and handed them to Frank.

He studied the IDs: Michelle Rodgers, the waitress, and Ernest Jackson, the doorman.

"You need me make copies?"

"No." Frank set the papers on the desk and took photos of them.

"Very sad they die," Wu said. But he didn't look sad. Expressionless, he said, "How long you cops be here?"

"As long as it takes to process the scene. Why?"

14

"Big mess in there. Must clean up broken glass. Put new carpet, clean walls and paint. Lose business for days."

Frank said nothing, thinking: Five people dead in your club, two of your workers and three customers, and you're worried about losing business?

"We need to know who came in here today, what time they came in and what time they left. How soon can you give us that information?"

Wu frowned. "Not normal to give this information—"

"Nothing is normal today," he snapped. "The people who were here when it happened are witnesses. You want me to get a search warrant from a judge, I will."

"No, no. Not necessary. I will access computer records and print out for you."

"Good. Have it by four o'clock. I'll have a patrol officer bring it to me."

Frank left the office just as the coroner stepped into the foyer. An older man in a baggy brown suit, Dr. Albert DeMayo carried a worn leather satchel with his tools. "Hi, Frank. The mayhem never ends, does it?"

"Not these days. I'm hoping you can help me out, Doctor DeMayo. I just got IDs for the two deceased employees from the owner. But I need to identify the other three victims."

"Sure thing. I'll take a look at them first."

When they got to the booth, DeMayo ssaid, "Ugly, but I've seen worse."

Frank pulled two evidence bags out of his canvas bag. "I hope you don't mind, but I was in a hurry to ID the victims. Didn't touch anything and managed to get two IDs, but ..." He gestured at the third man. "I didn't want to disturb the body. Could you get it for me? We need to notify the next of kin. By now this is all over the local news and people are probably worrying ...."

That wasn't the main reason he wanted the ID. The sooner he knew who the men in the booth were, the sooner he could get to work on solving the case.

Dr. DeMayo rolled his lips together, frowning now. "Well, I probably shouldn't. Let me take some pictures first." He took a Rolex camera out of his satchel and snapped several photos, wide angle shots, then closeups. Then he set the Rolex on top of his satchel, put on latex gloves and eased the third man over so he was facing them.

"One shot to the forehead," DeMayo said.

"Just like the other two victims." Frank said.

"There may be other wounds. I won't know until I get them to the morgue."

DeMayo took several more photos, medium shots and closeups.

Frank waited, silently cursing, wishing he'd hurry up, the minutes trickling by like the drip drip drip of a leaky faucet.

Finally DeMayo opened the man's jacket and searched the inside pockets. No wallet, no papers. DeMayo eased the man back against the wall and searched the pocket of his pants.

With a satisfied grunt, DeMayo pulled out a wallet and opened it. "Got a New Jersey DL. Dominic Marconi. Wonder what he was doing here."

"That's what we need to find out. Mind if I take a photo of it?"

"Not at all, go ahead."

He took a closeup and returned the DL. "Thanks a million, Doctor DeMayo. I really appreciate it."

"Glad I could help, Frank. Big club like this, busy at lunchtime, it's a wonder more people didn't die."

He nodded noncommittally. Three dead men in a booth, shot once in the forehead. Three killshots screaming a message, loud and clear.

This was a targeted hit.

But who paid the shooter? And why?

CHAPTER 3

Hunched over the table, he flexed his fingers, his wrists cuffed to a metal ring in the table. His cheek throbbed where they'd hit him, but what did it matter? His life was over.

Last night his employer had taken him for a ride and told him what would happen if he failed. "I'm paying you a lot of money. If you don't do your job, I'll find someone and pay him to kill you. Understand?"

Knowing how easily this could happen, he said, "I understand."

"Good. So do your job, collect the rest of your money and go home and have a happy life."

But he was not going to have a happy life. Never again would he see Katerina. His beautiful young bride did not know how he earned the money to wine and dine her at expensive restaurants and buy her fancy clothes.

He had no desire to kill those people. It was just a job. But he had failed. Never before had this happened. But never before had he killed five people on one job.

Seeking the cause of his failure, he reviewed what he had done.

Nursing a cup of coffee, he'd sat outside a coffee shop across from the club. No one paid him any attention. He was just a man in a black running suit and a Saint's ball cap, enjoying the mild weather. His employer had given him a photograph of the target and a diagram showing his escape route through the kitchen. His employer would be waiting outside to drive him away.

But things had not gone according to plan.

After he saw the target enter the club, he waited five minutes before he approached the entrance to make sure no one else was about to enter. When he pushed through the door, his weapon pressed against his thigh, a black man in the foyer asked for identification.

He set the gun barrel against the man's chest and fired. The man fell to the floor. The shot had been muffled somewhat, but there was no time to waste. He strode down the aisle between the bar and the line of booths to his right, seeking his target.

Thirty seconds later, he found him. But there were three men in the booth. He fired a shot into the target's forehead, another into his chest and shot the man beside him in the forehead. The fat man seated across the table screamed and raised his hands. He shot him in the head. But this cost him precious time.

When he ran toward the kitchen, a woman came through the door holding a metal serving tray. She saw the gun and screamed. He shot her and plunged through the door into the kitchen, seeking the exit door that would take him outside. A worker saw him and ran toward an open door off to his right. He fired at the man and missed. A fatal mistake.

He should have made sure no one else was in the kitchen. He ran toward the open door, but someone grabbed him from behind. Then something slammed his right arm. Excruciating pain shot up his arm and he dropped his weapon.

An assassin's worst nightmare. Never surrender your weapon.

He lashed out at his attackers, but they were too strong, punching him in the face, vicious blows that forced him to the floor. He curled up in a ball, trying to protect his head with his arms.

Shouting in some foreign language, they bound his wrists and ankles. Knowing it was useless to fight, he lay on the floor without speaking. Then two men in uniforms came into the kitchen, handcuffed him, slammed him against a wall and questioned him.

Resigned to his fate, he said nothing. Smelling the sweat-stink of his shirt. Imagining the tortures that awaited him. After a while, another man questioned him. No uniform, but he knew a cop when he saw one. And knew enough to keep his mouth shut.

Then the men in uniforms had driven him to a large building, marched him downstairs and locked him inside this room with no windows. He knew what that meant. Soon they would interrogate him. Beat him if he did not tell them what they wanted to know. He had memorized the number his employer had given him. The number to call if anything went wrong.

Things had gone terribly wrong, but he had not reached the age of twenty-three in his profession without understanding certain rules.

So. Should he call his employer or would he be safer in prison?

———

2:50 PM

Seated at his desk in the District 8 homicide office, Frank studied the photos he'd taken of the two Atlantic City DLs. Benny Green and Dominic Marconi. Most people think of Atlantic City, they picture flashy casinos, scantily-clad waitresses and slot machines. Cops picture mobsters.

The door opened and Kenyon Miller burst into the office, removing his jacket as he barreled toward Frank. It never ceased to amaze him that a six-foot-six guy who weighed 240 pounds could move that fast, quick and agile as an NFL linebacker. Not that Kenyon had played in the NFL, but he'd been a standout linebacker at Louisiana State University.

Kenyon leaned against the desk opposite Frank's and said, "Man, it took me forever to get across the bridge. Tuned in a local radio station and caught Zeke's statement. Five dead in the High Roller Club, but the shooter's in custody, no other suspects."

"Gotta calm the public. All kinds of rumors floating around thanks to the media."

"Zeke said the Superintendent would do a press conference this afternoon."

"Six o'clock last I heard. Vobitch wants a meeting at four-thirty." Lieutenant Detective Morgan Vobitch supervised the homicide detectives in Districts One, Five and Eight.

"How's he taking it? About to have a meltdown?"

Frank grinned. "The usual F-bombs, but no meltdown. In fact, he seemed energized, like he can't wait to tackle it. I got DLs for the men in the booth. One lives in Ponchatoula, the other two live in Atlantic City, New Jersey. Vobitch said he'd call and ask the locals to do the notifications. Richard Bauer lives in Ponchatoula."

"Name doesn't ring a bell."

"Second one's Benny Green."

A mischievous look appeared in Kenyon's dark eyes. "Who's on third?"

Frank burst out laughing, a welcome relief after the ugly scene at the club, enjoying Kenyon's droll sense of humor, another reason he loved the guy.

Going with the Abbott and Costello routine, he said, "I don't know."

Kenyon grinned and drew a one in the air with his finger.

"Name like Dominic Marconi, I'm thinking mob connection," Frank said. "I asked Vobitch for more detectives. We're already shorthanded." David Lee had taken a leave of absence. His mother was undergoing cancer treatments at a Boston hospital. David and his girlfriend, a graduate student at MIT, were helping her.

"He's putting Orville on the case," Frank said. "And Kelly."

"Mmm, mmm, mmm," Kenyon said. "The romantic duo rides again."

Jiving him about Kelly, his best friend and lover for the past five years. Not living together but he saw her at least twice a week. Kelly worked Domestic Violence now, but two years ago she had temporarily re-joined the D-8 Homicide Unit to help with a sniper case.

"Hey," Frank said, "Kelly's great at interviewing witnesses and possible suspects."

"Right," Kenyon said. "Unlike a certain guy I know who'd rather beat the crap out of 'em."

"Not today. Better tape the interview. Hot potato case like this, we gotta do it by the book."

19

"Tell me about the shooter," Kenyon said.

"Actually, I'd rather wait. I want to get your take on him first."

Ten minutes later they entered the interview room. The shooter raised his head, his expression bleak, gazing at them with sad eyes.

Frank felt no sympathy for him. The shooter wasn't sorry about killing five people. He was sorry he got caught.

A video camera in the ceiling was rolling. Later, Frank would study the man's body language and facial expressions, which often revealed more than a suspect's words.

He sat down opposite him, placed an audiotape recorder on the table and said, "Just to let you know, we're taping this." He pressed a button, announced the date and time, stated which officers were present, and identified the subject as John Doe, the man captured inside the High Roller Club who had refused to identify himself.

"What's your name, sir?"

The man looked at him and said nothing.

"This would go easier if you identify yourself," Kenyon said. "Otherwise we take you to the lockup and put you in a cell."

Silence in the room.

"You understand English?" Frank asked. Got back a nod.

He tapped the tape recorder. "We need you to speak into the recorder. Do you understand English?"

"Yaz."

"Murder's a capital crime in Louisiana," Kenyon said. "You could get the death penalty."

A flash of fear registered in the shooter's eyes, but he said nothing.

Frank took out his Miranda card and read him the warning. "You have the right to remain silent. Anything you say can and will be used against you in court. You have the right not to incriminate yourself. You have the right to the assistance of a lawyer, and if you cannot afford one, a lawyer will be appointed by the court to represent you without cost to you."

The shooter held his left hand to his head, fingers curled, the universal signal for a phone call.

"You want to make a phone call?" Frank asked.

"Yaz."

He turned to Kenyon, nodded at the door and announced for the recorders, "Interview paused at 3:19 PM while Detectives Renzi and Miller confer outside the room."

They went out in the hall and shut the door.

"Man," Kenyon said, "this guy's weird. Won't even give his name?"

"I'm not sure how much English he understands. He look foreign to you?"

"Not your average American boy next door, that's for sure."

"Maybe we can bargain with him. Tell him he can make a call if he gives us something."

Kenyon mopped beads of perspiration from his dark-skinned shaven pate. "Worth a shot, but I'm not gonna beg and say pretty please."

They went back in the room. Without starting the recorders, Frank said, "If you want to make a phone call, you need to give us something. Tell us your name and where you live."

"OK," the shooter said.

Frank turned on the recorders. "Please tell us your name, sir."

"Hans Nader. Come here from Mlll-wakee."

"Milwaukee?" Frank said. "Milwaukee, Wisconsin?"

"Yaz."

"How did you get here? Take a plane? A train? Drive a car?"

"Drive car."

"Where are you staying?" Kenyon asked.

"Garden Hotel."

"What's the address?"

The man shrugged and shook his head.

"Mr. Nader indicates he doesn't know the address. When did you get here?"

The shooter held up three fingers.

"Three days ago?"

"Yaz."

"Who did you talk to after you got here?" Frank asked.

"Phone call now."

He glanced at Kenyon, got back a shrug.

"Okay, Mr. Nader. We'll bring you a phone, but we'll stay here when you make the call and we'll be taping it, understand?" Tapping the tape recorder.

"Yaz."

Kenyon went to get the phone and hook it up to the recorder they used to tape calls.

The shooter stared at the table, gnawing his bottom lip.

Apprehensive? Maybe. Scared enough to call a lawyer anyway.

Two minutes later Kenyon brought in the phone and set it on the table.

The shooter picked up the receiver, punched in a number and waited. Moments later he let out a burst of gibberish that lasted twenty seconds tops, ended the call, and put his head in his hands.

Frank looked at Kenyon and jerked his head at the door.

Out in the hall, Kenyon said, "What the fuck was that? Sounded like Donald Duck on speed."

"Beats the hell out of me. Not any language I know. Not German or French, sure as hell not Italian."

"Man," Kenyon said, "this case just got a lot weirder. But at least we got his name and where he was staying."

"We got a name," Frank said. "I wouldn't bet the farm it's his real one."

CHAPTER 4

FRIDAY – OCTOBER 10, 2014 – 4:30 PM

"Frank! Don't go in yet."

Outside the conference room door, Frank turned and saw Detective Lieutenant Morgan Vobitch charging down the hall, a five-foot-nine Sherman tank with a take-no-prisoners attitude.

"What's up, Morgan? Looks like you're hot on something."

Raking stubby fingers through his thick mane of silvery-gray hair, Vobitch said, "Just got a tip from the Ponchatoula cops."

"Me too, from the coroner."

"Good news? Bad news?"

"Let's just say I'm gonna need a friendly judge for a search warrant."

Vobitch opened the conference room door. "Let's go see what else we got."

For covert meetings about hot-potato cases, they used the conference room on the second floor of the D-8 station. Vobitch wanted ammunition so he could give it to the Superintendent before the six o'clock press conference.

Armed with a Dunkin Donuts iced coffee, his second of the afternoon, Frank sat opposite Kelly O'Neil. She flicked an eyebrow at him but said nothing. Earlier, he'd called and said he couldn't come over for their customary Friday night dinner. Too busy with the case.

"Me too," she'd said, "but I'll be home by midnight."

The witching hour when he often stopped at her house to take a break from a fresh homicide.But not tonight. Not with a high-profile case and a million unanswered questions.

He raised a hand to greet Orville Wright, seated beside Kelly. An older black man with graying hair, Orville was the most experienced homicide detective in the city, worked homicides in D-1.

Orville nodded and said, "Got a helluva mess with this one, Frank."

Kenyon Miller slipped into the chair beside Frank and whispered, "Got some news."

"Me too," he said, and focused on Vobitch, seated at the head of the conference table. A middle-aged black woman sat beside him with a laptop computer.

"Lurleen's taking notes so I won't forget to tell the Super anything," Vobitch said, his steel-gray eyes frosty. "Especially the items we don't want released to the vultures."

Vobitch had a love-hate relationship with reporters, played nice when he needed them, railed against them when things didn't go his way.

"Frank was first on the scene," Vobitch said. "Run it down, Frank."

He took out his notes. "I went in the front door, found a deceased black male in the foyer. Nobody alive in the main room. They escaped when the shooting started. Three deceased white males were in the booth nearest the kitchen. Between the booth and the kitchen, a deceased white female, a waitress, lay on the floor. I got IDs for the employees and the three men in the booth."

"Leave that part out," Vobitch said to Noreen. "Go ahead, Frank."

"This was no random kill spree. This was a targeted hit on one of the men in the booth. Or maybe all three, too soon to tell at this point. Then he shot the waitress, ran in the kitchen, and Johnny Wu's boys captured him and held him until the first officers got there. You want names?"

"Not yet," Vobitch said.

"What about the shooter?" Orville said.

"No ID on him, wouldn't give his name," Frank said. "Kenyon and I grilled him later. We taped the interview, read him the Miranda. I'll let Kenyon tell you how that went."

"He makes like he wants to make a phone call," Kenyon said, holding a hand to his ear, "so we play let's make a deal. You give us something, we give you something. So he says he's Hans Nader, drove here from Milwaukee, says he was staying at the Garden Inn. But I just got back from there." He waved a sheet of paper. "Got a copy of a DL with his picture on it and a bogus Milwaukee address. It's a UPS store, and I don't think Hans is sleeping in a mailbox. Tell 'em the weird part, Frank."

"We bring him a phone, he punches in a number and spouts some foreign language. Not European. He's got a Slavic look about him, angular features, sharp cheek bones. Might be from Russia or one of those Baltic countries."

"But you taped it, right?" Orville said. "The local FBI office might have an agent who could translate the call for us."

"Fuck that," Vobitch said. "I'm not giving it to the feds and have them take over the case."

"Tony Coppola served in the Army during the Gulf War," Frank said. "Maybe he can ask around, find a veteran who speaks Russian or one of those Baltic languages. Tony's helped us before and he'll keep his mouth shut."

"Okay," Vobitch said. "Good follow-up on the shooter, Kenyon. Here's my news. Richard Bauer lived in Ponchatoula, so I asked the Ponchatoula Sheriff's department to do the notification. I just got a call from the Chief. He says Richard Bauer is an NBA referee."

"Hoo-eee!" Kenyon said. "Maybe somebody didn't like the calls he made."

Chuckles around the table, until Vobitch said sharply, "That's not for publication. The vultures will go ballistic when they find out. The other two vics lived in Atlantic City, New Jersey. Benny Green and Dominic Marconi. I called Atlantic City PD to do the notifications."

"Hold on," Frank said. "I just got off the phone with Doctor DeMayo. After the bodies got to the morgue, he removed Benny Green's clothes and found a mini-recorder taped to his chest."

"Jesus-fucking-Christ!" Vobitch exclaimed. "The guy was wired?"

"Looks like it," Frank said. "DeMayo preserved it as evidence, but it's personal property, so we'll need a search warrant to listen to it."

"You think he was the target?" Kelly asked, twirling a lock of dark hair around her finger.

"Coulda been him, coulda been the ref, coulda been Marconi," Vobitch said. "When I talked to Atlantic City PD, the detective said he didn't know Benny Green, but he knew Dominic Marconi, said he was an enforcer for the local mob."

"So it's mob connected," Frank said.

"No surprise there," Orville said, "but if Benny Green was wearing a wire, who was he taping? The ref or the mobster?"

"No way to know until we listen to the tape," Frank said. "And don't forget Johnny Wu. His gang might be running bets out of the club. Or dealing drugs."

"Or both," Vobitch said. "No shortage of suspects on this one."

"The spouse is always the first suspect," Kelly said. "Were any of them married?"

"The referee was," Vobitch said. "Also had two kids, age ten and five."

"Man, I got two kids of my own," Kenyon said. "I don't envy his wife. Gotta tell two little kids Daddy's not coming home tonight."

"But Kelly's right," Frank said. "For all we know she could be the Wicked Witch of the West. I want to talk to her, the sooner the better."

"Do it as soon as we wrap up," Vobitch said. "The other two weren't married. The Atlantic City detective said he knocked on Benny Green's door and got no response. A neighbor told him where Green's mother lived, so he went there and told her, said she just about fell apart."

"What about the mobster?" Frank asked.

"The detective knew Marconi's lawyer." Vobitch smiled tightly. "Marconi's been in court a few times. The lawyer said Marconi's brother, Niccolo Marconi, is his next of kin. The detective went over and laid it on him. But wiseguys don't weep and wail when they get news like that. He said the brother didn't seem all that surprised."

"Maybe he knew something we don't," Frank said.

"Plenty of people know something we don't," Vobitch snapped. "We need to find out what. We got the shooter and the gun. All we gotta do is figure out who the target was."

"No," Frank said. "Then we have to find the person who hired the shooter."

FOULSHOT

5:15 PM – New Orleans Central Lockup

He forced down the meal they shoved through a slot in the cell door. It smelled disgusting and tasted worse, brownish-gray meat, a slice of bread and soggy vegetables. But he kept eating.

Soon the cops would interrogate him again. And beat him when they found out he'd given them worthless information.

Hans Nader, who had driven here from Milwaukee, Wisconsin.

How long would it take them to find out he had not driven here from Milwaukee?

During their first meeting his employer had given him a driver's license with his picture on it and an address in Milwaukee. And a credit card, to be used only in an emergency.

But when he checked into the Garden Hotel, the clerk said he was required to make a copy of his driver's license. Even if he paid cash. When the police went there, they would use his driver's license to check the address and find out Hans Nader didn't live there.

Maybe Hans Nader used to live there and now he was dead.

Seated on the lumpy mattress, he forked up mushy carrots, chewed and swallowed.

When the cops let him make the phone call, he had dialed the number his employer had given him and spoke Russian. *The cops got me. I told them nothing. I need solicitor.*

His employer's reply. *I will send you a solicitor who speaks Russian. Until then, speak to no one. And remember what I said.*

He shuddered, imagining what might happen if he ratted out his employer.

Only idiots thought jails were safe. If someone paid you to beat the shit out of someone, a menacing appearance was an asset, but no good for assassins. A six-foot-four, 250 pound guy with bulging muscles attracted too much attention. He was five-foot-nine and weighed 155 pounds.

When they brought him here, he had shuffled past other cells. Men with hard eyes and muscular arms covered with elaborate tattoos. Daggers and crosses and gang tags.

An hour ago, two guards had come for him. Paralyzed with fear, he kept his face impassive.

Never show fear to guards or they would beat you. Never show fear to other inmates or they would consider you prey and do monstrous things to you.

The guards had taken him to a telephone, saying his lawyer wanted to speak to him, and told him all phone calls were taped. When he answered, a voice said in Russian, *Say nothing to the police. Do not talk to other inmates. I will come there soon to meet with you.*

His mind swirled with questions, but a loud click had ended the call.

He mopped up salty gravy with the bread and set the tray on the floor. When would his solicitor meet with him? Soon, he'd said. Which meant nothing. A clock beside the telephone had told him it was four-thirty.

By now it must be almost six.

When would they turn out the lights? Ten o'clock? Eleven?

From previous experience, he knew that's when the trouble would start. Prisoners banging on bars to communicate or shouting curses at one another.

Dawn would not come until five o'clock.

Until then, he would stay awake. Remain vigilant.

Perhaps he would be safe in his cell.

But if he screamed, would the guards help him?

Perhaps. Perhaps not. Not knowing was the worst part.

He pressed his back against the wall and thought about Katerina.

The beautiful wife he would never see again.

CHAPTER 5

FRIDAY OCTOBER 10, 2014 – 6:35 PM – Ponchatoula

Frank rang the bell and waited, keyed up and tense. Gut-wrenching images swirled in his mind. Death is a terrible thing, but murder is worse, multiple victims worst of all. Interviewing a woman whose husband had been murdered was never pleasant.

When the frantic 9-11 calls came in, they thought it was a random act by a crazed killer. Not any more. And the spouse is always a prime suspect.

Richard Bauer must have been making good money, living in a sprawling one-story house, flower beds along a curved driveway, shrubs along the house, a golf course right down the street.

A woman opened the door, her face pale and drawn, bloodshot blue eyes, a blank expression. Jackie Bauer seemed dazed, understandable given the circumstances.

He showed his photo ID. "Detective Frank Renzi, NOPD. I know this is a bad time, but I have a few questions. Can I come in?"

Forcing a smile, she said, "Of course."

She took him down a short hall lined with photographs. Two of Richard Bauer in his referee uniform. Others showed the proud parents beaming at a toddler. Another taken at Disney World with two kids, everyone smiling and happy. Back then, anyway.

He followed her to the living room. Her stylish blue dress didn't flatter her figure, stout for a woman in her forties. In the living room, rust-colored curtains covered the windows and orange throw-pillows decorated an L-shaped lemon-yellow couch.

Jackie sank onto the short part of the L. He took the seat around the corner.

"I'm sorry for your loss, Mrs. Bauer. I hate to intrude at a time like this, but given the circumstances, we have a few questions." He took out his notepad and pen.

"What sort of questions?" she said, gazing at him with her cornflower-blue eyes.

"Tell me about your day. Did you have breakfast together?"

She stared into space, as though recalling certain memories she was unlikely to share with him.

At last she said, "Richie always ate breakfast with the kids when he was home." She gave him a sharp look. "You know he's an NBA referee, right? He works a lot of games on the west coast."

"Yes. I'm a big NBA fan, so I'm familiar with the schedule."

"I made waffles this morning. The kids love them, but Richie watches his diet to stay in shape. He only had coffee and some fresh fruit. Then the bus came and Danny went to school."

"It must have been difficult, telling the kids their father wasn't coming home."

"Thank God they weren't here when the deputies came. After they left I fell apart. An hour later, the kids came home. Nora has playschool on Fridays. It was awful."

"What time did Richie leave today?"

"Around eleven I think."

"Did you know where he was going?"

Her lips tightened. "No."

"Did Richie have any enemies?"

"Why are you asking these questions? The deputies said you caught the man who did it."

He reflected on their theory. Jackie might have paid the shooter, but he couldn't afford to assume that. "There were two other men with him. They died too."

But Jackie didn't react to what he'd said. She jumped to her feet and said, "Do you want some dessert, Danny?"

A skinny boy with unruly dirty-blond hair came in the room and stared at him. Then a little girl appeared, a petite version of her mother, honey-blond hair in a ponytail, big blue eyes.

"I bought an apple pie yesterday," Jackie said. "Want me to cut you a slice, Danny?"

"No. I want to go play with Nicky."

Jackie leaned down to give him a hug, but he pushed her away.

"Me too!" the little girl exclaimed. "Can I go too, Mommy?"

"No!" Danny said. "Why do I always have to take Nora with me, Mom?"

Major meltdown coming up, Frank thought, watching Jackie to see what she'd do. But she didn't get angry, didn't yell at the kid. In a quiet voice, she said, "I know you're upset, Danny. And you have a right to be. But Nora's upset, too. I need you to be the big brother. Go play with Nicky and take Nora with you."

Danny's mouth quirked. "Okay. Thanks, Mom."

Jackie watched them go out the door and returned to the couch.

"Nicely done," Frank said. "Kids that age can be tough. How old is Danny?" Get her talking about the kids, maybe she'd open up about Richie.

"He's ten, going though the preteen rebellion these days. He's a good kid, but Nora wants to follow him around like a puppy. She'll be six next month."

"Sounds pretty normal to me. Good kids, but this is a tough time for them. You said Richie left around eleven. He didn't tell you where he was going?"

"No and I didn't ask. Why bother? Richie lies."

Now they were getting somewhere. "Lies about?"

"Where he's going and who he's with."

"You were having marriage difficulties?"

With a sardonic laugh, she rose from the couch and said, "Come in my office. I want to show you something."

He followed her to a bright sunny room at the rear of the house. A wall of windows faced a golf course. "Nice view," he said.

"Right. Richie spent more time playing golf than he did with me."

She yanked open a desk drawer, took out a DVD and plugged it into a desk-top computer. After a moment, the monitor blossomed into color.

To his surprise, LA Lakers cheerleaders appeared, doing their half-time routine, prancing around in short skirts and halter tops, bare midriffs.

Jackie paused the tape. "See the one front and center? Not bad, huh? Big tits, flat stomach, come-hither smile? That's Richie's girlfriend. He's forty-nine. Pom-Pom Girl is twenty-five."

Frank said nothing. This presented a whole new scenario. Husband cheats on his wife, wife finds out and does what? Files for divorce? Hires a hitman?

"She thought she was going to be the next Mrs. Bauer, get her picture taken with her NBA-ref husband and the Hollywood big-shots who come to Lakers games. While I take care of the kids. But she's in for a surprise, right? Her TV movie-of-the-week dream just went in the toilet."

Gazing at him now, her eyes brimming with tears.

Damn. He hated when women cried. He never knew what to say.

Came up with a question. "Did Richie have a life insurance policy?"

"I don't know. Why?"

"Do you know a man named Benny Green?"

"Yes. Richie grew up with him in Atlantic City. I never met him but I know they were good friends." She frowned as realization dawned. "Was he with Richie when … ?"

"Yes, but I'd appreciate it if you wouldn't mention that to anyone. We haven't released any names to the media yet. What about Dominic Marconi? Does that name ring a bell?"

"Never heard of him. Would you like a bottled water?"

"No thanks, but you go ahead."

She went to a mini-fridge, took out a bottled water and downed several gulps. "I don't know what the hell I'm going to do for money. The mortgage payment is due next week."

"Given the circumstances, the bank might cut you some slack. Do you have a lawyer?"

"Yes. Given the *circumstances*, as you call them."

"Were you planning to get a divorce?"

Or did paying someone to kill him seem like a better solution?

"Detective Renzi, I've got a bank account with a hundred bucks in it. When we lived in New York, I was working so I handled the finances, but after we moved here—"

"When was that?"

"Seven years ago. Richie said we had to cut back on expenses, opened his own bank account and started paying the bills. After Nora was born, it got worse. He said money was tight and started giving me a prepaid debit card every month, four hundred dollars."

Frank pretended to jot notes, thinking: Richie didn't want his wife knowing where the money went. Why? Where they really that hard up or was Richie dropping big bucks on drugs? Or gambling?

"Did Richie seem anxious lately? Nervous about anything?"

"If he was, he didn't tell me."

"Do you have family around here? To help you with the kids?"

Jackie clenched her jaw. "Are we done? I need to make some phone calls."

"Of course. I'm very sorry for your loss, Mrs. Bauer." He gave his card and said, "Call my cellphone any time, day or night, if you think of anything. Or if you need help with anything."

"Thank you." She took the card and put it in a mug that held pens and pencils on her desk.

Frank left the house and got in his car, planning his next move. Get the name of the Lakers cheerleader and go talk to her. Jackie might be good with the kids, but clearly she was angry. Given his experience with domestic homicides, he'd seen what angry women could do.

Jackie knew Richie was cheating on her, already had a lawyer.

To file for divorce? Maybe. Or did she hire a hitman? That seemed like a stretch, but he couldn't discount the possibility.

———

Slumped on the chair in her office, Jackie buried her face in her hands, sobbing as if her heart would break. She wanted this to be a horrible dream. Wanted to wake up and see Richie walk in the door.

But Detective Frank Renzi had destroyed any hope of that.

Richie was dead. Murdered.

Despite what he'd done, she still loved him.

31

Married twenty years and she'd never see him again. Never see his face light up in that beautiful smile. Never hear him laugh. Never make love to him.

She straightened up and blew her nose.

Saw Pom-Pom bitch on the computer screen and pounded her fist on the desk, torrents of fury gushing over her like Niagara Falls. After she'd stuck by him all those years, urging him to follow his dream, working to support them during the lean years, making a home for them in those shitty apartments.

A fat lot of good that did her.

Not only did Richie want a divorce so he could marry the fucking cheerleader, he wanted custody of Danny and Nora. Over my dead body, she'd screamed.

But she wasn't dead. Richie was.

She left her office, walked through the living room to the hall and studied the photograph she had photo-shopped from a game video. Richie in his uniform, a whistle clamped between his teeth, refereeing an NBA game at Madison Square Garden. Her surprise birthday present last year. Richie was thrilled. He told her how much he loved her, took her to bed and made passionate love to her. Like the night they got married in Las Vegas.

But enough with the trip down nostalgia lane. She had no money, and no matter how much she loathed her father, she had to call him.

She returned to her office, picked up the phone and dialed a number.

Her mother answered. Daddy Warbucks never answered the phone. Like Mom was his secretary.

"Jackie!" her mother trilled. "I'm so glad you called. What have you been doing lately?"

"I've got bad news, Mom. Richie is dead." No point sugar coating it.

Her mother gasped. "No! What happened? Has Richie been ill?"

"No. He was murdered."

"Murdered!" her mother shrieked.

Then her father grabbed the phone. "Jackie, what happened? Richie was murdered?"

"Yes. At a club in New Orleans."

"I'm coming down there right now. I'll book the next flight and—"

"No! I don't want you here. You hated Richie. You never wanted me to marry him."

"Because I loved you, Jackie. I always knew he was trouble."

"Don't start or I'll hang up," she said.

Silence for a moment. Then, "How are the kids? Are they okay?"

"Okay? How could they be okay? Their father is dead! They loved him and so did I!"

"Calm down, honey—"

"Don't tell me what to do! If you want to help, send me money."

"Tell me what you need. I'll wire it into your bank account right now."

"Five thousand dollars. But don't send it to my bank, use Western Union."

"I'll send it right away. Jackie, please, we love you so much. Why can't we come down and help you?"

"I've got friends to help me."

A heavy sigh. "All right. I hate arguing with you, Jackie. Call if you need us, okay?"

"Okay," she said and ended the call. One ordeal over with.

But others lay ahead. Renzi would probably question her again. She shouldn't have shown him the video, but what's done was done. She had too many other things to worry about. Renzi was right. She needed to call her lawyer and ask about life insurance. And a will.

She was certain her father would send the money, so she'd have enough to get by for a while.

But a three-day weekend loomed. Monday was Columbus Day.

No school Saturday, Sunday or Monday, endless hours to fill.

What would she do with Danny and Nora? How would she keep them busy?

She'd told her father she had friends to help her. The truth was, she had plenty of acquaintances at the golf club, but only one close friend.

Aware of the darkness outside the windows, she checked the time. 8:45.

Better call Nicky's mother and have her send the kids home.

What would she do without Martina?

CHAPTER 6

SATURDAY – OCTOBER 11, 2014 – 9:30 AM

Frank sat in the living room with Mrs. Rogers, sipping ice tea. He hated iced tea, but if it made her feel like this was just a social call, he'd drink it. "When did Michelle start working at the High Roller Club?"

Perched on a wooden rocking chair, Mrs. Rogers said, "I wish she'd never gone there. Mimi was smart enough to get into Tulane. She majored in theater. They gave her a big scholarship. She always played lead in the high school drama club productions, and she was gorgeous."

She rose from the chair and returned with Michelle's high school graduation photo. Mrs. Rogers was in her forties and still an attractive woman. Michelle was knock-out gorgeous, dark hair like her mother but frosted at the tips, a big smile and eyes that could light up a room.

Unlike the woman he'd seen yesterday at the High Roller Club.

"I hope that man gets what's coming to him."

"We haven't charged him yet, but the DA will probably go for murder-one."

"Not the killer, Mr. Wu. Gives her a part time job, then tells her to quit college and work there full time. Tells her she'd meet people from Hollywood who could get her into movies."

"When did she start working there?"

"Two years ago right after her twentieth birthday. Finished the spring semester at Tulane and never went back, started working at that dreadful club full time. Lord knows what that man had her doing. That man is evil. He didn't care about Mimi. All he cares about is making money."

Frank thought that was pretty accurate. "You met him then?"

"Damn right I did. I went and talked to him after Mimi told me she was going to quit Tulane." Her eyes filled with tears. "She would have been the first one in my family to graduate from college. I was working two jobs to help her out, but I didn't mind. Mimi and I were always close. I got divorced when she was two."

And worked your ass off to support her, Frank thought.

The apartment was near the Tulane campus, a two bedroom with a cozy living room, small but neat and tidy.

"Mimi was a good girl until she started working at that club. She got into drugs, started coming home stoned."

"You think she was dealing drugs there?"

"I hope not, but it wouldn't surprise me. She had plenty of money to buy new clothes."

Another angle to investigate. He rose to his feet. "Thanks for speaking with me, Mrs. Rogers. I'm very sorry for your loss."

Ten minutes later he met Kenyon at a coffee shop, got a black coffee to get the taste of iced tea out of his mouth. They sat at a table where other customers couldn't overhear. Frank yawned and massaged his eyes.

"What? Did Kelly keep you up all night?" Kenyon said. Jiving him.

"I wish. Called her from the homicide office at midnight after I wrote up a warrant application for the Benny Green tape and talked to a judge."

"Did you get it?"

"Yes. Judges watch TV. She knows we're under pressure from the politicians. I called Dr. DeMayo this morning, told him I'd pick up the tape today. Vobitch wants us to listen to it this afternoon."

Kenyon sipped his coffee. "What about the shooter phone call?"

"I called Tony Coppola and asked him to check with his Army buddies, see if he can find a veteran who speaks Russian. We'll see what he comes up with. Vobitch doesn't want to give it to the feds, but I've got a contact at the FBI office who might help us."

"Claudia, right?" Kenyon said. "Kelly's gonna love that."

Ignoring the jibe, he said, "Last night I spent two hours watching video of Lakers cheerleaders, trying to figure out which one was the referee's girlfriend."

Kenyon looked at him, deadpan. "Must have been quite a hardship. Watching sexy babes in halter tops and mini-skirts, shaking their booty."

"Cut the jive, Kenyon. I was focused on their faces."

"Ask Jack Nicholson. He's probably screwing half of 'em."

"Yeah, well, I haven't talked to Jack lately. But there's a Laker Girls website with photos and biographies. I skipped the girls with dark hair. Two of the blondes were the right age, twenty-five. I'm pretty sure I know which one was Bauer's girlfriend. I booked an early flight to LA tomorrow."

"You think she's gonna tell you something his wife didn't?"

"Get with it, Kenyon. After hot sex, you don't just roll over and go to sleep. Think pillow talk."

"No pillow talk for me last night," Kenyon grumbled. "Too busy doing my job. Ernest Jackson worked at the High Roller Club part-time while attending Southern University. No priors, got a couple speeding tickets, probably when he was racing from a class to his job at the club. I went to his house this morning. Not a fun visit."

"I'm sure it wasn't."

"Two little kids, age three and five, don't have a daddy anymore. His wife works for an accounting firm. Not today though. Man, she was shell-shocked. Trying to be a good mom, knowing her life will never be the same, worried about paying the bills. I asked if Ernest had any enemies. She said no, everyone loved Ernie, he was the sweetest man you'd ever want to meet. This guy was a family man. No leads there."

"Good," Frank said, "but we might have another one."

He recapped his conversation with Mrs. Rogers and the possibility of drug deals at the club. "I want to open the waitress's locker and see what's in there."

"Better get a warrant. Might want to get one for Johnny Wu's office while you're at it."

Frank smiled. "That too."

———

10:35 AM – Ponchatoula

Jackie knelt on the floor outside the door to Richie's office. Sounds floated down the hall from the family room, Nora watching her favorite show on TV, *Dora the Explorer.*

Last night she'd collected the five thousand dollars her father had sent to the Western Union office. But she had to make arrangements for Richie's funeral, no telling how much that would cost. She didn't even have a fucking credit card. For seven years, Richie had controlled their finances, paying the mortgage and all the other bills, doling out money to her.

She wanted to know what was in his bank accounts, but the door to his office was locked. She stuck a bobby-pin into the lock and jimmied it around. The cop shows on TV made it look easy, but it wasn't. Gritting her teeth, she twisted the bobby-pin this way and that.

"What are you doing, Mommy?"

Startled, she turned. Ten feet away, Nora stared at her, sucking her thumb.

"What's wrong, honey? Come give me a hug."

Nora put her arms around her neck and said, "I want Daddy to make me a waffle."

Jackie closed her eyes. Christ, would this ever end?

Danny was old enough to understand that Richie was never coming home again, but Nora didn't believe it, asking her over and over when Daddy would be home. Sucking her thumb for comfort, a habit she'd outgrown years ago.

"Let's go sit on the couch and watch Dora."

"Why can't I go next door with Danny?" Nora said, her big blue eyes sorrowful.

"Danny wants to play with Nicky, and his mother's busy this morning."

"Can I go to playschool then?"

"Not today, sweetheart. It's Saturday."

Nora pouted and set her jaw, a sure sign that a temper tantrum was coming.

"Nora, I need to make some phone calls. If you sit down and watch Dora, I'll take you to the Dollar Store after lunch and give you five dollars to spend."

Bribing her daughter to leave her alone for an hour.

But what else could she do? She wasn't going to bribe her with food and have her get fat like some of the kids at playschool. Richie would freak out.

Tears sprang to her eyes. No he wouldn't. Richie was dead and she had to look after herself. The only way to do that was to make sure she had enough money to pay for what she needed.

She got Nora settled in the play room, went in her office, got on the phone and dialed a number. "Good morning," said a woman's voice. "Law offices, Millstein and Shapiro."

"Good morning. This is Jackie Bauer. I need to talk to Mr. Millstein."

"I'm sorry, but he's with someone. I'll have him call you as soon as he's free."

Screw that. She didn't have time to wait.

"Tell him my husband was murdered yesterday."

"How terrible! I'm so sorry to hear that, Mrs. Bauer. Hold on and I'll get him."

After they moved to Ponchatoula, her father had told her to get a lawyer and recommended Millstein. At the time she'd blown him off, never dreaming she'd need one. But after the fight with Richie, she'd made an appointment and talked to him, an older man with deep soothing voice, calm and competent, telling her to call him Saul.

A click sounded. "Jackie, that's horrible news. How can I help you?"

"A homicide detective was here yesterday—"

"I hope you didn't talk to him without me being there."

She hesitated, then said, "He wasn't here long. He asked me if Richie had any enemies. I didn't tell him anything." Other than showing him the video of the fucking Pom-Pom bitch in LA.

"Have you made the identification yet?"

"What do you mean?"

"The police will need you to identify him at the morgue."

A mushroom cloud of dread descended upon her. Identify Richie's body?

"I'll be happy to go with you, Jackie."

She didn't want to think about it. "The detective asked if Richie had a life insurance policy. I said I didn't know. As I told you, Richie handled all the finances, but they're locked in his office. I can't get in there and I need to know about my financial situation."

"Of course you do. I'll call a locksmith and have him open the door for you. Bring the relevant documents to my office and I'll take a look at them. Would two o'clock be convenient?"

"Yes. Thank you so much."

"I don't want you worrying about anything right now. Just take care of your-self and the children. Goodness, how are Danny and Nora holding up?"

Amazed that Millstein remembered their names, she said, "They're devastat-ed, but thank you for asking. See you at two."

She put down the phone, sank back in her chair and smiled.

Nothing like a lawyer to solve problems. Let Millstein call a locksmith and have him open the fucking door to Richie's office.

CHAPTER 7

SATURDAY – OCTOBER 11, 2014 – 2:10 PM

Eager to hear the Benny tape, they gathered around the conference room table, Frank and Kenyon on one side, Kelly and Orville on the other. Vobitch gave them copies of the transcript Lurleen had prepared. "The sound isn't great in some places," Vobitch said, "but you'll get the gist."

A female voice asks the men what they'd like to drink—beers all around—then asks if they'd like an appetizer.

Unidentified male: *"Yeah, the Daily Double."*

Silence until the waitress delivered the beers and the appetizer.

Frank pictured Michelle Rogers dead on the floor with a bullet in her chest.

The sound of silverware clinking on plates. Faint voices in the background.

Voice #1: Benny Green. Did you see Kobe slam-dunk that breakaway layup?

Voice #2: Richard Bauer. Fantastic move. He's a great player.

Benny: The Lakers might make the playoffs this year.

Thirty seconds of silence.

Benny: Who do you like this weekend?

Silence for twelve seconds.

Richard: My wife. I'm not working this weekend so we're taking the kids to Disney World.

Benny: That's nice, Richie, but there's a lotta games this weekend—

Voice #3: Dominic Marconi: Benny. You talk too much.

Silence for twenty seconds.

Dominic: We got a shitload of Snickers in the warehouse. Our friends wanna know where to send them.

Silence for thirty-five seconds.

Richard: I gotta hit the men's room.

"Stop it there!" Frank said. "The ref saw him coming."

"You think he knew the shooter?" Orville asked.

"Maybe. Or maybe he saw the gun.." He gestured for Vobitch to roll tape.

Silence for fifteen seconds. Then gunshots and the intervals between them. One shot, followed by another 2.1 seconds later.

Another shot 3.8 seconds later.

A voice screams No! Another shot 1.2 seconds later.

Screams and garbled voices for 15 seconds. Fainter, another shot.

END of transcript.

Vobitch shut off the tape and said, "Reactions?"

"I'll tell you what happened," Frank said. "He shot the ref first, two shots close together, one to the head, one to the chest. Then he shot Benny in the head. The mobster knows what's coming, shouts No and the guy shot him in the head."

"We got the gun, Vobitch said, "but the serial number's filed off. Orville, can you ask around, see if anyone bought a throw-away snub-nosed .22 lately?"

A hitter's gun, Frank thought. Easily concealed, effective for close-in kills.

"I'll try," Orville said, "but those guns get passed around. Hard to nail down who bought 'em, and when."

"What's up with the Snickers?" Kelly said. "Sounds like some kind of code."

"Likely a drug deal," Orville said. "I hear it all the time." Switching to gang-speak, he said, "Got ten boxes of tamales, yo. Meet me on XYZ street, ten o'-clock." Orville shrugged. "Last week we busted two guys, search the trunk, find ten pounds of weed, three large in cash and two handguns. The dealer rats out his supplier, we go there and find eighty pounds of pot, four kilos of coke, thir-ty-five grand in cash, two sawed off shotguns and six handguns. No serial num-bers on any of 'em."

"Christ on a crutch! These motherfuckers make more money than I do," Vo-bitch said.

"The last shot was when he killed the waitress," Frank said. "I spoke to her mother this morning. She thinks Michelle might have been dealing drugs."

"Better search Wu's office," Kenyon said. "Before he gets a chance to hide anything."

"He won't," Vobitch said. "Zeke's patrol officers escorted him out of the club. He screams police brutality, says he wants his laptop, but they only let him take a picture of his family." Vobitch sneered. "Him and his wife and their gang-banger sons. The club is locked up tight. Nobody gets in but law enforcement."

"I want to be there when we search the place," Frank said.

"So noted," Vobitch said. "Write up a warrant. What else?"

"Big lie from the referee," Frank said. "Richie Bauer wasn't taking his wife and kids to Disney World or anywhere else this weekend. His wife says he's got a girlfriend, a Lakers cheerleader."

"Put 'em both on the suspect list," Vobitch said. "The wife and the girlfriend."

"I want to talk to her," Frank said, "already booked an early flight to LA for tomorrow. I think Kelly should go talk to Benny's mother in Atlantic City."

"It would be more productive than interviewing the witnesses," Kelly said. "You'd think the shooter was Godzilla. He was enormous, the gun was huge, he had scary eyes. But we already know what he looks like. Hell, we've got his prints and a mugshot. If I talk to Benny Green's mother, maybe I can find out why Benny was wired."

"Good point," Vobitch said. "If I tell the Super it will help us find out who hired the shooter, he'll spring for it." His cellphone rang. He checked the ID and answered. "Whaddaya got for me?" Listened for a moment, then smiled. "Beautiful. Spell it for me." Jotted notes on a yellow legal pad. Listened, then said, "Thanks. Text me the address."

He ended the call. "Popoffski or whatever the fuck his name is got himself a lawyer."

"Not Popovitch," Frank said. "He coaches the San Antonio Spurs."

"Yeah? Does he speak Russian?" Vobitch said sarcastically. "I got a pal at the lockup. He told me Attorney Boris Mosgov—M-O-S-G-O-V—just flew in from Las Vegas."

"Plenty of mobsters there," Kenyon said.

Vobitch flashed his evil smile. "You bet, Kenyon. You did a great job checking on the shooter. Dig up the dirt on Mosgov. Get me his wife's name, the names of his children and his known associates. I want to know where he got his law degree. If the guy's got a pimple on his ass, I want to know about it."

"Geez," Kenyon said. "You want me to pull down his pants and take a picture of it?"

"I want to be there when you do," Kelly said.

Even Vobitch laughed at that one. "Okay, we're done. Write up the warrant for the club, Frank. I'll call the Super and get travel allowances for you and Kelly. After you get back we toss the High Roller Club, see what we find."

As they left the conference room Frank caught up to Kelly and whispered, "Meet me in my car in ten minutes. I got a surprise for you."

In a low sultry voice, she murmured, "Oooh, I can hardly wait."

———

2:30 PM – Ponchatoula

Determined not to cry, Jackie marched into Millstein's office with a briefcase full of documents. To hell with crying. She wanted answers.

An older man with thick white hair, Millstein came around his desk and gave her a hug. "I'm so sorry for your loss, Jackie. You and Richard may not have been getting along lately, but I'm sure you have fond memories of better times."

He gestured at an easy chair in front of his desk. "Sit down and make yourself comfortable. Would you like coffee or tea? Bottled water?"

"Water would be great, thanks." Jackie set the briefcase on the floor beside her chair. Millstein's office was on the twentieth floor. Beyond the wall of windows behind his desk was an endless blue sky, not a cloud in sight.

An impressive view, but it didn't make her feel any better.

Millstein brought her a bottled water, sat at his desk and took out a legal pad.

"Thank you for sending the locksmith," she said. "He was great. Opened the door in a jiffy and unlocked Richie's file cabinet. I found lots of bills and bank statements but no will. It might be on in his desktop computer or his laptop, but they're password protected."

Millstein pressed a button on his intercom. "Grace, see if you can find a will for Richard Bauer. If you do, get me the lawyer's name and phone number."

"The savings account has a balance of three-hundred dollars," Jackie said. "How do I pay the bills? The mortgage payment is almost a thousand dollars a month and I have other bills to pay. Nora's playschool, the landscaper, the housekeeper comes in to clean once a week."

"I'm sure the bank will cut you some slack on the mortgage. I'll call them. Give me the latest bills and all the bank statements."

She took them out of the briefcase and put them on the desk. "I've got funeral expenses, too. I decided to bury Richie in upstate New York, near my parents."

"After the police release the body you'll need to sign some papers to transport it to New York."

"Jesus, does it ever end?"

He patted her hand. "Don't worry, Jackie. I'll take care of the paperwork. All you need to do is sign it. Have they asked you to make the identification yet?"

The question slapped her in the face like a dead fish. "No."

"Call me when they do, and I'll drive you there." Millstein paused a moment, looking uncomfortable. At last he said, "Where do you think the money went?"

"His fucking girlfriend's probably got it."

Millstein smiled. "You've got spirit, Jackie. I like that. What's her name?"

"Brandi Nylund. She's a cheerleader for the LA Lakers."

A tap sounded on the door and Grace entered the office.

"I found Richard Bauer's will, recorded two weeks ago in probate court." She put a slip of paper on the desk. "That's his lawyer's name and phone number."

"Thank you, Grace. You're a dear."

After Grace left the room, Millstein punched a number into his phone, listened a moment and put down the receiver. "The lawyer's office is closed for the holiday weekend, won't be open until Tuesday."

"Damn! Not until Tuesday?" *Two interminable days from now.*

Millstein said nothing, jotting notes on a yellow legal pad. At last, he raised his head and looked at her. Cleared his throat and said, "Do you think Richie might have been gambling?"

Not a question she wanted to answer. "I have no idea. I better go home and tend to the children. I left them with a neighbor."

2:35 PM – New Orleans

Outside in his car, Frank sipped his iced coffee, ruminating over the case. And the nagging questions in his mind. All without answers.

A tap on the window and Kelly slipped into the passenger seat. She pointed at an iced coffee container in one cup holder. "Is that my surprise?"

"No." He pulled her close and gave her a long lingering kiss, her pliant lips melding with his.

When they came up for air, Kelly said, "That was delicious. Wanna go for round two?"

Man, he loved this woman, five years together and she still turned him on. Her looks, her voice, her smarts, and her passionate lovemaking.

"Both of us are getting on planes tomorrow," he said. "I think we deserve a bon voyage party. After I finish work tonight, how about I pick up a bottle of wine and bring it to your house?"

Kelly combed fingers through her short dark hair, her sea-green eyes mischievous. "Oooh, a bon voyage party. How exciting! I can hardly wait. Let's see. What shall I wear?"

He smiled and said, "Your birthday suit. See you around six."

CHAPTER 8

SUNDAY OCTOBER 12, 2014 – 1:25 PM – Atlantic City

Kelly parked her rental car in front of Mrs. Greenblatt's house, a small white cottage with lime-green shutters. Carrying her all-purpose tote-bag, she went up the walk and rang the bell.

Mrs. Greenblatt opened the door right away. "Hello, Detective O'Neil."

She looked like a kindly grandmother, wrinkled cheeks, wispy gray hair, granny-glasses perched on her prominent nose. But she wasn't a grandmother and never would be. She was a mom, grieving for her son. "Thanks for seeing me on short notice, Mrs. Greenblatt."

"Oh, call me Ruth. Everybody else does. Come in and sit down."

Kelly stepped into a spotless living room filled with delicious aromas. A plate of cookies sat on a coffee table in front of a plum-colored three-cushion couch.

"Would you like coffee? It's no trouble. I just made a fresh pot."

"Coffee sounds wonderful. Those cookies look delicious."

She sat on the couch and put her tote-bag on the floor. In her experience, bereaved mothers didn't want to talk about their unbearable loss right away. They needed to keep busy, cooking and cleaning, offering coffee and cookies to the homicide detective who'd called from the airport asking to speak with her about Benny.

Two photographs stood on a side table, Benny's high school yearbook photo, a homely kid with a moon face and a prominent nose like his mother. The other showed him in an Army uniform, older but no more attractive, same round face and chubby cheeks.

Ruth returned and set a tray with two coffee mugs, cream and sugar on the coffee table. "Help yourself to the Linzer cookies. I make them with strawberry jam."

She took two cookies, set one on a plate and took a bite of the other. "These are marvelous, Ruth. Light and flaky and just the right amount of powdered sugar."

"Thank you. My doctor won't let me eat sweets, but my neighbors have kids so I bring them treats now and then."

"Benny must have loved them."

Ruth's eyes filled with tears and her face puckered. "I still can't believe it."

"I'm so sorry for your loss, Ruth. Tell me about Benny."

Ruth pulled a tissue out of the pocket of her flowery blue dress and blew her nose. "He was my only child. Two years after he was born, his father walked out one day and never came back."

"That must have been difficult, raising him by yourself."

"I couldn't afford an apartment so we had to live in a trailer park."

"Did you know Richard Bauer?"

"Oh yes! He and Benny were close friends."

"He was with Benny when he died. Richie died, too."

Fresh tears filled Ruth's eyes. "Goodness, they didn't tell me that. Richie was such a sweet kid. His family lived in the trailer opposite ours. Most every day he'd come over and play with Benny. They were in the same class in school."

"They spent a lot of time together?"

"Oh, yes! Hours and hours. Until Richie made the high school basketball team. He had practice after school and games on the weekend. After they graduated, Richie went off to college. Benny was smart, too, always got good grades, but I didn't have the money to send him to college. He was lost without Richie, so he joined the Army." Ruth showed her the Army photograph. "That's Benny in his uniform, after he finished basic training."

"You must have been so proud of him."

"I was. They taught him how to program computers." Ruth chuckled. "I can barely manage my email. But Benny got so good at it, they sent him to Germany."

"How wonderful. Whereabouts?" Army records were difficult to get, but not impossible.

"Ramstein Air Base. I looked it up on a map to see where it was. It's in the western part of Germany near the French border. Benny did really well over there."

"When did he change his name?" Kelly asked.

"After he graduated from high school. His birth name was Benjamin Greenblatt, but the kids used to tease him about it. So he changed it to Benny Green." Ruth smiled proudly. "He made lots of friends in Germany. He did really well over there, came home on leave one time and gave me the money for a downpayment to buy this house."

"Really? When was that?"

"In 1987. Benny came home for his birthday in August. Twenty-three years old and he gets me out of that horrid trailer park. He even paid the mortgage. I told him not to, but he said he wanted a nice place to live after he got out of the Army."

"So he could eat Mom's cooking," Kelly said.

Ruth smiled faintly. "Probably. I wanted him to get married and give me a grandson, but Benny never had much luck with girls. I used to feel guilty, him being overweight and all, but I loved cooking for him ..." Her face crumpled, a study in grief.

"When did he get out of the Army?"

Ruth mopped tears from her eyes. "Let's see, that would have been the summer of 'ninety-one. He bought me new furniture and moved into the spare bedroom. But it didn't work out."

"Why? What happened?"

"He didn't have any friends, spent all his time gambling at Bally's Casino. He had no life. He'd go to the casino, come home late, get up at noon and sit on the couch, watching basketball games, screaming at the TV when they didn't go the way he wanted." Ruth shook her head. "Gambling's worse than drugs. It's like he fell into a bottomless pit. I used to nag him. I'd say, gambling won't get you anywhere, Benny. You're good with computers. Get a real job."

"What did he say?"

"I'd clip want ads out of newspapers and leave them on the kitchen table, but he threw them away. Just about broke my heart. Finally I sat him down and gave him a choice. You can live here and get a job, or leave. And he says, I love you, Ma, but don't lay a guilt trip on me."

Ruth's eyes filled with tears. "Guilt trip? Imagine how I felt. Throwing my son out of the house. So he got his own place. But sometimes he'd stop by and eat dinner with me. He said he'd met some woman at Bally's Casino. I was thrilled. I thought he was going to get married. But he said no, she's just a friend."

"Do you know her name?"

"No. Some woman with red hair. He called her the Redhead."

Kelly ostentatiously checked her watch. "Sorry Ruth, I'm afraid I have to leave. I've got an appointment."

She didn't have an appointment but she sure did want to talk to the Redhead.

———

3:45 PM – Los Angeles

Brandi Nylund lived on the second floor of an apartment complex near the Staples Center. Frank rang the bell, sweating in the heat, wishing he'd worn shorts and a T-shirt like the young studs lounging around the pool downstairs. He had on a sports jacket and chinos. Show up unannounced in a police uniform, she might not let him in.

The cheerleader opened the door and beamed him a big smile.

"Hi, can I help you?"

46

He flashed his ID badge. "NOPD Detective Frank Renzi. Can we talk for a minute?"

Her big blue eyes widened in dismay. "What about?"

"Richard Bauer."

Her smile disappeared. She opened the door and let him into the living room.

"I'm afraid I have bad news," he said. "Someone shot Mr. Bauer."

She gasped and clutched her chest. "Someone shot Richie?"

"Yes. Last Friday, at a club in New Orleans."

"Where is he? Is he all right?"

"No. I'm sorry to have to tell you this, but he died."

"No!" she wailed. "He can't be dead. He can't be!"

He waited, knowing that nothing he could say would make the hurt go away. Eventually she stopped sobbing, looked at him and said, "Richie's really dead?"

"I'm afraid so. Can I get you something? A glass of water?"

A shaky sigh. "No. I've got bottled water in the kitchen. Want one?"

"No thanks, but you go ahead. Mind if I sit down?"

She gestured at a purple two-cushion sofa and left the room. He sat on the sofa and looked around. The living room was a shrine to the Lakers, purple-and-gold everywhere, two posters of the cheerleaders on gold-painted walls.

Brandi came back with a bottled water and a wad of tissues and sat beside him on the sofa.

He waited. Silence often elicited more information than questions.

"Richie called me Thursday night before the Lakers game."

"How did he seem when you talked to him?"

"I don't know. Same as usual, I guess."

"Did he seem worried about anything?"

"Not really. I mean, like, his wife was always giving him grief about something. Two weeks ago they had a huge fight. Richie said she found out about me." Gazing at him earnestly, she said, "We were going to get married. I loved him with all my heart. Richie wanted custody of the kids, but—"

"Divorces can be messy when children are involved." Years ago, his divorce had almost ruined his relationship with his daughter. Thankfully, they were as close as ever now.

"Did Richie have any enemies that you know of?"

A sardonic laugh. "Like his wife, you mean? No. Everyone loved Richie."

Somebody didn't.

Frank waited. He wasn't ready to ask the hard questions yet.

"Richie called me almost every night. He wasn't working this weekend. When he didn't call, I started getting worried, you know?"

Frank nodded. Clearly she hadn't seen the news about the massacre in New Orleans. Then again, if the news wasn't about Hollywood or the Lakers, it likely wasn't on Brandi's radar screen.

His cellphone rang. He checked the ID and said, "Sorry, I need to take this."

He rose to his feet, turned his back to Brandi and said, "Hi, honey. What's up? Is everything okay?"

Kelly laughed. "Are you that thrilled to hear my voice or are you with someone?"

"Sorry if I woke you this morning. I hate these early flights."

"Good catch. Listen, I just talked to Benny's mother. She said he was a heavy gambler. Ask the cheerleader if Richie was a gambler. That's who you're with, right?"

"Definitely. I'll take care of that right away."

"Is she beautiful? Big tits, nice ass?" Kelly busting him now.

"I'll be home tonight, hon. Can't wait to see you."

"I'll put on my birthday suit." Teasing him with her sexy come-hither voice.

"That sounds perfect. I can't wait."

"I'm headed for a casino as we speak. Benny's mom said he had a friend there. Come to my house when you get back so we can compare notes."

He put away the phone and sat down beside Brandi. "Sorry for the interruption. How'd you meet Richie?"

"At a party after a Lakers game. Richie and I got talking and we hit it off, you know? He's so friendly and easy to talk to. He was an all-star player in high school. Richie knows basketball better than some folks know the Bible. He loves movies, too. We talked for hours."

The realization that she would never do this again hit her like a rock-slide. Sobbing, she jumped up and ran into the kitchen. Frank jotted notes in his notepad. Five minutes later she came back and sat down.

"I'm sorry. This is so ... overwhelming."

"I can understand that. How long ago did you meet Richie?"

"Five years ago maybe?"

Five years ago when you were twenty and Richie was forty-four.

"Ever take trips with him? Go to Vegas maybe?"

Brandi smiled, showing her pearly whites. "Lots of times, especially when a Lakers game was the end of his road trip. Richie loved Vegas. We always stayed at Caesar's Palace because they'd comp him a room. That place is huge! I swear it's as big as the Staples Center."

"Richie liked to gamble?"

"He loved playing roulette. We'd sit in these plush chairs and waitresses would come by and bring us free cocktails."

48

"How about basketball? Did he ever bet on games?"

Aghast, she stared at him. "Richie would never do that! We went to Vegas to have fun and relax. Being an NBA ref is very stressful. Tons of pressure, especially in LA."

"Was he a high-roller?"

"Not really. Like, maybe if he was on a winning streak he'd bet more."

"Okay, what I mean is, did he owe someone a lot of money?"

Her eyes widened as the implication hit her. "Are you saying somebody killed him because ...?"

"It's been known to happen if you don't pay the vig."

"What's that?"

"The interest they charge when you owe certain people a lot of money. Depending on how much you owe, it can add up if you don't pay every week."

Brandi gnawed her lip, frowning now. "Richie never mentioned anything like that."

Didn't mention it to his wife, either.

The High Roller Club scenario was starting to look different.

Richie Bauer, an NBA ref who liked to gamble; his childhood friend Benny Green, a heavy gambler; and Dominic Marconi, a New Jersey mobster.

Frank rose from the couch. His flight back to New Orleans landed at 10:30 PM. Meet Kelly at her house, swap info over a glass of wine and celebrate their reunion in bed.

"I'm sorry I had to deliver such terrible news, Brandi."

Solemn eyed, she said, "I guess that comes with your job, right?"

"Yes, unfortunately." He gave her his card. "If you think of anything important, call me any time, day or night, and I'll get back to you."

CHAPTER 9

SUNDAY OCTOBER 12, 2014 – 2:35 PM – Atlantic City, NJ

Bally's Casino was pure madness. Mesmerized, Kelly stood in the lobby, absorbing the sights, sounds and smells. A whirlwind of people, upbeat music blasting, the odor of fast-food.

A sign above an enormous room to her left flashed in red neon:

5,000 SLOT MACHINES ... EVERYONE'S A WINNER

Two armed security guards stood beside much smaller signs: **MUST BE 21 TO ENTER.**

Opposite the slots were two other rooms. Roulette and blackjack tables in one. No sense looking there. Benny's mom said he and his friend were gambling on sports. The second room was the sports book area.

She stepped into a huge U-shaped room, cigarette smoke and the smell of greasy hamburgers floating in the air. No music, no sound on dozens of TV screens that lined the walls, just people shouting into cellphones or screaming at the TV screens.

But even if the Redhead was here, how would she find her?

Other than red hair, she had no idea what the woman looked like.

Along the left-hand wall, several men sat on stools at the bar, no women. Ahead of her at the bottom of a wide horseshoe-shaped U, a huge screen displayed an array of lines with the names of teams and a host of other numbers. None of which made any sense to Kelly.

To her right were dozens of tables, four chairs on each side. Waitresses delivered drinks and food, pausing to empty butt-filled ashtrays on their way back to the kitchen. Searching for women, Kelly methodically checked the tables. Plenty of men, no women. In the next to the last row, two women sat together at one table but they were too young and had long blond hair.

Maybe this was a waste of time.

She checked the last row, closest to the TV screens. Her heart sped up. A woman with flame-red hair sat by herself, watching a basketball game on one screen, a coffee mug, an ashtray and a notebook on the table in front of her.

Kelly eyeballed the woman: a scrawny neck, pale wrinkled skin, had to be in her mid-sixties at least, the flame-red hair definitely courtesy of L'Oreal or Clairol.

Approaching the table, she waited until the Redhead stopped jotted notes in her notebook and said, "Excuse me. Have you seen Benny Green around?"

The Redhead looked up and said in a raspy, chain-smoker's voice, "Benny? Hell's bells, I haven't seen Benny in years."

Kelly slipped onto the chair beside her. "I just stopped by to see his mother. She said you and Benny were friends." Got back a nasty look.

"What are you, a fuckin' cop?"

"No. His mother's a friend of mine." A lie, but Redhead wouldn't know that.

"So fucking what?"

"She said Benny admired you a lot."

The woman glanced at a TV screen and screamed, "You let that cocksucker dunk on you? Go back to fucking high school!"

An older man with a bushy white beard at the next table called, "Take it easy, Paula. You're gonna make me wet my pants."

Paula waved a hand. "Don't run your ballbuster trip on me." Turning to Kelly, she said, "You gonna pee your pants, *honey?*"

Kelly grinned. "Nah. My boss drops F-bombs all the time. Was Benny good at gambling?"

"Are you kidding? Benny didn't know his ass from his elbow. When I met him, he was a fuckin' loser like those old ladies that sit at slot machines waiting to hit the jackpot." Paula snorted. "Jackpot, my ass. A row of cherries gets them a bucket of quarters."

"But he got better after you helped him?"

"You better fuckin' believe it." She pointed at two men in Cornell sweatshirts at a nearby table. "See those dickheads? Watch the college games, think they're experts, come here on weekends with a wad of cash daddy gave them, don't care if they drop a bundle."

Kelly nodded, thinking, *To hell with college kids, tell me about Benny.*

A balding red-faced man at the next table screamed into his phone. "QX5A 452 three dimes."

"An hour before game-time, the asshole's gotta lay his bet," Paula muttered.

"I heard what he said, but what does it mean?"

"QX5A is his account number. He just bet three grand on team 452." She gestured at the board with all the lines. "See it? Cal-Tech, number 452. The asshole's gonna lose his shirt. I know better'n to put money on those cocksuckers." She stopped a passing waitress and said, "Wanna bring me a refill, hon? And a cup for my friend here?"

For my friend here. That made Kelly's heart go pitty-pat.

"What did Benny bet on?"

"Back then basketball was where the action was. ESPN was broadcasting all the college games, but Benny's head was up his ass, had no fuckin' clue about the over-under and point spreads. Said he made a shitload of money gambling when he was in the Army and he wanted to be a professional gambler. But he was losing big, begging me for help."

The waitress delivered their coffee and went to another table.

Kelly stirred the steaming hot coffee. "What's a professional gambler?"

"A wiseguy like me. That's what they call us. Wiseguys." Paula lit a cigarette and blew a cloud of smoke. "I got ten fuckin' three-ring binders fulla notes at home. This is a full time job, gotta work at it twenty hours a day sometimes. Some wiseguys use runners to stake out different books and lay money down when the spread changes, but I work alone."

"So you didn't work with Benny?"

"Not after he started making money. Sometimes we'd compare notes, but that's it."

"I hear a lot of gamblers get into drugs."

Paula blew a plume of smoke. "Not me. Benny didn't either, far as I know."

"When did you get into gambling?"

"When I figured out working at IHOP wasn't gonna pay the rent unless it's a fuckin' closet with cockroaches." Paula gave her a hard stare. "Wasn't gonna start hooking either, like a lotta babes in this town. Didn't have a boyfriend, didn't want one. They expect you to wait on them, do their fuckin' laundry, shit like that."

"I hear you. I've got a boyfriend, but he doesn't live with me. And I don't do his laundry."

"Yeah?" Paula puffed her cigarette. "Watch out. That might change."

"When I hear the word wiseguys, I think of mobsters."

"Plenty-a fuckin' mobsters in Atlantic City, but I stay clear of 'em."

Kelly sipped her coffee. "What about Benny?"

"I got no fucking clue, would tell ya if I did. Those cocksuckers know how to take care of rats."

The comment sent chills down her spine. "I gotta get going, Paula, but I sure did enjoy talking with you."

"Nice talkin' ta you too, sweetheart. If you see Benny, tell him I said hello."

"Good luck with your bets," Kelly said and walked away, wondering what Paula would think when Benny's name hit the news, murdered at the High Roller Club in New Orleans.

———

11:45 PM – New Orleans

Lost in the twilight zone between sleep and wakefulness, Frank traced his fingers over Kelly's bare skin, curves in all the right places, trim and fit from her workouts at the gym. No matter how jet-lagged and sleep deprived he was, he was never too tired to make love to her.

Earlier, they'd compared notes on their trips over a glass of wine, but then one thing led to another, and they wound up in bed.

Kelly's eyes fluttered open and she smiled. "Enough post-coital bliss. Let's have another glass of wine and talk about the case." She brushed his lips with a kiss and left the room.

Kelly was an excellent detective, so they often discussed the cases they were working. He loved her smarts and her sense of humor, except when she threatened to bake him a cake for his fiftieth birthday next month and make him blow out fifty candles. He didn't want to think about hitting the big five-O.

When he entered the kitchen, she was sitting at the table in a lacy white camisole and underpants, flipping through her notes. "What's up, Sherlock? You got a new suspect?"

"A new theory, maybe. Pour me a glass of wine, would you?"

He took clean glasses out of a cupboard, sat at the table and poured Merlot into them. "You don't deserve more wine. Busting my chops while I'm with the cheerleader."

"Just testing your reaction time and code-speak skills."

"Good thing you didn't call while we were in the bedroom."

She gave him a dead-eyed lizard stare.

"Hey, busty blondes don't do a thing for me. Tell me about Benny's friend, the redhead."

"She spouts more F-bombs than Vobitch. Her name's Paula. I never got her last name. She said Benny didn't know fuck-all about sports betting when she met him."

"When was that?"

Kelly checked her notes. "Mid-to-late '90s, maybe. She said she hadn't seen him in years. I told her I knew nothing about sports betting, which I don't, and she starts talking about the over-under and the spread." Kelly frowned at him. "Do you know these terms?"

"Sure. The spread evens the odds between two teams. Let's say the spread on an NBA game is Boston Celtics plus-five, Houston Rockets minus-five. You're betting on how many points each team is going to win or lose by. The Celtics need to win by more than five points, or lose by less than five, to cover the spread. The Rockets have to win by more than five to cover the spread."

"How do you know these things?"

He grinned. "If I told you I'd have to shoot you. Seriously? I've been watching Celtics games all my life, but I've never bet on one. When I asked the cheerleader if Richie bet on games, she said he'd never do that. Richie being a fine upstanding NBA referee and all."

"Maybe she didn't know. Why would he tell her?" Kelly twirled a lock of dark hair around one finger and said, "Do a lot of Russians play in the NBA?"

"A few. I'm not sure how many. Why?"

"What if a Russian player got pissed off at Richie and paid someone to kill him?"

"I'd say the odds on that are pretty steep. Like slim and none. I called Kenyon from the airport. He got a warrant to search the High Roller Club. Vobitch put a team together, looks like we'll hit the place tomorrow morning at nine."

"Less than eight hours from now. Want to sleep here?"

"Thanks, but I better sleep at my condo so I can meet Kenyon at the station early. We still don't know why Benny was wired. And we need more info on the New Jersey mobster."

"I still say Jackie's our prime suspect. What if she found out Richie was fixing games and betting on them? If he got caught and went to jail, the scandal would fuck up her life."

"I don't know," he said. "She was all torn up when I talked to her."

"What did she do, start crying? Every woman in the world knows guys hate it when they cry."

"All this time you been keeping crucial information like that from me?"

"You know it's true," she said. "But here's my point. When I was a kid, Dad would only take me to Cubs games. When I asked him why, he told me about the Chicago White Sox team that threw the 1919 World Series. Dad said an old retired cop told him about it."

Frank studied the scar tissue above her camisole, an ugly scar near her left clavicle above her heart where she'd been shot. Recalling the night he sat by her hospital bed, worried sick, thinking she might die. Her mother died when Kelly was ten, so her father had raised Kelly and her three brothers by himself. In the wee hours of the morning, Frank called him, identified himself and told him what had happened, the worst news a cop can ever get.

"I'm coming down there right now," her father bellowed. "Stay with her. Don't you fuckin' move until I get there, you got that, Renzi?"

That's how he'd met Chicago Police Captain Rico Zavarella.

"Did Kenyon tell you about the dirt he dug up on the shooter's lawyer?" she asked.

"No. Did he have a pimple on his ass?"

Kelly burst out laughing. "You are so baaad!"

"You know it," he said cheerfully. "I better go get my beauty sleep."

"Good luck with tossing the High Roller Club. After you finish, call and tell me what happened. I'll be researching Russian basketball players, to see if I find any likely suspects."

CHAPTER 10

DAY 4 MONDAY OCTOBER 13, 2014 – 9:30 AM

The High Roller Club break room stank of cigarette smoke and stale food. Two butt-filled ashtrays and a pile of paper napkins sat on a table in the corner. Frank checked the names taped to the lockers along one wall. Using bolt cutters, he snapped the padlock on Michelle's locker.

A half hour ago, armed with a search warrant, he and Kenyon, and a team of patrol cops and crime scene techs, had entered the High Roller Club to search for incriminating evidence. Johnny Wu had insisted on being here. Kenyon was holding Wu in his office.

Inside the locker, two clear plastic baggies lay on the top shelf, no cash, no wallet. A pink folder sat on the shelf below it. With gloved hands, he took out the baggies, a powdery substance that looked like coke in one, Oxy pills in the other. Below the shelves, a leather jacket dangled from a hook. He searched the pockets and found nothing.

In the pink folder, he found three photographs of Michelle on one side: a closeup of her face, a full-length shot standing in a casual pose, another lying on a blanket in a skimpy bikini. The other side held copies of her resume. Highlights of her academic record, scholarship awards and her starring roles in high school: Velma in *Chicago*, Maria in *West Side Story*, Glinda in *Wicked*.

Unfortunately, the only film Michelle would star in was the video the NOPD photographer had taken to document the crime scene.

He bagged the contents in evidence bags and gave them to a patrol cop in the foyer. Time to talk to Johnny Wu.

When he entered Wu's office, Kenyon gestured at a two-foot-square solid-steel safe in the corner. "Mr. Wu didn't want to open it, so I offered to call a locksmith and have him drill it open. Which, as I pointed out to Mr. Wu, would mean he'd have to buy another safe."

"We take in lotta money last week," Wu said. "Need to deposit in bank."

Frank looked in the safe and saw three bricks of hundred-dollar bills wrapped in clear plastic. He took them out and set them on the desk in front of Wu. "Do all your customers pay with hundred dollar bills? Most folks use credit cards these days."

Wu shrugged. "Lotta men like to impress people."

"Or maybe you place bets for them."

"No. Betting not allowed here."

"You fink on a big payout? Someone came here and shot up your club to send you a message?"

"Told you before," Wu said, glaring at him. "No gambling here."

"Where did all the cash come from then?" Kenyon asked.

Wu said nothing, lips clamped in an angry line.

"I found drugs in Michelle Rogers' locker," Frank said. "You selling drugs here?"

"No!" Wu said. "This is private club for sports fans. They not come here to buy drugs. We serve tasty food, good drinks, they relax, watch sports on TV."

Kenyon took a trash bag out of the safe and showed Frank the contents: wads of bills in smaller denominations.

"Looks like drug money to me," Frank said. "You got a coke habit, Mr. Wu?"

"You watch too many movies, think all Asians smoke dope."

"Do you test your employees for drugs? Have 'em pee in a cup?"

"No. Not my fault girl had coke habit."

Frank glanced at Kenyon, saw him thinking what he was thinking: *Cold calculating SOB.*

"Do you know Benny Green?" Frank asked.

"No."

"Richard Bauer?"

"No."

"They're members of your club and you don't know them?" Kenyon said.

Wu shrugged. "Not possible to know all member's names."

"What about Dominic Marconi?" Frank asked.

"Never heard of him. Who is he?"

Frank said to Kenyon, "Bag the contents of the safe and take it to the evidence lockers."

"That's my money!" Wu shouted. "You can't take it!"

Kenyon whipped out the search warrant. "Yes we can. Want me to read what the warrant says?"

"Fuck you," Wu said, his eyes glittering with anger.

A patrol cop tapped the office door and said, "Vobitch is here, Frank. Wants to talk to you."

He left Wu's office, saw Vobitch sitting at the end of the bar and slid onto the stool beside him. "What's up, Morgan? You look like you could chew nails."

"You would too if you were getting calls from the media vultures and local politicians, not to mention the NOPD bigwigs crawling up my ass. What's up with Johnny Wu? You find anything?"

"Three bricks of hundreds in his safe and a bag with bills in smaller denominations. Put a sniffer dog on 'em, we'd probably get an alert."

"You think he's selling drugs here?"

"Hard to say. I found two baggies with pills and what looks like coke in Michelle's locker, but it might have been her own private stash. No cash in the locker."

"You think the loot in Wu's safe is gambling money?"

"Wu denied it and I tend to believe him. Be tough to run a gambling operation in here without being obvious. Wu said he didn't know Benny Green, Richard Bauer or Dominic Marconi."

"So we got nothing," Vobitch said.

"Given the cash in the safe, we could nail Wu for money-laundering, but I don't think he hired the shooter. Why would he let his sons capture him?"

"Okay, cross him off the suspect list. An hour ago I got a call from the New Jersey FBI office." Vobitch smiled thinly. "Special Agent Fred Lewis wants me to send him the Benny Green tape. I ask why and he gives me the usual bullshit. Can't comment on an ongoing federal investigation."

"You gonna give it to him?"

"I ran it by the Super. He said to tell the New Jersey feds to put in a written request and when I get it, send them the tape."

"Good thing we already listened to it."

"Yeah. I didn't tell Fred about that."

"Did he ask you?"

Vobitch flashed his evil smile. "Yes. I said I couldn't comment on that due to our ongoing investigation of multiple murders." When Frank burst out laughing, Vobitch growled, "Wish I'd been there to see Fred's face when I said it."

"Want me to talk to Claudia Cohen? She might be able to find out what the New Jersey feds are up to."

"As long as she don't tell her asshole boss about it."

"She won't. Claudia doesn't like him any better than you do. She helped us a lot with that kidnapping case a few years ago."

"Okay," Vobitch said. "But on the QT, so nobody sees you. Lemme know what she says."

———

12:30 PM – Ponchatoula

No more damsel in distress when Frank talked to Jackie this time. He took a seat on the lemon-yellow couch, but Jackie didn't. Regarding him with a frosty stare, she waved the cellphone in her hand and said, "I'm busy right now. You said you had more questions?"

"Did you find out if Richie had a life insurance policy? Or a will?"

"I talked to my lawyer. He's handling that."

A non-answer, but he let it go. "Have you spoken with Richie's parents?"

57

"His mother died when Richie was a kid. I don't know where his father is. I never met him."

"He didn't come to the wedding?"

"No. He's an alcoholic. Richie didn't want him there. I didn't want *my* father there, either." A sardonic smile. "So we said to hell with them and eloped to Las Vegas."

A gambling mecca if ever there was one. Maybe Kelly was right. Forget drug deals. Maybe this was about gambling and Jackie was mixed up in it.

"Benny Green's mother spoke highly of Richie, said he used to come there a lot to play with Benny when they were kids."

"I wouldn't know. Richie never talked about his childhood. He was focused on his career. Worked his ass off for years until they hired him to referee NBA games."

"Do you think he was gambling?"

"What, you're blaming the victim now?" she snapped.

"No, but we need to find out why he—"

Jackie's cellphone rang. "I need to take this in my office," she said and left the room.

He jotted a few notes, looked up when Nora entered the room, carrying a stuffed bunny. "Hi Nora. What's your friend's name?"

She gave him a gap-tooth smile, one tooth missing in front. "Dora. What's your name?"

"Detective Frank," he said.

"Mom says Daddy's not coming home." Gazing at him with doleful eyes.

"And that makes you feel sad, right?"

Nora nodded, climbed up on the couch and sat beside him.

"Do you talk to Dora about it?"

"Sometimes. But it doesn't help."

"Where's your brother?"

"Next door playing with Nicky. I wanted to go too, but Danny said *nyet.* Do you know what that means?"

Frank didn't know much Russian but he knew that word. "Tell me."

"No," Nora said. "That's Danny's favorite word. Nicky's teaching him how to speak Russian."

"You're pretty smart, learning Russian words."

"That's the only one I know. Danny won't teach me how to say yes."

"What's Nicky's last name?"

"I'm not sure. I think it starts with Z." Smiling at him now. "I know all my letters. I learned them at playschool. But today's a holiday so there's no school."

"Okay," Frank said, "Nicky's last name starts with Z. What's the next letter?"

"It's hard to remember. I only saw it once. It's a U, I think. Want me to ask Mommy?"

"No, Mom's busy right now." He didn't want Jackie to know Nora was giving him information that might be crucial to the case.

Right on cue, Jackie came back in the living room.

"Can Detective Frank have lunch with me?" Nora said.

"Not today," he said quickly. "Your mom's busy. But next time I'm here we'll take Dora for a walk to the golf course. If Mom says it's okay."

Hoping she didn't say *nyet*.

Take Nora for a walk, she might give up more family secrets.

"Can I Mom, pleeze? That would be so fun!"

"We'll see, Nora. Go sit in the kitchen. I'll fix your lunch in a minute." After Nora went in the kitchen, Jackie said, "My lawyer advised me not to talk to you unless he's with me."

The bereaved wife lawyer's up.

"The two men in the booth with Richie were murdered, too. We want to know why someone wanted them dead." Hoping that would shake her up.

It didn't. She stood there stone-faced and silent.

He left the house and got in his car. Just when he'd started to think this was about gambling, a four-letter word changed his mind. *Nyet.*

The shooter spoke Russian. His lawyer spoke Russian. And now it turned out the referee's wife lived next door to a kid who spoke Russian.

If the kid spoke Russian, his parents probably did too.

Maybe when Jackie found out her husband was screwing around, she got pissed off, hooked up with the neighbor who speaks Russian and got him to hire the shooter.

RICHIE BAUER

TWENTY YEARS EARLIER

On Top of the World

FOULSHOT

January 2, 1994 – 10:30 AM – Las Vegas, Nevada

Buzzed with excitement, Richie wiped sweaty hands on his pant legs, shook the dice and tossed them on the coffee table. Yes! No boxcars, no snake eyes, another winner!

Last night at the roulette table, Jackie had urged him to play red 22, her favorite color and her birthday. He did and won $800. He wanted to double down, but Jackie, always the practical one, said, "No. We can use it to get a nicer apartment." Flashing the sexy smile that drove him wild, she said, "Let's go up to the room and celebrate." So they drank champagne and made mad passionate love and talked until the wee hours of the morning.

Jackie was still asleep. He always got up with the sun, eager to start his day. Eager to start a new life. Two days ago he and Jackie got married.

He'd been worried that Jackie would want a Jewish rabbi to officiate, but she said, "Hell, no. I've never been religious." So an older man with kindly blue eyes spoke the magic words, signed the necessary papers and wished them a long and happy life. They strolled out of the chapel, no parents to worry about, two lovebirds madly in love with each other.

Even now he could hardly believe it.

Ten years ago his life had gone in the toilet.

A highly-touted freshman with a big scholarship, starting point guard for the Marist College Red Foxes, he raced down the court for a breakaway layup, the crowd cheering like mad. A jolt of pain and he crumpled to the floor. At the hospital, they did an MRI. The surgeon said he'd torn the cartilage in his right knee. After the surgery, he would need six months of rehab.

Dark days and darker nights followed, worrying if the college would pay for the operation. His teammates came to visit, but he could tell they were uncomfortable. They didn't know whether to joke around like usual or do the doom-and-gloom thing. Four days later his girlfriend Ellen drove him to his dorm. He went in his room, shut out the lights and curled up in bed, sick with despair.

His dream of playing in the NBA was over.

A physical therapist came to his room and taught him the rehab exercises. Once he could get around on crutches, he did them at the gym. One day he stopped by to see the coach. "Richie," he said, "you're a talented player, but that knee is never gonna be the same. The financial aid office won't renew your scholarship."

End of basketball career. End of college too. He had no money for tuition.

So he called Ellen and said, "Let's pick up a six-pack and get blitzed."

The campus bordered the Hudson River, so they drank beer and watched boats sail down the river. It didn't make him feel any better. Not with his leg immobilized in a hard cast. Hell, he couldn't even make love to Ellen.

No sex, no money, no basketball and no future.

He hadn't felt this helpless since the night his mother died.

"My life is over."

"No it's not," Ellen said.

"Yes it is. No scholarship, I'll have to quit school."

Ellen was half Irish and had a temper. "You will not! You're really smart, Richie. Get off your butt and start studying."

"I don't have the money for tuition. I don't even have a fucking part-time job."

"There's scholarships for kids like you. Tell 'em you're an orphan or something."

He started laughing. That's exactly what he was, an orphan. The night Mom died, a cop came to the trailer and asked him if Mom and Dad had a fight before she left. He didn't dare tell the cop they fought most every night. Not with his father giving him the evil eye. So he said, "No, sir."

After that, Mom wasn't there to protect him when his father got drunk and beat him. So he avoided the asshole as much as possible. Before he left for college he went to the police station and asked to see the accident report. It confirmed what he'd suspected. They estimated her car was going sixty when it hit the bridge abutment. There were boxes for *Accident* and *Suicide*. The cops checked the *Inconclusive* box.

They didn't know what went on in the Bauer household.

Ellen helped him with the scholarship application and let him live in her apartment. He majored in marketing and got a part-time job at a ritzy golf club. Living cheap was nothing new. Even when Mom was alive, they'd never had any money.

But now things were different. Now he was honeymooning at Caesar's Palace Hotel with the woman he loved with all his heart.

But the road that got him here hadn't been easy.

One day when he was caddying for an older businessman, Richie showed him how to improve his swing. In return, Jacob Glazer offered him a part-time job at his Mercedes Benz dealership. He started out washing cars and detailing them, learned the different models and watched the salesmen to see how they closed deals.

After graduation, Ellen kissed him goodbye and moved back to California.

Mr. Glazer offered him a full time job

Thanks to his gift of gab, he did great, impressed buyers with his knowledge of different models. Glazer rewarded him with a bonus, took him out to dinner and asked what his goal in life was.

When Richie told him about his dream of playing in the NBA and how it had ended, Glazer said, "Never give up your dream. If you can't play in the NBA, why not be a referee instead?"

Stunned, he didn't know what to say. But the more he thought about it, the better he liked it.

He took the New York State Referee officiating class, passed the exam and got a job refereeing games at the local high school. But Mr. Glazer urged him to move up to college games.

Glazer had two daughters. Richie figured he was his surrogate son. Fine by him. Jacob Glazer was like the father he'd never had.

He joined the National College Athletic Association and aced the Officiating Exam. They let him referee Divisions 2 games: bigger crowds and more pressure, but he did okay. The next year they moved him up to Division 1. That was exponentially different. He was twenty-four, not much older than the players. Many of them intended to declare for the NBA draft, and the crowds were enormous, pressure to the max. Before each game his stomach would be in knots, but after a while he got more confident.

The big prize was March Madness, but only experienced refs worked those games. Determined to improve himself, he watched every game, taking notes on the players, intense and focused, like when he practiced shooting every day after school in the trailer park.

Officiating college games paid shit, so he sold cars at the dealership during the off season. Mr. Glazer found out most NBA referees worked the NBA D-League first. Richie registered his name, but you had to get invited to go to the D-League tryouts and he didn't get an invitation. The next year he got invited to a tryout but didn't make the cut. More determined than ever, he started running five miles a day and lifting weights three times a week.

In 1992, he got invited to a tryout, made the cut and attended the D-League training camp. He didn't make the final cut. Devastated, he thought about driving his car into a bridge abutment, like Mom.

Then he remembered his abusive alcoholic father.

The biggest loser that ever lived.

Richie Bauer wasn't a loser. Richie Bauer was going to be an NBA referee.

Someday his loser father would see him referee an NBA game on TV and realize his son had succeeded with no fucking help from him.

He heard water running in the bathroom. Great! Jackie was up. He couldn't wait to take her someplace neat for breakfast. Afterwards he'd try his luck at blackjack.

Last year he'd hit the jackpot. Fell in love with Jackie the minute she walked into the showroom. A blue-eyed blonde with a gorgeous smile and a vivacious personality to go with it, eager to buy a Mercedes Benz. She picked out a red one and he took her out for a test drive. He liked the way she drove. Not nervous or anxious like some women, decisive and confident.

Jackie said her father had given her money to buy a car for her birthday. "Daddy-O makes big bucks. He's a financial investment adviser. Every wealthy Jew in town depends on him."

That impressed the hell out of him, but he played it cool. "You're pretty smart yourself. What do you want to be when you grow up?" Teasing her to see what she'd say.

"Find a handsome guy like you and get married."

He almost swallowed his tongue. Jackie saw the look on his face and laughed. "I can be a ballbuster like my father sometimes."

"I think we should discuss this over drinks and dinner tonight."

So they did and fell madly in love with each other. But it wasn't all moonbeams and roses. When Jackie brought him home for dinner, her mother served a magnificent meal. Unlike Jackie, she was a mousy little thing, hardly opened her mouth. But Jackie's father took an instant dislike to him. "I assume you don't intend to be a car salesman for the rest of your life."

Like selling cars was one step up from garbage collector.

"Richie's going to be an NBA referee some day," Jackie said.

That sealed his fate. Daddy-O ran a background check on him, found out he grew up in a trailer park with an alcoholic father with several DUI arrests. He sat Jackie down and said, "Richie Bauer is trailer park trash. Dump him."

Jackie told him to go to hell. Stomped out of the house, moved in with Richie and got a job at a real estate agency. Daddy-O didn't like it, but what could he do? Jackie had a mind of her own.

And there she was! Stepping out of the bedroom, wearing a slinky dress and a triumphant smile. "Hey gorgeous," he said. "You look like a million bucks."

"I *feel* like a million bucks." She curled up beside him and said, "I just called my parents and told them we got married on New Year's Eve in Las Vegas."

"What did they say?" Dreading the verdict, his stomach in knots.

"Mom said that's wonderful, may you have good luck and happiness. Make me a grandchild."

"What did your father say?" Waiting for the bomb to drop.

Jackie laughed. "He was furious, but fuck him. Let's go have fun!"

His heart surged with joy. Now he knew how it felt to be on top of the world.

He'd just married the love of his life, made a bundle in the casino last night, might win more today.

Best of all, this year he'd start officiating NBA D-League games.

He could hardly wait.

CHAPTER 11

DAY 4 MONDAY OCTOBER 13, 2014 – 11:30 AM

Nicolas Zurik ended the call, slipped the cellphone in his pocket and glanced out the window of his second floor bedroom. Nicky and Danny were shooting around on the blacktopped rectangle beside the garage, their shouts audible through the window.

Ordinarily, he'd go out and join them, but not today.

In his walk-in closet, he selected a tie to go with his charcoal-gray jacket and took it in his bathroom. Martina had her own bathroom and closet on the opposite side of the room. Convenient when he came home late. Facing the mirror, he knotted the tie. Not bad for a man of forty-five, only a few flecks of gray in his black hair, still keeping his wife happy in bed.

When he went downstairs, Martina stood at the kitchen counter, paging through a Saks catalog. He nuzzled her neck and murmured, "You're looking splendid this morning."

She turned, her blue eyes sparkling with delight, and ran a hand over her hair, dark blonde with frosted tips. "So are you, my love. I bought Dover sole at the market yesterday. Shall we have it for dinner tonight?"

"Not tonight, luv. I'm meeting a new client this afternoon, might have to take him to dinner." Whoops and shouts floated through the window above the sink. "How's Danny doing?"

"Not so good. I try to get him to eat something but he says he's not hungry."

Nicky burst through the side door, followed closely by Danny.

"Guess what, Dad," Nicky said. "Danny almost beat me at Horse."

Nicolas smiled at his son, twelve years old and better-looking every day, blue eyes like his mum, black hair like his father, athletic and smart as a fox. "Danny's two years younger than you are. Pretty soon he'll catch up and start beating you."

Speaking rapidly in Russian, Nicky said, *"Nyet! I will still beat him."*

Responding in kind, Nicolas said, *"Be a good sport. Your friend is hurting right now."* To Martina, he said in English, "Have Nicky help you fix lunch while I talk to Danny."

He tousled Danny's unruly mop of dark-blonde hair. "Come in the playroom so we can talk."

He sat Danny down on a sofa facing a flat-screen TV, currently dark. Martina never let their son watch TV in the daytime, only after dinner, provided he'd finished his homework.

"I know you're hurting, Danny. My mother died when I was about your age. I thought it was the end of the world. But my father helped me get through it, just like your mum is helping you."

Danny's mouth quirked, but he said nothing.

"She's hurting too, so you've got to be strong. After my Mum died, I had no appetite, but my father made me eat Borscht." *Not to mention the many other things he'd done for him.*

"What's Borscht?"

"Beet soup. My father grew up in Moscow and Borscht was one of their basic foods. Served with piroshki, little dumplings stuffed with vegetables and cheese."

Danny smiled faintly. "I don't think that would go over too well with Mom."

"Probably not. But I ate the soup and got stronger. And figured out how to stop the pain."

Recalling the terrible nights when he lay in bed, wishing Mum would come in his room. Longing for the sweet smell of her Estée Lauder perfume as she read to him in French. And the words she spoke every night before she left: *I love you so much, Nicolas. Sleep well and I'll see you in the morning.*

"Every morning when I woke up, I'd think about the fun things Mum and I did. Playing in the park or riding our bikes to get ice cream. You had a lot of fun times with your dad, right?"

"Yes. But why was the cop at my house today, asking Mom if my dad had any enemies?"

"What did Mom say?"

"She said they caught the man who did it so why was he asking these questions."

"What did the cop say?"

"I don't know. Mom told me I had to come over here with Nora." Danny made a face. "Mom says I have to be the big brother."

"She's right, Danny. Nora is hurting too. Come on, let's go see what's for lunch. I'm pretty sure it's not Borscht."

When they went in the kitchen, Nicky was sitting on a stool at the island, waiting politely, a sandwich of cold cuts and a glass of milk in front of him. Danny climbed onto the stool beside Nicky and said, "Great. No beet soup."

"Beet soup?" Nicky wrinkled his nose. "What's that?"

Nicolas chanted in a sing-song voice, "Delicious. Nutritious. Makes you feel ambitious."

"Daaaad. That's so lame. Will you shoot hoop with us after we have lunch?"

"Sorry, sport. No can do. I've got to work today."

"But it's a holiday. How come you have to work?"

Speaking rapidly in Russian, he said, *"So I can make lots of money and let your mother buy fancy clothes so she always look pretty."*

Nicky grinned, his eyes sparkling with delight. Danny looked mystified and so did Martina. She could barely speak Russian now. Nicky was far more proficient. Every night they spent time conversing in Russian.

"Dad said he's gotta make lots of money, Mom. So you can buy fancy dresses and look pretty."

Beaming at him, Martina said, "That's right. Eat your lunch while I walk Mr. Moneybags to his car."

Nicolas put his arm around her as they walked along the driveway.

"What did you say when you talked to Danny?" Martina said.

"Nothing special. I think it cheered him up a bit." He stopped at the black BMW parked outside the garage. "If anyone asks, I'm away on business. You know the drill."

"Of course. Good luck with the new client. Talk to you when you get home."

He kissed her lips. "See you then, luv."

––––––

12:30 PM – Ponchatoula

Frank parked his unmarked Dodge in front of the Zurik residence. The Bauer family lived in a comfortable home overlooking a golf course. The Zurik abode was far more impressive, a two-story mansion with a large wing on the left-hand side. To the right beside the garage, a free-standing basketball hoop stood at one end of a blacktopped rectangle.

He didn't know what Nicolas Zurik did for a living, but he must be doing okay for himself. He strode up a field-stone walk lined with colorful flowers and rang the bell.

A woman opened the door. Smiling at him, she said, "Hi, can I help you?"

Martina Zurik, age 42, according to the information the Ponchatoula Sheriff's Department had given him, blue eyes, sleek blond hair with frosted tips, wearing an expensive-looking dress.

He flashed his NOPD badge. "Can I speak with Mr. Zurik?"

"Oh. I thought you were lost. It happens a lot here, so many twists and turns. Nicolas isn't home. He's away on business."

"When will he be back?"

"I don't know." Still smiling, she said, "I'd be happy to give him a message."

"I understand you're friendly with the Bauer family next door."

Her smile faded. "Such a tragedy. Jackie and the children are devastated."

"Maybe you could answer some of my questions."

"Not now. I'm about to go shopping at the Lakeside Mall. Lots of sales because of the holiday."

He thought about asking her when she'd be back, but why bother? He wanted to talk to Nicolas, and Martina didn't know when he'd be back. Or so she said.

She didn't seem eager to talk about the *tragedy*.

"Okay, I'll come back another time," he said and returned to his car. Next step, find out where Nicolas worked. Maybe someone there could tell him when Nicolas would be back.

He dialed a number on his cellphone and drove off along a street lined with red maples.

After two rings, a voice spoke into his ear. "Special Agent Cohen.

"Hi, Claudia. Frank Renzi. How you doing these days?"

"Hey, Frank, nice to hear from you. It's been a while. I'm doing okay, you?"

"Same old, same old. Any chance we could get together tomorrow?"

"Oh, this isn't a social call, huh? Are you working the shooting at that club last Friday?"

"Yes, and I'm hoping you can help me out."

"Hold on while I check my schedule." Moments later she was back. "How about tomorrow after lunch, two o'clock at our usual rendezvous?"

"Perfect. I'd appreciate it if you didn't mention this to your boss."

"Frank. He's the biggest asshole on the planet. Why would I tell him anything?"

He smiled. "That's what I figured. See you tomorrow."

————

12:30 PM – Ponchatoula

Jackie stood at the stove, stirring chicken noodle soup. She dipped in a spoon and tasted it. If it was too hot, Nora wouldn't eat it. Just right, she decided.

"Nora, do you want oyster crackers with the soup, or a piece of toast?"

Perched on a stool at the breakfast bar, Nora said, "Oyster crackers! I love oyster crackers."

"Then oyster crackers you shall have." She ladled soup into a bowl and set it in front of Nora.

"Aren't you having any?"

The thought of food made her want to puke. Earlier, Millstein had called and said she had to identify Richie's body tomorrow. "Just a quick look at his face. Don't worry, I'll drive you there."

Tears glazed her eyes. She couldn't bear the thought of seeing Richie, dead.

"Mom, what are you doing? I want my oyster crackers."

"Sorry, honey." She took a box out of the cupboard and poured crackers in a dish.

"Some for you too, Mom. To go with your soup."

She felt like her head would explode. She'd woken up with a headache and talking to Detective Renzi had made it worse. Then Millstein called. Now Nora was nagging her.

She wanted to scream and rage at the horrible fate that had befallen her.

The crushing responsibilities. Comfort the children. Talk to the police. Identify Richie's body. Decide where to bury it. And what about a funeral service? Should she ...

Nora tugged at her skirt. "Mommy, why are you crying?"

Startled, she swiped tears from her face and kissed Nora's cheek. "I was just feeling sad for a minute that's all. Come on, let's eat our soup."

"And oyster crackers," Nora said, smiling as she took the dish of crackers off the counter.

Resigned to it, Jackie ladled soup into a mug and took it to the breakfast bar.

"Detective Frank told me to talk to my bunny if I feel sad. Sometimes I do, but it doesn't help." Nora ate an oyster cracker. "But I like Detective Frank, don't you?"

"That was nice of him to tell you that." But Frank Renzi was no friend, grilling her, saying he wanted to find out who wanted Richie dead, and why. When the police released the names of the victims, her life would get exponentially worse. Her friends at the golf club would call, offering faux sympathy, asking why anyone would want to murder her husband.

Maybe she'd let her parents come down and help her. No, bad idea. Her father would take over and she didn't have the strength to fight him. Besides, Millstein had set up an appointment with Richie's lawyer tomorrow.

Two weeks ago Richie had changed his will.

Why? So he could leave all the money to the fucking cheerleader?

What about her and the kids?

"This soup is yummy, Mom. Can I have some more? And more oyster crackers, please?"

"Of course. You're my best girl in the whole world. Next month I'm going to bake you a big birthday cake and put six candles on it."

Nora kissed her cheek. "You're the best mom in the whole world."

CHAPTER 12

DAY 4 MONDAY OCTOBER 13, 2014 1:30 PM – New Orleans

Not until the cell door clanged shut behind him did he feel safe.

No more food delivered through the narrow slot in the door. Today they made him eat lunch in the cafeteria with the other prisoners.

He was still hungry.

An hour ago he'd shuffled past a line of metal containers, pointing at what he wanted. A female worker slapped food on his plate: a chicken leg, a scoop of mashed potatoes no bigger than a ping-pong ball, boiled carrots and a square of cornbread.

He put a half-pint container of milk on his tray and studied the rows of tables filled with other prisoners in orange jumpsuits. Prisoners who preyed on others. Prisoners who carved shivs out of toothbrushes. Prisoners to be avoided or you could wind up dead. He'd seen it happen.

He spotted an empty table near the wall, set down his tray and slid onto the bench on one side. But four prisoners suddenly appeared—schwartzers his father used to call them—huge men with dark skin, inked with elaborate tattoos. They penned him in, one on his left, one on his right.

The other two sat opposite him. The schwartzer on his left stole his corn bread, took a big bite, smiled and said, "Yummy." The one on his right took the chicken leg. The schwartzer across from him stole his milk. The other stuck his finger in the mashed potatoes, scooped some up and licked his finger, watching him with laughing eyes.

He glanced at the guard leaning against the wall fifteen feet away.

The schwartzer to his left said, "Donteventhinkaboudit, yo."

He didn't understand the words, but he knew what they meant. So he ate his boiled carrots and stared at the table. Look into the eyes of a predator, they regard it as a challenge and kill you.

At last, a bell clanged and the schwartzers left. He returned to the food line and said to a female worker, "They take my food." She took pity on him and gave him half of a grilled cheese sandwich, burnt black on both sides. Quickly hiding it inside his jumpsuit, he had returned to his cell.

Now, grateful to be alive, he sank onto the mattress, hitched himself back and leaned against the wall, his stomach rumbling with hunger. He took out the sandwich and crammed part of it in his mouth. Chewed and swallowed.

Focused on the meeting with his solicitor yesterday.

Boris Mosgov, an older man with snow-white hair and piercing blue eyes, who asked more questions than the cops, saying in Russian. *What did you tell them?*

Nothing. Just my name and I came here from MIllwaukee.

He didn't dare tell Mosgov he'd told them about the hotel.

When he asked if he could call Katerina, Mosgov said *No. They tape all phone calls. Give me her number, I will call her.*

So he recited her number. Mosgov wrote it down and asked what he wanted him to say. He wanted to say *I'm afraid for my life.*

But he didn't trust Mosgov. His employer was paying him.

So he said, *Tell her I miss her and I love her very much.*

Mosgov wrote this down in a notebook and picked up his briefcase.

Wait, he said. *Don't leave yet. The police say I could be put to death because I murdered five people. Is this true? If they decide I am guilty, will they kill me?*

Don't worry, I'll handle everything, Mosgov had said. End of meeting.

Don't worry? During the endless days and hours he'd been here, he had done nothing else, sitting in a shitty little cell, eating disgusting food, lying awake at night worrying.

How did they kill guilty men in America?

Hang them? Shoot them? Gas them?

He forced down the rest of the burnt cheese sandwich and thought about Katerina, waiting for him in London. His beloved wife who might never see him again.

———

2:30 PM – Slidell, Louisiana

Utterly spent, Nicolas lay in bed with his arms around Yvette. She reminded him of Marion Cotillard, the French actress: dark curly hair, alluring green eyes and sensuous lips. Martina was a fine mother, but he'd never been in love with her. She was ultra-conservative in bed, always the missionary position.

Yvette was far more adventurous.

Born in Paris thirty years ago, she was happy to converse with him in French or English. But there'd be hell to pay if Martina found out about their trysts. Her father was a powerful man. He could not afford to become this man's enemy. So he parked his BMW in a secluded spot and removed the battery from his cellphone so it couldn't be tracked. Yvette rented their hotel room. He reimbursed her in cash for the room and her services, and added a generous tip.

Tracing her fingers over his thigh, Yvette said, "Why do you wear a T-shirt when we make love?"

He caressed her cheek, smooth and flawless as a porcelain vase. "I don't want you to see my scars, *chéri*." He never called his lovers by name, a habit he had acquired many years ago, and he never took off his T-shirt when he went to bed with them. Only Martina saw the scars, and she knew enough not to ask how he got them.

"What happened?" Yvette said, her eyes mischievous. "Did you fight a duel with some terrible man and he stabbed you with a saber?"

"No, nothing like that." *Far worse things that you'll never know about.*

"Will we have dinner together tonight?"

"There's nothing I'd like better, but I have to work. Next week we'll sit outside our favorite restaurant with a glass of French wine and watch the sunset over Lake Pontchartrain."

"And smoke one of my **Gauloise** cigarettes?" she said, teasing him.

He laughed. "Yes."

She got on top of him, delicately feathering her tongue over his lips. Aroused by her delicious scent and her darting tongue, he groaned. But he had no time for another frolic, he needed to think.

"Go take a shower, my beautiful amour."

With a sultry laugh, she sauntered into the bathroom, a beguiling woman with creamy white skin and a curvy figure, who never failed to satisfy him.

He didn't love Yvette either, but he adored her *joie de vivre.*

At a university in Paris, she had earned degrees in languages and European history. Five years ago she had come to America with fine credentials, but teaching positions were difficult to find. She took a job as a teaching assistant at the University of Alabama and hated it.

Low pay, long hours and a dull life, she'd said.

Ever adventurous, she had run an ad in an adult magazine. No pimp, no madam, just a high-class call girl, who knew how to please men. Which was how he had found her two years ago. Now she lived in New Orleans. Twice a year she returned to Paris to see the latest fashions and French films.

He'd been to Paris once, but he hadn't watched any movies.

Back then he'd been too worried about staying alive.

He wished he could see Yvette more often, but what he'd told Nicky this morning was true. He had to make big bucks so Martina could maintain her lavish lifestyle and go on shopping sprees.

He stared at the ceiling, thinking about Richie, his longtime golf partner. His death had evoked sad memories of his own.

It wasn't hard to empathize with Danny this morning. He knew what it was like to lose a parent, both of them gone, many years ago.

FOULSHOT

His earliest memory was waiting for Papa to come home from work. He dearly loved his mum, but he idolized Papa, a man of few words but generous with praise when Nicolas did something to impress him. Each night after dinner, Papa set up a chessboard in his room and played a game of chess with himself. He let Nicolas watch and taught him how the pieces moved.

One night he pointed at the board. *Papa, why do you put the black knight there when you could put it here?*

Vladimir Kozlovich studied the board for a moment and began to laugh.

That night Nicolas got his first chess lesson. He was six years old.

Papa bought him a magazine with chess games printed in English and Russian, and made him play through them. For his seventh birthday, Papa gave him a chessboard with carved ivory pieces. The lessons continued. Nothing mattered but the chessboard, sixteen white pieces on one side, sixteen black on the other.

"To excel at chess," Papa said, "one must be able to see many moves ahead. You have natural talent, Nicolas, much more than I had at your age, but you must practice." Papa lit one of his Russian cigarettes and said, "Chess is like life. The ability to see many moves ahead allows you to anticipate when your opponent will make a mistake."

Unfortunately, it had not allowed Papa to escape his enemies.

Nicolas heard the water stop in the bathroom. Yvette was out of the shower. A tryst with Yvette was his reward for an arduous week, but his business wasn't a nine-to-five job. After a quick shower, he would drive to his office and get to work.

What he'd told Danny was true up to a point. Focus on the good times. When Mum died, Nicolas had lost himself in the world of chess, a ten-year-old reading adult magazines with chess games, solving the puzzles, determined to make his father proud.

But after Papa died, he had no time for chess. He was sixteen and focused on vengeance.

His thoughts returned to Richie. He'd warned Richie not to play around, but Richie had fallen for one of the Lakers cheerleaders. How much did she know?

More to the point, who else knew about her?

And what about Jackie?

This morning Danny said a cop had questioned her.

That might be a problem.

About what? he'd asked, but Danny said he didn't know.

Tomorrow he'd get Martina to find out.

She was much closer to Jackie than he was.

CHAPTER 13

DAY 4 MONDAY OCTOBER 13, 2014 – 2:00 PM

Frank set the Dunkin Donuts iced coffee he'd bought on his way back from Ponchatoula on the conference table. Vobitch didn't look happy, glowering at them, Frank and Kenyon on one side of the table, Orville and Kelly on the other. Fireworks coming for sure.

"From now on, we meet every day," Vobitch said. "The Super wants a daily report on this fucking case. Four days since the bloodbath and we still don't know who hired the shooter."

"Making progress though," Kenyon said. "Cross Johnny Wu off the list."

"Nothing incriminating at the club?" Orville asked.

"Nothing that ties him to the murders," Vobitch said. "How's it going with the gun search?"

"Took a walk through Treme yesterday, chatted with some folks to see what's shaking. Then I dropped by the corners on Orleans Avenue where pharmaceuticals and certain other items are sold, weapons and such. Asked some 'bangers was anyone looking to buy a snub-nosed .22 in the last week or two, hinted there might be a reward." Orville looked at Vobitch. "Didn't offer one, you know, just planted the seeds. Might think about offering a reward if we don't find out."

"We find out who bought the gun," Vobitch said, "we might find out who hired the shooter. Kenyon, mine your sources and compare notes with Orville. If we have to, we'll post a reward, but not yet. Kelly, you get anything in Atlantic City?"

"I talked to Benny's mother, Ruth Greenblatt. When I told her Richie died too, she got upset, said he lived in the trailer next door and she was very fond of him. He and Benny were pals all through school until Richie went off to college. Benny changed his name to Green and joined the Army. He wound up at Ramstein Airbase in Germany. But here's the important thing. He came home in August 1987 and gave her thirty grand for a down-payment on a house."

"Where'd he get that kind of money?" Vobitch said.

"We could ask one of his Army buddies," Kelly said, "but I don't think we need to, given what I found out later. Benny got out of the Army in 1991 and moved into his mother's house."

"How old was he?" Kenyon asked.

"Twenty-seven." Kelly grinned at Kenyon. "Yeah, I know. What guy lives with their mother at that age? But Benny wasn't a guy any girl would look at twice. Homely and overweight."

"Even if he had money?" Kenyon said. "Wined and dined her?

"No. Benny was married to Bally's Casino. Mom said he went their every night, got up at noon to watch basketball games on TV, screamed and yelled when his team lost. His only friend was a woman he met at Bally's Casino. So I went there, lucked out and found her. Profane Paula, I call her." Kelly grinned at Vobitch. "She's got a bigger arsenal of F-bombs than you do."

"Really?" Kenyon made his eyes go wide. "I didn't think that was possible."

Everyone laughed, including Frank. Over the years, he'd been in homicide units where back-biting was the rule, everyone looking out for themselves. Some supervisors loved the spotlight, basking in the media attention. Vobitch wasn't one of them. No favoritism, just do your job and get results.

"I'll see if I can remedy that," Vobitch said. "She give you anything?"

"She said Benny didn't know his ass from his elbow about betting on basketball until she taught him how. The place was wild, people screaming into cell-phones placing bets."

Orville nudged her elbow. "You win anything?"

"No chance," Frank said. "I had to explain the spread to her."

"Mr. Basketball knows how to live dangerously," Kelly retorted. "Wait till he tells you about the cheerleader. But let's get back to Paula."

"Please do," Vobitch said. "If it's not too much trouble."

"I asked if Benny was doing drugs. She said no, but when I asked if he was mob connected, she said ...." Kelly read from her notes, "I don't know, wouldn't tell you if I did. Those motherfuckers know how to take care of rats."

"But if the New Jersey mob wanted to whack Benny," Kenyon said, "why do it when Marconi was there?"

"He was expendable," Orville said. "Might even have been the lure. Get Benny and the ref into the club together, whack 'em all."

"Here's what I know for sure," Kelly said. "Benny and Richie were close friends, and Benny was a heavy gambler. I don't know if he was doing drugs or not."

"Great work, Kelly," Vobitch said. "Tell us about the cheerleader, Frank."

"Yeah," Kenyon chortled. "I can picture her already, a beautiful busty blonde in a halter top and a mini-skirt, shaking her booty."

"Not when I told her Richie was dead. Brandi Nylund said she talked to him the night before he died. I asked if he seemed worried about anything, she said no, but his wife was always giving him grief about something. Two weeks ago he told her Jackie found out he was having an affair. Brandi claimed they were going to get married. I ask if he had any enemies, she says no, everybody loved Richie. But somebody didn't."

"Right," Vobitch said. "The other woman always thinks her man is perfect."

Frank wasn't sure he agreed, but let it go. "She hooked up with Richie five years ago, right after his daughter was born. Nora will be six next month. Brandi said Richie used to take her to Las Vegas to play roulette. But when I asked if he bet on NBA games, she got huffy, said he would never do that."

"Oh yeah?" Orville said. "Man, I watch some of these games and wonder how the refs come up with these calls."

"Or no-calls," Frank said. "When I told Brandi certain people might retaliate if he didn't pay the vig, she freaked out. Bottom line, I don't think she knows anything."

"Okay," Vobitch said, "cross Brandi off the list. Tell us about the lawyer, Kenyon."

"He lives in Las Vegas," Kenyon said. "A fine city I've always wanted to visit, but the boss man wouldn't spring for the money."

"Wah, wah," Kelly teased, and Orville started laughing. Impatient to get on with it, Frank checked the time, almost three o'clock, and he had work to do.

"Boris Mosgov, age sixty-one," Kenyon said. "Born in London in 1953 during the Cold War when Khrushchev was calling the shots in Russia. His father, Dmitri Mosgov, had a low-level job at the Russian Embassy in London."

"A fucking spy," Vobitch growled.

"No doubt," Kenyon said. "Dmitri transferred to the embassy in Washington when Boris was ten, enrolled him in a private school. Boris did so well he got into Princeton in 1971. Princeton welcomed Boris with open arms and so did Virginia Wilson, a lovely blonde beauty with a rich father. They got married in 1976, whereupon Boris became an American citizen. He went to Yale law school, probably on Wilson's money, passed the bar on his first try in 1981."

Struggling not to laugh, Frank said, "Where the hell did you get all this?"

Kenyon grinned. "Clearly you have not begun to appreciate the wonders of the Internet, Frank. Find most anything, you look hard enough. But I got most of it off Boris's website."

"Get out," Kelly said. "He's got a website?"

"You bet. Complete with pictures of Mr. and Mrs. Mosgov and their three daughters. Oldest one's a dentist. Middle one's a chemical engineer. Youngest one owns a photography studio. Mrs. Mosgov is a lady of leisure, on the boards of two philanthropic organizations, in her spare time hangs out with the Garden Club ladies or some fucking thing."

Vobitch burst out laughing. "Kenyon, all this time you been hiding these skills from me?"

"Not to mention his comedy routine," Orville said. "He should go on Comedy Central."

"In good time, Orville, in good time." Kenyon studied his notepad. "Most important thing I dug up, Boris has been known to represent certain criminal elements in Las Vegas."

"They got Russian mobsters in Vegas?" Frank said.

"Boris doesn't discriminate, takes all the loot he can get from whoever."

Vobitch said, "Great job, Kenyon. While you guys were tossing the High Roller this morning, I got a phone call from the New Jersey feds. Special Agent Frederick Lewis wants the Benny tape."

"Fuck-all!" Kenyon exclaimed.

"Jesus," Kelly said. "The New Jersey feds wired Benny?"

"Looks like it. I told Fred to go fuck himself." Vobitch smiled faintly. "Well, I wanted to, but I didn't. Didn't tell him we listened to the tape either. I said I'd call him back and called the Super. He said if they send a written request, mail them the tape. Frank's got some news, too."

"I talked to Jackie Bauer this morning," Frank said. "She wasn't thrilled to see me, got a phone call and went in her office. Nora, the five-going-on-six-year-old wandered in, also not happy. Says her brother's playing with the kid next door, and when she asked to go with him, Danny says *nyet.*"

"Hoo-ee!" Kenyon exclaimed. "This is better than *The Man from UNCLE!*"

"Exactly. She says *nyet* is Danny's favorite word these days because Nicky's teaching him how to speak Russian, Nicky being the kid next door. So I ask Nora for Nicky's last name. She could only remember the first two letters. Then Jackie came back and told me her lawyer won't allow her to talk to me if he's not with her."

"She lawyered up," Kelly said.

"Exactly. The Ponchatoula Sheriff's Department got me the scoop on the Nicolas Zurik family. But when I went to their house, his wife said Nicolas was away on business and she didn't know when he'd be back."

"Sounds like a solid lead," Orville said. "What's your theory, Frank?"

"Maybe Jackie got pissed that Richie was screwing around and asked Nicolas to hire a hitman to kill him instead of getting a divorce."

"Or maybe she's in bed with Nicolas," Kelly said, "and Nicolas wants her all to himself."

"Sounds like *The Dating Game* for horny married people," Vobitch said. "Kelly, I want you to talk to Jackie's parents. Richie's parents, too."

"I don't know if I can match Kenyon's dazzling report on Mosgov," Kelly said. "But I'll do my best."

"Richie's mother is dead," Frank said. "Jackie told me she had no idea where his father is."

"We should put Tony C in a surveillance van," Orville said, "have him watch both houses. He's good at stuff like that."

"Excellent idea," Frank said, and looked at Vobitch.

"I'll call Zeke and set it up," Vobitch said. His cellphone rang. He answered and glanced around the table, his slate-gray eyes frosty. "Good afternoon to you too, Helen. What can I do for you and your fine news organization?"

Dead silence in the conference room, all eyes on Vobitch.

Vobitch frowned, his face mottled with anger. "I can't confirm that."

They sat there, waiting for the explosion.

"I don't give a flying fuck who you call, Helen. I AM NOT CONFIRMING that."

Vobitch slammed the phone on the table, a vein pulsing in his forehead.

"Helen heard a rumor the shooter's Russian, can't speak English, and wanted me to confirm it."

"Damn," Kenyon said. "Next thing you know Nancy Grace be all over it."

"Yeah?" Vobitch snapped, glaring at him. "You watch her show?"

"Not if I can help it," Kenyon said. "But now and then I get up to get a beer and when I come back the lady of the house and our teenage daughter are watching Nancy Grace."

Frank stifled a smile and glanced at Kelly, who looked away, about to crack up laughing.

"Fuck Nancy Grace," Vobitch said. "We got a leak at the Orleans Parish Prison."

"Nancy and her network got big bucks," Orville said. "Bribe some lowlife to spy on the shooter, you know, listen in on his phone calls. Or a guard looking to augment his paycheck."

"Jesus-fucking-Christ!" Vobitch bellowed. "Nobody talks to that fucking woman, you hear me? I never want to hear that name again."

"Don't worry," Frank said. "Nobody will get anything out of us."

"All well and good," Vobitch said morosely. "But Helen's probably talking to the bigwigs at Headquarters right now. So get busy and solve this motherfucking case."

BENNY GREEN

TEN YEARS EARLIER

An Old Friend, A Desperate Gamble

November 4, 2004 – Continental Airlines Arena, New Jersey

Benny leaned against the wall, his hands in the pockets of his windbreaker, watching a mob of fans stream past him, the Miami Heat fans whooping it up because Shaq and Dwayne Wade had slaughtered the Nets, the Nets fans quiet, eager to jump in their cars and go home.

He wasn't. He couldn't wait to see Richie.

He'd never forget the first time he laid eyes on him. Back then he was eight years old, living with Ma in a trailer park near Atlantic City. One day he saw movers loading stuff into the trailer opposite theirs. After the movers left, he went outside and heard yelling inside the trailer.

Then a kid stormed out the door and started throwing rocks at a tree.

Not many kids lived in the trailer park, so he walked over and said, "Hi, my name's Benny. What's yours?"

"Richie," the kid said, and threw another rock, like he was mad about something.

"Wanna come in my trailer and play? I got this great game. Payday."

"I'm not in the mood for games." Frowning at him now, taller than he was, but skinny.

"Come have some apple strudel then. Ma makes great strudel." Get Richie out of his bad mood, maybe they could be friends.

So he took him inside and told Ma that Richie had just moved into the trailer next door. Ma said, "You look hungry, Richie. I bet you haven't even had breakfast."

That's how they got to be best friends.

But elementary school was tough. On the playground the other third graders made fun of Richie because of his shabby clothes. They made fun of Benny too, called him Fatty Blatty because his name was Greenblatt. But Richie stuck up for him, told them to get lost.

"Fuck these middle school kids," Richie said. "They're assholes."

Ma got mad if she heard him swear, but he'd heard Richie's father swearing a lot. F-words mostly, floating out the window of their trailer.

So after school they went home and played Payday, dealing out fake money, pretending it was real, eating the snacks Ma gave them. Richie could eat whatever he wanted and never gain weight, partly because he was so competitive, wanted to win every game, partly because Richie was always angry.

At his father mostly.

Two years later when Richie's mother died, he and Ma went to the funeral. They sat four rows behind Richie, slouched in the front pew with his father but not talking to him, his jaw clenched. After that, Richie's father started taking him to the race track on weekends, like he thought Richie needed a distraction. Benny thought Richie needed his father to give him a hug.

Sometimes Richie came over for supper and they'd do homework together. Ma made sure he finished his, but the only homework Richie ever did was math. He was great at math. Then they watched TV. Richie liked *Charlie's Angels*. Bennie liked *Happy Days* better. Fonzie was great.

One day Richie said he'd figured out a way to make money. Neither of them had any spending money. Ma got a benefit check every month, but there wasn't much left after she paid the bills. Richie's father spent most of his money at the race track. Or on booze.

"My father taught me how a 5-play works," Richie said, "but let's start with a 4-play." Richie laughed, saying it sounded like foreplay for sex.

Benny didn't know anything about sex, but Richie was way ahead of him in a lot of ways. He was handsome even then, the girls in middle school making eyes at him.

So Richie laid out his plan. "High school kids are into baseball. We get them to bet on who gets the most hits in tomorrow's games, a buck a bet. The winner gets sixty percent of the pot; we get forty and split it. That way the winner will tell his friends and we'll get more bets for the next game."

The next day they went over to the high school athletic field. After baseball practice ended Richie asked some kids if they wanted to make some easy money. A few were Yankee fans, but most of them liked the Mets. They got ten kids to play. Ten dollars in the pot, the winner would get six bucks, they'd get four. Reggie Jackson got the most hits and it worked out the way Richie said.

The next day they took bets from twenty kids. It was exciting, watching the games on TV, wondering who'd win, knowing they'd collect either way. The second day Steve Henderson won. The winner got twelve bucks, he and Richie split eight. To celebrate they bought candy and Doritos at a convenience store and sat under a tree in the trailer park, laughing and joking, saying they'd be raking in a hundred bucks a month soon.

In October, what with the World Series, they did.

He bought Ma a new coffeemaker and asked her to help him open a savings account at the bank. Ma didn't ask how he got the money.

Richie bought a basketball and a hoop. He loved watching basketball on TV. He nailed the hoop to the roof of his trailer and practiced shooting every day after school, even in the winter. Benny sat on the steps of the trailer and watched him, not knowing that Richie's obsession with NBA basketball would eventually put an end to their friendship.

In high school, Richie tried out for the basketball team and made it. He was a natural athlete, even more handsome now, so the girls fell all over him. They paid no attention to Benny Greenblatt, homely, overweight, and Jewish.

Richie had practice every day after school. When they spent time together, which wasn't often, all Richie wanted to talk about was getting a basketball scholarship, fixated on his goal. Be the star point guard in college and get drafted to play in the NBA.

Benny had no idea what he'd do after high school.

Midway through their senior year, Richie came over, all excited, saying he'd gotten a basketball scholarship to attend Marist College, a liberal arts college in Poughkeepsie, New York. After they graduated, Richie got a summer job caddying at a golf course. Benny got a job clerking at a grocery store.

And then Richie was gone, and he was all alone. Well, he still lived with Ma, but he had no friends and he never saw Richie again.

Until three days ago, watching an NBA game on TV. One of the refs called a charging foul and they zoomed in on his face.

Benny couldn't believe his eyes. It was Richie! He got on his computer and checked the schedule to see when the next game was.

So here he was at the Meadowlands, anxiously waiting outside the Referee Locker Room. Now all the fans were gone, but the air still smelled of hot dogs and popcorn. He took out a Reese's Peanut Butter Cup and devoured it, wishing he had something else to ease his craving.

The door opened and his heart bolted into a gallop. Two refs came out and walked down the hall gabbing to each other. A minute later Richie stepped out the door, looking sharp in a gray-tweed sports jacket and black trousers, his face scrunched in a frown, like he was worried about something. Same old Richie.

"Richie!" he called.

Richie look puzzled for a second, then broke into a big smile. "Benny? Hey, great to see you!"

"Yeah, it's been a while. Wanna go have a drink and catch up on things?"

Richie hesitated, then said, "Sure. I know a great place near here."

The restaurant wasn't fancy, but it was a good place to talk. Richie got them a booth in the back and excused himself, said he hadda call his wife. That surprised him. Richie had lots of girlfriends in high school, but nobody serious, a different girl every month.

"You're married?" he said.

Richie laughed. "Yeah, she's Jewish. Her father makes big bucks."

"Gotta have the best of everything, right?"

"You got that right. No shopping at Target for Jackie. Gotta be Saks Fifth Avenue or Nordstrom's. How's your Ma doing? She made the best potato pancakes."

"Yeah, *latkes* with strawberry syrup. Ma knows how to cook."

"You still live with her? Benny, you gotta find yourself a nice Jewish girl!"

Marriage was the last thing on his mind. He had more important things to worry about. Like the money he owed certain people.

"I saw you on TV a couple nights ago, shocked the hell outta me. I figured you'd be playing, not refereeing. What happened?"

Richie waved a hand like he did when he didn't want to talk about something. "Tell me about you. Last time I saw you was in high school. Hate to think how long ago that was."

Thirty years ago, he wanted to say. *Why didn't you call me?*

But that would make Richie feel guilty and ruin everything.

"I joined the Army."

Richie stared at him. "You? In the Army? This I gotta hear."

He grinned. "Yeah. I barely passed the physical. Basic training was rough, but a coupla guys helped me. Remember how we ran those Pick-4 games? I set some up for the guys in my squad, made sure they did okay. When I took the aptitude test, they said I was good at math—"

"From figuring the odds, right?" Richie said.

"Right. So they put me in the computer unit. I learned a bunch of stuff and two years later they shipped me to Germany. I set up a gambling ring for guys on the base. Three years later I took a leave, went home with thirty large."

"Jesus Christ!" Richie said, staring at him. "Sounds like you did okay."

"I bought Ma a house with it. Well, not all of it. I used a chunk for the down-payment, got her a two bedroom cottage in the suburbs, so she could kiss the trailer park goodbye."

Richie didn't say anything, sipping his beer, staring into space.

He could tell Richie was thinking about his own mother, dead in a car accident so many years ago.

"You're a saint, Benny, helping your mom like that."

He waved a hand. "Yeah, well, it was the least I could do. Then I went back to Germany for four years." Benny grinned. "Figured I'd build up a stash so I could become a professional gambler."

Richie looked at him, expressionless. "So? Did you?"

"Yes. Got out in 1991 and moved in with Ma. Atlantic City was jumping. After ESPN started airing the college hoop games, lotta people got into sports betting. You ever bet on games?"

Richie flashed a fake smile, like he did when he was hiding something. "Not me. I'd lose my job. NBA refs can't bet on anything."

"Not NBA games. College games. Study the players, you'd know how to pick 'em."

"Nah. I'm too busy right now. Jackie's pregnant."

Damn! He needed money now. "Hey that's great. You must be excited."

Richie grinned, a genuine smile this time. "I can't wait to see the little guy."

"But kids are expensive, Richie. And your wife wants the best of everything, right?"

Richie looked at him, interested he could tell, but not saying anything.

"March Madness is huge. You could make a ton of money. Tell me who's gonna win, I place a bet for both of us, nobody knows you're involved."

Benny clasped sweaty hands in his lap, desperately needing Richie's help, hoping he'd say yes, terrified he'd say no.

"That might work," Richie said. "Give me your phone number."

His heart jumped for joy. He took out his card and set it on the table.

Richie put it in his pocket, slid out of the booth and said, "I better go. Jackie's waiting for me. I'll call you next weekend."

Benny watched him leave, feeling sick to his stomach.

Next weekend? Four agonizing sleepless nights from now?

But Richie called and it all worked out. For a while.

CHAPTER 14

Heartsick but determined, Jackie got out of Saul Millstein's car and marched into the building. Saul had offered to come with her, but she told him to wait in the parking lot. She wanted to be alone with Richie, wanted to touch him one last time.

The grim lobby filled her with dread: a black-and-white tile floor, dull gray walls, even the painting of the governor on the wall, a dour man in a black suit, with flinty blue eyes and thin lips.

The woman behind the information desk smiled and said, "Good morning, can I help you?"

Jackie wanted to slap her. *Help me? Only if you can bring Richie back to life.*

"I'm here to identify my husband's body. Richard Bauer."

The smile disappeared. "I'm sorry for your loss, Mrs. Bauer. The morgue is downstairs. Take the elevator down to Level 2 and follow the signs."

She got in the elevator, hit the button and waited. When the doors opened, she stepped into a deserted hallway. A huge yellow-and-black sign on the wall said BIO-HAZARD. Another said MORGUE and VIEWING ROOM, with an arrow pointing left.

Her palms dampened with sweat and her heart thundered inside her chest. How on earth would she get through this? She gritted her teeth and pushed through a set of stainless-steel doors, the cool air vaguely skanky, some odor she didn't recognize.

An older couple sat in the waiting room, a stone-faced black man with graying hair, the woman beside him clutching a wad of tissues. Avoiding their eyes, Jackie sank onto a yellow-plastic chair and studied a photograph on the wall. A golden sunset shimmering over Lake Pontchartrain. It seemed out of place, considering that people were here to identify the body of someone they loved.

Willing herself not to cry, she clenched her hands and pictured Richie five days ago in their kitchen, eating breakfast. Full of life and smiling at the kids. Now he lay on a slab somewhere in the morgue. Cold. Dead.

The door to her right opened. A tall black man in an NOPD uniform came in the room and said, "Dante Williams?"

The black man stood up and said, "Yes." The policeman escorted the couple through the door. Jackie wondered whose body they had to identify. Their son maybe, if the police were involved.

Would Detective Renzi come through the door when it was her turn? Damn it to hell! If he did, she'd tell him to get lost and let her spend a final moment alone with Richie.

But ten minutes later the door opened and a sallow-faced man in green scrubs said, "Mrs. Bauer? Come with me please."

He took her to the viewing room, a claustrophobic space the size of her bathroom, smelling of disinfectant. A horizontal rectangular window was set into one wall, but a maroon curtain blocked whatever was beyond the glass.

"Wait here please," said the man in green scrubs. "I'll bring Mr. Bauer's body out so you can view it through the window."

"No! I want to go in the room to see him."

"I'm sorry, but that's not possible."

"Why not? I want to touch him. Kiss him goodbye."

"Regulations won't allow it. Would you like us to have someone else identify him?"

She wanted to scream *Fuck the regulations!* But that wouldn't get her anywhere. "No. Let me see him at least."

The man left the room. A minute later he opened the maroon curtain and rolled a gurney over to the window. He positioned it lengthwise and pulled a white sheet down to Richie's waist.

She thought her heart would break.

Richie lay there, defenseless, eyes closed, his lips pulled back in a grimace. A small hole in his forehead, another in his chest near his left nipple. Holes where bullets had torn into Richie's body, ending his life.

Blinking back tears, she whispered, "Rest in peace, Richie. I always loved you and I always will."

On the drive home, she pretended her life was normal. Just another beautiful sunny day in New Orleans.

But her life would never be normal again.

———

2:00 PM – New Orleans

Frank parked in front of Lola's Cafe, eager to talk to Special Agent Claudia Cohen. Five years ago she'd helped him with a kidnapping case. Back then Claudia was thirty-five and had just been transferred to the New Orleans FBI office. For the past five years in the Chicago office, she had distinguished herself by solving a series of violent rape-murders.

Lola's Cafe occupied one corner of a strip mall in Lakeview, an upscale neighborhood near Lake Pontchartrain. No view of the lake but conveniently located two miles from the FBI office. He went inside and spotted Claudia at a table in the back. Petite and athletic-looking, she had on standard FBI attire, a charcoal pantsuit, a cream-colored blouse under the jacket. Her short dark hair was swept back from her heart-shaped face, exposing gold studs in her ears.

He took the chair opposite hers and said, "Hi Claudia, great to see you. What's shaking these days?"

"Same old, same old. It never ends, does it?"

He pictured the bloodbath at the High Roller Club, worse than any crime scene he'd ever encountered. Cops and first responders were usually the only ones who saw the grisly details. Visitors at the wake saw the victims laid out in a casket in a suit, eyes closed as though they were asleep. But viewing the carnage served as a powerful reminder to homicide detectives: the victims are real flesh-and-blood people who deserve justice.

Interrupting his ruminations, Claudia said, "I'm currently working a sex-trafficking case, staked out the bus station last week and collared a sleazeball who'd just picked up a ten-year-old girl."

"Jesus. How do they sleep at night?"

"They don't give a fuck. It's all about money, you know that."

"Indeed I do. Want coffee? My treat."

"Sure, same as yours, iced coffee, cream no sugar, right?"

He laughed. "You've got a good memory."

He went to the counter and put in the order, recalling Vobitch's warning. "Watch out. She reports to Walsh."

Vobitch's antipathy to Terrence Walsh, Special Agent in Charge of the New Orleans FBI office, was longstanding. The six-foot-three Irishman loved to throw his weight around and micro-manage his subordinates. That didn't intimidate Claudia. But Vobitch didn't trust her.

However, Vobitch hadn't been privy to his conversation with Claudia five years ago. When he'd asked why she joined the FBI, Claudia said she had Broadway ambitions. "I was gonna be the next Julie Andrews, but it didn't work out, so I joined the FBI."

"Quite a leap, Broadway to crime fighter in a single bound. What happened?"

"That's a story for another day." But when he pressed her, she said, "Back then if a woman cried rape, the defense lawyers crucified her and called her a slut. That's what happened to me. Not a gang-rape, but hey, who's counting when you get beat up and raped?"

Stunned, he said, "Did they get the guy?"

"I picked him out of a lineup and they charged him, but his lawyer got him off. For months I'd lie in bed at night, fantasizing that I had a gun and shot his balls off. But that only happens in the movies."

"Everything works out in the movies. Real life is different. How old were you?"

"Nineteen. He beat me up, broke my jaw and raped me."

Hoping to lighten things up, he said, "So you got into heavy metal. Metallica and Glock nines."

"You're pretty sharp for a homicide dick. Just for the record, I hate Metallica."

"Me, too. But you had every right to be angry when the rapist got off. A lot of them rape other women. And kill them."

"That's why I do what I do," she'd said. End of conversation.

He collected two iced-coffees, cream no sugar, and took them to their table. Claudia smiled and said, "Thanks, Frank, just what I needed. Tell me about the shooting."

"Two of the victims worked at the club. We checked them out and concluded they were collateral damage. We believe the three men seated in the same booth were targeted by the shooter. Could be one, could be all of them. One was an NBA referee, one was a bookie from Atlantic City, the third guy was an Atlantic City mobster."

"Jesus Christ!" Claudia exclaimed, and looked around to see if anyone had noticed. But the three women at the nearest table continued chattering. "Sorry, Frank, but that's a helluva situation."

"The media types are already busting Vobitch's balls. It'll get worse when we release the names."

"Which you'll have to do sooner or later."

"Exactly. And the reporters will dig up dirt on them in a New York minute." His cellphone rang. He checked the ID and said, "Sorry, I have to take this."

He punched on, his heart beating a tattoo against his ribs. "Hey Mo, is everything okay?"

"Better than okay, Dad. I just passed the board exams!"

Relieved, he said, "Fantastic! That's wonderful, Mo. Sorry I haven't called but I've been busy—"

"I know. It's all over the national news. Not that I had much time to watch it, what with studying for the exams and all. How's it going? You got any leads?"

Amused, he smiled. His daughter, always eager to play detective. "Not yet, but I'm working on it as we speak," he said, and glanced at Claudia, who was watching him.

"Got it. Call me later when you're not busy okay? Love you."

"Love you too." He ended the call and said, "My daughter, Maureen."

"So I gathered. Is something wrong? For a second there you seemed worried."

"She's had a rough year. But she just passed her board exams. She's an orthopedic surgical resident in Baltimore." He wasn't about to tell Claudia how rough last year had been. An Irish gangster from South Boston had murdered his father and kidnapped Maureen. Every time his phone rang and he saw Maureen's ID, he freaked out, fearing something had happened to her.

"And you're the proud papa," Claudia said, her brown eyes mischievous. "How can I help with the case?"

Frank grinned. "I thought you'd never ask. For openers, the bookie was wearing a wire."

"There's a kick in the ass. Who wired him up?"

"That's what I want to know. Could you find out if the New Jersey feds are involved?"

Claudia sipped her iced coffee. "I'll give it a shot. Murphy won't help me, but I have other sources. What else?"

"Anything you can find on the New Jersey mobster, Dominic Marconi, and the bookie. His name is Benny Green, but he changed it years ago, birth name Benjamin Greenblatt."

Claudia scribbled in her notepad and glanced at her watch. "Sorry, Frank, gotta go. This might take a day or two. Call you as soon as I've got something."

"Thanks a million, Claudia. I really appreciate it."

They got in their respective cars and he watched her drive off, certain she'd get the information. When Claudia Cohen wanted something, she was a pit bull.

In some ways she was a lot like Kelly. Five years ago he'd told Kelly about Claudia, who knew Kelly's father, a Chicago police officer.

"I told her you worked for NOPD, didn't mention we were involved."

"Uh-huh," Kelly said, regarding him with her sea-green eyes. "Is she a dog or a cat?" Kelly's classification system for evaluating the women he met. Dogs were loud and ugly. Cats were sleek and beautiful.

"She's gorgeous," he said, "looks like Holly Hunter, packs a gun."

Whereupon Kelly had laughed and said, "I better talk to my dad and see if you're lying."

Two feisty women. Frank would trust either of them to watch his back in a tight situation, but their response to the traumas they had suffered was dramatically different.

After being brutally raped, Claudia had dedicated her life to catching rapists and murderers. If she had a boyfriend—or a girlfriend for that matter, Frank didn't care—she'd never mentioned one, said she lived by herself and liked it.

Kelly hadn't been raped, but she had suffered a life-altering trauma, too. Now, five years later their relationship was as good as ever, and he was infinitely grateful for that.

91

CHAPTER 15

DAY 5 TUESDAY OCTOBER 14, 2014 2:25 PM – New Orleans

Late for the meeting, Frank hustled into the conference room and slipped into his chair. Seated across the table from him, Kelly arched an eyebrow but said nothing.

Vobitch gave him a look, but wasted no time getting started. "We're telling the media vultures the victims' next of kin don't live in New Orleans and we're waiting for them to make positive IDs. But we can't hold off releasing the names much longer."

"What about Benny's mother?" Kelly asked, frowning now. "She's not well enough to fly here."

"Doctor DeMayo had Benny's dentist send us X-rays of his teeth," Vobitch said. "A forensic dentist will make the ID. That might take a day or so. Dominic Marconi's brother will be at the morgue later today."

"Want me to talk to him?" Kenyon asked.

"Sure. Not that it will do any good. The asswipe will tell you his brother was a saint and it's our fault for not keeping him safe or some fucking thing."

"Did Jackie Bauer ID her husband yet?" Orville said.

"Yes. This morning at the morgue," Vobitch said. "We release the names, the vultures will go ballistic. I already told Lurleen to forward all media calls to Headquarters. Let the bigwigs upstairs handle it. They're the ones making the big bucks."

"Tony Coppola got me a translation of the shooter's phone call," Frank said. "He found an Army veteran who served in Afghanistan during the Gulf War. His mother's an American citizen, but she was born in Russia, so he knows the language. The shooter speaks first. *The cops got me. I told them nothing. I need solicitor.*"

"So he didn't call Mosgov," Kenyon said.

"Correct. I assume he called the guy who paid him."

"Or the woman," Kelly said. "Can we tell from the recording?"

"Sounded like a man to me," Kenyon said. "Low pitched voice."

"Definitely," Frank said. "Here's his response. *I will send you a solicitor who speaks Russian. Until then, speak to no one. And remember what I said.*"

"There's a threat if I ever heard one," Kelly said.

"To make sure the shooter keeps his mouth shut," Frank said.

"And hired Mosgov." Vobitch said. "At the arraignment today, Mosgov acted as the shooter's translator. Could have told him anything. The DA identified the defendant as John Doe, who calls himself Hans Nader but that has not been verified. They charged him with five counts of first degree murder. No bail. The motherfucker sits in jail until the trial."

"Can we find out when he talks to Mosgov?" Frank asked. "I want to be there, ask him a few questions, get a feel for how he interacts with Mosgov."

"Sure," Vobitch said. "I'll have my contact at the Orleans Parish Prison call me the next time Mosgov shows up to see him. What's happening on the gun search?"

"Kenyon and I are working it hard," Orville said. "Nothing yet, but we'll stay on it."

"Let's talk suspects," Vobitch said. "The referee's wife is still on the list, plus her next door neighbor, Nicolas Zurik. Who happens to speak Russian."

"I asked Tony to watch both houses," Frank said. "He needs to set up the surveillance van, figured he'll be ready to scout a good location this afternoon."

"What about the Atlantic City mob?" Kenyon said. "Maybe they found out Benny talked to the feds and killed him."

"I sent the Benny tape to the New Jersey FBI office." Vobitch did his imitation smile. "My pal Agent Fred faxed me a written request soon as I asked for one."

"We don't know what the feds were after," Frank said. "Could be drugs, could be gambling, given Benny's obsession with sports betting."

"When I was researching Russian NBA players," Kelly said, "I stumbled upon an article about Russian gangs that operate in London. Maybe the shooter came here from London."

"But how did he wind up here?" Vobitch asked. "As far as we know, none of our suspects ever lived in London."

"Get their passports," Orville said, "you'll know if they've been there recently."

"But how do we get them?" Kenyon said. "We'd need a warrant."

"Find a friendly judge and plead exigent circumstances," Orville said.

"I'll send the shooter's prints and mugshot to Interpol," Frank said. "Maybe they can get us something. The NOPD crime techs traced the shooter's call to a burner. No way to find out who bought it, but the guy speaks Russian, and it wasn't Mosgov."

Vobitch dialed a number on his cell phone and waited. After a moment he said, "I need to know when the motherfucker's lawyer comes to see him." He smiled. "Excellent." He ended the call and said, "Mosgov signed in five minutes ago. Go see what you can dig up, Frank."

———

3:15 PM – Ponchatoula

Jackie stifled a yawn as Millstein pulled into her driveway. This had been the longest day of her life. She wanted to crawl in bed and sleep for a week.

If only she could.

Danny and Nora had been at Martina's house since breakfast. Danny complained bitterly when she said he couldn't go to school, but teachers could be nosy and so could kids. Before she left the house, she'd called the school and told them Danny wouldn't be in today.

"I hope you're feeling better," Millstein said. "At least you know what's in the will." He handed her the copy Richie's lawyer had made for her after they went over it in his office.

"But there's no money in the bank accounts. All the money is tied up in a trust."

"I'll have Grace get me a copy of it. After I see what it says, I'll call you." Seemingly embarrassed, avoiding her eyes, Millstein cleared his throat. "At least he didn't leave anything to the cheerleader."

She bit back a laugh. Before Richie changed the will, he could have given Pompom Girl a big hunk of cash and now she was set for life, with no one the wiser. Including Saul Millstein.

"Thank you for everything, Saul. My father told me you were terrific and he was right."

Millstein patted her hand. "Get some rest, Jackie. Things will look better in the morning."

She clenched her jaw. Things weren't going to look better in the morning. They weren't going look better the next day either, or the day after that.

She unlocked the front door and went in the house. No welcoming whoops from Danny and Nora. Avoiding the photographs of Richie in the hallway, memories of happier days, she went to her office, put the copy of Richie's will in her desk drawer and massaged her forehead.

Another migraine lurked behind her eyes. Too much stress, too little sleep. She got on her cellphone and called Martina.

"Jackie," Martina said, "I've been so worried about you. Danny said a policeman came to your house yesterday and questioned you. What did he want?"

"Nothing much. He asked if Richie had any enemies, things like that. Danny tends to dramatize things."

"These kids watch too many cop shows on TV. But seriously, do you have a lawyer?"

"Of course. How are the kids doing?"

"They're fine. They're out on the patio playing a game. Where have you been all day?"

"I had to go to the morgue and identify Richie's body."

"Mother of God! I can't believe they made you do that. Come over here right now and have a glass of wine and we'll talk about it."

She didn't want to talk about it. She wanted to read Richie's will and figure out what to do.

"Thanks, Martina, but I've got a sick-headache. Send the kids home and I'll figure out something for dinner."

"Don't be silly. I've got a pan of lasagna ready to cook. Go take a nap. The kids can stay here for dinner. Call me when you wake up and I'll send them home with a plate of lasagna for you."

Tears filled her eyes. What would she do without Martina?

"Are you sure you don't mind?"

"Positive. Sleep as long as you want. The kids are fine here. Nicky is always happy to see them and so am I."

"Thanks, Martina. Call you later." But she had no intention of taking a nap.

She wanted to go over the will line by line. Two weeks ago Richie had added a codicil that specified several items be left to her.

His desktop computer and laptop, which was weird. She didn't have passwords for them. Plus his black file cabinet. It also listed several other items: his clothes, his shoes including the ones he wore to referee games, even the whistles he used to officiate games.

Almost like Richie was trying to tell her something. But what?

CHAPTER 16

Terrified, he clamped his trembling hands between his knees, seated beside Mosgov in a room with no windows. Two men sat across the table from them. The cop who had questioned him at the High Roller Club and later at the police station, the cop with the hawk nose and implacable eyes. The other man was black, but not the big schwartzer at the police station. This one was older, with bushy gray hair. Not a cop, but he knew the man was important.

This morning they had driven him somewhere and rushed him past a mob of screaming reporters and television cameras. Inside, Mosgov told him they would go in a courtroom and prosecutors would charge him for the crimes he had committed. In the courtroom there was only one reporter, and no television cameras. Was this normal?

Too afraid to ask, he sat beside Mosgov at a wooden table. Ahead of them on a raised platform, a judge in maroon robes sat at an ornate desk, an older man with pale skin and spectacles. The black man with bushy gray hair rose from a table to his right and spoke rapid English.

Peering at him over his spectacles, the judge asked if he understood. Mosgov told him to say yes, so he did. But he didn't understand. He had many questions. No matter, they had taken him back to his cell.

Ten minutes ago, two guards had come to his cell, saying he could talk to his solicitor. So here he was, trapped in a windowless room, unable to talk to Mosgov because the cop and the important schwartzer were here.

Beyond them, visible through a window in the door, two guards stood outside, watching him with hard eyes. To make sure he didn't make a fuss or try to escape. As if that was possible.

Mosgov said briskly in English, "Let's get started. I have an appointment at five o'clock."

The cop said, "We checked the Milwaukee address on your client's driver's license. No one named Hans Nader lives there."

"He moved," Mosgov said. "Forgot to change his address."

"We need a positive ID. Where's his passport?"

"He doesn't have one."

"Show me his birth certificate."

"Detective Renzi, his parents brought him to America from Afghanistan when he was an infant. They were lucky to escape with their lives, never mind documents like birth certificates."

He tugged on Mosgov's arm, whispered in Russian, *"You speak too fast. Tell me what is happening."*

"They asked for your passport. I told them you didn't have one. Same with the birth certificate."

"What about charges in court this morning? When do we talk about that?"

"After they leave. Say nothing unless I tap your foot. Be careful what you say."

He clenched his hands. *Be careful what you say.* He knew what that meant.

"Who paid you?" Renzi said, fixing him with his implacable eyes.

A tap on his foot.

Shudders of dread rippled through him. He knew enough English to understand the question. And how he must answer it.

"No one pay me."

Renzi said, "Do you know Richard Bauer?"

A tap on his foot. "No," he said.

"Do you know Benny Green?"

"No."

"Dominic Marconi?"

"No."

"So why did you shoot them?"

"You can't prove he shot them," Mosgov said.

"He was captured in the kitchen right after the shooting."

"He was running away."

"Don't play games," Renzi said. "We've got the gun he used to shoot them."

"Without his prints on it."

"Why was he wearing gloves?"

Mosgov looked at his watch. "We're wasting time."

The black man leaned forward and spoke rapidly, too rapidly for him to understand. He tapped Mosgov's arm and said in Russian, *"What does he say?"*

They offer you a deal if you confess, but if you confess they will put you in the electric chair and kill you. Is that what you want?"

"Nyet," he said, shaking his head emphatically.

In English, Mosgov said, "My client declines the deal. Interview over."

Renzi and the black man rose from their chairs.

"Wait," he said in English. "Very afraid, me. Other prisoners—"

Mosgov squeezed his arm, silencing him. "Detective Renzi, my client feels very alone here. A young man, twenty-three years old, who can't even talk to his girlfriend on the phone because all his calls are taped."

More afraid than ever, he gazed at Renzi, trying to send a message with his eyes. But Renzi turned and signaled the guards to open the door.

"Tell your client to take the deal," the schwartzer said, and followed Renzi out the door.

He lowered his head, put his face in his hands.

Very alone here, Mosgov had said.

Exactly. Very alone with no one to protect him.

———

5:10 PM – Ponchatoula

On the verge of tears, Jackie gulped some Merlot. It would make her headache worse, but so fucking what? She had searched every drawer in Richie's desk, hunting for passwords that would get her into his computers, pawing through Bic pens, pads of yellow stickies, boxes of staples, paper clips and felt-tipped highlighters. And found nothing.

Jesus! Everyone hid their passwords somewhere.

Hers were on a pink sticky in the top drawer of her desk.

She rolled Richie's desk chair to the black filing cabinet and opened the top drawer. Hanging files held manila folders with bank statements and household bills. She'd searched them before, had taken the bank statements and bills to Millstein.

She closed the top drawer and opened the bottom one. More hanging files with color-coded folders. Insurance policies for both cars, maintenance and re-pair bills. Insurance policies for the contents of the house. Nine years of state-ments from their medical insurance company, listing every medical treatment under the sun for everyone in the family. No yellow sticky.

"Damn it to hell!"

She rolled the chair back to the desk, gulped more wine and pictured Richie in the morgue this morning. Did the man who shot him feel anything when he pulled the trigger? Or was he just a hired gun, like Renzi said, eager to collect whatever disgusting amount of money he'd been paid?

But the prick-bastard would never spend it. Now he was in jail.

Why would Richie add a codicil to his will? There had to be a reason.

She stared at the file cabinet. A quarter-inch gap showed along the sides of the top drawer. Thinking a folder was sticking up, preventing it from closing all the way, she went to the cabinet and opened the drawer. No folders sticking up.

She pushed the drawer, but it still wouldn't close.

She got down on her knees and looked underneath the drawer.

Her heart jolted, racing like a runaway freight train. A manila envelope was Scotch-taped to the underside of the drawer. Using her fingernail, she dug off the tape and took out the envelope.

Her name was on the front, printed in capital letters. **JACKIE**

Tears filled her eyes. She was right. Richie had left her a message.

With trembling hands, she opened the envelope.

Shocked to the core, she gasped. It wasn't a love letter.

It was a warrant, ordering Richard Bauer to appear in a federal courtroom in Atlantic City, New Jersey, on Monday, November 3, 2014 at 9 AM.

What the hell was that?

Unwilling to believe it, she took the warrant to the desk and sank onto the chair. Richie had signed for it on September 22, 2014.

Less than a month before he was murdered. Three days later, Richie had gone to see his lawyer and revised his will.

Bile rose in her throat. She ran to the bathroom and vomited into the toilet. Panting, she gripped the toilet bowl and spewed more vomit. At last she rose to her feet and brushed her teeth. Pressing a wet facecloth to her aching temples, she returned to Richie's office.

No more wine. She had to think. She tried to remember if Richie had dropped any hints about this. She couldn't remember any.

Jesus, why didn't he tell her? He must have been devastated. Out of his mind with worry.

But why did the feds want to question him?

Doubt crept into her mind. Richie had always been a gambler.

On their honeymoon in Vegas, he'd spent hours at the roulette table, winning more than he lost for the most part.

Was he gambling on NBA games? No. Richie would never do that.

He loved his job, had endured years of hardship and endless hours of work to land a job as an NBA ref.

Her next thought. Federal warrants were a matter of public record.

What if the reporters found it?

"Jesus," she whispered. "My life is ruined."

NICOLAS

THIRTY-FIVE YEARS EARLIER

Death, Vengeance, a New Job

October, 1979 – London

Nicolas sat at the kitchen table, analyzing moves on his chessboard, waiting for Mum to come home and fix dinner. But when the door opened, Vladimir Kozlovich, a strapping bear of a man with dark hair, dark eyes and sharp cheekbones, stepped inside and slammed the door.

Mum called him Vladi. Nicolas was only ten and called him Papa.

His face seemed different tonight. Expressionless.

"Papa, how come you're home early?"

His father silently hung Mum's coat on a hook by the door.

Anxious now, Nicolas said, "Where's Mum?"

"She's dead."

Stunned, he said, "No, Papa. She just went out to buy groceries."

"Your mother is dead, Nicolas. She was crossing the street and a bus ran over her."

Papa took a liter of Stolichnaya out of the refrigerator, went in his bedroom and shut the door.

For an hour Nicolas waited for him to come out. Finally he tiptoed to the door and heard Papa sobbing, calling Mum's name. *Celeste, Celeste.*

He took the chess book Papa had given him and played through five games, blotting out everything but the chess pieces.

Blotting out the fact that Mum was dead.

But when he went to bed he had to face it. Mum wasn't coming home. Mum wasn't going to cook dinner or come in his room and tell him she loved him with all her heart. He curled up into a ball and cried himself to sleep.

For two days, Papa stayed in his room, only coming out to use the toilet, his face pale as death. Nicolas ate leftovers from the refrigerator. Borscht that Mum had made and piroshki, dumplings stuffed with vegetables and cheese.

To avoid thinking about Mum, he focused on what Papa had told him about what it was like growing up in Moscow after The Great Patriotic War. Foraging for scraps in garbage bins, rubble everywhere, living in a hovel because artillery fire had destroyed the apartment where he'd lived with his mother. His father had died fighting the Germans.

After Khrushchev took over, Papa and his mother got an apartment. But when Papa was sixteen, everyone was worried about the Cuban Missile Crisis. Fearing he would be forced into the army, hiding from soldiers with rifles, Papa fled Moscow. Days later, he swam across a river to safety. At last he arrived in Paris, made his way to Calais and took a boat across the English Channel. He met Mum on the boat. They fell in love and Mum taught Papa how to speak French and English.

When he told him this, Papa said sternly, "Never forget your heritage, Nicolas. Or how to speak Russian."

In London, Papa worked menial jobs that barely paid enough to rent a room in a boarding house. In 1969, Nicolas was born. Papa smiled when he said this, saying they were overjoyed. Papa was twenty-three. Mum was twenty. But they still lived in a boarding house. Papa wanted to rent an apartment, so he asked one of his Russian friends for advice.

"Join the *vory*," his friend said. "Russian gang, very powerful."

So Papa joined the *vory*. Two months later he rented a two bedroom apartment. Papa had not told him what he did to earn the money. That came later.

The third morning after Mum died, Papa came out of his room and said, "Let's go out and have breakfast, Nicolas." As though nothing had happened.

Papa began teaching him the tools of his trade. How to be a lookout. How to follow a person without being seen. Eager to learn, Nicolas mastered this quickly. Then Papa took him to an underpass outside the city, taught him how to use his gun and had him shoot at a target.

On his thirteenth birthday, Nicolas joined the gang.

At first he acted as a lookout during robberies, tooting a whistle if any cops drove by. Then he moved up to surveillance, watching a building and following a man when he came out. It was exciting, a bit like a chess match, anticipating where the man might go. Usually the men had done something to displease the gang leader. Sometimes they became Papa's target.

By then Nicolas knew what Papa did for the vory. He was their top assassin.

Then Alexei joined the gang. They were the same age and when they weren't on duty, they played chess. Most of the time Nicolas won, but Alexei didn't mind. They listened to pop music, British groups like the Eurythmics and Def Leppard, and danced with pretty girls at London clubs. Soon they were making bets about who would get laid first.

Nicolas won. Alexei was smart, but rather homely. One night Nicolas snared a sixteen-year-old dark-haired vixen, his heart pounding with excitement until he climaxed. Fourteen years old and he thought he'd died and gone to heaven. Not that he believed in heaven.

Life was good. But in 1985, Papa's ability to see many moves ahead in chess failed him in life. Two rival gang members ambushed him.

A policeman came to the apartment and told him Vladimir Kozlovich was dead. Nicolas was sixteen. At first he felt nothing, too stunned to comprehend. Then the cop took him to the morgue to identify Papa's bullet-riddled body.

That made it real.

He went home and took a liter of vodka out of the refrigerator, drank the whole bottle and got violently sick.

That day Nicolas vowed he would never love anyone again. His second, equally important vow: the men who murdered his father must die.

After months of reconnaissance, he and Alexei identified the cowardly dogs who murdered Papa, mowing him down with Kalashnikov AK-47s when he left the cafe where he ate lunch.

For months Nicolas stalked them, waiting outside their apartment, following them to see where they went. Finally, a pattern emerged.

One dark October night in 1986, Nicolas, now seventeen, armed himself with a Beretta and a buck-knife and set out to kill them. Alexei offered to help, but Nicolas said, "No. It is my job to avenge my father."

Beneath a moonless dark sky, he waited outside their apartment. When the men approached their car, Nicolas sprang from his hiding place.

"Stop or you die!"

One man went for his gun. Nicolas shot him in the heart.

The other man stood very still, his eyes wide with fear.

"You murdered my father," Nicolas said. "Vladimir Kozlovich."

"I just follow orders. Please don't shoot me."

"May you rot in hell." Nicolas drew his knife and slit the man's throat.

But such killings do not pass without notice. The police questioned Nicolas. Thanks to Alexei, he had an ironclad alibi, but the gang leader who hired the assassins put out a contract on Nicolas. 5,000 British pounds for anyone who delivered a photo of his corpse.

Alexei helped him escape, converting the British pounds Nicolas had saved and money the vory leader had given him to American dollars. Bidding his friend a sad farewell, Nicolas took a train to Rotterdam and boarded a freighter bound for New York. To insure his cooperation, Nicolas paid the captain a thousand dollars. Six days later in New York City, he vanished into the darkness. No passport required. No questions from customs agents.

He walked the streets, observing people to see how they walked, purposeful and determined. He mimicked them, striding along like he didn't have a care in the world. But there were many problems to solve. He figured out the subway system, rode a train to the last stop and found a cheap hotel.

Hidden in his knapsack were four thousand dollars in cash. His British passport was also in the knapsack, but he didn't want to use it. Russian gangs had contacts all over the world.

He told the desk clerk he wanted to rent a room for a week.

The man asked for his driver's license.

Nicolas put two hundred dollars on the counter. "I don't have one."

The man took the cash and gave him a room key.

Incessant traffic roared past the hotel on a nearby highway, but there were clean sheets on the bed and clean towels. Exhausted, he stretched out on the bed and stared at the ceiling. Pretended this was a chess match, figured out what he needed to do and fell asleep.

The next day he rode the train into the city. The streets were easy to navigate, laid out in a grid pattern. In London, there were chess games on the street, no papers needed, just balls of steel and a sharp mind. And right now his mind was as sharp as a scimitar. In Central Park he came upon some men playing chess and won a few dollars.

But what he really needed was a permanent place to live and a job.

Three weeks later, on his eighteenth birthday in November, he went to a cafeteria, eating cheap to conserve cash. He put in his order and noticed a young guy eating soup and black bread at a table by himself. He had a foreign look about him, black hair, Slavic features, dark eyes.

In fact, he looked very much like Nicolas.

He paid for his dinner—onion soup, a ham sandwich and a small container of milk—and went to the guy's table. Feigning broken English, he said, "Excuse, please. Okay I sit here?"

The guy looked up and smiled. "Yah. No problem."

Nicolas sat down, ate a spoonful of soup and said, "Not know much about New York. Just come here. You been here long?"

"Almost a year. Big city with many people. Where you from?"

Nicolas glanced around, acting furtive. "Uzbekistan. Sneak in without papers. You?"

"I come here from Serbia. Bad things happening there, so they let me in. My name is Roland."

"I am Vladi," he said. "You have job?"

"Yah." Smiling at him. "Work at Stock Exchange, sweep floors."

"Great." He drank some milk. "You know cheap place to stay? I not have much money."

Roland slurped some soup. Nicolas could see his mind working.

"Want to share my apartment? Help pay the rent? You sleep on futon in living room."

"That would be great!"

"We finish dinner and I show you."

On the way, Nicolas bought four muffins at a pastry shop, to thank Roland for helping him. Eventually they came to a street lined with run-down buildings, some with plywood covering the windows. They passed a vacant lot strewn with bald tires and discarded car parts.

Beside it was Roland's four-story apartment building.

On the sidewalk, a filthy mattress was draped over trash bags. Spray-painted graffiti marked the front door. In the foyer, mailboxes lined one wall, and a light bulb dangled from the ceiling. No elevator, so they walked up to Roland's flat. Cigarette butts littered the halls and the air stank of stale beer and urine.

On the fourth floor Roland stopped at a door, took out a key ring and let them inside. Beaming as if he lived in a palace, Roland showed him around. A cramped bedroom. A galley kitchen, a bathroom with a sink, a toilet and an ancient bathtub. In the corner beside the kitchen was a card table, no chairs. The tiny living room had one window. Nicolas looked out the window and saw a brick wall and a rusty fire escape.

Roland filled two glasses with water, added ice from a half-sized refrigerator and they sat on a black futon, facing a small television on a milk crate. A cheap rug covered the wooden floor.

"Tell me about your job. Where is this stock exchange?"

"Wall Street. I work at night, sweeping the floors after trading stops at four o'clock."

"What do you wear?"

"Keep uniform in my locker, go in at three-thirty and change." Roland grinned. "Easy work, no heavy lifting. Finish at eleven-thirty and come home."

"Sounds great. Okay I come when you go to work tomorrow?"

"Sure, no problem."

They watched TV for a while, a stupid program with squalling amateur singers. Then Roland gave him a clean sheet and a pillow, helped him set up the futon, and went in his bedroom.

The next day, Roland made coffee and they sat on the futon to eat their muffins. At two-thirty they rode a train to the Wall Street stop. No panhandlers or homeless people outside, just men and women in business suits. The stock exchange building blew his mind, an enormous structure seven-stories high with ornate pillars and a line of American flags flapping in the breeze.

Roland took him around a corner and pointed. "I go in that door. You want come in with me? Get application to work here?"

"No. I have no papers. I go look for job at a restaurant. See you tonight."

He went to a restaurant, but not to apply for a job. He ate a roast beef dinner and drank red wine to fortify himself for what came next. On the way back to the apartment, he stopped at a hardware store and bought a roll of steel bailing wire. For two hours he sat on a stoop across from Roland's apartment, watching. Off to his right in a narrow alley, a drug deal went down. Cooking odors wafted from open windows. Delivery drivers brought pizza to other occupants.

His surveillance completed, he went upstairs. Using the spare key Roland had given him, he entered the apartment and fashioned the bailing wire into a garrote. Then he watched TV, surfing the channels. Dozens of sports channels. Americans were obsessed with sports.

Roland came home after midnight, carrying his work uniform. "Must go to laundromat tomorrow and wash clothes. How did it go today? You get a restaurant job?"

"No," Nicolas said, "but I'm sure to get one tomorrow." Not at a restaurant, though.

Roland went in the bathroom to wash up. A half hour later, he came out in his bathrobe. Nicolas strangled him with the garrote. Roland put up a fight, but it was useless. Four minutes and he was dead.

Papa had taught him how to dispose of bodies. Nicolas stripped off Roland's bathrobe and rolled him up in the rug. Two hours later, he opened the door and made sure no one was in the hall. Grunting, he hoisted the rug with Roland's body over his shoulder and crept downstairs to the foyer. Along the way he met no one. Outside in the darkness, he shoved the rolled-up rug into the stinky dumpster in the dark alley beside building.

The next morning, he made coffee and ate a muffin. At two-thirty, he put on Roland's uniform, an olive-green shirt and brown trousers. The shirt smelled funky, but so what? He was a cleaner, after all. The arms were a bit short and so were the pant legs, but not enough to draw attention. He draped Roland Marić's laminated lanyard with the photo ID around his neck, took Roland's keys off the counter and left.

A half hour later he got off at the Wall Street stop and walked around the corner of the stock exchange. Now came the hard part.

He looked a bit like Roland, black hair, dark eyes, but he was taller and huskier. If the guard scrutinized the ID badge, he might stop him.

When in doubt, act like you belong there. His heart thumped his chest when he showed his ID badge to the guard.

The guard didn't even look at it, just waved him inside.

Nicolas walked through the door, unable to resist a triumphant smile.

A month ago he had escaped from London, not knowing what would become of him. Now he had an apartment in New York City, a new ID and a job at the New York Stock Exchange.

CHAPTER 17

Frank sprinted the last two blocks to Kelly's house. Usually he did a five-mile run along the Mississippi River three blocks from his condo, but he'd slept at Kelly's last night. Their passionate love session had taken him to another place. One that didn't involve dead bodies and blood spatter.

He toweled sweat off his face and went in the garage. Kelly was pedaling her stationary bike, pumping furiously, like she was racing Lance Armstrong, her face pink with exertion. "Hey!" she said, "Be done in ten."

"Great. I'll start the coffee."

After a quick shower and shave, he raided the stash of clothes he kept at Kelly's house—clean underwear and fresh white shirts—got dressed and went in the kitchen.

Kelly was leaning against the counter with a towel draped around her neck, sipping from a coffee mug. "Thanks for making the coffee, even if it is industrial-strength."

He laughed. "Maybe I'll give you an espresso machine for Christmas."

"You're as bad as my father, gotta have his espresso hit. Got time to talk before you go?"

"Always got time for you, Kelly. Go hit the shower while I gear up for my day."

He poured himself a cup of coffee and sat at the table, planning his day. Check his messages at the office, and provided none of them were urgent, watch the ten o'clock press conference. The NOPD Super wanted Vobitch to update the media on the High Roller case and take questions. Frank hoped Vobitch wouldn't go on a tirade, figured the odds were fifty-fifty at best. Vobitch's favorite reporter, Nancy Grace, would surely be there.

On the positive side, he'd located Nicolas Zurik's place of business. An office in New Orleans conveniently located near the Causeway, the twenty-three mile bridge across Lake Pontchartrain to the north shore. After the presser Frank intended to go there and grill him.

Kelly came in the kitchen, dressed in slacks and a V-necked teal shirt, her hair still damp. She never used a dryer, wore her dark hair in a pixie cut that framed her oval face.

"What happened when you talked to the shooter yesterday?"

"Mosgov did most of the talking, jabbered at him in Russian, so I don't know what he said, but just before we left, the shooter said, in English, *Very afraid, me.* Seemed like he wanted to say more, but Mosgov cut him off and terminated the interview."

"Shit happens," Kelly said, "even in jails."

"Maybe I'll talk to him when Mosgov's not around. What's on your agenda today?"

"Find Jackie's parents. I got her maiden name off their marriage license in Las Vegas, but Rosenstein is a very common name."

"Jackie said they live in New York. If her father's a wheeler-dealer, he might have a website."

"You sound like Kenyon. Find whatever you want on the Internet."

"Give it a shot, you never know. Maureen called me yesterday. She passed her board exam."

"Great! How's she doing these days?" Kelly knew Maureen had been kidnapped last year.

"She's doing fine, still involved with the new boyfriend, the insurance fraud investigator."

"Ditched the dentist and found a crime fighter like her dad."

"Yeah, well, the thing is, this guy lives in Philadelphia and she's thinking about moving in with him."

"She's a grownup, Frank. You're a great parent. Trust her to make the right decision."

He sipped his coffee. Was he a great parent? Maybe. Maureen had survived the kidnapping by staying calm and using her wits, but he still worried about her.

He got up and put his mug in the dishwasher. "I better get to the office. I want to watch the ten o'clock presser. The Super's got Vobitch doing an update and taking questions."

"I forgot about that. Let's hope Vobitch doesn't drop any F-bombs."

Frank smiled. "Not gonna call on Nancy Grace, that's for sure."

————

9:45 AM – New Orleans

Seated at her kitchen table, Kelly picked up her cellphone. After searching on Rosenstein + New York she'd found several websites. She skipped the ones for lawyers, electricians and plumbers, found one for Jack Rosenstein, a financial adviser, with offices in Manhattan and Crown Heights. A photograph showed an older man with white hair and sagging jowls. His wife's name was Leah.

The best part? His bio listed a daughter named Jackie.

A search on Jack Rosenstein yielded his home address and phone number. Almost ten AM in New Orleans, eleven in Crown Heights. Hoping Jack was at work, she dialed a number and waited. Jackie had told Frank that her father was very domineering. Kelly figured she'd have better luck with the mother.

After two rings, a female voice said, "Hello?"

"Mrs Rosenstein? This is Kelly O'Neil, with the New Orleans police department. Is this a bad time to call?"

"What's wrong? Did something happen to Jackie? Are the children all right?"

"Jackie's fine and so are the children, but I have a few questions—"

"You're not a reporter, are you? Jack warned me not to talk to any reporters."

"Heaven's no! I work for the New Orleans Police Department."

The desk officer would confirm that she worked for NOPD, but she didn't want Jackie's parents to tell her an NOPD cop had called to question them. That would alert her to the fact they considered her a suspect.

The prime suspect as far as Kelly was concerned.

To distract the woman, she said, "I feel bad for Jackie. She seems like a wonderful person."

"Yes she is, and a wonderful daughter. Very independent though, knows her own mind. Jack raised her like a boy right from the start." A faint laugh. "Got more than he bargained for."

Kelly smiled. Jackie wasn't the only one who was independent.

"Seems like Jackie is very intelligent. What was she like, growing up?"

"She started walking when she was ten months old. She never played with dolls. Jack helped her build an airplane with Legos. She was very athletic too, played on the lacrosse team in high school. But after she joined the the debate club, she quit lacrosse. She was captain of the debate team her senior year."

"So she didn't date much?"

Mrs. Rosenstein laughed. "Oh, Jackie had plenty of dates. She was beautiful. But I gave her some motherly advice. Boys don't like it if you act like a smarty-pants. Use your feminine wiles to get around them."

Like you, Kelly thought. "Where did she go to college?"

"Jack made her go to an all-women's school, Mount Holyoke in Massachusetts. He thought it might stop her from partying. It didn't. She'd find some boy with a car and go off campus to party. But then she met Richie and that was it. Jackie said they had the same outlook on life. Figure out what you want and go after it."

"Did you like him?"

A long silence. At last, Leah Rosenstein said, "Jack told her to bring him home for dinner. So I fixed a nice meal and hoped for the best. But Jack hated him, said he was trailer park trash."

"What about you? What did you think?"

"He seemed nice enough, handsome, good manners. Truthfully, he could have been ugly and I wouldn't have cared. A mother knows what to look for. I saw how he treated her, how he looked at her. I could tell he adored her. That's all any mother wants. Richie only came here once, but I know he loved my daughter. He would have done anything for her."

Did that include fixing NBA basketball games?

"Couldn't your husband see that?"

"Maybe, deep in his heart. But as far as Jack was concerned no man was good enough for Jackie. The next day he told her never to see him again. Jackie was furious. She packed a suitcase and moved in with Richie." A heavy sigh. "She's never been back."

Kelly sipped some bottled water. The woman sounded bereft. Heartbroken. The father sounded like an asshole.

"Jackie called us from Las Vegas after they got married. I was happy for her. She'd found the love of her life. I wished her the best and told her to make me some grandchildren. That's what finally brought Jack around. Danny and Nora. Jack can't do enough for them. When Jackie called and told us about Richie, Jack wanted to fly down there right away so we could help her, but Jackie wouldn't let us. She said she had friends to help her."

Like the neighbor who speaks Russian? "I'm very sorry for your loss, Mrs. Rosenstein. I'm sure Jackie will want the kids to see you soon."

"I'd love to have her bring the kids here. Let Jackie go out shopping, you know? Take her mind off things. I know she's grieving for Richie."

"Do you know where Richie's father lives?"

"No. We never met him. Somewhere near Atlantic City I imagine."

"Thanks for speaking with me," Kelly said. "I feel like I know Jackie a lot better now."

"She's a wonderful girl. Maybe we can patch things up now that Richie's gone. Not that I'm glad he's dead, mind you. Jackie loved him so."

Kelly thanked her and ended the call. Jackie's mother made it sound like Jackie was more of a victim than a perpetrator. But was she?

Or was she the mastermind behind the shooting?

———

11:05 AM – New Orleans

Zurik's office was in a 16-story building with a gleaming glass exterior. A sign on the gated garage said Employees Only, so Frank parked in a visitor slot beside the building, still seething about the press conference.

The NOPD Super had introduced Vobitch who recapped the investigation. The two deceased employees were collateral damage. They believed the three white males seated in one booth were the intended targets. They were not residents of New Orleans and NOPD would release their names as soon as their next of kin identified them. Then came the questions.

Studiously ignoring Nancy Grace, Vobitch answered the obvious ones. *Do you know why the shooter killed the three men in the booth?* Vobitch: No but we intend to find out. *Have you spoken to their families?* Vobitch: Yes, but I can't comment on what they said. *Do the three male victims have children?* Vobitch: There were five victims and yes, some of them have children.

The last question came from a *Times-Picayune* reporter. Or as Vobitch called it, the fucking local rag. The reporter dropped a bomb on him.

"Do you have reason to believe he was a paid assassin?"

Vobitch glanced at the Super, who had stepped to the podium and said, "We have several theories about these murders. When we have definitive information, we will issue an update." End of press conference.

Frank clenched his jaw. *Do you have reason to believe he was a paid assassin?* Where the hell did that come from? Leaks, leaks and more leaks.

To be dealt with later.

Right now he wanted to get some answers from Nicolas Zurik.

In the lobby a directory between two elevators told him Zurik Investment Services was on the twelfth floor. He rode an elevator up to twelve and walked down a plush-carpeted hall with various offices.

A metal plaque on one door said: **Zurik Investment Services**. To the right of the door, Venetian blinds covered a large window. He pressed the bell beside the door and waited.

A minute later he pressed it again. Still no response.

He turned and looked at the office across the hall, an insurance company. No blinds on that window. An older woman in a frilly white blouse sat at a desk, working on a computer. Nobody sitting the visitor chairs opposite her desk.

When he stepped inside, the woman gave him a welcoming smile. "Hi, can I help you?"

"I'm looking for Nicolas Zurik, but no one's answering the bell."

"He's not usually there in the morning."

"Have you ever talked to him?"

"Not really, just a quick hello if I run into him in the hall. He's friendly enough, but I don't know how his business is going. I don't see many clients going in the office."

Frank weighed his options. He had no reason to think the woman would tell Zurik he'd been here, but looks could be deceiving. He'd had serial killers look him in the eye and swear they'd never killed anyone.

On the other hand, the woman had a birds-eye view of Zurik's office, a useful asset if he played his cards right. He flashed his ID badge and said, "I need to speak to Mr. Zurik about an urgent police matter."

Her eyes widened. "That sounds ominous. Has he done something I should know about?"

Frank smiled. "Sorry, I'm not at liberty to say. Are you in the office every day?"

"Not every day. We're closed on Sunday. But I'm here Monday through Friday eight to five. Eight to noon on Saturdays."

"So you'd see Mr. Zurik if he went in the office, right?"

She smiled faintly. "I would if I was looking for him."

He put his card on the desk. "Could you call me the next time you see him?"

She picked up the card, studied it a moment and extended her hand. "Nice to meet you, Detective Renzi. I'm Helen."

He shook her hand and said, "Happy to meet you, Helen. I'd rather you didn't tell Mr. Zurik I was here today." He wanted to catch Zurik off guard, gauge his reactions before he had time to rehearse his answers.

Helen smiled. "That's what I figured. Next time I see him I'll call you right away."

"Thank you," he said. "That would help me a lot."

He rode the elevator down to the lobby and went out and got in his car, ruminating about the High Roller case. All homicides were ugly. But some were uglier than others. *Did any of the victims have children?*

Damn right they did. Danny and Nora Bauer, age ten and age five. Two innocent kids who would never have breakfast with their father again.

The shooter was the key to the case, but Frank wanted to know who hired him. Who was the mastermind behind the massacre?

After any homicide, his goal was always the same: get justice for the victims. All of them, no matter who they were or what they'd done.

Find the mastermind and make the motherfucker pay.

113

CHAPTER 18

Jackie forced down a bite of grilled chicken. Martina had offered to treat her and the kids to lunch in the French Quarter, saying a change of scenery would do her good. Considering what she'd found yesterday, she needed more than a change of scenery.

How about a new life on Pluto where no one could find her?

It was a gorgeous day so they were sitting at a table outside The Louisiana Pizza Kitchen, shielded from the sun by a fire-engine-red umbrella. She was glad to get out of the house and so was Nora, but Danny was sulking. He wanted to go to school and she wouldn't let him.

Across the table from her, dressed to the nines in a red silk blouse and slim black skirt, Martina said, "My grilled chicken sandwich is delicious! How's yours, Danny?"

"Okay. But I'd rather eat lunch in the cafeteria with Nicky."

Jackie nudged his foot. "How about a thank-you? Martina's treating us to lunch."

Danny gave her a dirty look and mumbled, "Thank you for treating us, Mrs. Zurik."

"My pleasure," Martina said, and gave her a look that said *No worries. I know he's upset.*

Nora piped up in her I-want-to-please-voice and said, "Thank you for taking us out for lunch, Mrs. Zurik. I love my pizza!"

Martina smiled at Nora. "Why don't you and Danny go sit in the shade beside the Mint so Mom and I can talk."

Eager to escape, Danny sprang to his feet. Nora looked disappointed.

"Look both ways before you cross the street, Danny."

He gave her a surly look. "I always do, Mom."

She watched them cross the street with their drinks, Pepsi for Danny, milk for Nora. Once they were settled on a shady bench outside the Mint, she said to Martina, "I'm sorry Danny's acting rude. He's mad because I won't let him go to school."

"No problem," Martina said. "Yesterday he told me a cop asked you if his father had any enemies. And asked me why the cop would do that."

Shocked, Jackie stared at her. "He did?"

"I think he saw something on the news."

"I don't let him watch the news."

"Maybe he saw it on his cellphone."

"He doesn't have a cellphone. Richie and I were planning to get him one for his—" Tears filled her eyes. Another thing they would never do together. Buy Danny a birthday present.

"But Nicky has one," Martina said. "You can't hide much from kids these days. On the news last night, a reporter said three of the victims were sitting in the same booth and maybe the killer targeted them intentionally."

Her heart began to pound. "But they caught the killer."

"Yes, but … " Avoiding her eyes, Martina took a sip of Chablis.

"But what?"

"Maybe someone paid him to do it. That's what the reporter said."

Jackie gulped some Chablis, her mind churning. Someone paid the bastard to kill Richie? She wiped sweaty palms on her napkin. Who would want Richie dead? And why? Then she remembered what Renzi said before he left her house one day. Christ Almighty, she couldn't even remember which day it was, the days blurring together like scenes from a horror movie.

But Renzi's words were clear as a bell.

Richie wasn't the only one who was murdered. The two men in the booth with him were murdered, too, and we want to know why someone wanted them dead.

Her mind flitted to the subpoena. Was that why someone wanted him dead?

"Have you made the funeral arrangements?" Martina asked.

"I'll probably bury him near my parent's house in New York. My lawyer will help me get him there." She couldn't bear to say *body*. So cold and lifeless. Like Richie, lying in the morgue with a bullet hole in his head and another in his chest.

What if Richie was gambling on NBA games? Why else would they send him a subpoena forcing him to testify in a federal courtroom?

"Are you okay for money?" Martina asked. "I can lend you some if you need it."

Irritated, Jackie rose from her chair. "Let's go see how the kids are doing."

Martina could be rather domineering at times, not as bad as her father but annoying. Still, she couldn't afford to alienate Martina. She needed her to mind the kids. Now more than ever.

They crossed the street. Outside the Old US Mint, Nora and Danny were sitting on a cement bench in the shade of the building. Nora saw them coming and smiled. Danny didn't. He looked utterly despondent, shoulders slumped, eyes fixed on the pavement.

Her heart ached for him. A ten-year-old boy, grieving for the father he dearly loved, grappling with the idea that someone wanted his father dead.

―――

3:35 PM – New Orleans

"They think Benny was the target," Claudia said.

Surprised, Frank said, "Not Richie Bauer?"

They were sitting in the back corner of Lola's Cafe, but unlike their previous visit, today the place was almost deserted. The only other customer was a UNO student working on a laptop at a table near the door.

"That's just the tip of the iceberg, Frank. Wait till you hear the rest."

"You sure your source is reliable?"

"She's works at the Chicago FBI office. Prior to that she was a forensic accountant for a big law firm, which involved accessing public records and banking information. Forensic accountants are like detectives. They hunt for shady financial deals and bank transactions. That's why the Chicago FBI office hired her. Trust me, she won't talk."

"Follow the money and keep your mouth shut."

"Exactly. She can use FBI computers to access all sorts of data bases, including records on Dominic Marconi. He's an enforcer for the Atlantic City mob."

"We knew that. But why was he sitting with Benny and Richie at the High Roller Club?"

"It's complicated. Marconi was the root cause of the New Jersey FBI investigation. He beat up a gambler who borrowed money from the mob and wasn't paying the vig. Marconi said pay up or he'd grab his kid some day after school and slit his throat."

Appalled, Frank said, "Grab a kid and slit his throat?"

"These mobsters don't fuck around. Scared the shit out of the guy, so he contacted the New Jersey FBI office and asked for protection."

"How'd they get onto Benny?"

"The New Jersey feds had an informant inside the Sargetti gang in Atlantic City. In November 2012, he told them the gang was making millions of dollars on sports betting. Mobs have been a problem in Atlantic City for years: drug deals, prostitution, loan-sharking, protection rackets. The New Jersey feds have been trying to bust the Sargetti gang for years."

"Benny grew up in Atlantic City and so did Richie Bauer."

"I'm getting to that. In January 2013, the New Jersey FBI office set up LOOK-SHARP, a special unit to nail the Sargetti gang, and assigned ten agents to it."

"Sounds like the old Gillette commercial. Look sharp, feel sharp, be sharp."

Claudia burst out laughing. "That's it! I couldn't figure out why they called it that."

Frank shrugged. "I'm a trumpet player. Soon as you said it, the jingle started playing in my head. Some agent got pissed off because he can't wear a mustache probably named it."

"In any case, FBI bureaucracy being what it is, their investigation didn't bear fruit overnight. The NBA has taken certain steps to detect game-fixing. Monitoring foul calls, suspicious betting-line fluctuations. The LOOK-SHARP team had their top analyst review NBA games for the prior two seasons. For the 2010-2011 season, the win percentages for certain teams looked suspicious. It's not about which team won—"

"It's about the point spread."

Claudia grinned. "The hidden talents of Detective Frank Renzi never cease to amaze me. Plays trumpet, instantly recognizes shaving cream commercials, knows how betting on NBA games works."

Frank sipped his iced coffee. He had other hidden talents, but she would never know about them. Claudia was smart and very attractive, but he had no interest in going to bed with her.

"Sometimes it's about the spread," Claudia said, "but not always. The analyst discounted games where one team beat the other so badly the spread wasn't in doubt. But for competitive games that attracted big wagers for the 2010-2011 season, the favorite won and consistently beat the point spread almost seventy percent of the time."

"Was Richie Bauer officiating those games?"

"The analyst listed the referees for the games in question. Richie was on every list. There were fewer suspicious games for the 2011-2012 season, because of the lockout."

"I remember that," Frank said. "About salary caps, right?"

"And a few other things. The lockout didn't end until December eighth. They played the first games on Christmas. Instead of a season with 82 games, there were only 66. The analyst tagged twenty-three out of thirty games as suspicious. The winning team beat the spread almost seventy-percent of the time. In case you're wondering, the odds of that happening are 6,155 to one."

"Did Richie Bauer officiate all of them?"

"Yes." She gestured at her briefcase. "I've got printouts. The analyst used a betting information service that lets you see betting line fluctuations for individual games. If the spread widens, it means gamblers are betting more on the favorite. The games Richie officiated drew more bets than the others and the winning team pulled in heavier bets."

Frank thought about it, imagining how Danny and Nora would feel when the news came out, as it surely would at some point. Especially Danny, wondering why his father cheated. If Jackie knew Richie was gambling on NBA games, was that motive for murder?

"You're thinking about his kids," Claudia said. "After this comes out."

"Yes. Especially his ten-year-old son."

"If it's any comfort, the New Jersey feds haven't told the NBA front office about the investigation yet. To prevent any leaks."

"Where'd Richie's money go? How much was he making?"

Claudia shook her head. "Don't know. My friend can't access private bank accounts without a warrant. Here's what got them to Benny. They got a warrant to access the phone records of Sargetti mob associates. In February 2014 they found Benny's number in Marconi's phone records. They already knew Richie grew up in Atlantic City. They ran Benny's name and found out he grew up in Atlantic City, too."

"Big brother is always watching. Was this the guy who wanted the Benny tape?"

"Yes. Special Agent Fred Lewis took Benny to his office in March 2014 and put him through the wringer." Claudia shrugged. "I don't have a transcript, just the summary report. When Fred asked Benny if he knew Richard Bauer, Benny said he hasn't seen him since high school. Fred asked him ten times if he and Richie were betting on NBA games, but Benny refused tell him."

"Best friends for life," Frank said.

"Who told you that?"

"Kelly went to Atlantic City and talked to Benny's mother. That's what she said."

"How's Kelly these days?" Claudia said. "You're still …. ?"

Frank smiled. "Definitely. These days she works Special Victims-Domestic Violence, but Vobitch pulled her back into Homicide to help with the High Roller case."

"I remember her father in Chicago. Big beefy Italian, more F-bombs than Vobitch. But underneath it all he was a sweetheart."

"Yeah? That's not my take."

"Frank, you're in bed with his daughter. What would you do if your daughter decided to marry some guy you didn't like?"

"Throw him off a tall building." In fact he'd come close to doing that last year.

Claudia burst out laughing. "No you wouldn't."

He gave her his *Don't fuck with me or I'll rip your balls off* look.

"Okaaay," she said, "Moving right along. Agent Lewis put a surveillance team on Benny, got word a week later that a prostitute visited Benny. The feds knew she distributed drugs for the mob, so they squeezed her and found out Benny was buying coke from the mob."

"Man, this is like a bad made-for-TV movie."

"To cut to the chase, in April 2014, Fred squeezed Benny hard. You know how it goes. *We know you do coke, probably hide money from the IRS, so you're looking at twenty years in a federal pen.* Like that. Benny refused to give Richie up, but he admitted he told Marconi which team to bet on. They used a candy-bar code."

"Snickers," Frank said.

Claudia stared at him. "How did you know?"

"We listened to the Benny-tape before Vobitch sent it to Fred. Marconi said *We got a lotta Snickers in the warehouse and we need to know where to send them.*"

"Exactly. By September the New Jersey FBI office decided they had enough evidence to convene a Grand Jury. Set it up for the first Monday in November."

"Three weeks before the murders. Did Benny tell Richie about this?"

"I don't know. Maybe, maybe not. I assume Fred wired him up for the meeting at the High Roller Club."

"I really appreciate this, Claudia. Any chance you can keep me posted on any updates?"

"As long as the information flows both ways." Claudia shrugged. "To be honest, I want in on the case."

"I'll call Vobitch and see if we can meet to talk about it."

"You think he'll agree to it?" Claudia said, clearly skeptical.

"Positive." Frank grinned. "He'd love to see you again. The Poorhouse Pub is a local burger joint, so you might want to swap your fibbie outfit for something a bit more casual."

––––––

6:00 PM – New Orleans

Frank waited for Claudia in the Poorhouse Pub parking lot. He and Vobitch often met here to discuss delicate matters—no interruptions, no other cops around, just tasty burgers and reasonably priced booze.

At six on the dot, Claudia drove into the lot, parked beside him and got out, had on jeans and a boat-necked blue jersey, her short dark hair freshly styled.

"Vobitch is waiting for us," he said, "got us our usual table in the back."

The Pub was crowded, blue-collar workers drinking beers at the bar, watching a football game on TV. Most of the booths were occupied.

In the back corner, Vobitch was ensconced in their usual booth, his back to the wall, nursing a Glenlivet on the rocks. Frank slid into the red-leather booth beside him to let Claudia sit by herself on the other side.

With a pleasant smile, she said, "Nice to see you, Lieutenant Vobitch. What's new?"

"The pig valve in my heart."

"Jesus! When did that happen? Are you okay?"

Vobitch patted his chest. "Seems to be working okay so far."

Amused, Frank suppressed a smile, watching them circle each other, a grumpy bloodhound and a sleek Siamese cat.

"Thanks for getting us the lowdown on the New Jersey feds," Vobitch said. "I hear you want in on the High Roller investigation."

"Richie Bauer had a wife and two children," Claudia said somberly. "I'll monitor what the New Jersey feds are doing, as long as NOPD shares their information with me."

"I got no problem with that," Vobitch said.

"Tell me about the shooter. I gather he's got a lawyer?"

Vobitch sipped his Glenlivet. "Boris Mosgov, who speaks Russian. We figure whoever paid the shooter hired him."

"The plot thickens," Claudia said.

"Indeed it does," Frank said. "Jackie Bauer told me Richie had a mistress in LA."

"So Richie was playing around and she found out about it."

"It gets better," Vobitch said. "Tell her about the next-door neighbor, Frank."

"He speaks Russian, too. We've got surveillance on both houses monitoring when the cars come and go, who's in the car."

Claudia took a notepad out of her handbag. "Who's the neighbor?"

"Nicolas Zurik," Frank said. "Z-U-R-I-K. I went to his place of business, an office tower near Causeway Boulevard, rang the bell and got no answer."

"What are your theories so far?" Claudia asked. "Who hired the shooter?"

Vobitch ran them down. "The New Jersey mob hit Benny because they were afraid he would talk. The ref's wife was pissed he was fucking around and hired the neighbor to kill him."

"Kelly thinks maybe she was in bed with Zurik," Frank added.

Claudia smiled. "The scorned woman. Maybe my contact can dig up something on Zurik."

Vobitch smiled. "Great! Frank will keep you informed about what we get."

Frank grinned at Claudia. "See? I told you he'd be happy to see you. Pay no attention to what he said at the press conference. We're not telling the media much."

"Right," Vobitch growled. "Especially Nancy-fucking-Grace."

NICOLAS

TWENTY-FIVE YEARS EARLIER

A Big Gamble and a New Life

February 1990 – New York City

Nicolas sat on the futon, eating a bowl of hot oatmeal sprinkled with brown sugar. For three years he had lived in Roland's apartment as Roland Marić, working five days a week at the New York Stock Exchange.

But he didn't intend to sweep floors forever.

Papa had taught him many things: covert surveillance, how to follow a man undetected, and how to kill him. But other than his ability to speak fluent Russian, French and English, he had no job skills.

The newspapers featured no want-ads for assassins. In truth, he didn't want to be an assassin. He never wanted to kill anyone again.

Last year, to celebrate his twentieth birthday, he had bought an elegant suit, black with gray pinstripes. He went to an upscale wine bar, sat at a table beside a window, ordered a glass of French Bordeaux and lighted a Gauloise Blonde.

And thought about Papa. Murdered four years ago in London, a big bear of a man and a wonderful father.

If he had a son, would he be a good father like Papa? Teach the boy to speak Russian and how to play chess? Tell him the ability to see many moves ahead, in chess and in life, was crucial to his survival?

Outside on the sidewalk, well-dressed men and women strolled past the wine bar. He swept floors for a living. Would he ever make love to a beautiful woman again? Not until he found a job that would make Vladimir Kozlovich proud of him.

After he killed Roland, he'd bought an untraceable burner, called Alexei and told him he had an apartment and worked at the NYSE as a cleaner.

Alexei congratulated him and they made a pact. On the last day of each month, they would talk on the phone. Each time he heard his friend's voice, Nicolas rejoiced. It was lonely, living in New York.

Alexei urged him to get a computer so they could communicate via email, so he bought a computer and asked the clerk about email. Four days later, he emailed Alexei and received an immediate reply. *So glad you have joined the computer nerds!! Keep me posted on what you're doing.*

Now he and Alexei exchanged emails almost every day.

A chime interrupted his ruminations, his clock radio alerting him. Time to go to work. He ate the last bite of oatmeal, rinsed his coffee mug and put it in the sink. At least it was Friday. The end of another long work week.

Wearing his insulated jacket, Nicolas left the apartment. When he emerged from the subway, he trudged to work, cursing the bitter cold, his breath showing in the frigid air, dirty snowbanks along the sidewalk, slush in the gutters.

Inside the stock exchange, he hung his jacket in his locker and took out his uniform. Turk sat down beside him on the bench, a muscular six-foot-three, 220 pounds. He didn't speak much English, so Nicolas had helped him a few times. Turk lived with his wife who cleaned toilets in a ritzy hotel.

"You want make some money?" Turk asked, and took out a slip of paper.

"Sure. How?"

"Is time for March Madness."

Mystified, Nicolas said, "What's that?"

"College boys play basketball. I watch on TV. You pick winner, win money. I help you."

So Nicolas marked the squares Turk told him to and won twenty-five dollars.

Usually after he got home from work, he played through games in his chess magazine, moving the pieces on his folding chessboard. That night he watched basketball on ESPN. The next day he bought a book that explained how the game worked. ESPN replayed highlights from the games, gave the team standings and listed information about the players.

The following Friday, he and Turk filled out their slips. This time Nicolas bet more money. He won a hundred dollars, and kept watching ESPN. Betting on basketball was a bit like playing chess. Instead of seeing many moves ahead, he had to watch games and figure out which team was most likely to win.

By the end of March Madness he had won two thousand dollars.

One night in the neighborhood bar, Nicolas overheard a man tell his companion that he placed bets with the cigar-smoker at the newsstand outside the subway. The next morning, Nicolas told Cigar Man he wanted to bet on a game. The man said he needed a cash deposit first, five hundred dollars. If Nicolas won, Cigar Man took ten percent of his winnings. If he lost, Cigar Man kept all his money.

The next day Nicolas gave him the five hundred dollar deposit and bet a hundred bucks on Duke to win the Louisville-Duke game. Duke won. Nicolas made two-hundred dollars.

He continued to bet on games and told Alexei about it.

"Lady luck is with you," Alexei said. "When will you start betting on NBA games?"

Nicolas laughed. "After I figure out who's good and who isn't."

This took quite a while. The NBA season began late in October. After six weeks he'd won more than he lost. Winning gave him a huge rush, but he wasn't satisfied. In a chess match, his ability to see many moves ahead allowed him to beat his opponent, but when NBA teams played, the outcome was not within his control. Unless he could figure out how to improve his odds of winning.

Most NBA teams had one outstanding player. If he was injured, the opposing team usually won. Moreover, some teams were better at offense, others at defense. Usually the best defensive team won. Teams that excelled at offense and defense were the best of all. Weaker teams usually lost to them. In that case, the bookies made it harder to win. They imposed a spread, the number of points the dominant team had to exceed for the bettor to win.

Nicolas conducted an experiment. For one week he chose the team he believed would win, but placed no bets. At the end of the week he compared his choices with the actual winners. Seventy percent of the time he'd been right. He adjusted his bets accordingly. His winnings doubled.

But he hated giving a percentage to Cigar Man. He called Alexei and asked about offshore betting. To open an account, you needed a credit card. Nicolas didn't have one, but Alexei did. So Nicolas told him which team to bet on, Alexei placed the bet and they split the winnings.

By the end of the NBA finals, Nicolas had won $22,000 and decided he wanted a credit card of his own. For this, he needed a new identity. He asked Alexei to get him the name of a Russian gang leader in New York City.

One fine Sunday afternoon, a week after his twenty-second birthday in 1991, Nicolas put on his elegant suit and rode the subway to Brighton Beach in Brooklyn. Surrounded by an eight-foot security fence, the gang leader's house was an enormous two-story Victorian with a Spanish tile roof and a glass-enclosed greenhouse along one side.

When he rang the bell, a man with hard eyes opened the door and said in Russian, *"You have weapon?"*

"Nyet. I am a member of the London vory." He unbuttoned his jacket, then his shirt and showed him the distinctive tattoo. *"My father was their premier assassin."*

The man searched him anyway. Then he took him to a sunlit room and introduced him to Pavel Volkovich, boss of the largest vory in New York. Volkovich was only five-foot-nine, but he exuded power. An imposing presence with piercing black eyes, he extended his hand and said in Russian, *"I am pleased to meet the son of Vladimir Kozlovich."*

Nicolas smiled courteously and shook his hand. *"The pleasure is mine."*

Two guards stationed behind Volkovich regarded him with amusement. *Let them be cocky and sure of themselves,* he thought.

Underestimation had always worked in his favor.

With a flick of his wrist, Volkovich dismissed the guards and took him to an interior courtyard. Cooking odors wafted from one side of the house, the sound of young voices from the other. At the far end of the courtyard, Volkovich unlocked a door and they entered a greenhouse with a towering glass-and-steel ceiling. A canopy of greenery shaded the tiled floor.

Beyond the greenhouse, a secluded area held a wooden table surrounded by four rattan chairs.

Volkovich sat down, selected a Partagas cigar from a humidor and offered him one. Nicolas declined.

"Cigars aren't a vice of yours?" Volkovich said in accented English.

"I have no vices. Vladimir Kozlovich would not allow it. You've done well here in America. Your home is very impressive."

Volkovich made a modest gesture. "I've been blessed."

"Not just blessed. You are a man wise in the ways of leadership."

Volkovich fixed him with a stare. "What is it you need?"

"A new identity, a US passport, birth certificate and driver's license." He had no intention of revealing that he had killed two members of another gang in London and their leader had put out a contract on him.

"How old are you?"

"Twenty-two. I have a British passport, but due to my work for the London vory I need to disappear for a while."

"You are healthy?" Volkovich asked. "No infectious diseases? No debilitating conditions?"

"Very healthy. No hereditary diseases. And no vices as I told you. "

Volkovich puffed his cigar, sending clouds of smoke billowing into the air. "I will get you a birth certificate, a US passport and a valid New York State driver's license with your photo." Volkovich locked eyes with him. "Here is what you will do for me."

Nicolas waited, desperately hoping Volkovich would not order him to kill someone.

"I have four sons and a daughter. The girl is fifteen and she is driving me crazy. Martina is willful and headstrong, goes to bars and flirts with boys, some of them older than you. Now you will be her boyfriend. Entertain her. Movies, dinner, dancing perhaps, but no alcohol. And no sex."

Nicolas waited, knowing the deal had to be more complicated.

"I have spoken with your vory boss in London. He told me you were a fine worker, following orders, completing assignments. A fine testament to your character." Volkovich leveled his cigar at him. "Make Martina fall in love with you. If all goes well, when she turns eighteen, you will marry her."

He sat there, stunned. Marry a girl he'd never seen?

What if he couldn't stand her?

"Then you will become part of my family."

Part of my family. The hackles rose on the back of his neck. Marry the boss's daughter and be under his thumb for the rest of his life? Not if he could help it.

But this was not the time to object. This was a time to project confidence and sincerity, even when he told bald-faced lies.

Volkovich placed an envelope on the table. "For you. To make sure you don't skimp when you entertain Martina."

Inside the envelope were two bricks of hundred-dollar-bills.

For that much money he could romance a toad.

Nicolas smiled and extended his hand. "You've got a deal."

Volkovich pumped his hand and said, "Come, you must meet her. I think she will like you."

As it turned out, Martina was no toad. Headstrong, but pleasant enough and reasonably smart. So he took her out twice a week and made sure she fell in love with him. Knowing she would tell Pavel Volkovich how much she adored her charming new boyfriend.

Six months later Volkovich gave him the items he so desperately wanted.

Now he was Nicolas Zurik and no longer worked at the stock exchange. He made money betting on basketball games.

When Martina turned eighteen in 1994, Nicolas married her. For a wedding present, her father bought them a condo near the Volkovich home. Martina was happy enough to play house, as long as he fucked her three times a week. Every day he went to the tiny office he'd rented and bet on basketball. Later, watching the games on TV, he got a huge rush when his team won.

But Volkovich wanted a grandson. Martina was willing, but Nicolas made her take birth control pills and warned her not to tell her father. He began looking for another place to live. Somewhere far away from Martina's powerful controlling father, Pavel Volkovich.

In January 1998, he flew to New Orleans where real estate was cheap. Here he could rent an office for half what it cost in New York. A real estate agent found him the perfect house in Ponchatoula, a forty minute drive from New Orleans. He signed an offer sheet, gave the agent five grand in cash and said he needed to show it to his wife.

Let Martina convince her father this was the perfect place to raise his grandson.

A week later he flew her to New Orleans and showed her the house. A master bedroom with husband-and-wife dressing areas, a gleaming kitchen with stainless steel appliances. Last and most important, the large sunny bedroom on the second floor.

"A fine room for the son we shall have," he said.

Gazing at him adoringly, Martina said, "I love you so much, Nicolas."

"No more than I love you," he said and kissed her deeply.

A week later he signed the papers to purchase the house.

CHAPTER 19

Standing at her office window, Jackie watched Danny and Nora walk along the sidewalk beside the golf course, Nora skipping along, happy to be with her big brother. She'd told Danny he could stay up late and watch a movie in the play room if he'd take take Nora for a long walk.

Bribing him.

Anything to get them out of the house so she could watch the ten o'clock press conference on the TV in her office.

The NOPD Superintendent had released the names of the men seated together at the High Roller Club. Benny Green, Richard Bauer, Dominic Marconi. Names but no addresses, saying their relatives had requested privacy and asking the media not to contact them.

A fat lot of good that did.

Moments later her phone started ringing. Calls from nosy neighbors probably, eager to offer faux sympathy and ask her what really happened. Calls from reporters would come soon enough. She had unplugged every phone in the house. That solved that problem.

But what if the reporters found out where she lived? She'd seen that enough on TV to know what would happen. A horde of reporters and TV crews would camp out at her house, screaming questions, sticking boom microphones in their faces if she and the kids went outside.

Fuck that! There had to be a legal way to keep them out. But that meant she had to call Saul Millstein. Her palms grew sweaty. She hadn't spoken to him since Tuesday, the day they met with Richie's lawyer. The day she'd found the subpoena hidden in Richie's file cabinet. A subpoena that required him to testify in a federal courtroom in New Jersey on the second of November.

If Detective Renzi was to be believed—and why would he lie to her?—the killer had targeted Richie and his companions, Benny and Dominic Marconi. Renzi wanted to know why.

He had also implied that someone had paid the bastard to kill them.

Someone wanted Richie dead. At the time, she had dismissed the idea. Not after her latest discovery.

The funeral director had asked her to bring him some clothes for Richie. So she went in his closet and took out his gray blazer and charcoal gray trousers, an outfit he often wore after games. When she checked the pockets to make sure they were empty, she found a roll of hundred-dollar bills. Shocked, she counted them. Three thousand dollars. What was Richie doing with that much cash in his pocket?

The possibilities had frightened her.

They still did. Just thinking about it made her heart pound, beating her chest like a hammer.

Why would Richie have three thousand dollars in his blazer pocket?

Maybe he never got a chance to deposit it in the bank.

Maybe he gave it to fucking Pompom Girl. Or maybe he used it to bet on a basketball game.

Twenty years ago on their honeymoon, all Richie wanted to do, other than drink champagne and make love, was gamble. For all she knew, he still did. It would be easy enough to stop in Las Vegas after his western road trips.

Richie and Benny had grown up in Atlantic City. Plenty of opportunities to gamble there. Maybe Benny was gambling on NBA games and got Richie to help him.

The subpoena had been served three weeks before Richie was shot. Did he want her to find it? Was that why he added the codicil to his will, listing the items he wanted her to have?

The feds didn't want to talk to Richie about golf, they wanted to talk to him because he was an NBA referee. A man who could control the flow of the game with his whistle. And possibly the outcome.

Unwilling to think about it, she massaged her temples. Maybe Dominic Marconi was the target. Plenty of gangsters in Atlantic City. But if Marconi was a gangster, why was Richie sitting with him?

Jesus, the questions were endless. And the clock was ticking.

She had to call Millstein and ask him to fend off the media. If she told him about the subpoena and the cash in Richie's blazer, would he make her tell the police? She took Renzi's card out of the pen-holder on her desk.

Should she tell Renzi about the cash and the subpoena? And likely face more questions she didn't want to answer? She sure as hell wasn't going to tell her father. That would only fuel his disdain for Richie.

Tears glazed her eyes. Too many decisions to make and no one to help her. She felt so alone.

Richie was dead, and Danny and Nora were grieving children.

She dialed Millstein's number and waited.

"Millstein and Shapiro Law Offices," chirped a female voice. "May I help you?"

"Hi Grace, this is Jackie Bauer. Could I speak to Saul?" On a first name basis with Grace now.

"Of course, Mrs. Bauer. No one is with him now. Hold on."

Moments later, Millstein came on the line. "Jackie, how are you holding up?"

"The NOPD just released Richie's name to the media. Two minutes later my phone started ringing so I unplugged it, but if the reporters find out where I live they'll come here and—"

"No, no, we can't have that. Is there just the one entrance to the Ponchatoula Estates?"

"Yes. Could the Ponchatoula Sheriff's Department post a guard at the entrance?"

"Let me think for a moment," Millstein said.

Jackie sipped her bottled water. The other residents wouldn't be happy to have a guard posted at the entrance. An icy chill wracked her.

Jesus! What if they found out about the subpoena?

"We could install a gate at the entrance," Millstein said, "and give residents key cards to open it. But that would take time and it would be expensive. I think posting a security guard at the entrance is the best solution. No media allowed, just residents and utility workers."

"That would be great," she said. "Would he stay there all night?"

"Let's go for six AM to midnight for now. I'll call the Sheriff and ask him."

"Wonderful. Could you contact the Neighborhood Association and have them notify the residents to let them know what's going on?"

"Of course. I don't want you dealing with this, Jackie. How are the kids?"

"Not great, but okay. I'll sit them down and tell them not to talk to anyone."

"Good idea. Anything else I can do for you?"

Jackie hesitated. Should she tell him about the subpoena she'd found, and the two grand in cash?

No. Why add another complication?

"I've decided to bury Richie in Crown Heights, New York. Can you help me ship the casket up there?"

"Of course. I'll draw up the necessary papers. I'll need the name and address of a funeral home to accept the body."

"I'll get that for you today and call you. Thanks for everything, Saul."

"You're welcome, Jackie. I'll let you know what the Sheriff says about the guards."

Jackie ended the call and massaged her eyes. She didn't want to call her parents to ask about a funeral director.

To hell with that. She'd find one online. Another chore to do.

Would this ordeal ever end?

———

10:45 AM – New Orleans

Frank sat at his desk in the Homicide office, sorting the pink message slips he'd collected from the desk officer. After yesterday's meeting, Vobitch had authorized a two-thousand dollar reward for information about the gun. An hour later Crimestoppers had put out the word.

At the desk opposite his, Kenyon was multi-tasking, sorting message slips while talking on the phone. Kenyon ended the call and said, "You think Vobitch watched the Super's press conference?"

"No doubt. By now Lurleen's probably getting a ton of calls from reporters."

"Won't take them long to find Jackie's address," Kenyon said.

"They probably had it two minutes after the Super read his name."

His cellphone rang. He saw the ID and answered. "Hey, Tony, what's doing?"

"I'm inside the surveillance van in the golf club parking lot. I can see both houses with my binoculars. Jackie's kids are taking a walk near the golf course. Her red Toyota's in the driveway, but Zurik got in a black SUV at ten o'clock and left. I'll text you the tag numbers."

"Great. Too bad we can't put a bug on it."

"Yeah, that'd be good," Tony chortled.

"Keep me posted." He ended the call put the cellphone on his desk.

"You think Tony could bug Zurik's car?" Kenyon asked.

"I'd like to. Zurik left a half hour ago. Be nice to know where he went."

"Damn straight. Seven days since the massacre and we got nothing. I'm not getting anywhere on the gun and neither is Orville."

"Claudia found out the New Jersey feds knew Benny was connected to Marconi."

"Really!" Kenyon said. "You think they wired him up?"

"That's what I figure, but Claudia wasn't positive. Vobitch and I had a sit-down with her."

"Hoo-ee! I bet that was fun!" Kenyon said.

Frank smiled. "Actually, it was. She wants in on the case. Her source can access the FBI computers. Needless to say, Vobitch was thrilled, so we agreed to swap info."

His cellphone rang. He didn't recognize the number and answered warily, "Detective Renzi."

"Hi, Detective Renzi? This is Helen at the office building on Causeway Boulevard. Nicolas Zurik just went in his office."

His heart sped up. "Great to hear from you, Helen. Thank you for calling me."

"You're welcome," she said cheerily. "We aim to please."

He ended the call, opened a drawer in his desk and took out his SIG.

"The woman in the office tower just saw Zurik go in his office." Frank checked the SIG to make sure it was loaded, put it in his shoulder holster and put on his jacket.

Kenyon said, "Armed and dangerous. You want backup?"

Frank shook his head. "Not this time. We'll see what he has to say."

CHAPTER 20

Frank rang the bell and waited. If Zurik was in his office, why were the blinds on the window beside the door closed? Yesterday he'd gotten a copy of Zurik's driver's license from the RMV so he knew what to expect.

Height: six-one. Weight: 200 pounds. Hair: black. Eyes: brown. Gazing into the camera for the photograph, expressionless.

A man in a business suit and a red-striped tie opened the door. Zurik.

Smiling at him, Zurik said, "Yes? Can I help you?"

His first impression: an engaging smile and a hint of wariness in his eyes. He flashed his NOPD badge. "Homicide Detective Frank Renzi. I've got a few questions. Can I come in?"

Still smiling, Zurik waved him inside. "Of course."

Frank assessed the room. To his right, a small desk with a chair. No phone. No computer. On the wall behind the desk, a security system keypad. To his left, two easy chairs and a low table with several magazines. Ahead of him on the far wall was a closed door.

What was behind Door Number Two?

"I was here a couple of days ago and rang the bell, but no one answered."

"I might have been with a client. Sometimes I meet them closer to my home in Ponchatoula," Zurik said, standing by the desk with his feet apart, his arms by his sides.

A fighting stance if ever Frank saw one. Poised like a street-brawler in a dark alley. He'd run into a few of those, but they weren't wearing business suits. Frank unbuttoned his jacket to expose his shoulder holster and flashed a smile. He could play the Charm Game, too.

"Your house is very impressive, Mr. Zurik. I spoke with your wife on Monday. She said you were away on business."

"Really? She didn't mention it. How can I help you?"

"I hear your son is teaching Danny Bauer how to speak Russian."

Zurik frowned. "Such a terrible thing, this shooting. Martina and I try to help Jackie whenever we can. Danny's a great kid. My son loves to hang out with him."

"So you speak Russian?"

After a slight hesitation, Zurik said, "I grew up in Paris. My mother was French, but my father was Russian, so I grew up speaking both languages."

What about English? You speak that pretty well.

Aloud he said, "Does Martina speak Russian?"

"I try to teach her, but she'd rather go shopping." A charming smile. "*Parlez vous Français?*"

"No. But my grandparents came here from Sicily. *Parla Italiano?*"

"No. I've never been to Italy."

"What did your father do for a living?" Watching Zurik to clock his reaction, closely enough to discern an almost imperceptible flinch.

Zurik held up his hands. Strong muscular hands. "My father did manual labor all his life. We could barely afford a tiny apartment in the onze arrondissement. The eleventh district in Paris. It was on the fifth floor. No elevator."

"Where is he now?"

"He died many years ago."

"How much time did you spend with Richie Bauer?"

Zurik didn't answer immediately, his eyes somber, his expression melancholy. "Not a lot. We played golf when he wasn't traveling. I will miss him. Richie was a nice guy. He doted on his kids."

What about Jackie? Did he dote on her? Did you know Richie had a mistress?

Aloud he said, "Did you ever talk about basketball?"

"Not really. I'm not much of a fan." Gesturing at a poster on the wall, an advertisement for a chess tournament, he said, "Many years ago I used to play chess. Now I'm too busy. So many stock exchanges in different time zones. Advising clients about stocks is complicated."

"I'm sure it is. Did you study that in college or ...?"

Zurik smiled, clearly amused. "Many years ago I worked at the New York Stock Exchange, sweeping floors. But an older man, a stock broker, took an interest in me and taught me about buying and selling stock." He shrugged. "I was always good at math."

"Looks like you've done very well. A big house in an exclusive neighborhood."

No response from Zurik, who gazed at him. Waiting for him to leave, no doubt.

"Do you know Hans Nader? Or Boris Mosgov?"

Zurik went still, his head tipped to the left. "The names don't ring a bell. Who are they?"

Deceptive, Frank thought. Jazz trumpeters talked about right-brain, left-brain improvisations. Some said their best performances came when they used their left brain, the creative side, to improvise. The right-brain was the rational side.

Presented with a sudden question about the shooter and his lawyer, Zurik's head had tipped left, while he composed his answer.

"Do you know anyone who wanted Richie dead?" Frank asked.

"I can't imagine it. Richie was a wonderful guy. Full of life, a great sense of humor. Why would anyone want him dead?"

Another crock of shit answer. "Thanks for your time, Mr. Zurik. I'll let you get back to work."

"No problem. Anytime." Flashing his charming smile.

Frank left the office and paused at the window of the office across the hall. Helen saw him and smiled. He gave her a thumbs-up and got in the elevator. On the surface, Zurik seemed like a well-dressed businessman plying his trade, good-looking, well groomed and clearly in good physical shape.

But his answers were too pat, smiling at him, eyes wide with innocence.

Frank had interviews dozens of convicted killers who maintained their innocence, smiling as they lied to him. Killers with engaging personalities and deceptive as hell. Like Zurik.

Complaining about how busy he was, unaware that Helen had told him she never saw anyone but Zurik enter the office. Another deflection when Frank said he knew Zurik's son was teaching Danny to speak Russian, saying what a terrible thing about the shooting. He and Martina did their best to help Jackie.

The hesitation when he asked what his father did for a living. Manual labor, holding up his hands. Strong powerful hands.

The denial when he asked Zurik if he knew Hans Nader and Boris Mosgov. Gazing at him with a puzzled frown, asking who they were.

Just an innocent businessman who lived in Ponchatoula Estates, an exclusive neighborhood with expensive homes, manicured lawns, and a private golf course.

Moreover, Zurik spoke damn good English, considering it wasn't his native language. No accent. No awkward phrasing.

Growing up in Paris seemed too convenient.

No way for Homicide Detective Frank Renzi to check that, right? Wrong.

He would send a copy of Zurik's DL to Interpol, see if they came up with something. Give it to Claudia and find out if the FBI had anything on Zurik.

But the biggest question remained.

What was behind Door Number Two?

Cheap furniture in the waiting room, so whatever was behind the other door must be expensive.

Otherwise, why would Zurik have a security system?

———

Nicolas armed the security system, strode into his work room and slammed the door, his mind racing, his body shaking with fury.

Did you spend much time with Richie Bauer?

Did you ever talk about basketball?

He glanced at the eight flat-screen TV sets mounted on the wall to his right, four on the top row, another four beneath it, running highlights of yesterday's NBA games.

Venetian blinds covered the window facing the door, closed to keep out the sun. No worries about prying eyes. That's why he'd rented an office on the twelfth floor. An L-shaped computer desk opposite the television monitors held a laser printer, a state-of-the-art desktop computer, and an executive phone with three lines. His open laptop sat on the short L.

Nicolas sank onto his padded-leather swivel chair. Homicide Detective Frank Renzi said his grandparents came from Sicily, known for its vicious Mafia gangs. Was this supposed to scare him?

Renzi appeared physically fit, strong and wiry, opening his jacket to make sure he saw the gun in his shoulder holster. Flashing a disarming smile, one that did not reach his penetrating dark eyes.

A dangerous man.

He reviewed his answers, examining them like moves in a chess match. He found no flaws, but that didn't mean there weren't any.

This game was far from over.

Do you know Hans Nader? Boris Mosgov?

The most dangerous questions of all.

He studied the photographs on his desk, the only personal items in his office.

His beloved son, two hours after he was born, black hair, large dark eyes and red-faced, his mouth open wailing for attention. Another taken on Nicky's third birthday outside the house in Ponchatoula, Nicky beaming up at him, holding a basketball in his pudgy little hands.

The most recent photo, taken earlier this year, Nicky standing beside him in his basketball uniform after he scored the winning basket for his team.

His heart swelled with pride.

After Papa died, he could not imagine ever loving anyone again. Not until he was thirty-two years old when Nicky was born had he felt such devotion to another human being. Holding his infant son, his own flesh and blood, in arms. The intensity of it still amazed him.

A month after Nicky was born, Martina's father had flown them to New York City for the christening, showering them with gifts, asking when they would give him another grandson.

Nicolas had smiled at Pavel Volkovich, thinking: *Never. You want him in your gang. No son of mine will ever work in your ugly business. Nor will I, now that we live in New Orleans.*

But last month everything changed. Not for the better.

And now Renzi was complicating matters.

Do you know Hans Nader? Boris Mosgov?

Nicolas took a fresh burner out of the carton beside his chair, dialed an international code, then Alexei's number in London.

Alexei answered after the second ring. "*Privyet!*" His familiar Russian greeting.

Speaking in Russian, Nicolas said, *My Pawn is weak.*

"*The Bishop can't control it?*"

"*Perhaps. Perhaps not.*"

"*Better take care of that or the game is lost.*"

"*Difficult. The Pawn is protected where it is.*"

Silence. Then, "*A black Pawn might take care of this.*"

"*Good idea. I'll see to it.*" Nicolas ended the call.

No matter how complicated the game, there was always a solution.

CHAPTER 21

Vobitch held the daily briefing at his house. They needed a break, he said, and a home-cooked lunch, courtesy of Juliana. She'd set the dining room table for five, with fresh salads at each place.

They helped themselves from pots of seafood gumbo, shrimp Creole and rice on a sideboard along one wall. Vobitch distributed beer bottles around the table, plunked onto his captain's chair and told them to dig in. Frank sat beside Kelly. Orville and Kenyon sat opposite them.

At one time or another, they'd all been to Vobitch's house, less than a mile from the Poorhouse Pub, a small two-story cottage. The perfect place to meet. No leaks, no shortage of beer, and no discussion of the case while they ate, just compliments on the delicious food.

Finally, Vobitch set aside his plate and said, "Shall we start?"

"I'll start by saying thanks for the fabulous lunch," Kelly said.

Orville nodded and raised his beer bottle at Vobitch. "Mighty fine gesture, Boss."

"You've been working your asses off for a week, I figured you deserved a treat." Patting his belly, Vobitch said, "Pecan pie for dessert. If Juliana lets me have any."

"I'll put in a good word," Frank said. "Or maybe I'll just eat mine and yours, too."

Vobitch allowed them a few guffaws, then said, "The Super told the vultures not to contact the victims' next of kin, but I wouldn't count on it. By now the fuckwads know where each victim lived and whether he's got a fucking pimple on his ass."

Kenyon smiled mischievously. "Give 'em an hour, the pimple be all over the Internet."

"But they don't know Benny was wired, right?" Orville said.

"Jesus-fucking Christ!" Vobitch said. "I hope not. If that gets out, we're in trouble."

"I don't know if this is relevant," Kelly said, "but Richie's mother may have committed suicide. Benny's mother said Mrs. Bauer died in a car accident when Richie was ten, so I called the Atlantic City PD and got a copy of the police report." Kelly checked her notes. "On November 15, 1974, Mrs. Bauer drove her car into a concrete bridge abutment."

"Was she alone in the car?" Vobitch asked.

"Yes. According to the police report, it was a clear night, the cops found no brake marks and estimated the car was going sixty miles an hour when it hit the abutment."

Frank clenched his jaw, thinking about his father. Last year, Judge Salvatore Renzi had driven his car into a tree, but it was no accident. It wasn't suicide either, but he still wound up dead.

As if she'd read his mind, Kelly glanced at him, her eyes somber. After a moment she said, "They checked inconclusive for the cause, not accident or suicide. Mr. Bauer was listed as next of kin. Richie was only ten at the time, but police reports are public records, so he might have found out about it later. I'm still trying to locate his father."

"If you find him," Vobitch said, "get him talking about Richie. The Lakers cheerleader said he took her to Vegas on trips, so we know he liked to gamble, and we know Benny was a gambler. Frank got us some information on the New Jersey feds. Run it down, Frank."

Without mentioning that Claudia was now a silent partner in the High Roller investigation, he recapped what she'd told him about Dominic Marconi and the New Jersey FBI office. He ran down the LOOK-SHARP investigation into NBA games during the two prior NBA seasons. "The team favored to win beat the spread almost seventy percent of the time. The odds on that astronomical. Richie Bauer was officiating all of them."

"Mmm, mmm, mmm," Kenyon said. "Don't get much better than that."

"Oh, but it does. Morgan's favorite FBI agent, Special Agent Fred Lewis, hauled Benny in and raked him over the coals."

"And wired Benny up," Orville said.

"Probably. My contact couldn't confirm that. But when Fred asked Benny if he and Richie were betting on NBA games, Benny refused to rat him out, only admitted he gave tips to Marconi."

"What's up with the gun search?" Vobitch said.

"Nothing on my end yet," Orville said, "but I'm on it."

"Not much on my end either." Kenyon grimaced. "Other than the tips we're getting since Crimestoppers posted the reward. The usual crackpots plus the dime-droppers and grudge-settlers. But we'll stay on it. Gotta catch a break sooner or later."

"I talked to Zurik this morning at his office," Frank said. "What I could see of it. Not much in the waiting room other than a desk and a security keypad on the wall. Zurik smiles and acts helpful, but I don't trust him. I asked if he knew Nader and Mosgov. Never heard of them. When I asked if he spent much time with Richie, he said he'd miss him, such a nice guy, devoted to his kids. Didn't say Richie was devoted to Jackie though."

"Maybe he knew about the cheerleader," Kelly said. "Maybe he figured Richie's not paying attention to Jackie, why not jump her and see how it goes. Did you ask him if he spoke Russian?"

"Yes. He said he grew up in Paris. His mother was French, but his father was Russian. No reason why he shouldn't teach his son to speak Russian, but the shooter speaks Russian, Mosgov speaks Russian and so does Zurik. I want to talk to the shooter when Mosgov isn't there."

"My guy at the lockup says Mosgov usually sees the shooter in the afternoon after lunch," Vobitch said. "Give it a shot tomorrow."

"If he'll agree to see me," Frank said. "I can't force him."

Vobitch gave him his evil smile. "Give it a try. He might be lonely."

Kenyon said, "Did you show Zurik your SIG?"

"Oh, he saw it all right. When I asked if he and Richie talked about basketball, he said he wasn't a hoop fan, said he used to play chess, but now he's too busy. Making the big bucks to pay for his mansion in Ponchatoula. I want to get a search warrant for Zurik's office and car."

"Good idea," Vobitch said. "Write one up and take it to a judge."

"Will do," he said. "Tony parked the surveillance van in the golf course parking lot where he can see both houses and the cars parked outside. Jackie's, Zurik's and his wife's car. Tony sent me the makes, models and tag numbers."

"Okay," Vobitch said. "Anybody got anything else? If not, time for pecan pie!" When Kelly started to get up, Vobitch said, "Let Frank do the honors. Juliana wants to talk to him."

Frank tossed him a mock salute and hustled into the kitchen where the aroma of garlic and spices permeated the air. Juliana smiled and rose from her chair. A tall willowy black woman, she'd been a prima ballerina for a New York City ballet company three decades ago. One night after she left the theater, NYPD patrolman Morgan Vobitch had rescued her from a mugger and one thing led to another. Thirty years later they were still devoted to each other.

"Fantastic lunch," Frank said. "You outdid yourself, Juliana."

"Nothing but the best for Morgan's best detectives. How are you doing, Frank? Almost a year since the funeral, but I'm sure you still miss your father."

Juliana and Morgan, accompanied by Kenyon and Tanya Miller, had flown to Massachusetts for his father's funeral. A poignant gesture of support, one he would never forget. Nor would he forget how much his father meant to him. Cheering him on at high school basketball games. Taking him to Celtics games at Boston Garden. And years later, after Frank got his detective shield, discussing law enforcement issues.

"How's Maureen doing?" Juliana asked. "That was a terrible ordeal she went through."

"Doing great. She passed the board exams."

"Wonderful!" Juliana exclaimed. "Have her come down for a visit. Tell her I'll make some seafood gumbo. Morgan and I would love to see her."

"And she'd love to see you." Frank smiled. "Before the funeral, I warned her about Morgan and his F-bombs, but she said he wouldn't dare do it when you're around."

Juliana laughed. "Smart girl. But I'm hearing too many of them these days. Morgan's obsessed with this High Roller case. Are you close to solving it?"

"I hope so, but every time we think we're on the right track, we get another curve ball. And if I don't bring Morgan some pie pretty soon, I'll be in trouble."

But as he watched Juliana put pecan pie slices on plates, his thoughts returned to his father. Juliana was right.

Losing a father wasn't something you got over right away.

He hadn't, and neither would Danny Bauer, whose father would never cheer him on at school basketball games, never take him to a New Orleans Saints game, never give him a golf lesson.

And what about Nora? Gazing at Frank with forlorn eyes, sitting beside him on the couch when it was obvious she wanted him to give her a hug. Something he would gladly have done, but every police officer knew this was verboten. A lawsuit waiting to happen if the parent found out about it.

The jury was still out on Jackie.

Was she another innocent victim of Richie's bad choices?

Or had Jackie been making bad choices of her own?

―――

2:30 PM – New Orleans

He flinched as the door clanged shut behind him. His new cell had bunk beds along the right wall, a metal toilet and sink on the left. Ahead of him, a chair welded to a metal desk stood underneath a narrow vertical window.

The biggest difference?

The schwartzer who'd stolen his cornbread sat on the top bunk.

Glaring at him, his eyes dark with fury, the schwartzer swung his legs over the side of the bed. Jumped off and landed on the floor with a loud *thump*. Six-foot-four, brawny tattooed arms, his face screwed up in a frown. "Whatchoo doing here, white boy? Think you gonna take over my territory?"

White boy. He didn't understand the rest, but he knew hostility when he saw it in a man's eyes.

"Hans," he said, and offered a smile, hoping to placate the man.

"Hands? I ain't shaking yo hand. I ain't no homo."

Homo. He knew what that meant, too.

140

"That whatchoo you are, white boy? Gonna bend over so I can fuck you up the ass?"

He stood very still, heart pounding, hands sweaty, knowing exactly how easy it was to make someone to disappear from the face of the earth. The man outweighed him by fifty pounds. Could snap his neck in an instant.

The schwartzer wrenched the plastic bin out of his hands. Supplies for his new cell: a new toothbrush, a fresh towel and clean sheets for the bed. Set the bin on the lower bunk and grabbed the pillow, smiling at him as he put a clean pillow case on it. Tossed the pillow onto the upper bunk and said, "Thanks for the extra pillow."

He said nothing, weighing his options. His employers in London had taught him various tactical moves. Eye gouging. A quick thrust with the flat of your hand to the throat …

"Gonna escort you to breakfast tomorrow, Pussy." The schwartzer smiled but his eyes were hard as agates. "You order up one a them waffles so's I can have an extra one."

He went to the door and peered through narrow opening. Not a guard in sight. He pounded the door with his fists and yelled, "Phone call! I must make phone call!!"

"Shut up!" The schwartzer grabbed his arm, clamping it like a vise.

If he gouged his eyes out, the man would scream, but ….

The schwartzer picked him up as if he were no heavier than the pillow and flung him onto the lower bunk. "Shut up, Pussy, and stay out of my sight."

He curled up on the bare mattress, his back against the wall and thought about Katerina, the beautiful bride he would never see again.

Would he live to see another day?

Maybe. As long as he stayed awake.

In the bunk above him, the schwartzer chuckled, a nasty rumble. "Yo, white boy, you 'bout ready to nod off in dreamland?"

He dug his fingernails into his palms. Visualizing Katerina, silently speaking her name in his mind. *Katerina. Katerina. Katerina.*

The best day of my life was the day that I met you.

I love you with all my heart.

CHAPTER 22

DAY 7 THURSDAY OCTOBER 16, 2014 – 6:15 PM – Ponchatoula

Jackie slid a slice of pepperoni pizza onto Danny's plate, turned to Nora and said, "What would you like, Nora? Cheese with mushrooms or pepperoni?"

She had ordered delivery of takeout pizza so they could have a pizza party on the playroom floor. Spread out a quilt like they did when it got cold in the winter and they couldn't eat outside on the patio.

Sometimes they watched TV, but not tonight. Not tomorrow, either.

Maybe they'd never watch TV again.

"Cheese," Nora said, wrinkling her nose. "I hate pepperoni."

"Why can't we watch TV?" Danny said.

She put a slice of cheese pizza on Nora's plate. "Because we need to talk about something."

Danny gave her a sullen look and ate a bite of pizza. "Why? I'd rather watch TV."

"I don't want you watching TV, or the news. The police held a press conference this morning and gave your father's name to the reporters. And I don't want you talking to them."

"Why would I talk to them?" Danny picked up his can of Pepsi, took two big gulps and let out a loud burp, knowing this would annoy her.

She chose to ignore it. "They might ask you questions about your father."

"Will they ask me questions?" Nora asked, gazing at her, oblivious to the grease dripping from the pizza slice in her hand.

"They might, but I don't want you talking to them. Now that they have Daddy's name, it will be easy enough for them to find out where we live."

"So?" Danny said. "It's not like they're outside ringing our doorbell. Besides, I want to go to school tomorrow."

"Me too, me too!" Nora exclaimed. "Can I, Mommy? I'm sick of staying home all the time."

Jackie clenched her jaw and took a deep breath. Calm. She had to stay calm or things would get out of hand. "You can't go to school tomorrow and neither can Danny. The reporters will find your school and stand out in front and scream questions at you."

"I don't care," Danny said. "Why can't I hang out with my friends at school?"

"Maybe next week after things die down."

"Next week?" Danny stared at her, incredulous. "I have to stay home for a week?"

"I want to go to playschool," Nora said, pouting now.

"Playschool," Danny sneered. "They don't teach you anything there. You don't even have homework. I'm missing all my classes, Mom! I'm way behind!"

"You'll catch up, Danny. You've only missed three days. Besides, you always complain about the homework you have to do every night. Pretend you're on vacation."

"Some vacation," Danny said. "Sitting here pretending we're at the beach is stupid, Mom. It's like Nora, talking to her stuffed bunny, pretending it's a real person. Nicky asked me to come to his basketball game at the YMCA tonight. Will you take me?"

Ready to pull her hair out, Jackie massaged her temples, picturing the lineup of reporters she'd have to face if she drove him to the game. Millstein had convinced the Ponchatoula Sheriff to post a deputy at the entrance to the Ponchatoula Estates to keep the media out.

But the deputy wouldn't stop the reporters from following her.

"Not tonight, Danny. Maybe next week. By then maybe this will be old news."

She sure as hell hoped so. She felt like a hostage, hounded on all sides. The media outside the gate, rebellious children inside the house.

"No!" Danny said. "That's all you ever say, Mom." He flung his half-eaten pizza slice on the floor. "I'M NOT THE ONE THAT'S DEAD!" he screamed. "DAD IS!!!

He scrambled to his feet and ran out of the room, his feet thundering down the hall. Shocked to the core, she clutched her stomach, her heart pounding.

Should she go talk to Danny and try to comfort him?

Nora crawled into her lap, sobbing, "Where's Daddy? I want my Daddy."

Jolted into Good-Mother mode, Jackie patted her back. "Hush, Nora. It's all right. Hush."

But Nora wouldn't be placated, sobbing, "Where's Daddy? Where's Daddy?"

Tears flooded her eyes. *Daddy's in a casket on a train bound for Crown Heights, New York.*

If only she were with him. But she wasn't. She had too many decisions to make. Life-changing decisions and unpleasant tasks.

Tomorrow she had to call her father and ask him to contact the funeral home she'd found on the Internet. And listen to him berate her for choosing someone who wasn't Jewish, no doubt.

Eventually, she wanted to hold a memorial service for Richie.

But she couldn't think about that now.

She had too much to do before she left Ponchatoula.

11:45 PM – New Orleans

Nicolas turned left on Orleans Avenue, muscled his BMW over a curb onto the two-block-long concrete slab under the I-10 and killed the headlights. Years ago after Katrina, the NOPD had towed thousands of abandoned cars here, to be claimed if and when the owners returned. Those cars were long gone.

No cars here now, abandoned or otherwise, just his.

But soon there would be. He checked the time. Almost midnight.

This afternoon he'd used his burner to text Big Dawgg. He didn't know his real name and didn't want to know. Big Dawgg didn't know his real name either, called him "Whitey."

It never ceased to amaze him how many people wanted other people dead. There were men in London ready, willing and able to kill them. If you paid them enough. New Orleans was no different.

Many years ago Nicolas had learned to exploit a crucial concept. All men maintain certain rituals.

Those with jobs were most predictable. Wake up, eat, go to work, go home, eat again, watch TV and go to bed. The best time to strike was between midnight and dawn, when they were asleep. Woken from a deep sleep, a man is less able to defend himself.

The next best thing was to strike when the target least expected it.

Other times a situation yielded an opening so glaringly obvious, it was impossible to ignore. Such was the situation in this case.

Alert for any sudden movement, he checked his rearview, then the side mirrors. The only sign of life: a blinking neon beer sign outside a convenience store two blocks away. At this hour, the dark shadowy wasteland beneath the highway was frightening: cars, motorcycles and trucks thundering along on the I-10 above his head. Frightening and dangerous.

He touched the Beretta, hidden in his waistband under his windbreaker. Trust no one. Especially a black gangbanger who bought and sold untraceable guns.

Headlights flashed behind him and went dark.

Nicolas went on full alert, his heart racing, palms sweaty. Now came the dangerous part. He lowered his window.

A sleek black Cadillac passed his BMW, reversed direction and pulled up beside him.

The driver's side window lowered and Big Dawgg said, "Yo, Whitey. Need another gun?"

"No, something else. You got any friends in the lockup?"

Big Dawgg's pudgy moon-face lit up in a smile. "Got friends everywhere. Whatchoo need?"

"Need somebody dead." Nicolas took an envelope stuffed with hundred-dollar bills out of the cup-holder and showed it to him. "Five large in here, five more when it's done."

Big Dawgg reached out and snatched the envelope. "Who you want daid?"

"This guy," he said, and handed him a photograph.

Big Dawgg glanced at the photograph and put it in his pocket. "When you want him gone?"

"The sooner the better."

"No problem. Be here tomorrow night and pay me the rest." Big Dawgg's window rolled up and the black Cadillac zoomed away.

Drenched in sweat, Nicolas sat very still.

So far so good, but his brain churned with bad scenarios.

What if Big Dawgg took the five grand and did nothing?

What if Detective Frank Renzi told the warden to put the Pawn in solitary?

A sudden yearning seized him. He wanted to call Yvette, have her meet him at the hotel and let her whisper sweet nothings in his ear in French. Lose himself in an orgy and forget how many things could go wrong.

The worse scenario of all: What if Big Dawgg found out his real name and ratted him out? Gangsters like Big Dawgg had ways to dig up information.

He massaged his aching temples.

Sometimes his need to see many moves ahead caused him unnecessary agita.

Sometimes you placed a bet and hoped for the best.

He put the BMW in gear and left the shadowy concrete wasteland.

No frolic with Yvette tonight.

Better to drive home to Ponchatoula and sleep with Martina, knowing his beloved son Nicky was safely tucked in bed.

CHAPTER 23

Frank got out of the shower, eager to visit the Orleans Parish Prison and see if the shooter would talk to him without Mosgov.

No telling how that would go. *I will send you a solicitor who speaks Russian. Until then, speak to no one. And remember what I said.*

The person who hired him delivering a veiled threat.

Remember what I said.

Two days ago in the interview room, the shooter had said in English. *"Very afraid, me. Other prisoners—"*

But Boris Mosgov had shut him up.

Even if the shooter agreed to talk to him, he might not reveal who hired him, especially if whoever hired him was paying Mosgov. Crucial information when the case went to trial.

After he left the OPP, he'd call Claudia to see if she'd found any information about Hans Nader, the shooter, and Nicolas Zurik, the man Frank now believed was the mastermind.

After a quick shower and shave, he got dressed and went in the kitchen.

Kelly stood at the counter, sipping coffee. She handed him a mug and said, "Dark. Very dark."

He leaned against the counter beside her and took a sip. "Not bad. Better than Starbucks."

She laughed. "Frank, your obsession with Dunkin Donuts coffee is turning into a fetish."

"You're my fetish, but duty calls so we'll get into that later. I talked to Maureen after the lunch meeting at Vobitch's house. Her new boyfriend wants her to move to Philadelphia."

"You worry too much, Frank. He might be Mr. Right."

"Or Mr. Wrong," he said, thinking of the dentist in Baltimore. "The judge wouldn't okay the warrant to search Zurik's office and his car. She said I didn't have probable cause, told me to bring her something concrete."

"Like what?" Kelly said, twirling a lock of dark hair around her finger.

"Who the fuck knows? How about a gun with Zurik's prints on it? Or a signed confession from the SOB." He drank some coffee. "Maybe Claudia will get us something."

Kelly arched an eyebrow. "She's your source for the New Jersey feds, right?"

"Yes, but don't let on I told you. She agreed to help us. Might get us something on Zurik."

"That would be good." Kelly sipped her coffee. "You think he's in bed with Jackie?"

"I'm not sure." His cellphone vibrated in his pocket. He took it out, checked the ID and answered. "Tony, what's going on?"

"Jackie's home with the kids. So is Zurik but he came home late last night. After midnight."

"I wonder what he's up to."

"Bug his car, we'd know. But here's the important thing. A deputy sheriff is screening cars at the entrance to Ponchatoula Estates, set up a barricade to keep out the media. Gotta be two dozen pissed-off reporters and TV vans parked outside the gate."

"Smart move on Jackie's part. Maybe her lawyer's got clout with the Ponchatoula Sheriff."

"Looks like it," Tony said. "I told the deputy about the NOPD surveillance van in the golf club parking lot. He said they knock off at midnight. Another deputy comes on at six in the morning."

"Thanks, Tony. Keep me posted." He ended the call and said, "We better check the news."

They went in the living room and Kelly tuned in a local news channel. The lead story was about Jackie Bauer.

Doing a stand-up outside the barricaded entrance to Ponchatoula Estates, a female reporter said, "Jackie Bauer, the widow of deceased NBA referee Richard Bauer, lives here at Ponchatoula Estates, but police won't allow any media inside. We tried to speak with a resident at the checkpoint, but he said the Neighborhood Association sent an email to the residents warning them not to talk to the media."

Kelly muted the sound and said, "You think Jackie had her lawyer set it up."

"Yes, and I don't blame her. That's why Vobitch calls them vultures. Picture a mob of reporters outside her house, shouting *How do you feel about your husband being murdered, Mrs. Bauer? Do you know who wanted to kill him?* The kids aren't deaf. Danny's ten and Nora's five. Imagine what they're thinking."

"I can't," Kelly said. "It's too horrible."

"Exactly, and this is only the beginning. Pretty soon the reporters will find out Benny's a gambler and he grew up with Richie in Atlantic City."

"And figure the same thing we did," Kelly said. "Richie was fixing games so he could make money gambling on them."

They went back in the kitchen. His cellphone vibrated again. Vobitch this time. He answered and said, "What's shaking, Morgan?"

Agitated, Vobitch snarled, "The shooter's dead."

He felt like a mule had kicked him in the gut. "Dead?" He looked at Kelly, who stared at him, eyes wide, her mouth gaping open.

"Jesus Christ!" he said. "When? How?"

"Ten minutes ago at the fucking OPP," Vobitch said. "My contact called me, said there was some kind of rumble at breakfast. I'm going there now."

"Be there in five," he said, and grabbed his jacket.

"The shooter?" Kelly said, pouring coffee into a metal travel mug.

"Yes. They killed him at the lockup. I'm meeting Vobitch there now."

She handed him the mug and said, "This will cause a shitstorm."

"Yes it will. I should have done more to protect him. Last time I talked to him he said he was afraid."

"Not your responsibility, Frank. Call me when you get a chance."

"Will do. Thanks for the coffee," he said and hustled out the door.

———

10:30 AM – New Orleans

The mood in the conference room was grim as they took their seats around the table. Vobitch had called them in for an emergency meeting. Frank sipped coffee from his travel mug and looked at Kelly, who frowned and shook her head.

"In case you haven't already heard," Vobitch said sarcastically, "a bunch of fucking maggots at the Orleans Parish Prison ganged up on the shooter and beat him to death."

"Someone was afraid he'd talk," Kenyon said. "Whacked the guy to shut him up."

Fighting the rage boiling inside him, Frank said, "The motherfucker that hired him. No matter what we do, the mastermind is always a step ahead of us."

"Premeditated murder," Kelly said emphatically.

"Gang related?" Orville said, his eyes solemn as he sipped his coffee.

"No doubt," Kenyon said. "You got a thousand prisoners in the OPP. Public Defenders call it Off Prisoners Pronto. Already got a shitload of lawsuits filed by relatives of prisoners who died there. If they're not a gang member when they get there, they join one damn quick."

Orville nodded. "For protection."

"The media's all over it," Kelly said. "I caught the bulletin on TV. At seven-thirty they were talking about a riot at the OPP, ten minutes later they said the man charged with the shooting at the High Roller Club was dead. How did they find out?"

"The OPP leaks like a sieve," Kenyon said.

"And smells worse," Orville said. "The stench alone be enough to kill you."

"But it's not our worry," Vobitch said. "Let the Orleans Parish Sheriff take the heat. He's the one that has to investigate the murder. Him and his deputies."

"That'll go nowhere fast," Orville said. "Forty-four inmates have died there over the past nine years, only one of 'em ruled a homicide."

"Last year a local TV reporter got hold of some jailhouse videos,"Kenyon said. "Clips of inmates partying in the cell blocks, drinking beer, using drugs. Gambling, all kinds of shit."

"An out-of-control snake-pit," Kelly said. "If one of my domestic violence victims files a restraining order, I go there to make sure the asshole surrenders his guns. Two years ago a class action lawsuit claimed pretrial inmates were at risk of serious harm. Forget inmates with mental health issues. They just hand-cuff them to the bars in their cells."

"Hold it!" Vobitch commanded. "We know the fucking OPP is a shithole. Focus on what happened. Frank and I watched videotape from the surveillance cameras. What there was of it. Half the cameras in the cafeteria don't work "

"And the inmates know it," Frank said. "This was no rumble, it was planned ahead of time. From what I saw, which wasn't much, a bunch of prisoners started milling around, a fight breaks out and the shooter's in the middle of it."

"What about the guards?" Kelly asked. "Did they try to stop it?"

"Not that I saw," Vobitch said. "The maggots would eat them for breakfast."

"You got that right," Orville said. "Inmates got half the guards in their pocket. Guards make shit money, the inmates pay 'em to look the other way, smuggle in dope, cellphones, even guns. No place to be if you're innocent. Too many inmates, not enough guards. Even if he's guilty, a man's got a right to be safe."

"Don't shed any tears over him," Frank snapped. "He murdered five people in cold blood."

"Most of the inmates involved were black," Vobitch said. "But the video footage was fuzzy and they kept their heads down. Gonna be hard to identify a specific prisoner."

"Last time I saw him," Frank said, "the shooter said he was afraid, but Mosgov shut him up."

"Mosgov was in this from the get-go," Vobitch said. "He's as guilty as the shooter."

"So was the person who hired him," Frank said. "Zurik's at the top of my suspect list."

He clenched his jaw, thinking of Danny and Nora, two fatherless kids who deserved justice. No way was he going to let the bastard who ordered the shooting get away with it.

"We need to find the 'banger that sold the gun to whoever ordered the hit at the High Roller," Vobitch said. "Maybe the motherfucker paid the same 'banger to set up the murder at the OPP."

"Plenty of 'bangers in the OPP," Orville said. "Me and Kenyon best squeeze some 'bangers on the outside. Dangle an accessory-to-murder charge over 'em."

"Do it!" Vobitch said. "Frank, did you get the search warrant for Zurik's office?"

"No," he said. "The judge said we don't have probable cause."

Vobitch grimaced. "Fucking judges. Pretty soon we'll need PC to brush our teeth. Talk to Jackie and find out what she's up to. Grill her about Zurik."

"If she'll talk to me," Frank said. "Her lawyer told her not to. I don't think she's in bed with Zurik. He's the one I'm after. Tony told me a Ponchatoula deputy sheriff is guarding the entrance to the Ponchatoula Estates, only lets residents in, no media."

"Good," Vobitch snarled. "The media fuckwits don't give a rat's ass about grieving relatives, think they're road-kill, ripe and ready for pecking. Stick a microphone in a kid's face and ask 'em if they miss their daddy or some fucking thing."

"I better call Benny's mother," Kelly said. "If the reporters found out where Jackie lives, they'll find her too, and start calling her."

"They're already calling me," Vobitch growled. "But I tell them to call the Super. Christ! Just when we think we're getting somewhere, something worse happens." Icing them with a look, he said, "Get me something! We need to nail the prick that planned this before he kills someone else."

"Will the Super do a press conference?" Orville asked.

"Hell if I know," Vobitch said.

"The Orleans Parish Sheriff is the one who should take the heat," Frank said. "They didn't protect the shooter and now he's dead."

And I'm gonna get the motherfucker who paid someone to whack him.

CHAPTER 24

Alone in the homicide office, Kelly sat at Detective David Lee's desk, hers temporarily while she worked the High Roller case. After the emergency meeting with Vobitch, Kenyon had bought her a turkey sandwich for lunch, but she didn't feel like eating.

Too many people dying these days. Violent premeditated deaths. The bloodbath at the High Roller Club last Friday, the shooter beaten to death at the OPP this morning. A major setback.

Frank was furious. By now he was probably in Ponchatoula, questioning Jackie. She wouldn't want to be in Jackie's shoes right now. Frank had a reputation: Don't cross him or you'll regret it.

A half hour ago, Kenyon had left to meet one of his CIs, hoping to find out who bought the shooter's gun. Kelly was looking for Richie Bauer's father, hoping to squeeze him for information about their current theory: Richie was betting on NBA games.

Five minutes ago she had obtained a copy of his father's most recent driver's license from the Atlantic City RMV. Henry Bauer, age 72, but no one by that name lived at the listed address. After his third DUI arrest two years ago, Henry had lost his license. He was probably getting a Social Security check, but to get information from Social Security she'd need a warrant.

Screw that. She wanted to talk to Henry Bauer today.

She got on the computer and Googled Alcoholics Anonymous in Atlantic City. Plenty of meetings listed, but she wouldn't get anything from them. That's why they called it anonymous. She scrolled past the AA meetings and found two listings for alcoholic treatment centers.

Blessed Recovery was first on the list.

She got on her cellphone, dialed their number and waited.

Moments later, a deep male voice said, "The Lord's Blessings upon you. This is Reverend Bob. Are you an alcoholic seeking redemption? We can help you."

Kelly grimaced. Just what she needed, a religious freak. "Hello, Reverend Bob. NOPD Detective Kelly O'Neil speaking. I'm trying to reach Henry Bauer. Do you know him?"

"Of course I do! Henry came to live with us at Blessed Recovery over a year ago. Thanks to the Good Lord he's made great progress."

Her heart skyrocketed into the stratosphere. Henry Bauer lived there!

"Has Henry done something wrong?"

"No, nothing like that. But I need to speak with him about his son."

"Lord Be Praised! I feared Henry might have strayed from the Lord's path. Demon Alcohol lurks everywhere."

"Could you tell me how I can speak with him?"

"Certainly. Do you take comfort in the Lord, Detective O'Neil?"

Give me the number, asshole! "I need to speak to Henry. Could you give me his phone number?"

"Just a moment." She waited. Thirty seconds later, he recited a telephone number and added in deep stentorian tones, "May you find peace in your journey through life, Detective O'Neil. Should trouble befall you, rest assured the Lord will look after you."

"Thank you," she said and ended the call. She doubted the Lord was going to furnish the name of the man who'd paid the shooter. But Richie's father might give her something useful. Over the years she'd dealt with more than a few alcoholics, and they could be devious as hell, so she had to stay alert.

She dialed the number and waited.

"'lo," said a male voice.

"Hi, Mr. Bauer? Is Richie Bauer your son? The NBA referee?"

"Sure is," Bauer said, more animated now. "Why? Are you a reporter?"

"No, but I've seen him a lot on TV." She could be devious too. "Richie's a great referee.

"You got that right. Are you gonna write a book about him?"

Damn it to hell! She didn't want to lie to him, but Henry Bauer was the only person who could give her the information she needed. "Maybe. What was he like as a kid?"

"Back then we was living in a trailer park. I got laid off from my job so we couldn't afford nothing better."

Kelly rolled her eyes, thinking: *Because you spent all your money on gambling and booze.*

"Smart as a whip, Richie was. I used to take him to the track when he was a kid. Taught him how to play the ponies. Caught on real quick, Richie did. We had a great time."

"Did he play basketball back then?"

"Lordy, you couldn't keep him away from it. Bought his own hoop when he was eleven and nailed it to the roof of our trailer. I asked him where he got the money, but he wouldn't tell me. Said it wasn't none of my business. Well, that wasn't exactly what he said. The kid had a mouth on him even then, I can tell you that."

"Uh-huh," she said, encouraging him.

"Him and the fat kid next door, I forget his name, I think him and Richie set up a gambling scheme over at the high school."

Her heart sped up. "What made you think that?"

Bauer chuckled, a phlemy gurgle that ended in a smoker's cough. "Found the betting slips in his room while he was in school. When I took him to the track, sometimes I'd buy a few Six-Play tickets, you know? Pretty good odds, if you know how to pick 'em."

"So you found Six-Play betting slips in Richie's room?"

"No, no. Richie was smart enough to know Six-Play odds are tough to beat. Him and the fat kid was running Four-Plays on baseball."

"Baseball?"

"Yeah. Back then all the kids were into baseball. Richie ran Four-Plays on the Mets and the Yankees. Know how I could tell? Richie marked the slips with Ms and Ys."

"How much do you think they were making?"

"Got no clue about that. Wouldn't do me no good to ask, neither. After Richie got into basketball, I hardly ever saw him, spent hours shooting around outside, even in the winter. Don't get to see him much nowadays, neither. Reverend Bob don't let us watch TV until after dinner, got all kinds of meetings during the day, praying to the Lord and such."

Kelly hesitated. Didn't he know Richie was dead?

"You don't watch the news?"

"No. Reverend Bob won't let us. Says those reporters lie about stuff."

"So you didn't hear about the shooting in New Orleans last week?"

"Just told you! Reverend Bob don't let us watch that stuff, says it's the work of the Devil."

"Richie was murdered at a club in New Orleans last Friday."

Dead silence for ten seconds. Then a plaintive wail. "Richie's dead? Christ Almighty! I was so proud of him. Got out of Atlantic City and made something of himself, and now you tell me he's dead?"

"I'm very sorry for your loss, Mr. Bauer," she said, and ended the call. Richie's father was a bit of a braggart, claiming he took Richie to the racetrack and taught him how to bet, but most of what he said rang true.

The fat kid next door had to be Benny, and the part about the betting slips was too detailed to be fabricated.

Which meant Richie and Benny had begun gambling long before they got out of high school. Information Vobitch would be happy to have.

But she felt like a sleazeball, mining Henry Bauer for information about Richie, then dropping the bomb on him. His son was dead.

———

12:05 PM – Ponchatoula

Frank rang the doorbell and waited, his fury unabated. Maybe Jackie knew who ordered the shooter killed and maybe she didn't. Either way he intended to grill her like a suspect.

She opened the door, her face pale, dark hollows beneath wary blue eyes.

"Can we talk in your office?" he said. Forget pleasantries. He wanted answers. "I've got some news I don't want the kids to hear."

Her mouth quirked, but she opened the door and took him into the living room.

"Hi Detective Frank," Nora called from the kitchen doorway. "Can we go for a walk?"

He smiled at her and said, "Not right now, Nora. Maybe after I talk to your mother."

"Finish your lunch, Nora," Jackie said, and took him to her office. Clearly not happy to see him, she leaned against the desk, arms crossed over her chest in a defensive posture.

Frank shut the door and said, "The man who murdered your husband was beaten to death at the Orleans Parish Prison this morning."

Jackie gasped, staring at him, slack-jawed. Seconds later her shock morphed into anger. "So the sonofabitch won't go on trial for murder, right? What the hell kind of justice is that? I wanted him to fry in the electric chair and celebrate when he was dead."

He'd seen the same reaction from relatives of other homicide victims. But those relatives weren't on the suspect list. Jackie was.

"We believe someone set up the beating."

Jackie rubbed her arms and muttered, "It never ends."

"What never ends?"

"Everything!" she snapped. "Paying security guards to keep the fucking reporters away from my house. Danny wants to go to school, but I won't let him. The reporters will go there and yell questions at him. The kids are sick of staying home, hiding inside the house. And so am I."

"I want justice for Richie, too. But his friend Benny was a bookie, and Dominic Marconi was a known mobster in Atlantic City. Why were they sitting with Richie last Friday?"

"I don't know. I told you that before!" Glaring at him belligerently.

"We believe someone paid the shooter to kill them. We want to know who."

"And why, right? Isn't that what you said?"

"Yes. Any idea who it was?"

Jackie took two bottles of water out of the mini-refrigerator, handed him one and drank from the other. Not answering his question.

"We think the person who hired the shooter arranged to have him killed this morning. To keep him quiet." Watching her to see how she'd react.

She clamped her lips together in a grim line and said nothing.

"What's your relationship with Nicolas Zurik?"

"He's my neighbor. I talk to him once in a while. Why?"

Frank drank some water, weighing his next move. "I talked to him at his office the other day. He's a charming guy, good-looking, got plenty of money. Are you sleeping with him?"

"Jesus Christ!" she exclaimed, her eyes blazing fury. "Is that what you think?"

He said nothing. She seemed outraged, but she could be faking.

"I'm not sleeping with him," she said. "His wife is my best friend."

"Be careful," Frank said. "He's dangerous."

The door opened and Nora stepped into the room. "When can we go for our walk, Mom? You promised."

Frank said, "I'm pretty busy, Nora. But maybe we can take a ten minute walk to the golf course and back." To give Jackie a chance to think about what he'd said.

"Can we, Mom? Pleeeeze?" Nora said.

"Not today," Jackie said. "Maybe next time."

Nora stamped her foot and yelled, "Not next time! I want to take a walk with Detective Frank today!"

Big tantrum coming up, Frank thought.

Jackie clenched her jaw, looking frazzled. Opened her mouth to speak. Stopped when her cellphone rang. She checked the ID and let the call go to voicemail. Lowered the phone and said, "Okay, Nora, take a walk with Detective Frank while I return a phone call."

"Yea!" Nora said. "Can I bring my bunny, Detective Frank?"

"Of course. We can't take a walk without Dora. I'll meet you outside."

After Nora dashed off to get her stuffed bunny, Frank said, "If you know something, now's the time to tell me, Jackie."

Her lips tightened. "Take Nora for a walk, but bring her back in ten minutes."

Frank went outside to wait for Nora. He got the feeling Jackie knew something but was afraid to tell him about it. Was she scared of Zurik? Or was she part of the murder scheme? Maybe she was afraid Homicide Detective Frank Renzi would find out and arrest her.

Nora raced out the door with her stuffed bunny, smiling at him, saying, "It's a beautiful day, right, Detective Frank?"

"It sure is," he said, unwilling to dampen her enthusiasm. But his day was far from beautiful. *Very afraid, me.*

The shooter knew he was in danger. Knew he was a liability to the person who hired him. And now he was dead.

Careful to shorten his stride, he strolled down the sidewalk with Nora. Off to their right, the midday sun beat down on two golfers as they lined up their shots on a neatly trimmed putting green.

Nora slipped her tiny hand into his and said, "What did you have for lunch, Detective Frank?"

He laughed. "I haven't had lunch yet. What did you have?"

"Chicken noodle soup," she said, giving him a gap-toothed smile. "With oyster crackers!"

"That sounds yummy. How's it going with the Russian? Did you learn any more words?"

"Nyet," she said, pouting. "Danny won't teach me any more and neither will Nicky."

"What about Mr. Zurik? Maybe he'd teach you some."

"No," Nora said, gazing at him, her eyes fearful. "I don't like him."

"Why not?"

"He doesn't like me. He doesn't even like Danny that much. He only cares about Nicky. They talk in Russian a lot so other people don't know what they're saying."

Frank's neck prickled. *So other people don't know what they're saying.*

His gut told him Nicolas Zurik was a killer.

The problem was he had no evidence to prove it.

––––

Jackie watched Nora walk along the sidewalk with Renzi.

What did Renzi know? More than he'd told her, for sure. Telling her to be careful, Nicolas was dangerous.

But she had more immediate problems to worry about.

Danny's emotional meltdown yesterday. Should she make an appointment with a therapist?

Her father, complaining about the funeral director she'd chosen. The man wasn't Jewish and he didn't want to deal with him. Asking about a memorial service. Trying to take over, as usual.

Her biggest worry was Homicide Detective Frank Renzi.

Should she tell him about the subpoena and the cash she'd found in Richie's blazer? No way could he know about the cash, but what if he found out she had the subpoena?

Her stomach twisted into a tense knot. Subpoenas were public records, easily accessed by police.

If she didn't tell Renzi about it, he'd think she was lying.

Jesus! What if Richie was gambling on NBA games and the cops thought she was in on it?

Her eyes brimmed with tears. She felt so alone.

No one to talk to. No one to confide in.

And no one to trust.

RICHIE BAUER

TEN YEARS EARLIER

A Deal with the Devil

October 15, 2004 – 12:30 PM – Ponchatoula, LA

Richie stepped out onto the sunlit patio and smiled. The air smelled of gardenias and carnations. And Ponchatoula Estates smelled like money.

Jackie would love it here. No ice, no snow, just glorious sunshine, not a cloud in the sky. The perfect place to raise their son.

Last year had been the best year of his life. When Danny was born in June, he was overjoyed. A month later life got even better. For three years he had worked NBA games on short notice when a referee needed a day off, his stomach in knots, knowing they'd be evaluating him. In July he got the long-awaited call. When the next season started, he would be a full-time NBA referee.

But the season didn't end until June after the playoffs, eight grueling months, and he traveled a lot, often for weeks at a time while Jackie took care of Danny in their apartment in upstate New York. Jackie hated cold weather. Hated living near her father even more.

Living in Louisiana would solve both problems.

But the house was expensive.

Ever since he ran into Benny at the Meadowlands three years ago, he'd been giving Benny his picks on NCAA games. Benny placed their bets and gave him his winnings in cash. He locked the cash in a file cabinet in his office so Jackie wouldn't find it. The IRS wouldn't either.

That might be a problem.

He'd better talk to the real estate agent. It was almost one o'clock and he had to officiate a game in New Orleans, a forty minute drive from here, at six.

When he went in the house, Desiree and said, "What do you think, Mr. Bauer? Want to make an offer?"

He shifted into car salesman mode. "The price is pretty steep. What can you do for me?"

Desiree studied the sales sheet and said, "The seller might take a bit less than the asking price."

Which was way too high as far as Richie was concerned, but the house was perfect: three bedrooms, a playroom, a kitchen with a breakfast bar, and a gorgeous patio. The best part? You could see a golf course from the house.

But even if he offered six-fifty, he'd still need twenty percent for a down payment: $130,000. Twenty grand in their savings account, plus the hidden cash, he could maybe scrape up another seventy-five.

He'd have to mortgage the rest. $575,000.

Christ on a crutch! No bank would give him that kind of money, not on his referee salary. Jackie had quit her job to take care of Danny so they wouldn't count her income.

"Let me think about it and get back to you."

"Certainly, Mr. Bauer. I know it's a big investment."

The rest of the day passed in a blur. During the game, he stood in the end zone during timeouts, thinking about the house. He hadn't wanted something this bad in a long time.

The next day he called Benny and said he needed favor.

"Yeah? What's up? Is Jackie pregnant again?"

"Jesus, I hope not. I'm barely making it now. Kids are expensive."

Benny laughed. "What did Jackie do, buy the crib and the baby carriage at Nordstrom's?"

Exasperated, he said, "It's not just the money. Jackie hates living near her father. The bastard despises me, says I'm trailer park trash."

"He's a fucking asshole."

"That he is. But I'm gone a lot, so Jackie's gotta deal with him when he brings her mom over to babysit. So Jackie can go out once in a while, you know? And she hates the winter."

"Uh-huh," Benny said. "So what's the favor?"

"I found the perfect house for us. Jackie will love it."

"But?"

"It's expensive, and we don't have much in the bank. Twenty grand tops. Even with the cash from *you know what* I can only put down seventy-five grand."

"How much is the house?"

"Including closing costs, I figure six-hundred grand."

"Jesus! What is it? A palace?"

"Benny, I need this house. When I'm on the road, Jackie calls me, bitching that I'm never home and it's snowing. The house is perfect, next to a golf course! But I'll never get a mortgage for five hundred large on my salary. I need to knock it down to … three-fifty or so."

"Jeez, Richie, that'd be what, two-fifty large I gotta front you?"

Richie smiled. "How about two and a quarter?"

After a while Benny said, "Cash, right? Nobody knows about it?"

"Right. I'll pay you back, Benny. You know I'm good for it."

So he had Desiree fax Jackie the papers to sign, so her name would be on the deed. In January 2005, he closed on the house.

A week later, Jackie flew down with Danny and they moved in. Jackie loved the house, loved the patio and the lawn out front. Danny was eighteen months old and already walking. Life was good.

Until Benny called a month later and said he needed a favor.

He flew to Atlantic City. Benny picked him up at the airport, said he wanted him to meet someone and drove him to a flashy joint with a big red neon sign: DINE, DANCE & DAMES.

He got a bad feeling when they went inside. Men with hard eyes, waitresses in skimpy outfits, posters of half-naked strippers on the walls.

Christ! This was a Mafia club.

Benny took him to a booth in the back and introduced him to Dominic Marconi, an older man with slicked back hair and a beer gut bulging over his belt.

"They call me the Macaroni Man," he said and stuck out his hand.

Big fucking deal, Richie thought as he shook the man's sweaty paw.

They ordered beers all around. Marconi drained half of his in one gulp and said, "I hear you know how to pick winners."

Stunned, he looked at Benny, who mumbled, "College games."

"How about picking some winners for NBA games?" Marconi said.

"Not the games you work," Benny said quickly. "Other games."

Richie saw sweat on Benny's forehead and half-moon circles under the armpits of his shirt. Not good. Benny looked worried. And scared.

"We'd give you a cut," Marconi said. "Two large for every winner you give us."

He studied Benny's eyes, pinprick irises. Definitely on something. Coke maybe. "No way," he said. "I could lose my job."

Benny gripped his arm, pleading with him. "Help me out, Richie. Last month you called and said you needed a favor, right?"

"Yeah," he said, wishing he hadn't.

"And I came through for you!" Benny smiled. "How does Jackie like the house in Ponchatoula? Nice warm weather, no snow."

Richie couldn't believe it. *The motherfucking idiot!* Running his mouth, mentioning the house in Ponchatoula, speaking Jackie's name.

What else had he told this fucking gangster?

"One good turn deserves another," Marconi said, his eyes cold as an iceberg in winter.

"Right," Benny said. "I need this house, you said. Remember?"

He remembered all right. Remembered his desperation because he wanted the house so bad. So Jackie would stop bitching about his road trips, make friends with the neighbors and let him play golf every day when he wasn't working. And that's what happened. Jackie made friends with Martina and he played golf with her husband, Nicolas.

If Benny hadn't given him the cash to swing the deal, he'd still be living in New York, listening to Jackie bitch about road trips and snow storms.

He drank some beer and said, "So how would it work?"

Benny's face lit up like a Christmas tree. "Same as the college games. You give me the picks and I take care of everything else."

"He gives me the tips," Marconi said, "we pass your cut to Benny, he gives it to you in cash. Two large for every winner you pick."

Richie clenched his hands, his gut teeming with acid, his mind screaming *Mafia!* Marconi knew where he lived. Knew Jackie's name. Did he know about Danny?

But then he did the math. Each NBA team played 82 games in a season. No bets on games he was officiating. If he picked four winners a week, he'd collect eight grand in cash. Multiply by four, he'd make thirty-two large a month. Pay Benny what he owed him and keep the rest.

Jesus! In one NBA season, he could make a quarter million in cash. Easy money. No one the wiser. Stop off in Vegas after his western road trips and have fun at the casinos.

"Okay," he said. "On one condition."

"What's that?" Marconi said, gazing at him, eyes black as agates.

"You and I never see each other again."

So he made his deal with the devil and everything worked fine, for a while.

CHAPTER 25

After the noon meeting with Vobitch, Frank and Kenyon collected their messages from the desk officer and went up to the homicide office. Kelly went out to buy groceries, said her refrigerator was full of containers with stuff she didn't dare look at.

Deciphering scribbled notes on pink slips, Frank threw messages from reporters in the trash and put the rest in two piles, Pursue and Not Credible. Most of them were from people eager to collect the two-grand reward they'd posted for info on the gun. No tips on the murder at the OPP.

Why rat out an inmate if he'd killed someone? Inmates had friends outside the OPP. Killer friends.

Kenyon set his message slips aside and said, "Pretty weird, Richie's father didn't know he got murdered. It's all over the news on TV."

"Confirmed Richie and Benny started gambling when they were kids, though."

"Too bad we can't prove they were gambling on NBA games."

"Richie was worried about something. According to the toxicology report Dr. DeMayo sent me, Richie was taking Xanax, a tranquilizer."

"No shit!" Kenyon said. "What about Benny?"

Frank took the report out of his desk drawer. "Benny had traces of coke in his system, plus traces of Valium, an anti-anxiety drug."

"Worried about the New Jersey feds? Or something else?"

"Nervous about the meeting, maybe. No drugs in Marconi's blood, just alcohol. Richie and Benny had alcohol in their blood, too. Not surprising. I saw a lot of beer bottles on their table."

He set the report aside. Every investigation was a story, painstakingly assembled piece by piece. Not just about the murder, about everyone involved. Each piece of the story had to fit exactly the right way at the exact right time. But there were too damn many missing pieces.

"My CI says the Dirty Doggz sell a shitload of guns," Kenyon said. "Guns with serial numbers filed off like the one the shooter used. A black gang with a violent rep. Get caught talking to cops, you're dead."

"That's all they do? No drug deals? No protection racket?"

"Nope, just gun deals. Plenty of buyers in this town. Big Dawgg runs the gang but my CI has never seen him, says Big Dawgg never leaves his house.

Has his 'bangers buy guns all over the South and sell them to local buyers. Says he's as big as an elephant, must weigh three hundred pounds."

Kenyon spread his hands apart and grinned. "No empty refrigerator at Big Dawgg's house, no shortage of booze either, parties with his girlfriend when he's not chowing down chitlins."

"What's that? Some kind of black soul food?" Frank said, jiving him.

"For some folks maybe. Take small intestines from a pig, fry 'em up, you got a mighty tasty dish." Kenyon grimaced. "Not that I've ever eaten any. Too disgusting."

Frank laughed, but the moment of levity quickly dissipated. "Jackie's hiding something. Either she was in on the High Roller shooting, or she knew Richie was gambling on NBA games."

"You think she's in cahoots with Zurik?"

"I'm not sure. When I asked if she was sleeping with him, she got pissed, or a good imitation thereof. But when I took Nora for a walk, she said she didn't like Mr. Zurik. Said he was always talking Russian with his son, so nobody would know what they were saying."

"Like Mosgov talking to the shooter," Kenyon said.

"Exactly. But I can't prove Zurik is involved, and the shooter's dead."

"Maybe Claudia will get us something."

"Let's hope so, because right now we've got nothing."

He got back to his message slips and ditched most of them. People giving wildly inaccurate descriptions of the shooter: wrong race, wrong age, wrong build. Some claimed the shooter lived in Texas or Detroit. An old lady in the lower Ninth Ward said her son lived in California but he could have flown in for this. He did that all the time.

But some went into his Pursue pile. One tipster said she overheard a guy in Baton Rouge say he knew who did it and he had a gun. Another nailed the gun caliber but didn't know the name of the man who owned it. Others came from 'bangers calling to drop a dime on a rival: so-and-so from Treme or Hollygrove who runs with so-and-so.

His desk phone rang. Frank set aside the message slips and answered the call. "Homicide."

"Who am I speaking to?" said a female voice.

Annoyed, Frank said, "Who wants to know?"

"Um, it's me, calling about the reward?"

Frank jerked his chin at Kenyon, who mouthed, *You got something?*

The voice on the phone said, "There's this guy, Larry, and I heard him bragging about it."

"Yeah?" Frank said. "Does Larry have a gun?"

"Sure does. Definitely."

"Do you know the caliber?"

"I think it might be a .22."

"A .22," Frank said, and saw Kenyon's eyes widen. "How do you know Larry?"

"He was in Angola with my brother. He just got out."

"Who got out, your brother?"

"No, Larry. My brother's still in."

"What was he in for?" Frank asked, Kenyon watching him now, rapt.

"Larry or my brother?"

Frank rolled his eyes heavenward. "Larry."

"Larry got sent up for armed robbery, held up a store in East Baton Rouge."

"Does Larry have a last name?" Silence on the other end.

"You know where he is right now?"

"Shacked up with his girlfriend."

Frank wanted to ask if she was the girlfriend, but didn't.

"When did he get out?"

"Yesterday."

He grimaced and shook his head at Kenyon.

"So," the woman said, "you coming over now?"

"Sure," Frank said. He wrote down the address and ended the call.

"You get something?" Kenyon said eagerly.

"Got a woman ratting out her boyfriend for the reward on the gun. He got out of Angola yesterday, but guys like that usually know other guys. We might as well talk to him."

————

Kenyon drove, Frank riding shotgun, giving him directions. The tipster lived in Hollygrove, a mostly working-class black neighborhood, some law abiding, others not. Some of the homes were well-tended, fresh painted trim, flowerpots in the windows, neatly mowed lawns.

Unlike the tipster's house, a depressing shack with dirty clapboard siding, asphalt shingles missing from the roof, a sagging front porch.

When they approached the door, curtains on a window parted slightly. Someone watching them.

Frank knocked on the door. He heard security chains fall, a deadbolt twist and the door opened. An older white woman appeared, looked to be in her sixties, wrinkled skin and gray hair, five-foot-two and scrawny, gazing at them with suspicious gray eyes.

"You called about Larry?" Frank said.

"Uh-huh. He ain't here right now, went out to buy booze." She let them into a darkened parlor. All the shades drawn, a rickety table beside a beat-up sofa held an open bag of Cheetos and a glass of amber liquid, likely whiskey. They followed her into a kitchen that smelled of bacon grease. The linoleum floor looked like it hadn't been washed in months, dirty dishes in the sink, more on the counter. Unfolded laundry piled on the kitchen table beside stacks of mail and magazines.

Frank introduced himself, then Kenyon, and said, "What's your name?"

"Josie."

"What's your last name?"

Josie frowned. "'Sposed to be anonymous. That's what it says on Crimestoppers."

Frank let it go. "What's the story with Larry?"

She took a pack of Best Buy cigarettes off the counter, lit up and spewed a cloud of smoke. "He told me he bought a gun from some guy lives around here, a .22 he said."

"When was this? You said he only got out of Angola yesterday."

Josie shrugged. "Larry always gotta have a gun. For protection."

Kenyon stepped closer, looming over Josie. "Protection from who?"

"Tough neighborhood, Hollygrove. Lotta criminals around here done worse things than Larry. Least he never killed nobody."

"Who do you know around here that's killing people?" Frank said.

"Not gonna give you no names, get myself killed."

"What about Big Dawgg?" Kenyon said. "You know him?"

The woman took a deep drag on her cigarette, her hand shaking. "Know Big Dawgg gonna kill me, he finds out I talked to the po-lice."

"Did Larry buy a gun from Big Dawgg?" Frank said.

"Lord-a-mercy, don't ask me that!" Shaking her head violently. "Thought you was here to gimme the reward! Two thousand dollars!"

Kenyon took a twenty out of his wallet. "We don't care about Larry. Tell us where Big Dawgg lives, gets you the twenty."

She snatched the twenty and said, "Lives over on Rye Street near the abandoned mill. Get on outta here, before Larry gets back. Don't tell Big Dawgg I tol' you nuthin' or he'll kill me."

When they got in the car, Kenyon said, "Shall we take a look?"

"Might as well," Frank said. "She didn't give us the house number, but maybe Big Dawgg will be out on his porch eating chitlins."

Kenyon chuckled mirthlessly. "Don't bet on it."

166

Two minutes later they cruised down Rye Street. "There's the abandoned mill," Frank said, clocking the houses on both sides of the street. "You see Big Dawgg anywhere?"

"Not jumping out at me. Houses pretty much look the same. Nothing fancy but not falling apart like Josie's dump."

Kenyon did a U-turn and they cruised the street again.

"Damn it to hell!" Frank said. "If Big Dawgg lives here, nobody's going to point us to him. Even if we had the address, I couldn't get a search warrant. I can just hear the judge. You want me to issue a search warrant for a house be-cause some woman who won't give her last name said someone on Rye Street sold somebody a gun?"

"But I got the feeling Josie knows what she's talking about," Kenyon said. "Looked mighty scared to me. We might not be able to get a warrant for Big Dawgg, but the Orleans Parish Sheriff likely could. Why should we waste our time trying to figure out where the asshole lives?"

"Tell the OPP investigators about Big Dawgg and the approximate location of his house?" Frank said.

"Maybe get 'em to put a surveillance team on Rye Street."

"I like it. You want me to call them?"

Kenyon gave him a sly look. "Nah. I'm due for some entertainment. I'll call and put a bug in their ear about Big Dawgg, see what happens."

CHAPTER 26

DAY 9 SATURDAY OCTOBER 18, 2014 – 8:35 PM – Ponchatoula

Cloaked in darkness, Nicolas skulked along the side of Jackie's house and stopped at the kitchen door. Off to the south, he saw tiny red flashes, jetliners taking off from Armstrong Airport. Above him, the sky was dark and gloomy, like his mood. Another unpleasant chore to do.

Unlike some homes in Ponchatoula Estates, Jackie's door had a cheap lock, easily thwarted with the right tools. He took out a small pick and got to work. A minute later he opened the door, stepped inside and waited, his heart racing inside his chest.

No beeping alarm.

Relieved, he put the lock-pick in his pocket. Security guards were screening cars at the entrance to Ponchatoula Estates, a major pain in the ass, and he'd feared Jackie might have installed a security system. Which would have ended tonight's mission.

Martina had taken Jackie and the kids out for dinner at a restaurant in Kenner, a good hour away. He'd told Martina to call him when they left the restaurant, stressing this was very important.

He hadn't told her what he'd be doing.

Using a small penlight, he made his way to Richie's office and tried the door. Unlocked. He stepped inside and shut the door behind him. He'd never been in Richie's office. Richie was secretive about a lot of things, especially lately.

It hadn't always been that way. He'd met Richie nine years ago when the Bauers moved into the house next door. Jackie and Martina hit it off right away, and Nicky loved playing with Danny. Nicolas invited Richie to play eighteen holes at the golf club.

At the first tee, he said, *Twenty bucks says I'll beat you.* He duffed a few shots to let Richie win. To make him feel important.

Later they had a few beers in the clubhouse and started talking about work. When Richie said he was an NBA ref, Nicolas almost fell off his chair. Foreseeing a golden opportunity, he asked Richie if he bet on games.

But Richie said, "Hell no. If the NBA front office finds out an NBA ref is betting on games, forget it. Career over."

"What about March Madness? Everyone bets on those games."

"Yeah, well, I'm not everyone."

"Richie, if you bet on March Madness, you'd make big bucks."

After a moment Richie said, "Well, sometimes a friend of mine places a few bets for me."

"Yeah? Who's your friend?"

But Richie wouldn't tell him. The next time they played golf, he asked Richie for tips on college games, said he'd bet a hundred bucks a game and give Richie ten percent if he won. Richie agreed, and that's how it started. Nicolas gave Richie his cut in cash. A pittance.

In truth he bet five thousand dollars on the games, winning thousands more.

Three months and many more rounds of golf later, Richie finally admitted he was betting on NBA games. But not on games he officiated. Nicolas figured he was lying and offered him the same deal as before: tell him which team to bet on, he'd give Richie ten percent of his winnings in cash.

So Richie started giving him tips and Nicolas wagered thousands of dollars on NBA games. His take was huge so he gave Richie more cash to sweeten the deal. Life was good.

Until the last week in September.

Richie called and said he wanted to play golf before he left for a road trip on the west coast. Two days later, they played 18 holes at the Ponchatoula Estates golf course. When they went in the clubhouse, Richie said he had to take a leak, he'd meet him at the bar.

Nicolas had an ear for the spoken word and an excellent memory, honed by playing chess games in his head for many years. He watched the next part unfold like a movie. An unspeakably bad movie.

Richie joined him in the lounge and put his Smartphone on the bar between them. "I already ordered the beers," Nicolas said. "Got any tips on the west coast games?"

Richie leaned closer and said in a low voice, "No more tips on games, Nicolas. Benny called the other day and told me the feds are investigating sports betting, including NBA games. If the feds find out I'm betting on games, I could go to jail."

After the barman delivered their beers and left, Nicolas said, "How do you know Benny?"

Richie shrugged. "I grew up with him in Atlantic City."

"Is Benny mob connected?"

"What the fuck kind of question is that, Nicolas?"

That should have been the tip-off. When threatened, attack.

But he missed it.

Leaning closer, he'd said, "Does Benny know you're giving me tips on NBA games?"

"Don't worry, Nicolas. Benny doesn't know I tell you which teams to bet on. Doesn't know you give me a cut of your winnings either. But we need to stop for a while. And I need to go home and pack for the trip. See you after I get back." Whereupon Richie picked up his Smartphone and left.

The minute he went out the door, Nicolas had known with absolute certainty that Richie had taped their conversation on his Smartphone, deliberately saying his name repeatedly. If the feds questioned Richie about gambling, he might use their taped conversation to cut a deal.

Then the feds would question him, too. His life would be ruined.

Even then he'd tried to be merciful. Get Richie to give him the tape and warn him not to tell the feds anything. When Richie returned from his trip the first weekend in October, Nicolas called him.

Richie didn't answer, so he left a message, asking Richie to call him.

But Richie never called. Which had sealed his fate.

And necessitated tonight's break-in.

Richie was dead, but the tape wasn't.

Nicolas flashed the penlight around Richie's office. A desktop computer on a metal desk, a laser printer and a laptop beside it. Both computers were off. Assuming they were password protected, he opened the top drawer of the desk, hunting for passwords. Pens, magic markers and paper clips in the top drawer. He went through the other drawers. No luck there either.

Forget the computers. He doubted Richie kept anything incriminating on them. But Richie could have hidden the tape somewhere else. The problem was, he didn't know what to look for. A thumb drive? A cassette tape?

He studied the black file cabinet opposite the desk. The file cabinets in his office were protected with digital locks. Only he knew the code to open them. But Richie's file cabinet had a single lock at the top, one that opened with a key. No key in the lock, but the top drawer opened when he tried it.

He flipped through the folders: household bills, insurance documents for the house and the cars, medical bills, receipts from insurance companies. He checked his watch. 8:45. He didn't have time to search all the folders. If a cassette tape or a thumb drive was in the drawer, he would have seen it.

Making sure the office was exactly as he'd found it, he left the room and shut the door. Hurrying now, he located the master bedroom. Jackie's clothes were in one closet. The other held Richie's clothes: shirts, trousers and jackets.

He checked the pockets of the jackets and found nothing. Where else would he hide the tape?

On the top shelf were several shoe boxes. He took one down and opened it. Running shoes. Checked another box. More shoes. Another and another. Forget shoe boxes, maybe Richie had a safe.

He swept his penlight over the floor. No safe, just two suitcases. He opened one. Empty. Opened the other. Empty.

Damn it to hell! He returned to the kitchen and opened the refrigerator. Condiments and salad dressing on the door, a gallon of milk, hot dogs, a carton of eggs and plastic food containers on the shelves. He opened the freezer. Nothing there either, just a half gallon of chocolate ice cream and boxes of frozen pizza and waffles.

His cellphone rang. Martina calling him.

He took out the phone and answered. "Yes?"

"Hi," Martina said. "We just left the restaurant, should be home in forty-five minutes."

Forty-five minutes. He needed more time.

"Drive slow, luv. Stop at a gas station and fill the tank."

"But we—"

"Just do it, luv. Please. It's important."

He ended the call and swept his penlight over the kitchen cabinets. Opened a door. Dishes. Opened another door. Glassware. Checked another cabinet. Boxes of cereal and oyster crackers and cans of soup.

Frustrated beyond measure, he massaged his temples.

Where would Richie hide the tape? In the kid's rooms? No, too dangerous. They might find it and listen to it. He went into the living room. Flashed his penlight around. On the end table beside the sofa was a photograph, Richie and Jackie and the kids at Disney World, smiling at the camera.

A handsome husband with secrets, now dead, and three very unhappy survivors, Jackie and two kids.

Maybe Jackie found the tape and hid it in her office.

He checked his watch, mentally willing Martina to take her time. Enough time for him to find the tape and anything else that might incriminate him.

In Jackie's office, he took care to aim the penlight on the floor. The windows faced the golf course and the shades were open, the trees on the golf course vague outlines against the dark sky. He doubted anyone was out there at this hour, but never take chances.

Life is like chess. Study your opponent's moves. Trust no one. Papa's words.

Words that had served him well for the most part.

Until Richie betrayed him.

He flashed the penlight over Jackie's desk. A desktop computer and a laptop. He opened the top drawer and smiled. On top was a pink sticky with passwords. Sometimes Jackie gave him attitude, acting like she was smarter than anyone else. She might be smarter than some people, but not smarter than Nicolas Zurik. Not when he was hellbent on finding evidence that could destroy him.

He booted up Jackie's laptop and accessed her the email to see if Richie had sent her a message. Working backwards in time, he scrolled through the inbox, closer and closer to the day of the murders. No messages from Richie.

He checked the Sent messages. None sent to Richie.

Jesus, didn't they talk to each other? He massaged his temples, silently cursing Richie and his smartass wife.

Where else might Jackie have hidden something? He opened the left-hand desk drawer. His heart skyrocketed into his throat.

Stunned, he stared at the document, his heart pounding.

A subpoena ordering Richard Bauer to appear in a federal courtroom in Atlantic City on Monday, November 3, 2014 at 9 AM.

Richie had signed for it on September 22, 2014. More than two weeks before he died. And said nothing to him. Not a word about a subpoena that could end the comfortable life Nicolas had enjoyed in Ponchatoula for nine years.

Richie was a weasel, intent on covering his ass.

What if he already talked to the feds?

A fulminating fury rose inside him, his heart racing like a killer torpedo seeking its target.

He photographed the subpoena with his cellphone.

Jackie had the subpoena. Maybe she also had the tape.

If she did, she might not want to give it to him.

Murderous thoughts crept into his mind.

Images of Roland in the New York City apartment, dead on the floor.

CHAPTER 27

Frank devoured the last bite of his steak. He rarely ate beef, but every now and then he craved a juicy rib-eye, medium-rare, and a big baked potato slathered with butter. No worries about calories. Two days ago his bathroom scale told him he'd lost five pounds.

Ten days since the massacre, no decent leads, he wasn't eating much.

Across the table in their booth at the Poorhouse Pub, Claudia Cohen was eating a salmon filet. No baked potato, just fresh broccoli and a garden salad. Claudia watching her calorie intake.

Vobitch could have polished off both dinners, but he wasn't here. This morning Vobitch had told him to update Claudia on their progress, see what she had on her end.

Frank set aside his plate and said, "Kelly talked to Richie's father. Henry Bauer, age seventy-two, currently living in a halfway house for alcoholics in Atlantic City."

"Good for her. What did Henry say about Richie?"

"Said he used to take Richie to the track when he was kid, taught him how to play the ponies. More importantly, he said Richie and Benny were running betting games when they were in school together, said he found betting slips in Richie's room."

"Okay," Claudia said, "but I'd rather know what Richie was doing last month, wouldn't you?"

"I'd like to know what a lot of people were doing last month. Want another glass of wine?"

"Sure, why not live dangerously? Like Richie."

Frank signaled the waitress for another round and said, "You think he was a compulsive gambler?"

"We admire people who take risks." Claudia smiled. "You're a risk-taker yourself, Frank. Willing to walk into a dangerous situation, even a deadly one, to take down the bad guy. We admire people who take risks and *win* even more. Like *Rocky*."

"Great movie," he said. "Big dumb Italian loses a lot of fights, never gives up and wins it all."

"But for compulsive gamblers, it's not just the win. It's the rush they get. The bigger the risk, the bigger the rush. Tempting the odds is sexy, dangerous even. Not just physically, emotionally dangerous. Dangerous to the psyche."

The waitress brought their wine and said, "Would you folks like dessert?"

Claudia shook her head, so Frank said, "No thanks, just the check."

"We live in an ultra-competitive culture," Claudia said. "We root for the dark horse or the underdog. Put on a poker face, call somebody's bluff."

"True. But most people don't turn into compulsive gamblers."

"They're social gamblers. For them, it's about the camaraderie. They watch the Super Bowl together, join the office pool during March Madness, watch the games and talk about them the next day. But they don't go crazy and bet the farm. They know if they lose big they'd go into debt, maybe lose the house. Compulsive gamblers are different."

Frank drank some Chianti. "They don't care if they lose the house?"

"That's not even a blip on their radar. The risk and the rush are what drives them. They want to prove they're smarter than the losers, and nobody better get in their way. Not a wife nagging about bills, not even a bankruptcy lawyer. They need to live on the edge."

"Like sports bettors?" Frank said.

"Especially sports bettors."

"You think Richie's wife knew he was gambling?"

Claudia combed her fingers through her short dark hair. "They bought an expensive house in a ritzy neighborhood, way beyond what an NBA ref could afford. Maybe she knew and pretended she didn't. She didn't want to know."

Frank nodded, thinking of his ex-wife, who likely knew he was having an affair, but chose to ignore it, so she wouldn't have to do anything about it. Until her girlfriend goaded her into it.

"But some sports bettors make money at it," Claudia said. "A lot of money."

"And 'bangers make big bucks selling guns." He recapped what the woman said when he and Kenyon talked to her yesterday. "We drove by the location, no sign of Big Dawgg."

"Grab him on some bullshit charge and interrogate him."

"Easier said than done. He never leaves his house. Kenyon called the OPP folks and said Big Dawgg might have set up the murder in the OPP. They said they'd put a surveillance team on him. Maybe we'll get lucky. But the shooter's a phantom. We ran his prints, his picture and his DNA and got nothing."

"My contact didn't either," Claudia said. "But she's got clout with Interpol, feeds them intel now and then. I might have something on Zurik."

"Music to my ears. What have you got?"

"Interpol ran his DL photograph through their face-recognition program and got a match. Interpol put an Orange Notice on Nicolas Kozlovich way back in 1987. The London cops wanted him for killing two men, revenge for murdering his father, Vladimir Kozlovich." Claudia smiled. "You're gonna love this part. Vladimir was an assassin for a Russian gang in London."

Stunned, he said, "Zurik's father was an assassin? In London?"

"Correct. The London cops were after him for a dozen murders, but he left no evidence. Or witnesses. After Nicolas murdered his father's killers, he disappeared. No trace of him after 1987."

She opened her briefcase, took out two photographs and set them side by side on the table. "The right height, about the right age. Close resemblance, yes?"

Frank studied the photos. Nicolas Kozlovich, age 17, the other taken almost thirty years later, Nicolas Zurik, age 45.

"Zurik looks a lot older, but the resemblance is there. Same hairline, same bone structure, same eyes."

"I agree," Claudia said. "So what do we do with it?"

"Let me talk to Vobitch, see what he says." Frank grinned. "One thing for sure. Dinner's on me tonight. Great information. I can't wait to see what you come up with next."

———

10:45 PM – Ponchatoula

Seated at the desk in her office, Jackie poured more Merlot into her wine-glass. Thoughts buzzed her mind like angry hornets. Renzi had a helluva nerve, coming here to tell her the shooter had been murdered in the Orleans Parish Prison. That was just a ploy to interrogate her.

He believed someone paid the shooter to kill Richie, implying that she knew who it was. Like she was a suspect!

She gulped some wine. Then he'd asked if she was sleeping with Nicolas.

Jesus-fucking-Christ! Not in her wildest imagination would she even think about sleeping with Nicolas. When she denied it, Renzi said, "Be careful. He's dangerous."

She went to the window and studied the Zurik house. She liked Martina, but she didn't trust Nicolas. A handsome self-centered man, who used his charm to persuade people to do his bidding.

But forget Nicolas. Focus on Richie. She'd found the subpoena taped to the underside of a drawer in the black file cabinet. She was certain Richie wanted her to find it. But she had the nagging feeling that wasn't the only thing he wanted her to find.

An hour ago when she'd checked the kids, Nora was fast asleep in her room. Danny was sitting in bed in his pajamas, reading a book, but by now he was probably asleep.

She studied the list in the codicil. In addition to the file cabinet, it listed the clothes and shoes in his closet, his luggage, even the whistles he used to officiate games. She ran her finger down the list: three suits, three blazers, eight pairs of trousers. Dress shirts, polo shirts and running suits. Three leather belts.

Six NBA uniforms. Five shoes for work. Four pair of running shoes. A numbered list of his everyday shoes.

The third one on the list caught her eye: 1231.

Her heart lurched. Not 1231, 12-31. The date of their wedding.

Back in the day, Richie told her he used it as a pin number because nobody would know what it was except for him. And her.

She ran to the bedroom. Flung open the closet door. The box labeled 1231 sat on the top shelf. She took the box down and set it on the bed. With trembling hands, she removed the lid.

Polished black shoes wrapped in tissue paper, but under the shoes she found a plastic bag with bundles of hundred dollar bills, a business envelope and a smaller envelope with a thumb drive.

She opened the business envelope. Her heart began to race, thumping against her ribs. She was right! Richie had left her a message.

Printed on a single sheet of paper.

Jackie, if you're reading this, I'm probably dead. Don't tell Nicolas. Take the money and run.

Her heart exploded inside her chest. Jesus! What did that mean?

If you're reading this, I'm probably dead.

Tears flooded her eyes and spilled down her cheeks.

Richie knew he was in danger. Knew he might die and loved her enough to leave a warning.

Last Friday Renzi had told her Nicolas was dangerous.

But so was Renzi. He wanted to find out who paid the man to kill Richie and suspected it might be her.

Don't tell Nicolas. Take the money and run.

One thing was certain. Richie was dead. And she was in danger.

———

11:30 PM – New Orleans

Nicolas unlocked his office door. No Ms. Busybody in the office across the hall, waving and smiling him, like they were friends. At this hour she was home, fast asleep in bed.

That's where he should be, not sneaking into his office at this hour.

Because the New Jersey feds had sent Richie a subpoena and Richie hadn't told him about it. Keeping secrets from him. Damning secrets.

He armed the security system, stalked across the foyer to his workroom and shut the door. He punched in the code that unlocked one file cabinet. Yanked out a folder and fed documents into the shredder, hearing the machine hum and whir, spewing out tiny strips of paper.

Richie wouldn't be telling the feds anything, but Jackie had found the subpoena. What if she told Renzi about it? He'd seen Renzi's car outside her house last Friday.

The shredder stopped. Nicolas stuffed strips of paper into a trash bag, took out another folder and fed more documents into the machine.

Recalling the day he and Richie sat in the clubhouse after a round of golf, Richie sucking down beers, moaning about the many tragedies in his life. His mother committed suicide when he was ten, and his alcoholic father used to beat him, but after he went to college, he never saw the prick again.

Feigning sympathy, Nicolas pictured his own mother, who'd taught him to speak fluent English and French, reading to him every night before he went to sleep. Until her life was snuffed out by a bus on a London street.

What would have become of him, if she'd lived?

But then Richie started yammering about his next tragedy. His dream in life was to play in the NBA, but his freshman year in college he blew out his knee. Gazing at him, saying his dream was over and he'd wanted to kill himself, like his mother.

Nicolas said nothing, recalling his early life in London. Papa teaching him to play chess and speak Russian. Murdered by two rival gang members. Months later he'd killed them, but then he had to flee the country, only to encounter more adversity in New York. Until he found Roland.

Picturing Roland, dead on the floor, he'd said, "I killed a man once."

Shocked, Richie stared at him, his mouth gaping open in disbelief.

Whereupon, Nicolas had said, "I'm joking. I really did want to kill him. We applied for the same job, but they hired him instead."

Nicolas fed more documents into the shredder. Richie was weak.

Richie had no idea what real hardship was, sweeping floors at the New York Stock Exchange. The hours he'd spent watching basketball games to devise a winning formula.

Until his deal with the devil. Pavel Volkovich got him legal documents with a new name and Nicolas had married Martina. Ever since he'd bought the house in Ponchatoula, life had been good.

But if the feds found out he was getting tips on NBA games from Richie, they would question him. Martina's father would not be pleased if he heard about this, as he surely would, given the media's obsession with scandal.

After Renzi came to his office, he had assumed NOPD was watching him at home and at his office. He'd paid a man at his service station to check his BMW for a tracker. These days they were small, half the size of a cigarette pack, and powerful. Attached to the car's engine block, they sent a GPS signal strong enough so the person tracking the car could watch its movements on a laptop fifty miles away. Fortunately, the man hadn't found one.

Nicolas glanced at the TV screens on the opposite wall, currently dark. With no tips from Richie, his winnings had fallen dramatically. Now he had to spend hours, calculating which teams to bet on and how much to wager.

Hours he would prefer to spend with Yvette.

But he still got a rush when his team won. That euphoric feeling of excitement, living on the edge and winning, thanks to his wits and intelligence. He was smarter than most sports bettors, which allowed him to make an enormous amount of money.

But his comfortable life in Ponchatoula was about to implode.

Life is like chess. Always consider what will happen before you make a move.

Papa's voice, alive in his mind, even this many years later.

The night he took revenge on Papa's killers, he had rejoiced, his heart surging with joy. With Roland, he had only done what had to be done.

Soon he might need to kill again.

Papa had taught him various methods. With Roland, he'd used a garrote. No blood, which made for easier cleanup. Other situations required a handgun or a rifle. But even with a silencer, these weapons were not silent. In such cases, a sharp knife was best.

He fed the last documents in the file cabinet into the shredder. The other cabinet contained items for a fast getaway. Weapons in the bottom drawer, cash in the top drawer, more than enough to get him far away from New Orleans, enough to leave the country if necessary.

If Richie had already talked to the feds, there was nothing he could do about it. His only option was to leave New Orleans and begin life again somewhere else with a new name and a new identity.

He sank into his desk chair and massaged his temples.

Richie had taped their conversation to implicate him, intending to use it to bargain with the feds. The feds used plea bargains to arrest associates of criminals all the time.

If the media found out Richie was gambling on NBA games, fixing them to make sure the winning team covered the point spread, it would cause a scandal. Jackie's life would never be the same.

What if she cut a deal with the feds? Keep Richie's name out of the news in exchange for a tape that would let them arrest others involved in the scandal. Like Nicolas Zurik.

He took out a fresh burner and called Alexei in London and said in Russian, *"I need my emergency documents right away, both identities. Send them overnight express."*

"Of course. I will do this immediately. You seem ... worried. Need anything else?"

"Not now. Thanks for the help."

Nicolas ended the call, his shirt damp with sweat despite the air-conditioning.

No Big Dawgg to take care of Jackie.

He would have to do that himself.

RICHIE BAUER

ONE MONTH EARLIER

The Death Spiral

Stunned speechless, Richie ended the call and set his Smartphone on his desk. Jesus, his hands were shaking. What the fuck was this? Benny calling from Atlantic City, agitated, saying no more bets on games, the feds were investigating sports betting.

He got up and shut his office door, sat at his desk and opened the drawer where he hid his Zannies. Shook out two tablets and washed them down with a gulp of bottled water. No Valium today. Then he'd be zonked out, and Jackie might notice when she came home. She'd taken the kids grocery shopping,

Jackie was noticing too many things these days, questioning him about their finances, saying she needed more money to run the household and where the hell did all the money go?

His palms dampened with sweat.

Christ, what if she found out about Brandi?

But then the Xanax kicked in, a comforting warmth flowing through his body. Now he felt better, not great, but calmer.

Calm enough to focus on Benny. *No more bets on games. The Atlantic City feds are investigating sports betting.*

Jesus-fucking-Christ! The very idea terrified him.

But how would the feds know he was betting on games? He never placed the bets, Benny did. And Benny would never tell anyone about it. That was the deal. Give Benny his picks and tell him how much he wanted to bet on each game.

The Macaroni Man was the wild card.

He never wanted to see that motherfucker again. Once was plenty. But Atlantic City mobsters knew how to hurt people. And Marconi knew where he lived. With Jackie and the kids.

He gave Nicolas tips on games too, but Benny didn't know that.

So why did Benny say: *Don't tell anyone, not even your golf buddy.*

He didn't recall mentioning Nicolas to Benny, but sometimes his mind got fuzzy when he'd taken a few Zannies. Besides, Benny had his own problems, coked up half the time when he gave him the cash: his payoff from the mob for his winning picks.

Forget Benny and his paranoid delusions. Life was good these days so why not enjoy it? He had a gorgeous house in Ponchatoula, a wife who loved him, a mistress in LA and best of all, two beautiful children.

But three days later his life went in the toilet.

On September twenty-second, a Monday afternoon, a deputy sheriff came to the door and served him with a subpoena.

Richard Bauer was required to appear in a federal courtroom in Atlantic City, New Jersey, on Monday, November 3, 2014 at 9 AM.

After he signed for it, the asshole said, "Thank you very much and have a nice day."

Have a nice day? Fucking forget about it! His life was over.

His only consolation: Jackie and the kids weren't there to see it.

He took the subpoena in his office, locked the door and took two Zannies and a Valium. He wasn't supposed to take them together, but after some trial and error, he'd learned this would get him through most anything.

No more nights plagued with nightmares. No visions of his mother driving her car into a bridge abutment. No visions of his father's angry eyes as he beat him with a leather belt. No visions of wrecking his knee, career over.

But testify in a federal courtroom? That was the nightmare from hell.

Jesus-fucking-Christ! If they asked if he was betting on games, what would he say? If he lied, they might nail him on a perjury charge and put him in jail.

If he admitted he was gambling on games, his career as an NBA referee would be over!

He left a note for Jackie saying he had an appointment, and drove to the High Roller Club in New Orleans. He thought of it as his safe house. The sort of place John Le Carré might create for a spy in his espionage novels. No one paid any attention to him at the High Roller. All the other members cared about was drinking fancy cocktails, watching sports on TV and talking about what teams they'd wagered on, rejoicing if they'd won, lamenting if they'd lost.

He put on a Saints cap, checked into the High Roller Club, sat at the bar and ordered a seltzer water. No booze tonight. He needed to figure out what to do.

He tuned out the nearby chatter, contemplating the death spiral of his life.

Starting in July 2006 when he made the deal with the devil.

The Macaroni Man.

Things went okay for a while, plenty of money coming in, enough to pay back the money Benny had loaned him with enough left over to live comfortably. But three years later Jackie sat him down one sunny day in April 2009 and said she was pregnant, beaming at him, saying it's a girl, she'd already had an ultrasound. When Nora was born that November, he fell in love with her, his adorable baby girl smiling at him when he held her. But Nora was colicky, awake half the night, and Jackie was always tired. Too tired to have sex.

Then he met Brandi, a gorgeous Lakers cheerleader eager to talk about basketball. Fun to be with and great in bed. He started paying the rent on her apartment and took her to Vegas. They had a great time, but sometimes he dropped big bucks on roulette.

Worse, before the 2010-2011 NBA season started, Benny came to New Orleans, met him at the High Roller and said the Macaroni Man was pressuring him for tips on games Richie was officiating, saying they'd give him three large on those games.

Mindful of his growing expenses and dwindling cash, he agreed and started blowing his whistle more often, especially at the end of games, to control the spread.

Then came the Lockout during the 2011-2012 season. No games for weeks, no cash coming in, Benny's unhappy, the Macaroni Man's unhappy. Even Nicolas was unhappy. By then he was giving Nicolas tips on NBA games for a percentage of his winnings.

He didn't think Benny would rat him out, but if the feds pressured the Macaroni Man, he'd throw Richie Bauer under the bus without a second thought.

And what about Nicolas?

Richie drank some seltzer water. Deep down inside, he didn't trust the man. Not since the day in the clubhouse after a round of golf, when Nicolas said he'd killed a man once. But then Nicolas smiled and said, "I'm joking. I really did want to kill him. We applied for the same job, but they hired him instead."

Maybe Nicolas was joking and maybe he wasn't. Over the years, there had been times when he'd seen the heart of darkness in his neighbor's eyes: cold, cruel and calculating.

Richie thought about the subpoena. One thing was crystal clear.

If he was going down, he wasn't going alone.

Four days from now he was leaving for a road trip, wouldn't be back until the first Saturday in October. Too little time, too much to do.

He paid the check and went out to his car, prioritizing his tasks. Set up a golf match with Nicolas before he left, get him in the clubhouse and tape their conversation on his Smartphone.

But he had to warn Jackie. Leave a hint for her that nobody else would decipher. Add a codicil to his will maybe.

Something his lawyer wouldn't understand but Jackie would.

One thing for sure. He wouldn't be testifying in a federal courtroom in November. That would end his career. Not only that, he'd be a pariah.

Shame and humiliation to the max. Nora was too young to understand, but Danny wasn't. Danny would know that his father had cheated, bringing shame upon himself and his family. So would Jackie.

But there were plenty of bridge abutments near Ponchatoula.

All he had to do was find the right one.

CHAPTER 28

Jackie leaned against the kitchen counter, sipping coffee, watching Danny and Nora at the breakfast bar. Not eating, Danny pushing scrambled eggs around his plate.

He gave her a sullen look and said, "Why can't we have waffles, Mom?"

"You had waffles yesterday."

"I hate bacon," Danny said.

"Me too," Nora said. "I like waffles better."

The headache lurking behind her eyes stabbed her like an ice pick. She set her coffee mug on the counter and went to the breakfast bar.

"Listen to me!" she said sternly. "Both of you. I was awake half the night, worrying about all the things I have to do. Even so, I got up and cooked scrambled eggs and bacon for you because I love you and I want you to eat a good breakfast. But all you do is complain."

Danny and Nora stared at her, wide-eyed.

"So you can fix lunch, Danny. Heat some soup for you and Nora. Maybe you'd like to cook dinner too, so I can take a break and relax."

Looking contrite now, Danny said, "Sorry, Mom. I know you've got a lot on your mind."

She tousled his hair and took a slice of bacon off his plate. "One for you, one for me, okay?"

"Okay," Danny said, and got started on his scrambled eggs.

"Want my bacon?" Nora said, smiling at her. "I don't mind sharing."

"Thanks, Nora." She took a slice off Nora's plate and returned to the counter. She'd dump the bacon later. She couldn't eat anything now, her stomach a seething cauldron of acid. Danny was right. She had a lot on her mind, but not what Danny was thinking.

Last night she had taken the thumb drive to her office, plugged it into her laptop and made a copy of it. Then she played one of the audio files. It blew her mind. Richie talking to Nicolas, saying Benny told him no more bets on games, the feds were investigating sports bettors. Which meant Benny was placing bets on NBA games for Richie. Then Richie told Nicolas not to worry, Benny didn't know he was giving Nicolas tips on NBA games too.

Implicating Benny and Nicolas, before he had to testify in a federal courtroom in New Jersey. Which Richie would never do, nor would Benny.

They were dead. But Nicolas wasn't.

If Nicolas found out Richie had taped their conversation, he had good reason to want Richie dead. Should she tell Renzi about the tape? Maybe she'd call him tomorrow. Then she had listened to the other audio file. Heartbreaking.

Richie saying goodbye to her and the kids. After she stopped crying, she had locked the thumb drive, her laptop, and Richie's laptop in the trunk of her car.

Now, relieved that Danny and Nora were eating breakfast, most of the scrambled eggs gone, Jackie sipped her coffee.

A tap sounded on the kitchen door. She looked over and saw Nicolas.

The last person she wanted to see.

Her stomach clenched into a hard knot. Pasting on a smile, she opened the door and said, "Hi, Nicolas, you're up early today."

"Busy day," he said, and strode to the breakfast bar. Smiling at Danny, he said, "Hey, Sport, how's it going today?"

Danny grinned at him. "Great. No Borscht for breakfast."

Nicolas laughed. "Do me a favor and take your sister outside so I can talk to your mum."

"I don't want to go outside," Nora said. "I want to stay with Mom."

Nicolas picked her up off her chair and set her on her feet. "Be a good girl and go outside with your brother. Mom and I need to talk."

"Yeah," Danny said. "Come outside and finish your milk."

Pouting, Nora took her glass of milk and followed Danny outside.

Annoyed, Jackie waited, arms folded across her chest.

Nicolas wanted to talk? Fine. Let him talk.

"What did Richie tell you about the gambling?" Nicolas said.

The question hit her like a hand grenade, sucking the wind out of her.

When all else fails, plead ignorance. "What are you talking about?"

Nicolas came closer, looming over her. "You know what I'm talking about."

"Get out of my face, Nicolas. Don't come here before I've finished my coffee and yell at me."

His dark eyes bored into her. "I'm not yelling. I asked a simple question. What did Richie tell you about gambling on basketball games?"

"Nothing," she said, her palms damp with sweat.

"I don't believe it. Show me what you found in his office."

"Fuck you! I don't have to show—"

He grabbed her arm and dragged her down the hall to Richie's office. Opened the door and shoved her inside.

"Show me what you found."

Her heart slammed her chest, Renzi's words echoing in her mind.

Nicolas is dangerous.

But he wouldn't dare hurt her now, would he? Not with the kids right outside.

He released her arm and shut the office door. "Don't pretend you didn't know Richie was gambling on NBA games. Where did you think all the money came from? What did he tell you?"

Beyond angry now, she said, "Did you know he had a mistress?"

That stopped him. But not for long.

"I told him that was a mistake. I tried to look out for you, Jackie."

No you didn't. You only look out for yourself, you narcissistic prick.

"Thanks," she said sarcastically. "Too bad he didn't listen. Was he sharing her with you?"

Fury blazed in Zurik's eyes. "Watch your mouth, Jackie. Don't say something you'll regret."

"I'll say whatever I want. This is my house."

He gestured at Richie's desk. "Where's Richie's laptop?"

Her heart pounded. How did he know Richie's laptop was in here?

"The cops took it."

"No they didn't. Don't lie to me, Jackie."

"Don't threaten me! Get out of my house."

Nicolas stepped closer. "Where's Richie's laptop?"

"The cops took it when they took his car."

"You're lying," he said, skewering her with a look.

Jesus Christ! If looks could kill, she'd be dead.

"What did Renzi say to you last Friday? I know he was here."

The office door opened. Startled, they both turned.

From the doorway, Nora said, "I don't want to stay outside, Mom. I want to watch *Dora the Explorer.*"

Saved by Dora. "Okay," Jackie said. "I'll turn it on for you right now."

Still glaring at her, his eyes hard and cold as granite, Nicolas said, "Be careful what you say to the cops, Jackie. It could get you in trouble. Don't talk to Renzi, or you'll *really* be in trouble."

After Nicolas left the room, Nora said, "I don't like Mr. Zurik, Mom. He scares me."

Jackie hugged her and said, "Don't worry, Nora, I'll protect you."

But Nicolas scared her, too.

Time to get out of Ponchatoula. Today.

———

187

7:40 AM – New Orleans

Exhausted, Frank sat at his desk. After a few hours of fitful sleep, he'd gotten up at five to go for a run, filled with a vague sense that he was missing something. After a quick shower and shave he'd come directly to the office.

Desperate to find evidence that would allow him to arrest Zurik.

Desperate to solve this fucking nightmare of a case.

Last night he'd called Vobitch and recapped what Claudia told him, including the Interpol alert on Nicholas Kozlovich, who had killed two men in London, men who had murdered his father, Vladimir Kozlovich, an assassin for a Russian gang. Father of the man they knew as Nicolas Zurik.

"Good," Vobitch said, "but we need more than that to nail the motherfucker."

"Jackie's the key to this case. I get the feeling she's hiding something."

"Talk to her again, before the meeting tomorrow," Vobitch had said.

Fighting a headache, Frank massaged his temples.

Another meeting. Another day of frustration.

The door opened and Kelly strolled into the office, accompanied by the delightful aroma of coffee. "Surprise!" she said, and put a large Dunkin Donuts coffee on his desk.

He took the lid off his coffee. "The answer to my dreams."

"Me or the coffee? Make the wrong choice you're in trouble."

"My shameless hussy, of course." He sipped his coffee. "Excellent. Dunkin Donuts dark roast."

"Nothing but the best for my favorite caffeine-deprived detective. Plus a pumpkin muffin."

He cleared a space on his desk. "Pull up a chair and join me."

Kelly rolled her desk chair over and drank her coffee while he recapped what Claudia had found.

"You were right all along," she said. "Zurik's a killer. Did you tell Vobitch?"

"Yes, last night." Frank ate a bite of muffin. "But he said it won't get us anywhere, and he's right. Doesn't matter that I know Zurik's a killer. Doesn't matter that I think he bought the gun for the shooter and got somebody to murder him. We need evidence."

Kelly broke off a piece of his pumpkin muffin and ate it. "I still think Jackie's involved."

"Maybe. Hiding something, for sure."

His cellphone vibrated on his desk. Tony Coppola calling.

"What's up, Tony?"

"Something's going on in Ponchatoula. At seven-thirty, Zurik went over to Jackie's house. A minute later the kids came outside and sat on the patio."

"Wanted to talk to her alone," Frank said, looking at Kelly.

"Seems like it," Tony said. "He spent fifteen minutes with Jackie and went home. He just got in his black BMW and left. You want me to follow him or watch Jackie?"

"Follow Zurik. I don't know what's going on, but I'm afraid he might run. If he goes to the airport, don't let him get on a plane!"

"Okay," Tony said. "But how do I stop him?"

"Hell if I know. Don't let him get in the TSA line. Get a couple of airport cops to help you. I'm going to his office in case he shows up there. Keep me posted."

He ended the call and took his SIG out of the bottom drawer of his desk.

"Jesus," Kelly said, "you really think he'll try to get on a plane?"

"I don't know and I'm not waiting until it happens to find out." He rose from his chair, strapped on his holster and checked to make sure the SIG was loaded. It was.

Gazing at him, her sea-green eyes full of concern, Kelly said, "Be careful or he'll kill you too."

"I'm always careful."

"So you say. Think about it, Frank. He's a killer. His father was an assassin!"

"Taught him how to do it."

"Exactly." He kissed her lips. "Don't worry. I'll see you at the meeting."

She said nothing, frowning at him.

"See you at two o'clock," he said, and left the office, buzzed with adrenaline-fueled energy.

Finally, a break in the case. Zurik was on the move.

CHAPTER 29

Jackie shut off her desktop computer. Ten minutes ago she'd found a non-stop flight to JFK in New York with three seats together and paid for their tickets. The flight didn't leave until tomorrow.

Not from the airport in Kenner. NOPD cops might be watching Armstrong Airport. If she was a suspect, they might not let her leave. Unfortunately, it would take at least five hours to drive to the other airport. She needed to book them a room for tonight, but she'd do that later with her cellphone.

Be careful what you say to the cops, Jackie. It could get you in trouble.

Don't talk to Renzi, or you'll really be trouble.

Nicolas threatening her. A cold wet blanket of dread made her shiver.

How did he know she'd taken Richie's laptop?

Nicolas is dangerous. Renzi's warning last Friday.

She took his card out of her pen holder and put it in her purse.

Too bad it wasn't a gun.

Jesus, what was she thinking? She was no gunslinger. She was a forty-five-year-old mother with two children, who needed to get out of here, pronto. But some sort of weapon would be good.

She went in the kitchen and took a serrated knife with a steel handle out of the wooden butcher block on the counter. If the need arose, and it very well might, she would use it.

After Richie was murdered, she'd gone through the usual stages of grief: denial, anger, then acceptance and deep sorrow. Now, terror.

Nicolas thought he could intimidate her. Wrong!

If he threatened her again, she'd stab him and damn the consequences.

In her bedroom, she took her suitcase out of the closet and set it on the bed. She couldn't take the knife through security, but if she got to the airport tomorrow, she would no longer need it. Ditch the knife, get on a plane and fly to New York. Her father would protect them.

She packed enough clothes for two days and returned to her closet. Eased a shoe box off the top shelf and took out a thick envelope with the cash Richie had left her. Three thousand dollars in hundreds.

She put two of the hundreds in her wallet and slid the envelope under her clothes beside the knife.

Now for the hard part. Get Danny and Nora packed and get out of here.

Danny would be her biggest problem.

Dreading another confrontation, she went to his room.

"I need you to pack some clothes." She took his suitcase out of the closet and set it on his bed.

Seated at his work table, he said, "Why? Where are we going?"

"We're flying to New York to visit Gramma and Grandpa."

"But you promised I could go to school this week!"

"I've already booked the tickets. We're flying to New York."

"I'll miss too much school!" Danny screamed. "You're the worst mother in the whole world!"

She gripped his chin in her hand. "I've had it with your temper tantrums. Pack your suitcase. We're leaving in half an hour. I'm going to help Nora pack her suitcase. When I came back, yours better be packed and ready to go."

She hurried down the hall to Nora's room. Nora sat on her bed, playing with her stuffed bunny. "Help me pack your clothes, Nora. We're flying to New York to see Gramma and Grandpa."

"Yea!" Nora said, her face wreathed in a smile. "I've never flown on a plane before!"

"Yes you have, but you were only a baby, so you don't remember it."

She took Nora's pink suitcase out of the closet, the one they'd used when they took the kids to Disney World. Back when they were a happy family with two great kids, a husband and wife madly in love with each other.

At least she'd thought so at the time. Now she wasn't so sure.

Was Pom-Pom Girl already in the picture even then?

Nora brought her a stack of shirts and said, "Can I bring Dora?"

"Of course! We can't leave without Dora, but don't put her in the suitcase. We'll let her sit in your lap while we ride in the plane."

Nora danced around the room. "This is so fun! When do we get on the plane?"

"Not till tomorrow, but we have to leave now so we can check into a hotel near the airport. That will be fun too. A new adventure for us."

As long as nobody knew where they were.

She went to the door and called, "Danny are you ready?"

No answer. Why did Danny have to act up when she desperately needed him to cooperate? She went back to his room.

His suitcase was open on his bed. Empty.

Glaring at her defiantly, Danny said, "I'm not going, Mom."

"Yes you are," she snapped. "Pack your clothes now or I'll do it for you."

"Why can't I stay with Nicky?"

"STOP ARGUING!" she screamed. "We're leaving NOW. If you're not in the kitchen with your suitcase in ten minutes, I'll drag you down to the car and lock you in the trunk."

Danny stared at her, speechless. "Do it," she snapped, and left the room.

Jesus, what kind of a mother was she? Screaming at her son, threatening him.

If her friends at the golf club heard her, they'd be appalled. But they didn't have to deal with an NOPD detective who thought she might have paid a man to kill her husband. Or a neighbor who'd threatened her. They were mealy-mouthed women worried about play dates and after-school activities for their kids. They weren't terrified, carrying a knife to protect themselves.

What kind of a mother was she?

A mother determined to protect herself and her children, that's who.

She collected her suitcase from her bedroom and towed it to Nora's room. Nora looked at her, not smiling now, her eyes full of unspoken questions.

"Sorry, Nora. Danny's not being very helpful and right now I need all the help I can get. Can you tow your suitcase in the kitchen for me?"

"Yes," Nora said, and followed her down the hall to the kitchen.

Jackie opened the kitchen door. "Can you wait here while I put our suitcases in the trunk?"

"Are you scared of Mr. Zurik, Mom?"

She knelt down and looked Nora in the eye. "No, but I don't trust him. That's why I'm upset."

Nora patted her cheek. "It's okay, Mommy. Don't worry. I understand."

Tears sprang to her eyes. Dear sweet Nora.

Her cellphone rang. She checked the ID. Damn! Another problem.

When she answered, Martina said, "Hi Jackie, let's go out for lunch. My treat! We can take the kids to that place in Kenner. We had so much fun there the other day."

Damn, damn, damn! A lie sprang from her mouth "Thanks, Martina, but I'm about to take the kids grocery shopping."

"That's no fun," Martina said. "Do your shopping later."

"No can do. I'm out of a bunch of things. Let's do lunch tomorrow. I'll call you later." She ended the call, thinking, *In a pig's eye.*

Nora looked at her, frowning. "I thought we were going to get on an airplane."

"We are, but it's a surprise, so I don't want anyone to know about it."

"Like Mr. Zurik?" Nora said, gazing at her solemnly.

"Yes. Wait here while I put our suitcases in the car."

———

9:40 AM – New Orleans

Nicolas sat at the computer in his office, waiting for program Alexei had sent him to finish. "Nothing really disappears when you delete computer files," Alexei had said. "A good forensic expert can reconstruct them. This program will not allow them to do this."

The program ended with a ping and a word appeared on his screen. *Cleaned!*

He shut off the computer and rose from his desk. The file cabinet where he kept his documents was empty, the shredded files already in the dump.

The other file cabinet held his weapons and cash. He took a trash bag out of a box and stuffed bundles of cash into the bag. If the busybody across the hall saw him leave with them, she'd think he was taking out the trash.

In the bottom drawer was a snub-nosed .22 caliber revolver, easy to conceal, effective for close kills. He had procured a similar gun for his hitman. Recalling his surprise, the first time he'd set eyes on him, a scrawny little man, black hair and a sallow complexion, seated at a table nursing a cup of coffee, nervously watching pedestrians. Like a bird of prey, not a hunter.

The man had insisted he could pass as an American, but Nicolas had his doubts. The man hardly spoke English. Despite his reservations, he'd gone ahead with the plan. But his hitman had screwed up.

A fatal error with cascading consequences. All of them bad.

He unrolled two trash bags, put one inside the other, wrapped the .22 in a soft cloth and put it into the double-thick bag. Wrapped his Beretta nine-millimeter in another cloth and added it to the bag. Both were fully loaded. He added the silencer, the garrote and the scabbard with his buck knife to the bag and knotted the bag closed.

His burner chimed and he answered. "Yes?"

Maybe it was Martina and maybe it wasn't.

Martina spoke into his ear. "I invited Jackie and the kids for lunch, but she said she had to go grocery shopping."

"Watch the house. If she leaves with the kids, follow her, call me and tell me where she goes."

He ended the call and massaged his eyes. Could he depend on Martina to do what was necessary? Perhaps. Up to a point, anyway.

Last year on Nicky's birthday he had taken him for a drive and revealed his true origins. "The day may come when we must leave suddenly," he'd said. "This must remain strictly between you and me."

Nicky had nodded solemnly, his dark eyes serious.

Now, that day had arrived.

CHAPTER 30

Alone in the elevator, Frank unbuttoned his jacket and took out his SIG. The last time he'd flashed it as a warning. Now he knew Zurik was a killer. To hell with warrants. If Zurik was in his office, he would arrest him.

At gunpoint if necessary.

The elevator doors opened on the twelfth floor. He hustled down the hall to Zurik's office. The Venetian blinds on the window were shut, but that didn't mean Zurik wasn't there. Most killers kept their weapons handy, loaded with ammo that could penetrate doors.

Frank moved past the door and extended his left hand to ring the bell.

"He's not there," said a woman's voice.

Startled, Frank turned and saw Helen in the doorway of the office across the hall.

"He left about ten minutes ago," she said. "He was carrying trash bags so I thought he was putting them in the dumpster outside. But he never came back."

"Thanks. If he comes back, call me right away," Frank said and ran back to the elevator.

Two minutes later he got in his unmarked and called Tony.

"No sign of Zurik at the airport," Tony said. "But he gave me the slip in Ponchatoula."

"I'm at his office. The woman across the hall said he left ten minutes ago."

"My backup just called from Ponchatoula, said all the cars are gone."

"All of them?" Frank said as he drove out of the parking lot.

"Yup. Jackie's red Kia, no sign of Martina's silver Toyota, either. Want me to stay at the airport in case Zurik shows up?"

"For now, yes. I'm headed for Jackie's house. If she's not there, I'll break in. Could be she's out running an errand. Could be she's running, period. Call Vobitch and update him. But don't tell him I'm gonna break into Jackie's house."

Tony chuckled. "Frank. Why would I tell him a thing like that? Keep me posted."

"You too," Frank said, and drove up a steep incline onto the Causeway, the fastest way to Jackie's house, but not fast enough for him. Twenty-three miles across Lake Pontchartrain, another ten to Ponchatoula, it would take him a while to get there.

He got on his cellphone and called Claudia.

She answered right away. "What's up, Frank?"

"I just left Zurik's office, missed him by ten minutes." He recapped what Tony had told him and said, "I'm headed for Jackie's house now. Any possibility you can track the cars for me? Jackie's and the two Zurik cars."

"I'll try. Send me the details and the tag numbers. The Louisiana State Police patrol the state highways. I'll call and ask them to put out a BOLO on the cars."

"Hold on." Driving one-handed, he accessed a document, attached the file to an email and hit Send. "I just emailed you the information. Call me right away if you get anything."

"Will do, Frank. Do you think Jackie's running scared? Or leaving so you won't question her?"

"I'll know more when I get to her house, should be there in forty minutes."

He got in the high speed lane, ugly scenarios running through his mind. Zurik was a killer. Jackie was a widow with two kids.

Would he kill them before he got there?

————

10:10 AM – Mandeville, LA

Nicolas exited the Causeway and got on Route 22 headed west toward Ponchatoula. Twenty minutes ago Martina had called and said Jackie filled the tank at a gas station and got on Route 55 headed north. Martina was following her, saying the red Kia was easy to track.

He clenched his jaw. By now Jackie was miles ahead of him. She had the kids with her, which would make things more difficult. But he'd worry about that later. If she got on an airplane, he was screwed.

This morning she'd told him the cops had taken Richie's laptop, unaware that he'd seen it in Richie's office last night. Lying to him. From personal experience he knew that one lie often necessitated others.

Jackie had taken Richie's laptop because something important was on it. What else was she lying about?

He was certain Richie had taped their conversation at the golf club, a tape that incriminated Nicolas Zurik. If the feds got hold of it, they would send him a subpoena to testify in that federal courtroom in New Jersey on the second of November. He could not allow this to happen.

Jackie had the tape. Of this he was certain.

Her parents lived in New York. Would she drive there? Doubtful. Not in her sporty red Kia with two restless kids yammering at her.

The handguns in his trunk were fully loaded. Get Jackie alone, make her give him Richie's laptop and the tape, then shoot her.

Problem solved. Except for the kids.

He couldn't imagine shooting Danny and Nora.

His burner chimed. Martina calling him.

"I'm still following her on Route 55. She just crossed into Mississippi, heading north. Maybe she's going to St. Louis."

"Why would she go there?"

"Maybe she's tired of staying home with the kids. There's plenty to do in St. Louis for kids. A big zoo with an aquarium—"

"There's an aquarium in New Orleans if she wanted to do that."

"I know. But the reporters would follow her if she took them there."

A sudden thought struck him. "How come they're not following her now?"

"She gave them the slip. Drove behind Pop's Service Station near the railroad tracks, zipped over to the next street, drove down an alley, circled back to Pop's and filled her tank."

Exactly what he had done, to avoid the suspicious white van that had been following him.

Martina trilled a laugh. "She didn't fool me. I figured that was where she was going."

Martina was better at this than he'd thought. His plan might work after all.

"Good work, Martina. I'll be on Route 55 in ten minutes. Keep me posted."

He ended the call and clenched his fists. What Martina had failed to mention: the airport in St. Louis could fly Jackie and whatever incriminating evidence she possessed directly to New York.

Or anywhere else, for that matter.

Time to leave his comfortable life in Ponchatoula and disappear.

Everything he needed was in the trunk: cash, weapons, a canvas bag with a few clothes and the documents Alexei had sent him. He'd collected them this morning at the mail-drop they used in Ponchatoula: passports, credit cards and driver's licenses with two different names.

Many years ago he had disappeared from London and begun a new life in America. Now he would do it again.

But not until he got the incriminating items from Jackie.

CHAPTER 31

Frank stood outside Jackie's kitchen door, his SIG in hand. The deputy guarding the entrance to Ponchatoula Estates had quickly waved him through, but the local reporters had recognized him. By now they'd be talking about him on the local news.

But that wasn't his biggest worry.

No lights visible in the house when he drove into the driveway and his gut told him something was wrong. An hour ago Zurik had left his office with a ten minute head start on him.

Enough time to beat him to Jackie's house, kill her and leave.

He tried the doorknob. Locked. He went around the corner, looked through the kitchen window and saw no one. He returned to the door. No one in the kitchen that he could see. He took off his jacket and wrapped it around his left elbow.

Holding the SIG in his right hand, he rammed his left elbow against the glass near the doorknob. The glass shattered and fell into the kitchen, leaving jagged shards around the frame.

He unlocked the door with his left hand and entered the kitchen.

"Police!" he shouted. "Anybody home?"

Silence. The hackles rose on the back of his neck. If the kids were home, they would have come running. Were they out riding around in the car with Jackie? Or were all three of them dead?

It took him seven minutes to clear the house, crouching outside each door then springing into the room, his SIG at the ready, then checking the closets.

Relieved that he'd found no bodies, Frank returned to the kitchen. A coffee mug in the sink. No dirty dishes. If Jackie decided to split with the kids, where would she go?

He ran down the hall to her office. The shades on the windows facing the golf course were shut. Was Jackie afraid Zurik was watching her?

Nothing to indicate where she'd gone on her desk. Her desktop computer was off and her laptop was gone.

Why take your laptop if you were only going shopping?

Damn it to hell! Jackie wasn't shopping, she was getting out of Dodge. By now she could be anywhere.

Something jogged his memory. He went in the living room and studied the snapshot of the Bauer family at Disney World on the table beside the sofa.

Jackie and Richie, Danny and Nora, smiling at the camera. Off to one side were four suitcases. Two big ones, a smaller one with a Spider-man decal for Danny, a small pink suitcase for Nora.

He ran to the master bedroom and checked Jackie's closet. No suitcase. Ran down the hall to Nora's room. No pink suitcase in the closet. Checked Danny's closet, no suitcase there either.

Jackie had packed suitcases for herself and the kids, but where was she going? If she wanted to get on a plane, why not go to Armstrong Airport? But Tony hadn't seen them.

Then he remembered Natalie, his longtime adversary, fleeing New Orleans after she shot him. Going to St. Louis and getting on a plane to … somewhere.

He called up a map on his Smartphone. If Jackie got on Route 55 in Ponchatoula, she could drive north through Louisiana, Mississippi and Tennessee into Missouri. And St. Louis.

He'd given Jackie his cellphone number, but she'd never called him, so he didn't have hers. But every mother in the world left a cellphone number to call in case of emergency. Usually in a prominent place. He dashed back to the kitchen. And there it was on the refrigerator.

A pink sticky, with Mom's cellphone number.

He entered the number on his cellphone and hit Call. One ring and it went to voicemail. He left a message: *Jackie, call me right away when you get this. It's urgent.*

Then he called Tony. "No sign of Jackie," Tony said. "Or Zurik."

"I'm at Jackie's house. She packed suitcases for her and the kids. If she's getting on a plane, she might be on Route 55, headed north to St. Louis."

"Or Memphis," Tony said. "There's an airport there too, and it's closer. I updated Vobitch, didn't say a word about your plans to break into Jackie's house. How'd that go?"

"Broke the glass in the kitchen door. Can you come up here and watch both houses? Maybe nail some plywood over the broken window to secure the house?"

"I can do that, no problem. Should be there in forty minutes. What's our next move?"

"Claudia put out a BOLO on the cars. Talk to you later." He ended the call, hit the speed-dial for Claudia. When she answered, he said, "I'm at Jackie's house. She packed suitcases and split with the kids. Any news from the State police on the BOLO?"

"Not yet," Claudia said. "Any idea where she's headed?"

"I figure she's heading north on Route 55. Maybe to an airport in St. Louis or Memphis."

"No clues in the house as to where she's going?"

"None. I found her cellphone number and called her, but it went straight to voicemail. I left a message, told her to call me."

"Probably shut off her cellphone so we couldn't track it," Claudia said. "Smart."

Frustrated, he paced the kitchen. "Smart enough to give us the slip. She knows something, I'm certain of it. Tony said she left her house three hours ago. If she's got plane tickets, she could get on a plane and we'll never find out what she knows."

"Meet me in the cafeteria at North Oaks Medical Center in Hammond," Claudia said. "I'm in my office so it'll take me forty-five minutes to get there."

Mystified, Frank said, "Why? If you want to eat lunch, I can think of better places."

"So can I, but they don't have helipads on the roof."

His heart almost jumped out of his chest. "You can get us a chopper? Fantastic!"

"Calm down, Frank. I haven't asked for one yet, but I'll alert the pilot to make sure he's got one ready to go. I don't want to ask my asshole boss face to face. I'll call him from the hospital."

"Good move. Then he can't pull his John Wayne act. You know: I'm way more powerful than you are so don't get uppity."

Claudia chuckled. "How perceptive. See you soon, Frank."

He ended the call and hit the speed-dial for Kelly's number.

"Frank!" she exclaimed, agitated. "Where the hell are you?"

"In Jackie's kitchen. Zurik wasn't in his office. I missed him by ten minutes."

"Jesus Christ! You could be dead, Frank. Why didn't you call me?"

Picturing her angry sea-green eyes, he said, "Sorry, Kelly. Too many things were happening. Jackie split with the kids. Tony and I figure she's headed north, maybe to an airport in Memphis or St. Louis. What's doing on your end?"

"I'm in the homicide office. Vobitch is at Headquarters updating the Super."

"Can you do me a favor? I called Jackie's cellphone, but she might have turned it off so we can't track where she is. Can you call her, in case she turned it back on?"

"Sure," Kelly said, "but what do I say?"

"Nothing. Hang up and call me right away. I'm leaving to meet Claudia at the North Shore Medical Center in Hammond. They've got a helipad. Claudia might get us an FBI chopper."

"Frank," Kelly said, her voice somber. "Be careful."

"I will," he said. "And you be careful too."

FOULSHOT

12:20 PM – New Orleans

Kelly set her cellphone on the desk, Frank's parting words ringing in her ears. *Be careful.* Their terms of endearment when one of them was in danger.

Now Frank was chasing Nicolas Zurik, a stone killer, the son of an assassin. Frank was a first-rate detective, but when he was hot on the trail of a murder suspect, he could be border-line reckless.

She took her Glock out of a desk drawer.

Packing a gun was reassuring to cops, not just the physical weight of it, the power. Deadly force, if you needed it. Not always a good thing.

A cop could walk into a dicey situation, knowing that if things went bad, deadly force was a trigger-pull away. Like Frank.

Kenyon was quick with a joke, using humor to diffuse situations. Frank was the department time-bomb, dark and brooding, living life on the edge. Because he cared about homicide victims and wanted to get justice for them.

Frank also had a certain reputation; he didn't play well with others.

Before they worked a case together five years ago, she'd been a tad afraid of him. Until they went out for a beer one night after work, and she told him what happened to her husband.

Most people mouthed platitudes. *How awful*, or *I'm so sorry to hear that.* Frank didn't. He just listened, gazing into her eyes until she finished. Then he took her hands in his and told her to remember the good times, laughing at her husband's silly jokes or knowing what he would say before he said it, or feeling his skin against hers when they made love.

Which told her Frank wasn't just a tough cop seeking justice for victims. Frank had lost someone he loved, too. Someone he'd loved deeply.

Now he was pursuing a killer.

Nicolas Zurik, no doubt armed, definitely dangerous.

She slid the Glock into her waistband holster. Her work outfit was designed to conceal it, a dark blazer and loose trousers with elastic waistbands. She buttoned the blazer to conceal the Glock.

Carrying a gun gave you options.

Terms of endearment were good.

Backup was better.

CHAPTER 32

Jackie forced down another bite of her Big Mac, hoping to induce Nora to hurry up and finish her Happy Meal. She wanted to get back on the road. Miraculously, seated across the table from them, Danny seemed happy, chowing down a Big Mac and sucking up Pepsi through a straw.

She glanced out the window beside their table. The glare from the sun was giving her a headache. She'd parked the red Kia in the front row so she could keep an eye on it. Everything important was locked in the trunk. Leaving it there made her nervous.

Would she ever return to the house she had shared with Richie in Ponchatoula? Tears stung her eyes. No time to think about that now.

Nicolas had threatened her this morning.

All that mattered now was getting away—as far away as possible.

"Can I go get another Pepsi?" Danny asked. "And more fries?"

Unwilling to upset their fragile truce, she said, "Okay, a Pepsi and a small order of fries."

"Can I go too?" Nora said. "I ate my apple slices and most of my cheeseburger."

"No, let Danny go by himself." She opened her wallet and gave him a twenty, thankful she'd used one of the hundreds Richie had left her to fill the tank at the local gas station. Paying at MacDonald's with a hundred dollar bill would draw too much attention. The clerk might ask the manager to okay the payment. "Get Nora a chocolate chip cookie."

"Cool," Danny said, and headed for the counter to put in his order.

"I love chocolate chip cookies!" Nora exclaimed, smiling up at her. "Thanks, Mom."

"Finish your cheeseburger, Nora. You can eat your cookie in the car."

"Why can't we stay here?" Nora pointed at the sign outside. "I love the big yellow french fries, don't you?"

Jackie wanted to scream. Gritting her teeth, she gathered Nora's Happy Meal items and put them in the box. One more day and she'd be safe.

Shoving the remains of her Big Mac into a paper bag, she watched Danny, smiling as he returned to the table with his order.

"Bring it out to the car, Danny. We need to get back on the road."

"How far do we have to go?" Danny said, not looking happy now.

"Not far, another hour or so." *More like three hours if they were lucky.*

The bad mother, bribing her kids with sweets and lying to them.

1:15 PM – Hammond, Louisiana

Seated in the North Oaks Medical Center cafeteria with Claudia, Frank got to work on his roast beef sub. Claudia had left her jacket, emblazoned with big yellow FBI letters, in her car, dressed casual today—bluejeans, a white T-shirt, and a jean jacket. And she clearly didn't plan to go hungry: a roast chicken sub, a garden salad, a cup of fresh fruit and an oatmeal cookie on her tray.

Jiving her, he said, "You sure you're not pregnant? Looks like you're eating for two."

Her lips twitched in a smile. "Damned if I know how long we'll have to wait for the chopper. Or where we'll go if it gets here. FBI helicopters carry a lot of equipment. Food isn't one of them."

He drew a one in the air with his finger. "Touche. What kind of weaponry does it carry?"

She looked at him, deadpan. "I told the pilot to load up like we're going to Afghanistan."

He wasn't sure if she was joking or not. "Can I take my SIG with me?"

"Why not? My Glock is in my tote bag."

"Good to know." He finished half of his sub and started on the other half. Claudia polished off her chicken sub and started on her salad. Her cellphone rang. Both of their phones were on the table, different ring tones.

Claudia answered, listened a moment, and said, "Thanks for the update. Keep me informed." She put her phone down on the table. "No sign of any of the cars on Route 55, but they'll keep looking. Call Kelly and see if she's been able to reach Jackie."

Special Agent Cohen giving him orders, showing him who was in charge. For the moment, anyway. He got on his cellphone and called Kelly.

"Hey, Frank, what's happening? Did you get the chopper?"

"Not yet. Did you call Jackie?"

"Yes, but it went to voicemail. I'm on my way to her house to see if I can find something."

"Good idea. Be on the lookout for Zurik."

"Don't worry, I will," Kelly said.

Frank ended the call and said, "Jackie's phone is still off. Kelly's going to her house, to see if she can find anything that indicates where Jackie's going."

"Good. Let's go somewhere more private. Now that I've eaten, I'm ready to call my asshole boss."

Frank collected their trash and threw it in a rubbish bin. Claudia put the oatmeal cookie in her tote bag and they left the cafeteria. As they walked down the hall, he said, "Do I get to see the helipad?"

She stopped at an elevator and pressed a button. "Yes. Right now."

The elevator took them to the roof, where a security guard said, "I need to see your ID."

Claudia flashed her FBI badge and said, "We might need to use your helipad today."

"Okay, but you'll need to tell us the ETA."

"No problem," Claudia said. "Homicide Detective Renzi will be flying with me. Okay if we go outside for a quick look?"

"Sure," the guard said, and opened a security door.

They went up a short ramp and stepped outside. Heat hit him like a bomb, the midday sun blazing down from a cloudless blue sky. He put on his Raybans and saw the landing spot: a huge white cross painted on the black asphalt roof.

Huffing wisps of dark hair off her forehead, Claudia said,"Seen enough? I'm fried."

"Me too," he said, and they went back inside.

They walked past three gurneys and cabinets with medical equipment to a deserted waiting area. They sat at a table with molded-plastic chairs. Claudia took out her cellphone. "When I talk to Murphy, I'll put it on speaker so you can listen, but don't say anything." She dialed, gave him a warning look, put the phone on speaker and set it on the table.

Murphy's voice boomed from the speaker. "What can I do for you, Claudia? You got a flat tire?"

"I need a chopper at the helipad in Hammond, Louisiana."

"Jesus Christ! What the hell for?"

"NOPD got a lead on the mastermind behind the High Roller shooting. He's running."

A moment of silence, then, "Who is he? What's his name?"

"NOPD believes he's gunning for Jackie Bauer, the widow of the NBA referee that was murdered at the High Roller Club."

"Claudia, are you deaf? What the fuck is his NAME!!"

Claudia glanced at him. Frank shrugged and motioned with his hand. *Tell him.*

"Nicolas Zurik," she said, "and I need a chopper now. Unless you'd rather have NOPD capture him and take all the credit."

"Oh, I get it. This is a glory move, right? Grab him all by yourself and make headlines?"

Claudia's lips tightened. "I already told Roger to get a chopper ready. Will you send it or not?"

"Christ Almighty," Murphy muttered. "All right, I'll give him the okay. But you're not doing this alone. I'm sending Tonto with him."

"Thank you, sir. I'll be waiting." Claudia ended the call and pumped her fist, smiling at him.

"Who the hell is Tonto?" Frank said.

"One of Murphy's watchdogs. We call him Tonto because he's like the proverbial Cigar Store Indian, expressionless no matter what. Hands out cigars when his son was born, nary a smile. In the middle of a fucking shootout, he acts like he's eating cake on his front porch."

"Hey, you got a watchdog, but at least we get the chopper."

"And as you probably noticed, I didn't mention that you were with me."

"I did. Murphy and I being such good pals and all."

Grinning at him, Claudia said, "That'll be the day."

———

2:15 PM – Ponchatoula

Kelly parked in Jackie's driveway and got out of her car. Standing at the side door with a sheet of plywood, Tony waved and said, "Hey, Kelly, good to see ya. Wanna hammer some nails for me?"

She laughed and joined him at the door. "Not really. How about I bake you a cake instead?"

"That'd be good. I prefer chocolate." Grinning at her.

"Good luck with that. Last time I baked a cake was last November for Frank's birthday. I talked to him a few minutes ago. He's with Claudia, waiting for a helicopter."

"So I heard. Be good if you could find something to tell 'em where to go."

"That's why I'm here."

Tony opened the door and said, "Have at it."

She stepped into the kitchen, her senses on full alert. The house was quiet and still. Entering Jackie's home without a search warrant wasn't her first choice. But desperate times called for desperate measures.

Frank thought Jackie wanted to get on a plane to escape from Nicolas.

Kelly wasn't so sure. Maybe Jackie was getting on a plane to fly somewhere to meet Nicolas.

Figuring Frank had already checked obvious places like the freezer and the refrigerator, she went in the living room and stopped. Jesus, what a hideous sofa, an L-shaped monstrosity upholstered in bright yellow.

A framed photograph was on the end table. A smiling happy family, allegedly, until Richie was murdered.

She opened the drawer in the end table. Empty. Dozens of books sat on the bookshelves along one wall. If Jackie had hidden something in a book, it would take her hours to find it.

But why do that if she was hellbent on leaving as fast as possible?

Seeking possible hiding places, Kelly explored the house. A master bedroom, two smaller bedrooms for the kids. Richie's office. A desktop computer but no laptop, and a black filing cabinet to be explored later.

She went down the hall to Jackie's office.

If Jackie had planned to escape, this was the mostly likely place to do it. She sat down at Jackie's desk and started her search.

———

3:05 PM – Mississippi

Frustrated and angry, Nicolas drove north on Route 55 at 65 mph, the posted speed limit. Stomp the accelerator and his BMW would easily top 100 mph, but State cops patrolled the two-lane highway. He couldn't afford to get stopped by a cop.

Martina was following Jackie's red Kia. He'd given her strict orders to call him if Jackie got off the highway. Two hours ago Jackie had stopped for lunch at a MacDonald's.

Renzi was the wild card. Where was he and what was he doing?

His burner chimed. He grabbed it out of the console and answered.

"Jackie just took the exit for Memphis," Martina said. "I'm following her."

"If they go to the airport, don't let them get on a plane!"

"But how do I stop them?"

He clenched his jaw. Martina was an idiot. Too stupid to figure out what to do in an emergency.

"Follow them to the parking garage. Tell them they forgot something and you've got it in your car. I'll be there in ten minutes."

He ended the call and saw a highway sign up ahead. 40 miles to Memphis.

Fuck the State cops. He stomped the accelerator.

In twenty minutes he'd be in Memphis.

CHAPTER 33

Tonto was pretty much as advertised, though taller than Frank had expected, six-foot-four and rail thin. Standing with Claudia in the heliport doorway, Frank watched him duck under the whirling rotors and march toward them, stiffly erect and expressionless.

Ex-military, Frank thought, early fifties, gray hair in a military buzz-cut, pale skin, a humorless mouth.

Claudia did the introductions. Upon learning that NOPD Homicide Detective Frank Renzi would be riding with them, Tonto's expression didn't change, but his eyes got squinty. Like he saw trouble ahead.

"You two go ahead and board," Tonto said. "After I complete the required paperwork and get clearance to leave, we'll be on our way."

Frank studied the helicopter, white with a wide blue stripe running from nose to tail, six black numbers on the side. Nothing to indicate it was FBI. No surprise there. The federales liked to travel incognito.

He wished he hadn't eaten the roast beef sub. His stomach felt queasy, his brain telling him they'd be flying at least 500 feet above the ground, flashing images he'd seen of downed helicopters, broken wreckage and debris scattered over the ground.

But Claudia was already jogging toward the chopper. He didn't want to look like a wimp so he followed her. Up close the noise was deafening, the rotors whipping hot smelly air in his face.

Claudia ducked under the rotors and climbed into the helicopter.

Frank set his jaw, muttered *Fuck it*, and did the same.

Waiting for him inside, Claudia pointed at the cockpit and yelled over the rotor noise, "Say hello to Special Agent Roger Beltré."

"Welcome aboard," Beltré said, a light-skinned black man with a two-inch scar near his right eye. It lent character to his face, Frank thought. Like the scar on his own chin, distinctive but not disfiguring.

"Frank Renzi," he said, and shook Beltré's hand. "No need to get Tonto in a dither with titles."

Beltré grinned. "Cool. Call me Roger."

Frank nodded absently, gazing at the instrument panel, a multitude of knobs and switches, more lights than a Christmas tree, and a large map.

"Your first chopper flight?" Roger said.

"Yes. So be kind to my stomach, okay? No swoops and quick plunges."

"No promises, but I'll try. The pocket under your seat has a barf bag."

"Good to know. Can we skip the car search and fly directly to Memphis? The woman we're tracking might already be there. I'm afraid she'll get on a plane."

Roger grimaced. "Sorry, no can do. Tonto's got orders from Murphy. I'm just the pilot, gotta go where he tells me."

"Just thought I'd ask," he said, thinking *Claudia's not in charge, Murphy is.*

"Here comes Tonto, better strap yourself in, we'll be airborne soon."

He stepped into the cabin of the chopper, which seated five passengers. Two seats in one row, two more slightly behind them on the other side, one seat in the rear. Seated beside the window in the front row, Claudia waved him over.

"Sit beside me, so I won't have to talk to Tonto."

He sank into the leather seat, buckled his seatbelt and said, "Can we use cell-phones in here?"

"Not for long conversations," she said. "Better to text. Why?"

"Figured I'd call Kelly, see if she found anything."

"Text her. If she found something, call her."

Frank thumbed in a text: *Find anything?* and hit Send.

Watched Tonto pull the door shut and thought, Oh boy, here we go.

Got back a text from Kelly: *Not yet. Still searching. Where are you?*

On the chopper. Take off imminent.

He added a fear emoticon and hit Send.

Got back a smiley.

The rotor noise suddenly got louder and the chopper lunged into the air as if shot from a cannon.

His stomach lurched. Man, this wasn't his idea of fun.

3:45 PM – Memphis, TN

Nicolas swerved into the right lane. Two miles to the Memphis exit.

Off in the distance he saw the hazy outlines of tall buildings, the gray sky filled with ominous dark clouds.

He eased off the accelerator, the speedometer slowing to sixty, then fifty-five.

Fear slashed him like a bullwhip, his mind screaming: *Don't let Jackie get on a plane!*

His burner rang, jangling his already-frazzled nerves. Martina.

Fearing the worst, he grabbed it off the console. "Yes?"

"Jackie just parked outside a Holiday Inn Express. Looks like she's not going to the airport."

Relieved, he said, "Excellent. Give me the address."

She recited the address and said, "What do you want me to do?"

"Hold on." He plugged the address into his GPS and a map appeared on his dashboard.

"Park where you can watch them," he said, "but don't let them see your car. I'll be there in five minutes. Find out which room they're in and wait in your car. I'll meet you there."

He ended the call and let out a triumphant scream.

"Now I've got you, bitch!"

He'd be inside the hotel room by four. Have Martina take the kids for a ride in her car. So he could be alone with Jackie.

———

3:45 PM – Memphis

Jackie parked the Kia around the corner from the hotel entrance and exclaimed, "We're here! Let's unload our suitcases and get settled in our room."

"About time," Danny grumbled. "My butt's got pins and needles from sitting so long."

Danny wasn't the only one happy to get here. She got out and stretched her aching muscles, arms first, then her legs. She'd been driving for hours, checking the rearview mirror, fearing Nicolas might be following her. She'd seen plenty of black SUVs but not the distinctive black BMW that Nicolas drove.

Finally, she was safe.

She opened the trunk and took out their suitcases. The air was muggy, the sky filled with dark clouds, looked like it might rain any minute. She pulled up the handle of her suitcase. The one she didn't intend to let out of her sight.

The one with the thumb drive and the cash. And the knife.

"Let's get inside before it rains," she said, urging Danny and Nora toward the entrance.

The hotel wasn't as nice as the pictures on the website. A two-story building with a faded red-brick exterior, dirty windows, cracked tiles on the walkway.

But so what? Tomorrow they'd get on a plane, fly to New York and sleep comfortably at her parents' house. Well, they would, provided that she called Mom and told her they were coming.

The automatic doors opened and she towed her suitcase into the lobby, a narrow rectangular space with dingy green carpeting, green-plaid sofas, and tables with brochures about Memphis and Elvis Presley and Graceland.

She told Danny and Nora to sit on the sofa near the back window and towed her suitcase to the waist-high reservation counter.

A young female clerk smiled at her. "Good afternoon! Do you have a reservation?"

Jackie parked her suitcase beside the desk and said, "Yes. Hold on." She took out her cellphone, found the confirmation and showed it to the woman, Mae-Rose according to her name tag.

"Perfect." Mae-Rose tapped some keys on her computer. "Two double beds with a cot for your little girl, right? The maintenance man didn't put it in the room yet. Hold on while I call him." She picked up on a two-way radio and said, "Room 210 needs an extra cot right away."

Setting the two-way receiver on the desk, Mae-Rose and smiled and said, "I just need your credit card and a license."

Jackie put her driver's license on the counter and said, "Can I pay cash? I'm only staying one night. I can give it to you now."

Mae-Rose studied her license, frowning now. "We don't usually let guests with out of state licenses pay cash."

Damn it to hell! She didn't want to use a credit card. The cops might trace it.

She took two hundreds out of her wallet and set them on the counter.

"That covers the room." Flashing a persuasive smile, she said, "Here's an extra twenty. For your trouble."

Mae-Rose checked to see if the manager in the glassed-in office behind her was watching. He wasn't so she pocketed the twenty.

Smiling at her, she said, "Let me get you a receipt. I'll be right back."

Relieved, Jackie leaned against the counter. This had been an exhausting day, but tomorrow she'd get on a plane and get out of here.

No more worries about Nicolas.

Two minutes later Mae-Rose returned with a printout of her receipt and a key card. "Room 210 is on the second floor. The elevator is that way." Pointing to a hallway off the lobby, she chirped, "Have a pleasant stay!"

"Thank you." Jackie put the key card and receipt in her purse and towed her suitcase to the sofa where the kids were waiting.

"We're all set. Let's take the elevator up to the room."

As they passed an alcove with vending machines for snacks and soda, Danny said, "Can I get a Pepsi? I'm thirsty."

"Not now, Danny. Let's get settled in our room first."

She pressed the elevator call button and said to Nora, "This is our great adventure, right?"

"Right!" Nora said, her blue eyes sparking. "I can't wait to get on the plane tomorrow."

———

FOULSHOT

4:05 PM – Ponchatoula

Kelly entered the password for Jackie's desktop and the Windows screen appeared. Finally! After searching Jackie's office, Richie's office and Jackie's bedroom, she had returned to Jackie's office. And found the password on a crumpled pink sticky in the wastebasket.

She studied the document folders. Nothing about travel. She clicked on the browser and waited for Google Chrome to load. She clicked on Jackie's email. Excellent. Google had saved the password. She opened the email.

No emails sent or received today.

She accessed the cache to see where Jackie's browser had taken her.

Her heart almost jumped out of her chest. Jackie had visited four airline websites. The most recent one was Delta. She navigated to the Delta website, clicked *Manage my flights* and crossed her fingers.

Yes! Jackie had booked three seats on a flight to New York City, departing at ten AM tomorrow from Memphis International Airport.

She grabbed her cellphone, called Frank and waited.

Damn it to hell! Was he still on the helicopter, out of cellphone range? Three rings, four, five ....

At last, he answered, the connection fuzzy with static, "Kelly, wh ... up? You got ... thing?"

"Jackie and the kids are flying out of Memphis International Airport tomorrow. A Delta flight, departing at ten AM."

More static. "They must ... staying ... Memphis. Can ... find ... reservation?"

"I'll look. Figured you'd want to know about the fight first."

"Thanks. Call me if ... find ... hotel."

"Will do. How's the chopper ride?"

After a short silence, he said, "Tell you later. Find ... hotel."

"Will do." She ended the call. Frank didn't sound like he was enjoying the chopper ride.

She checked Jackie's browser cache again. No hotel websites on the list.

She searched on *Memphis Airport*, called up the map and hit the button for *Nearby Hotels*.

Damn it to hell! There were dozens of them dotting the map.

She heard footsteps in the hall and Tony entered the office.

"Is the cake done yet?" he said, his dark eyes mischievous.

"How about a plane reservation for Jackie instead?"

Tony's face lit up. "You found one?"

"Yes. Departing Memphis airport tomorrow morning. I just got off the phone with Frank."

"Fantastic! I now pronounce you ... Supersleuth!"

Kelly laughed. "For a second there I thought you were gonna say man and wife. But I need to find out where they're staying, and there must be three dozen hotels near the airport."

"Better update Vobitch," Tony said. "Your turn. I did it last time."

"He won't be thrilled that Frank's in a chopper with Claudia headed for Memphis."

"Use your charm, Kelly. Tell him we know Jackie's in Memphis. That should make him happy." Tony shrugged. "If you don't find their hotel, Frank can grab her at the Memphis airport tomorrow morning."

CHAPTER 34

Nicolas drove into the Holiday Inn Express parking lot and spotted Martina's silver Toyota off to his right, parked near a tall wooden fence at the far end of the property. He parked beside the Toyota and motioned her to join him.

She got out of her car and slid into the passenger seat, holding her purse and a bottle of water in her hand.

"Did you find out what room she's in?" he asked.

Martina looked at him, eyes narrowed, her mouth set in an ugly line. "Is that the best you can do? No hello? No thank you for spending my entire day doing what you asked me to do?"

He wanted to slap her.

Thought about what would happen if he did. Nothing good.

He caressed her cheek. "Sorry, Martina. I didn't mean to upset you. But I've been busy too."

"What about Nicky? It's almost dinner time. What will he eat for dinner?"

"He'll cook a frozen dinner or call out for pizza and have them deliver it. Nicky's very resourceful, thanks to you. You're a great mother."

Her expression softened. "And you're a great father, but I worry about you sometimes. You're so ..." Martina shrugged. "So Russian. That guy in the Woody Allen film described it perfectly. To love is to suffer. To avoid suffering one must not love, but then one suffers from not loving."

He stared at her. What the hell was this? Martina, the philosopher?

But deep down, he knew she was right. After his father died, had he not vowed never to love another person again?

"All Russians have dark moods," he said. "You should know. Your father is Russian."

"My father can be volatile, but ..." Martina licked her lips. "You're so detached, Nicolas. It's like you turn off your feelings."

He said nothing. Martina did not play chess. Did not understand that in chess there was danger everywhere, coming from many directions at once. Chess was a deadly game, to be played fearlessly. Ferociously.

Emotions got in the way. In chess and in life.

"Where's Jackie?" he said.

Martina sighed. "In Room 210 on the second floor."

He took the snub-nosed .22 revolver out of the glove compartment. "Show me where it is."

"Nicolas!" she gasped. "Why are you taking a gun?"

"Martina, when you were living with your father, you knew his men had guns. Did you ask what they would do with them? No. If you had, your father would have punished you. Take me to Jackie's room."

"What will you do when we get there?" Gazing at him, eyes fearful.

"Never mind. You will take the kids out to your car. I'll handle Jackie."

————

4:20 PM

Jackie dug the toiletry bag out of her suitcase and parked the suitcase between her bed and the wall. Maybe if she took a Tylenol, her head would stop throbbing. Danny was stretched out on the bed nearest the window with a pillow behind his head, a sour expression on his face, thumbing through the hotel brochure. Sulking.

She pointed at the table lamp between their beds. "Turn on the light, so you can see better."

"What's to see?" Danny flung the brochure on the bed. "This hotel sucks. It doesn't even have a swimming pool. There's nothing to do! And now it's raining. Can I go get a Pepsi?"

"Not now. It's too close to dinner. I'll order takeout pizza and have them deliver it."

From her child-sized cot near the bathroom door, Nora said, "Mommy, I'm tired. And hungry."

Fearing she was coming down with something, Jackie pressed her hand to Nora's forehead. It didn't seem like she had a temperature. She was just tired after a long day in the car. "I'm going to order pizza soon," she said. "Take a little nap while I wash my face."

Inside the bathroom, she ran cool water over a facecloth and held it against her bloodshot eyes to soothe them. After a minute she hung it on a metal rack and gazed into the mirror. Her face was pale and dark hollows showed under her eyes. Would this nightmare ever end?

She took a bottle of Tylenol out of her toiletry bag, popped two in her mouth and washed them down with a plastic cupful of water. She had to be strong for the kids. Only one more day.

Then let Mom take over. And her father. She had to admit he was great with the kids.

All she wanted to do was sleep. But she wouldn't sleep much tonight, not with the drone of planes taking off from the airport and incessant traffic on the highway near the hotel.

"Mom," Danny called. "Can I watch TV?"

Her heart jolted. Fearing he might stumble upon a newscast, news that she didn't want him to see, she opened the bathroom door. Nora was dozing on the cot. Danny was holding the clicker.

"Not now, Danny. Give me the clicker."

He made a face and gave it to her. "I'm hungry, Mom. I need a snack and some Pepsi."

She massaged her aching forehead. Would the world come to an end if Danny didn't eat his dinner? Why not keep him happy? Then he'd stop nagging her.

"Okay. Hold on and I'll give you some money."

She took took her purse off the bed, took a ten dollar bill out of her wallet and gave it to him. "No junk food and no candy. Get a package of crackers and cheese, and a can of Pepsi."

"Thanks, Mom." Danny put the bill in his pocket and headed for the door.

"Can I go too?" Nora said, sitting up on her cot, rubbing her eyes.

She wanted to scream. *One more day.*

"Go get your snack, Danny, but leave the door open a crack so you can get back in the room. In case I'm taking a shower or something."

Smiling broadly, Danny went out the door but didn't close it completely, leaving it ajar.

"Why can't I go too?" Nora said in her whiny voice.

"Danny will share when he comes back. Come sit on my bed while I find a movie for you on TV, okay?"

"Okay." Hugging her stuffed bunny, Nora climbed onto the bed.

Jackie turned on the TV and surfed the Kids Channel.

After a moment, Nora said, "That's a good one. I saw it before, but let's watch it again."

Relieved, Jackie rose from the bed, took out her cellphone and said, "Stay here and watch the movie while I make a phone call."

Now that she was safe in Memphis, she could call Frank Renzi and tell him about the recording Richie had made.

Tell him she wasn't the one who wanted Richie dead, Nicolas was.

She stepped into the bathroom but left the door open so she could watch Nora.

———

4:30 PM – Memphis

Relieved to be out of the chopper, Frank walked along the hallway beside Claudia. Tonto and Roger were ten yards ahead of them. The Memphis FBI office had no helipad, so they had landed at a private airport, nine miles north of Memphis International Airport.

Striding along beside him, Claudia said, "Want to call Kelly and see if she found anything?"

"No. She'll call if she finds Jackie booked into a Memphis hotel."

His cellphone rang. He checked the ID. Grabbed Claudia's arm. "It's Jackie!" He stepped into an alcove beside a restroom and answered. "Frank Renzi."

"Frank, it's Jackie." Speaking rapidly in a low voice, she said, "I found something important. Richie left me a thumb drive with an audio tape of a conversation he had with Nicolas."

Frank locked eyes with Claudia. "A tape of Richie talking to Nicolas? What did he say?"

"They were talking about betting on NBA games. Richie said Benny was placing bets for him, but Benny didn't know he was giving tips on the games to Nicolas."

Blown away, Frank said, "Where are you now?"

"Two weeks before he was murdered, Richie got a subpoena ordering him to testify in a federal court in New Jersey. That's why he made the tape. To implicate Benny and Nicolas. To prove he wasn't doing it on his own. But Nicolas came to my house this morning and threatened me."

"Tell me where you are! We'll protect you."

"I'm flying to New York to stay with my parents. My father will protect us. Hold on, Danny went downstairs to get a snack and ... "

Frank waited, anxiously pacing back and forth. That explained what Nicolas was after. But Jackie had the tape and she wouldn't tell him where she was.

"What's going on?" Claudia said, frowning at him.

He shook his head. Pressed his cellphone against one ear, covered the other with his free hand to block out extraneous sounds from the nearby hallway.

Suddenly he heard some sort of commotion.

Then screams. Then nothing.

Agitated, he said to Claudia, "Jackie's in trouble. I think Nicolas got her. Go rent us a car at the nearest rental place."

"The BU-car will pick us up," she said. "Tonto called for one."

"I'm not riding with Tonto. Go rent us a fucking car. A dark sedan, powerful, with GPS." She stared at him, wide-eyed. "Go!" he said. "Pick me up outside after you get it. I'm calling Memphis PD."

He watched Claudia hustle down the hallway and dialed 911.

"What is your emergency?" said a female voice.

"This is Homicide Detective Frank Renzi, New Orleans police. I need to talk to a detective right away."

"Hold on, sir. I'll connect you."

A moment later a male voice said, "Detective Jones. What's your emergency?"

"An assault in a hotel near the airport. This is Frank Renzi speaking, NOPD homicide. A woman called me for help but then I heard a commotion and the line went dead."

"Why didn't she call 911?"

Asshole. Frank clenched his jaw. "She's got two kids with her and a man with a gun wants to kill her. I don't know where she's staying, but any minute now you're going to get a 911 call from a hotel. When you do, call me immediately."

He ended the call and dialed Jackie's number.

It went straight to voicemail.

CHAPTER 35

DAY 11 MONDAY OCTOBER 20, 2014 – 4:30 PM – Memphis

Rigid with fear, Jackie stood at the foot of her bed, her heart a wild animal, clawing her chest.

"Where's Nora? Why did Martina take her?"

Ten feet away, holding her cellphone in his hand, Nicolas stood in front of the television set. "Martina took her downstairs so I could talk to you alone. Where's Danny?"

She said nothing thinking, *Please don't come back now, Danny. Run away as fast as you can!*

"Danny!" Nicolas yelled. "If you're in the bathroom, come out now and talk to me."

Silence, but for the thumping of her heart.

"He's not here," she said, her voice quavering.

"Yes he is. His suitcase is on the bed." Nicolas came closer, looming over her, his cold granite-black eyes fixed on hers.

Her mouth went dry and her stomach clenched.

She thought about the knife in her suitcase. But the suitcase was behind her, wedged between the wall and her bed. She didn't dare turn and look at it.

"He wanted to … I let him go downstairs to get a snack. He said he was hungry."

Nicolas held up her cellphone. "Who were you talking to?"

"My parents. We're going to visit them. They'll worry if I don't call them back."

He studied her cellphone. "Liar. You called a Louisiana number ten minutes ago. Who were you talking talk to?"

His voice was dangerously quiet, which made it all the more unnerving. She tried to catch her breath and couldn't. Her fingertips went numb.

She had to do something. Distract him.

"I trusted you," she said. "So did Richie."

He looked at her with thinly disguised contempt. "I don't need to make excuses to you."

Of course not. Nicolas would never accept responsibility for what he and Richie had done. Which meant the responsibility lay elsewhere. With Richie. Or her.

"Where's Richie's laptop? You lied to me this morning. The cops didn't take it. His laptop was on the desk in his office last night."

She stared at him. How could he possibly know that?

Was he spying on her, prowling around outside her house at night? Having Martina watch her when he wasn't home?

"How do you know?"

A menacing smile. "I went in his office last night. While you were having dinner."

Dinner with Martina. Tears glazed her eyes. The idea that this despicable man had been in her house last night sickened her. And Martina, the woman she thought was her best friend, was helping him.

"Where's Richie's laptop?"

"In the trunk of my car." *Let him take it. The important items are in my suitcase.*

"You better not be lying." He slid her cellphone into the pocket of his windbreaker and took out a gun.

The air left her lungs in a whoosh. Frantic questions buzzed her mind, setting off skyrockets of fear. Traffic on the highway roared past the hotel. No help there. If she screamed, would anyone hear? The drapes on the window were closed. Nicolas had locked and bolted the door.

What if Danny came back?

She stared at the gun. Metallic black with a short barrel. The opening aimed at her heart.

Dead silence in the room. The drumbeat of her heart sounding in her ears.

"I know you've got the subpoena," Nicolas said, his implacable eyes boring into hers. "I saw it in your desk drawer last night in your office. What else did Richie give you?"

Overcome with dread, she couldn't speak. He was going to kill her.

Terrified, she dug her nails into the palms of her hands.

If Danny comes back, he'll kill us both.

———

Frustrated and angry, Nicolas gestured with the gun. "Stop stalling. I know you found the subpoena. What about the tape? Did Richie give it to you?"

Jackie flinched, gazing at him, her eyes fearful.

"Where is it? Tell me or I'll go downstairs and shoot Nora."

"No!" she screamed. "Bring Nora back to the room and I'll tell you."

"Don't try to bargain with me. Where's the tape?"

"Why should I tell you? If I do, you'll kill me and my children!"

He shoved her to the floor and aimed the gun at her heart.

"Tell me or you're dead."

Her face went slack with fear. "It's in my suitcase. Please don't shoot Nora."

"I will if you're lying." He put the suitcase on the bed and opened it. Flung aside pants, several tops and a pair of shoes in a plastic bag. Metal glinted in the bottom of the suitcase. A knife.

He turned and looked at her, curled up against the wall.

"What were you going to do? Stab me?"

She stared at him, slack-jawed, mouth open, chest heaving.

He explored the suitcase. Beside the knife were two envelopes. He opened one and his heart surged. A thumb drive. He looked in the other envelope. A wad of hundred-dollar bills.

"Where are your car keys?"

Her eyes brimmed with tears. And defeat.

"In my handbag. On the bedside table."

He went to the table and opened the handbag. Found her wallet and a set of keys. One was a fob to open her Kia. He tossed them on the bed beside the knife, the thumb drive and the cash.

Returning to Jackie, he stood over her with the gun.

"Don't shoot," she moaned. "I made a—"

Avoiding her eyes, he squeezed the trigger. Her body went slack on the floor, blood oozing from her head onto the carpet.

Conscious of the passing minutes, he took her shoes out of the plastic bag and tossed them aside. Put her cellphone, the thumb drive and the cash into the plastic bag, and shoved Jackie's keys in his pocket.

Martina had taken Nora down to her car, but where was Danny?

The shot from his .22 caliber revolver wasn't too loud, but someone in the adjacent room or the hallway might have heard it. No time to wipe down the room to eliminate fingerprints.

And no time to find Danny. He had to get out of here fast.

Gripping the revolver in his right hand, he went to the door. After Martina left with Nora, he'd bolted it so no one could interrupt him. With the knuckles of his left hand, he flipped the bolt on the door. Using the sleeve of his windbreaker, he opened the door a crack. Listened for sounds.

Hearing none, he eased open the door and checked the hallway.

No one in the hall. He shut the door behind him and ran down the hall. To the left of the elevator was an emergency staircase. He opened the door and raced down the stairs.

On the first floor, he peered through a window in the door. Only half the lobby was visible, not the registration desk, just an older man in a chair, reading a brochure. No Danny.

He opened the exterior door and stepped out into drizzly rain. Far off to the west, the sun was setting, an orange glow. To the north, the sky was black with clouds. Jackie's red Kia was parked around the corner from the front entrance. He wanted Richie's laptop, but first he had to tell Martina to get out of here. He put the revolver in the pocket of his windbreaker.

In the distance, he heard sirens approaching.

Damn! Someone had called the cops.

He ran to Martina's Toyota parked near the fence that enclosed three sides of the parking lot. When he tapped on Martina's window, she lowered it and cool air hit him in the face.

Clearly unhappy, she looked at him but said nothing.

In the back seat, Nora was buckled into a seat-belt, crying loudly.

"Nora," he said. "Be a good girl and stop crying."

"I want Mommy," she wailed. "Where's Mommy?"

"Mommy is fine," he said. "Stop crying."

The sirens were closer now.

Leaning closer to Martina, he whispered, "You need to get out of here. The police are coming. Get on the highway and drive to your father's house."

Martina frowned. "Why? What do—"

"Just do it," he hissed. "I don't have time to explain. I need to get something out of my trunk. Don't wait for me. I'll be right behind you."

"What about Nicky?"

"Martina," he said sternly. "Just go. I'll call Nicky and tell him what to do. After you get on the highway, stop at a rest area and get Nora something to eat. Tell her Danny's with Mom and everything will be fine. Buy some NyQuil and give it to her, so she'll fall asleep."

"I hate you!" Nora screamed from the back seat. "Mommy hates you, too!"

He locked eyes with Martina. "Go. Now. I'll catch up with you on the highway."

Like hell he would. Grab Richie's laptop and he was out of here.

Martina put up the window and drove toward the entrance of the parking lot.

He ran to Jackie's Kia and opened the trunk with her key fob. Two laptops. One was Richie's, the other must be Jackie's. Holding one in each hand, he sprinted to his car. Martina's car was gone. But the sirens were closer.

In a minute they'd be here.

He tossed the laptops on the back seat of the BMW and got behind the wheel.

Without turning on the headlights, he drove toward the street and stopped at the exit.

His heart catapulted into his throat. Flashing blue lights were a half block away and closing fast, sirens whooping.

He held his breath.

Heaved a sigh of relief as the police car flew past him, heading east.

He turned left, heading west, and floored the accelerator.

The cops weren't after him yet, but soon they would be.

CHAPTER 36

DAY 11 MONDAY OCTOBER 20, 2014 – 4:45 PM – Memphis

A bolt of lightning flashed, then rolling thunder, the sky black with clouds. Sheltered by the overhang outside the helipad terminal, Frank waited impatiently, Jackie's truncated scream ringing in his mind.

He needed to find her ASAP. She had to be staying near the airport, but here he was, miles away, no car, no control over anything, and no news about Jackie. Now it was rush hour. Traffic would be heavy and heavy rain would cause even more delays. Sick with anxiety, he clenched his fists.

What about Danny and Nora? Where were they?

A navy-blue four-door sedan pulled to the curb, Claudia behind the wheel. Rain splattered the sidewalk as he dashed to the car. He opened the back door and slung his gym bag on the seat.

He slammed the door shut, got in the shotgun seat and said, "Good choice. Dark and innocuous, no antennas."

"Two out of three was the best I could do. The only one they had with GPS wasn't ready." Claudia looked over and said, "And we're in a hurry, right?"

"Damn right we are. Head for the Memphis Airport. Jackie must have rented a room nearby." A deluge of rain splattered the windshield. Claudia turned on the wipers and pulled away from the curb.

When they reached the main road, two lanes of traffic were inching along, but Claudia muscled her way into the right hand lane and said, "Jesus, at this rate it will take us a while to get there. Did you talk to Memphis PD?"

"Yes. Detective Jones didn't seem too interested until I told him a man with a gun was threatening a woman with two kids in a hotel. He's got my number, said he'd call me if Memphis PD gets any 9-11 calls from a hotel."

"How did Zurik know Jackie and the kids were in Memphis?"

"His wife is helping him. Probably saw Jackie leave her house."

"And followed them." Claudia cut into the left lane which was moving faster. "Can you start calling the hotels on your Smartphone?"

"No. I'm waiting for Jones to call me." A sea of red brake lights lit up ahead of them. If they'd landed the chopper at the Memphis airport, they'd already be there. But Tonto was in charge and Murphy had told him where to land.

"I already called Kelly," he said. "She's calling the airport hotels looking for Jackie, said she'd called nine of them, sixteen more to go."

They passed a big green sign that said: **3 Miles to Memphis International Airport.** A minute later traffic loosened up as several cars took another exit.

"Did you talk to Tonto?" Frank said.

"Yes. He wasn't happy about me renting a car."

"Fuck Tonto. He reports to Murphy and Murphy doesn't give a shit about Jackie."

"You're worried about the kids," Claudia said.

"Aren't you?"

"Of course. But do you really think Zurik would harm Jackie while the kids are there?"

Frank pictured Nicolas Zurik, the man with the genial smile and the cold hard eyes. If Zurik wanted something badly enough, he would kill anyone who got in his way.

"He might have killed them too. Before someone took the phone away from her, Jackie told me Zurik threatened her this morning. She's got a tape that Richie made before he was murdered. A tape that implicates Zurik in the betting scheme. You think he wouldn't kill to get it?"

Claudia looked over, somber-eyed. "I think we better find Jackie and the kids pronto."

———

4:55 PM – Memphis

Nicolas drove into the motel parking lot, a two-story Mom and Pop motel with outside walkways. Four vehicles with Tennessee plates were parked in front near the rental office, two cheap sedans and two trucks with NRA decals.

He circled the gray stucco building, ten rooms facing the roadway in front, ten more above them. Same thing in back. The first floor rooms had blue doors, yellow doors on the upper level.

On the westbound side of the roadway opposite the motel, bright lights on tall poles lit up a 24-hour Shell station with a convenience store. He was certain the station had security cameras but none that would show the parking lot behind the motel. Still, he backed the BMW into a space against a low metal fence so his Louisiana plate wasn't visible.

He had not played a serious game of chess for many years. But one reason he'd stayed alive this long was by thinking many moves ahead.

That, and trusting his instincts.

Rain spattered the windshield and distant thunder rumbled. He put the .22 in his duffle bag, took out a pair of horn-rimmed glasses and a St. Louis Cardinals baseball cap and put them on. Papa had taught him well.

To create a disguise, begin with the face, then the clothing. "Build up enough layers," Papa had said, "you disappear and become another person."

Which was exactly what Nicolas intended to do. As soon as possible.

Pelted by rain, he got out and dashed around the motel to the office.

A twenty-something kid behind the registration desk looked up and said, "Rotten weather, ain't it?"

"The pits," Nicolas said. "I need a room for two nights, but traffic noise keeps me awake. Got anything around back?"

"No problem," the kid said, brushing lank brown hair from his face. "Rooms in back cost you forty bucks a night. First floor or second?"

"Second." He gave the kid a credit card. The name on it was Anthony King.

The kid smiled, revealing nicotine stained teeth. "I need your driver's license too."

He gave him the one Alexei had sent him. Anthony King's DL, with an address in St. Louis, Missouri. The kid glanced at it and gestured at his baseball cap. "You a Cardinals fan?"

"Big time," he said, smiling. "Ever since I can remember."

Tapping on his computer, the clerk entered Anthony King's credit card and license information.

Five minutes later, a flight of cement stairs took him up to the second floor. The motel had no restaurant and no room service, but on the way to his room he'd passed an ice maker and a vending machine with soda and snacks. Using the key card, he open the door and entered the room.

The hot stuffy air smelled of cigarette smoke. He flicked a light switch, lowered the temperature on the air conditioner unit beside the door and turned the fan on high. Hung his black windbreaker in the closet on the other side of the door and set his canvas duffle on the luggage rack beside the closet. Inside were his weapons, a trash bag full of cash, and items from Jackie's suitcase: her cellphone, the thumb drive, an envelope with hundred dollar bills, and the knife.

Ahead of him was an open bathroom door. To his right, set against the wall, a double bed was neatly made. Enticing after this interminable, exhausting day, but sleep could wait. He needed a shower.

He put his laptop on the bed. Richie's laptop and Jackie's were locked in his trunk. Stifling a yawn, he turned on the lamp on the bedside table, opened the drawer and laughed. A naked woman smiled up at him from the cover of an adult magazine with ads for strippers, call girls and massage parlors. Tempting, but he couldn't afford to waste what little energy he had left on sex.

Opposite the bed, a three-drawer dresser held a television set. After he took a shower, he'd check the news to see if they'd found Jackie.

In the bathroom fresh towels and toiletries sat on the vanity, a small tube of toothpaste, sample-sized bottles of shampoo and body wash.

He stripped off his clothes, got in the shower and let hot water beat on his body. Soaped every inch of his skin, scrubbing it until it turned red.

But no amount of scrubbing could erase the guilt he felt or Jackie's accusing eyes, still vivid in his mind.

He had never killed a woman.

Recalling the tepid water in Roland's apartment, he shut his eyes and saw Roland's face. The image shifted to Jackie, dead on the hotel floor. His mind guilt-tripping him.

What would Papa think? Had he ever killed a woman?

Nicolas groaned and banged his forehead against the tile.

Stop agonizing over Jackie. What's done is done. Focus on the goal.

Get out of Memphis and disappear.

In London, many men had been made to disappear on orders from the vory leader. They vanished, never to be seen again. They were dead. But he wasn't.

He got out of the shower, toweled off and a prodigious yawn wracked him.

Gathering his soiled clothes, he took them in the room and dumped them on the floor beside his duffle. He put on clean underwear and his black running suit. Exhausted, he stretched out on the bed and reviewed his endless day.

Threatening Jackie this morning. Eliminating evidence in his office. Following Martina and Jackie to Memphis.

Jackie was dead. Martina had Nora, but where was Danny?

Then he remembered Jackie's cellphone. He got up and retrieved it from his duffle and sat on the bed. It was low on power and the message light was blinking. He accessed her voicemail and listened to the message.

He knew that voice. Renzi! Telling her to call him back, it was urgent.

What did she tell Renzi before he took the phone away from her? Did she tell him where she was? Equally crucial, where was Renzi?

In New Orleans? Or in a car headed for Memphis?

He had to leave Memphis as soon as possible. But not on a plane.

After the cops found Jackie, they would monitor the airport, and he was certain Renzi had the plate number on his BMW.

That's why he'd chosen a motel near the train station. Take a train to Canada, use his new passport and fly to London. Alexei would help him.

His cellphone buzzed. He grabbed it off the bedside table. Martina calling him. He dismissed the call and blocked her number.

He didn't want to talk to Martina. He might never talk to her again.

But he would never abandon Nicky. That would require a different plan.

CHAPTER 37

"Where the hell is she?" Frank said. "I talked to her more than an hour ago."

Beside him in the rental car, Claudia said, "Maybe Zurik took her cellphone and she locked herself in the bathroom."

"She's not in the bathroom," he snapped. "She's dead."

Claudia looked at him but said nothing. They were parked outside a Days Inn, the first hotel on the airport access road. He'd already gone in to see if Jackie Bauer was registered there. She wasn't.

Holding her iPad, Claudia said, "The map shows nearby hotels. Want to try the next one?"

"No. It's a waste of time. Kelly said there were dozens of hotels near the airport."

"By now she must have eliminated some of them. Call her and—"

"I don't want to tie up the phone."

"You really think Zurik killed her?"

"Claudia, he's got a gun. And we know he's a killer."

His cellphone rang and he grabbed it. "Frank Renzi."

"This is Detective Larry Jones. We spoke a few minutes ago. I'm at the Holiday Inn Express a couple of miles south of the airport. We got a dead female in one of the rooms."

Even though he expected it, Frank felt like someone punched him in the gut. "What's the address?"

Jones told him and he repeated it for Claudia, who plugged it into her iPad.

"What happened?" Frank said.

"Her son left the room to get a snack, came back and the door was locked. He knocked on the door, but nobody answered, so he peeked through a gap in the window curtain and saw his mom on the floor, bleeding. He ran down to the desk and told them to call 911. We got there four minutes later, found the mother dead on the floor. One gunshot to the head."

"Where's the girl? Danny's sister."

"She wasn't in the room when we got here."

"They took her."

"Jesus Christ!" Jones said. "This is a kidnapping?"

"Yes. Put out a BOLO on two cars. I'll text you the info." He showed Claudia the phone number and said to Jones, "She's in one of the cars. Put out the BOLO. Now! Where's Danny?"

"In a squad car with Detective Billups. He's pretty shook up, but Nadine's good with kids."

"I need to talk to him. What's Nadine's phone number?"

"I need you to tell me what the hell is going on," Jones said.

"Someone murdered Danny's father and we believe the killer was after Jackie. I'll explain when I get there. What's Nadine's phone number?"

Jones gave it to him. Frank dialed the number and motioned to Claudia. "Get us to the hotel ASAP while I talk to Danny."

A female voice spoke in his ear, "Nadine Billups."

He heard sobbing in the background. "Nadine, this is NOPD Homicide Detective Frank Renzi. Detective Jones gave me your number. How's Danny? He must be freaking out."

"Affirmative," Nadine said quietly. "Keeps saying it's his fault. I told him it wasn't, but ..."

"Let me talk to him. He knows me. Tell him it's Detective Frank Renzi."

Moments later a quavery voice said, "Hello?"

"Danny, I know you feel terrible right now, but Nadine will help you and—"

"Where's Nora? My mom's dead and Nora's gone!"

"And we're going to find her. Was Nora in the room when you left to get a snack?"

"I should never have left! It's my fault Mom is dead. I should have protected her!"

"Danny, it's not your fault."

"Yes it is!! All day long I was mean to her. Complaining that I didn't want to go."

"Danny, here's the important thing. You're safe and we're going to find Nora. But you've got a right to be upset. Someone killed your dad, and now your mother is gone."

"She's not GONE! She's dead!! Nora's the one that's gone."

Frank puffed his cheeks, groping for words. "Dozens of cops are looking for her, Danny. But we need you to help us. When you came back to the room, did you see anyone in the hall?"

"No. I shouldn't have left. I should have stayed—"

"Danny, listen to me. You were very brave. You did exactly the right thing. Went downstairs and told the desk clerk to call the police. If you'd been in the room, you might be dead, too."

"Why did they kill her?"

Frank hesitated a moment, debating with himself, then said, "Did Mr. Zurik come to your house this morning?"

"Yes. To talk to Mom. But I don't know what they talked about. Nora and I went outside."

"Does your friend Nicky ever talk about his mother's family? Maybe mention where they live?"

"I'm not sure. I think he said they lived in New York City."

"New York City," Frank said. "That's a big help, Danny."

"Why? Is Nicky here in Memphis?"

"Thanks for your help, Danny. Can I talk to Nadine?"

"You have to find Nora! Right away! I'm worried about her."

"I am too, Danny, but we're going to find her." *Hopefully alive.*

After a moment Nadine spoke into his ear. "Frank, we need to contact Danny's relatives."

"My colleague will call them, but I'm worried about Danny. I'm not big on meds, but he needs something to calm him down and help him sleep. Can you call social services? Get him some meds and find him a place to sleep? He can't stay there."

"Totally agree on all fronts. I'll make some calls and take care of that."

"Thanks. I'll have my NOPD colleague call Danny's grandparents. She's talked to them before. Can you keep me informed on what's happening with Danny? I'd really appreciate it."

"Of course. I'll call you after I get things organized."

Frank ended the call. "Damn it to hell! They took Nora. And Danny's in bad shape."

Barreling down the roadway, gripping the wheel, Claudia said, "I can't imagine what the poor kid is thinking. But you did what you could. Said all the right things, calmed him down. You even got some information. Martina's parents live in New York City?"

"Maybe. Danny wasn't sure. It was risky, asking him about Nicolas. Seemed like he didn't make the connection—Mom's dead and Zurik was at his house this morning—but later he might."

He called Kelly and told her what had happened.

"That's horrible!" Kelly said. "They took Nora? And Danny's down there all by himself?"

"Exactly. Right now he's with a female detective. She'll get him a place to stay. I told her you'd contact his grandparents. Can you call Jackie's parents and get them down here? Don't tell them Nora's missing. They'll already be freaking out about Jackie."

"I'll try, but Jackie's father will want to know what's going on, control freak that he is. You think Martina's got Nora?"

"I'm not sure. Better Martina than Nicolas. Memphis PD put out a BOLO on both their cars. Tell Jackie's father that Danny's with a female police detective, and they need to get down here ASAP. At this point I'm not telling Memphis PD much. Too many agencies with different agendas. Claudia and I are on our way to the crime scene."

"I'll call Jackie's parents," Kelly said. "Call me right away with any news about Nora."

———

Nicolas paced his motel room, his cellphone clamped to his ear. The manager at Executive Limo Service was calculating how much it would cost to drive Nicky from Ponchatoula to O'Hare Airport in Chicago. Nicky was too young to fly or take a train by himself. Someone had to be with him when he boarded.

That wasn't going to happen.

He had to get Nicky out of the house before the cops went there.

"Hello, Mr. King?" the limo manager said. "One of our drivers can make the trip tonight, but he'd need to drive back, so the round-trip is rather expensive. Twenty-five hundred dollars."

"Not a problem. I'm calling at the last minute, so let's round it up to three thousand, provided he can pick up my nephew tonight."

"Joe can be here in thirty minutes. Another forty minutes to Ponchatoula, he could pick up your nephew by seven at the latest."

"Excellent. Let me give you my credit card." He recited Anthony King's credit card information and said, "Please run it now, so I'll know it's all set."

"Certainly, sir. One moment."

Again he waited, anxiously pacing the room. So much to do, so little time. Call Nicky and give him instructions, book his own ticket to Chicago ...

"You're all set, Mr. King. I just need the address where Joe will pick him up."

"He'll be eating dinner with his mom at Pizza Pronto. Tom loves pizza."

"Don't they all. Seems like that's all they eat at that age."

He recited the address and said, "It's not far from Route 55. Easy to find."

"No worries. The car has GPS. Anything else you need?"

"What color is the car? So I can tell Tom what to look for."

"It's a silver Audi, a four-door sedan, air-conditioned, clean and comfortable. Bottled water and snacks in the back seat."

"Perfect. Thanks for accommodating me on short notice."

"My pleasure, Mr. King. I'm texting you a receipt for payment. Have a great evening."

Nicolas ended the call and massaged his eyes, desperate for sleep. But he had to call Nicky. He hit a speed dial number on his cellphone and waited.

Nicky answered right away. "Hey Dad, what's up? You working late?"

"Not exactly. Remember that day when I told you we might have to leave town someday?"

"Yes. You told me not to talk about it. Just between you and me, you said."

"Correct. That day has arrived so listen carefully. Mum's driving to New York to stay with her father for a while. I'm headed to Chicago and I need you to meet me there."

"Cool!" Nicky said. "Tell me what to do."

"Go upstairs to my bedroom. In my closet you'll find a safe with a digital keypad. Punch in your birth year and it will open, got it?"

"Got it. What's in the safe?"

"Your passport and an envelope with two grand in cash. Take the passport and the cash and shut the safe. It will lock by itself. Put the passport and the money in your knapsack and pack enough clothes for two or three days. Be sure to take your cellphone. Have you had dinner?"

"Not yet. I was waiting for you and Mom."

"Okay, here's the fun part. When you're ready to go, lock the house and leave by the back door. Remember the path behind the house we use when we go for pizza?"

"Sure. The one that takes us to Pizza Pronto."

"Exactly. Walk to Pizza Pronto and have dinner. Get whatever you like and pay cash for it. I've hired a limo service to drive you to O'Hare Airport in Chicago."

"Wow! That is so cool! Is that where I meet you?"

"Hold on. The limo driver's name is Joe. Your name is Tom. Here's your cover story. You've been staying in Ponchatoula with your aunt and you're meeting your father in Chicago. Got that?"

Nicky laughed. "You mean like Double-O-Seven?"

Amused, he said, "Yes, but you won't be having any martinis. Repeat what I told you, so I know you won't forget anything."

"Open your safe with my birth year. Take my passport and the cash and close the safe. Put the passport and the money in my knapsack with my clothes. Don't forget my cellphone. Lock the house and walk to Pizza Pronto. Eat dinner, pay with cash and the limo will pick me up."

"Excellent. The limo will be there by seven, a silver Audi sedan. It's a long drive to Chicago, fourteen hours, so try to sleep. When Joe lets you off at the airport, don't let him come in with you. Tell him you know where to meet me. Tip him with a couple of twenties. Okay so far?"

"Got it, Dad. Is this my first assignment as an operative? Like the ones you used to do when you were in London?"

Pained at the thought, Nicolas closed his eyes. Years ago he had vowed never to let his beloved son get involved in this filthy business.

But unforeseen events had blindsided him. You might think you know what's going to happen in life, but you don't.

And unforeseen surprises were rarely good ones.

"You're not an operative, Nicky. This is a field test, like the ones I did when I was your age. I won't be at O'Hare Airport when you get there. I can't get to Chicago until tomorrow. I'll meet you at the train station tomorrow afternoon."

As long as everything goes as planned.

"So how come I'm going to the airport?"

"When you get to the airport, it will already be ten o'clock tomorrow morning. Go inside and walk around, stretch your legs and see the shops. Find the food court and eat breakfast. Okay, so far?"

"Yes. Tell me the rest, Dad! I can't wait to get going!"

"If anyone asks… I doubt that they will, but if they do, tell them your father's plane is arriving in two hours and you're waiting to meet him. Find a place to sit down and relax. But keep an eye on the time. At two o'clock, take a taxi to the train station. Are we okay?"

"Yes. Hang out at O'Hare until two o'clock, take a taxi to the train station and you'll be there."

"Very good. I'm texting you a phone number. If you run into a problem, call Alexei. He's a friend of mine in London."

"What kind of problem, Dad?"

In case I don't show up, which means I'm dead.

"Don't worry, Nicky. See you tomorrow."

Exhausted, he ended the call and sank onto the bed. Sleep. He needed to sleep. But first, he'd better find out if the Memphis cops had found Jackie.

He used the clicker to turn on the TV and found a local station.

Damn it to bloody hell! A news bulletin about a missing girl, possibly kidnapped. Then two photos flashed on the screen: his black BMW and Martina's silver Toyota, including the plate numbers.

"If you see these cars," the reporter said, "call Memphis Police."

He shut off the TV and massaged his throbbing temples. At the moment his BMW was safe where it was, the Louisiana license plate on the back hidden.

But later it wouldn't be.

Another problem to solve.

CHAPTER 38

They got to Jackie's hotel in record time, Claudia cutting off other drivers, ignoring curses and middle fingers. Strobe lights on four MPD cruisers pulsed red and blue light over the Holiday Inn Express exterior. A wide swath of crime scene tape blocked the entrance.

"No discussion about Jackie or Zurik," Frank said. "Our first priority is finding Nora."

"I agree," Claudia said. "But Detective Jones won't be thrilled about having an FBI agent walk through his crime scene."

"Won't be happy to see me either, but he better not fuck with me."

He got out of the car and hot air hit him like a blast furnace. Even at twilight it had to be over ninety. No rain now, just misty drizzle. They approached a sweaty-faced cop in a bright yellow rain slicker outside the police tape.

Frank flashed his badge. "Homicide Detective Frank Renzi, NOPD. Where's Detective Jones?"

The cop frowned. "Upstairs in the room, but—"

"Call him and tell him I'm here. We need to talk to him."

"Right now," Claudia said firmly.

The cop stepped away and spoke into his radio handset. Took his time coming back. Gave them a sullen look and lifted the police tape. "He's upstairs in Room 210."

On the second floor, Detective Jones stood in the hallway outside the room, a large black man, almost as big as Kenyon Miller, but without the charm. Glowering at them. No friendly greeting.

He looked at Frank and said, "Who's your partner?"

Claudia flashed her FBI creds. "Special Agent Claudia Cohen. We need to see the room."

"You need to tell me what's going on. Why the big interest in this woman?"

"Show us the room and we'll tell you," Frank said.

Jones shut his mouth, a muscle working in his jaw, and jerked open the door.

Frank went inside and stopped two paces from the door, studying the room. No sign of a struggle, no overturned chairs, no broken lamps. But in his experience, violence had a certain energy that lingered in the air. Like now.

"The body was in the far corner," Jones said. "Beyond the TV."

Cursing under his breath, Frank moved closer. No body now, just a chalk out-line on the floor. Blood stained the carpet where Jackie's head had been, blood spatter on the wall behind it.

Claudia joined him, saw the chalked outline and gave him a look. *What the hell?*

"Tell me why you're here," Jones said.

"Tell me why you waited so long to call me," Frank said.

"Just doing my job. Had to secure the crime scene and get the forensic team over here."

"And removed the body before we could see it."

"This is my investigation," Jones said belligerently. "I'll run it as I see fit."

"The victim is a resident of Louisiana," Frank said. "Her five-year-old daughter is missing. We gave you information on two cars so you could put out a BOLO."

"And you said you'd explain what was going on when you got here. So start talking."

"The victim is related to a recent murder in New Orleans, a case the NOPD Superintendent is very eager to solve. If you don't call me *immediately* when you find Nora and the cars, I'll call the NOPD Super and have him call your boss. Got it?"

Clearly unhappy, Jones glowered at him. "Who was she?"

"Detective Jones," Claudia said. "The New Orleans FBI office is involved in that case. Call Frank *immediately* with any information you get on Nora's whereabouts. You really don't want my boss to call your boss, trust me."

Jones took out a handkerchief and mopped his forehead. "Okay, you've made your point. I'll call you *immediately* when I get any information. I had a patrol cop take the boy's suitcase to the room Nadine rented for him."

Irritated, Frank said, "His name is Danny. His sister's name is Nora." He pointed at the small pink suitcase on a cot. "That's her suitcase. Have one of your officers take it to Danny's room."

"If you haven't found Nora by daybreak," Claudia said, "my FBI colleagues will go up in a chopper and start looking for her."

"You've got my number, correct?" Frank said.

"Yes I've got your number," Jones snapped. "I'll call you right away if we get anything."

"Thank you for your cooperation." He left the room and said to Claudia as they went down the stairs, "Just doing his job. Fucking asshole. But I think he got the message."

"Let's hope they find her fast," Claudia said.

When they got in the rental car, Frank said, "I need a shower. We need to rent a room."

"Tonto already rented one for him and Roger." When Frank looked over, she said, "I called him while you were in the Days Inn asking about Jackie. He wants to have a meeting."

"Okay, but I need a shower first. And dinner."

"That's what I figured. I rented us two rooms on the same floor. I'll order dinner from the hotel dining room and have it sent to my room for the meeting."

"Not before seven-thirty. I need to make some calls."

The first one wouldn't be pleasant. Vobitch would be bullshit.

Jackie dead, Nora missing, and no sign of Zurik.

———

7:00 PM

Nicolas paid for his train ticket with his Carl Birch credit card. A precautionary move. The limo service and the motel had his Anthony King credit card information. Exhausted, he sank onto the bed in his room, leaned back against the headboard and massaged his forehead.

At nine o'clock tomorrow morning he would board a train to Chicago. One problem solved, but others remained.

Was Renzi still in New Orleans or here in Memphis?

What did Jackie tell him? The Woman Who Knew Too Much.

Renzi also knew too much. A dangerous man. Cops could access driver's licenses and car registration information. He jerked upright.

Bloody hell! His photograph was on his license. Not a great likeness, but enough to identify him if he wasn't careful.

He had the skills to disappear, trade craft mastered years ago, once learned, never forgotten. He never walked into a room without assessing potential threats and locating the exits. His life depended upon it. Now more than ever.

When the stakes are life and death, analyze each move and weigh the risks. Only then could he determine his best moves. In life and in chess.

Driving around Memphis in a car with a Louisiana plate was a risk, but there were remedies for that. He'd pack his weapons, fake documents and credit cards in his duffle with half of his cash and lock the rest in the trunk with his laptop until he got to the train station.

A prodigious yawn wracked him. He desperately needed sleep, but he needed to know what the cops were doing. Know your enemy. Trust no one.

Jackie had told him Danny had gone downstairs to get a snack, but that was two hours ago. Danny must have returned to the room by now. Which meant the police must have found Jackie's body.

He flicked on the TV with the clicker. Damn it to hell! The same two photos appeared on the screen: his black BMW, Martina's silver Toyota, and their plate numbers. But now the Memphis police were seeking the drivers in connection with a shooting at a local hotel.

When Martina called earlier, he should have answered. If the cops caught her, Martina would call her father. A powerful mobster who ruled his gang by fear. To Pavel Volkovich, loyalty was a one-way street.

You will marry Martina and keep her happy.

An icy chill prickled his spine. He imagined Volkovich telling his hitman, "Nicolas abandoned my daughter. From now on, he is dead to me. Make him go away permanently." Cold. Bloodless.

Pavel Volkovich had connections all over the world.

Forget leaving Memphis. He had to leave the country as soon as possible.

After he moved to Ponchatoula, he'd begun sending money to Alexei in London. Alexei deposited it into an offshore account. Now he had amassed enough to finance several different escape routes: flights from cities in Canada and Mexico to other cities thousands of miles away.

Study the chessboard. Determine your opponent's weaknesses and strengths.

Papa's words. Nicolas would not make his move until he understood all the variables and possibilities, no matter how trivial.

Nothing was trivial, in life or in chess.

And he could not allow fatigue to dull his mind.

He shut off the TV and set the alarm on his cellphone for 2 AM.

To accomplish his tasks, he needed darkness.

Sleep a few hours, then go out and eliminate some problems.

———

7:35 PM

Frank's room at the Hamilton Suites Hotel sported a king-sized bed, a large TV set, a work desk and a comfortable easy chair. Nothing but the best for the fibbies. But now that he'd taken a shower and put on fresh clothes, he could no longer avoid the dreaded phone call.

He dialed a number on his cellphone and waited.

"Nice to hear from you, Frank. I thought you lost my number." Vobitch giving him sarcasm.

"Sorry, Morgan. But everything went to hell in Memphis. Kelly told you what happened, right?"

"Yes. Jackie's dead, Danny's safe and Nora's missing. Other than that everything's peachy."

"Zurik killed her. I'm not sure who's got Nora. The Memphis detective is a territorial asshole. By the time we got to Jackie's room, the body was gone. We leaned on him, told him he'd regret it if he didn't call me right away when they find Nora or the Zurik cars."

"Who's we? You and CC?"

"Morgan, she got us the chopper. But Murphy sent his minder."

"Fucking asswipe," Vobitch growled.

"Can you ask the NOPD Super to call Memphis PD and tell them to cooperate with us?"

"Sure, no problem. What's MPD doing to find the girl?"

"I told Detective Jones to put out a BOLO on the Zurik cars. The Tennessee state cops are looking for them. Nothing yet. Kelly's calling the grandparents to get them down here."

"Any idea where Zurik is?"

"No, but we figure he'll get out of Memphis as soon as he can."

"You think his wife's got the girl?"

"I hope so. Why would Nicolas take her? She's a liability."

"Exactly," Vobitch said. "He'd kill her and dump her somewhere. You better find him before Memphis PD grabs him."

"Can you get a warrant to search his house and his office? Maybe locate his credit card information to see if he's used them? That might tell us where he is or where he's going."

"I'll do that now. Don't tell CC. She reports to Murphy and—"

"I'm not telling anybody anything. I'm gonna find the sonofabitch and rip his balls off."

Vobitch chuckled. "I like the sound of that. Keep me posted."

Frank called Claudia's cellphone and said, "Be there in ten."

"Okay," she said. "Dinner just arrived. We'll keep yours warm."

He went in the bathroom and took two Tylenol, hoping to thwart the headache lurking behind his eyes. It had been a long day with disastrous results. Jackie was dead and Nora was missing.

Claudia was helpful, but Tonto was following Murphy's orders. If they didn't find Nora tonight, Roger could take up the chopper tomorrow and hunt for Martina's car, but that was hours from now. Tony was watching the house in Ponchatoula, but he doubted Nicolas or Martina would go there.

His cellphone rang. He dashed into the room, grabbed the phone off the bed and answered. "Renzi."

"We found Nora," Detective Jones said. "I just got off the phone with the Tennessee State cops."

"How is she? Is she okay?" Expecting the worst, hoping for the best.

"She's pretty upset, crying and all, but physically okay. I told them to take her to the room where her brother is staying."

"Perfect. Thanks for calling me. Which car was she in?"

"The silver Toyota, driven by Martina Zurik. She claims her husband told her to drive to her parents house in New York and he'd follow her. But he didn't."

Of course not. He knows he's wanted for murder.

"Don't release any info about finding Nora to the media. It will spook the husband, no telling what he might do."

"I'll have to release it sooner or later," Jones said.

"Go for later," he said. "We don't want him killing anyone else."

"I'll have to run that by my boss."

Just doing my job. "Call me if you get any info on the BMW."

Jubilant that Nora had been found unharmed, he ended the call and dialed another number.

"Frank! What's going on?" Kelly said.

"They found Nora. She's okay."

"Fantastic! She must have been scared to death. How's she doing?"

"Very upset, but they're taking her to the room where Danny's staying. The Tennessee state cops found her in Martina's car. No sign of Nicolas."

"I talked to Leah and Jack Rosenstein. Their plane lands in Memphis tomorrow at one-thirty."

"Excellent! I'll call Nadine and let her know. She's staying in the hotel room with Danny."

"Be careful, Frank. Nicolas is a killer. He won't go down without a fight. I wish I was in Memphis to back you up."

"Me too. But Claudia's got a weapon."

"Yeah? Tell Claudia if you get shot I'm gonna come after her."

Frank stifled a smile. "I'll be sure to pass that along. She's waiting for me in her room."

"Where are you?"

"At the Hamilton Suites Hotel. Tonto and Roger are in one room. Claudia and I are in separate rooms down the hall. She set up a meeting in her room. Tonto's orders. From Murphy."

"To hell with Murphy. Go catch the bastard who killed Jackie."

"Sounds good to me." He ended the call and dialed another number.

When Nadine answered, he said, "Good news! They found Nora. She's okay, but she's pretty shaken up. I told them to bring her to your room so she could be with Danny. My colleague spoke to the grandparents. They'll fly to Memphis tomorrow, arrival at one-thirty."

"Great!" Nadine exclaimed. "Hold on while I tell Danny."

He heard her call, "Danny, they found Nora! She's okay. They're bringing her here." After a moment, Nadine came back on the line and said, "That's the first time I've seen him smile. Thanks for calling me, Frank. This makes my day."

"Mine too," he said. "Now all we gotta do is capture the bastard who killed their mother."

CHAPTER 39

DAY 11 MONDAY OCTOBER 20, 2014 – 7:50 PM – Memphis

Twenty minutes late for the meeting, Frank tapped on Claudia's door. She opened it and took him straight to a room service cart near the door that held platters of food with enticing aromas. "Tonto and Roger are just finishing dinner," she said. "Fill up a plate and join us."

Beyond a seating area with a big-screen TV facing a plush couch, Tonto sat beside Roger at a square table with four chairs. But Frank didn't want company, he wanted food. A pumpkin muffin twelve hours ago and no lunch, he could eat a steak as big as Rhode Island, two baked potatoes slathered with butter and a strawberry shortcake, no trouble at all.

His stomach rumbled as he filled his plate: a boneless chicken breast, roasted potatoes, broccoli and candied carrots. He carried it to the table and sat down beside Claudia. Across the table, Tonto nodded a greeting, expressionless. Roger smiled and said, "Good to see you, Frank."

Frank nodded, working on a mouthful of roasted potatoes. Forget chitchat. He was ravenous.

"Great dinner," Roger said to Claudia, who smiled and said, "Can't work on an empty stomach."

Roger went to the room service cart, returned with two bottled waters and gave one to Frank.

"Thanks," he said, and got to work on his chicken breast.

Tonto pushed his plate aside and said, "Now that we're all here, let's get started."

"Jones called me," Frank said. "They found Nora."

Stunned silence. Then Claudia exclaimed, "Fantastic! Is she okay?"

"Okay physically, but very distraught."

"How did they find her?" Tonto said, stone-faced.

"The Tennessee state police caught Martina before she left the state. I told Jones to have them take Nora to Danny's room at the Midtown Hotel. I also told him not to tell the media about finding Nora. We'll see how that goes. I'm sure Nicolas is watching the news on TV."

"If he hasn't left town already," Tonto said. "We need to find him immediately."

"He won't drive," Frank said. "Not with the photos of his BMW and the license plate on TV."

"What about the airport?" Roger said. "That's the fastest way out."

"No chance," Frank said. "He won't give up his guns to get on a plane."

"He could take a bus," Tonto said. "No worries about weapons, no need for a passport."

"Too slow," Claudia said. "He knows we're after him. He wants to get out of Memphis fast."

"Check the train schedule," Frank said, and kept eating, shoveling down chicken and roasted potatoes, feeding a bottomless pit.

Claudia got out her iPad and poked at it. "No more trains leaving Memphis tonight. The first train out tomorrow goes to Canada, departs at eight AM."

"Forget Canada," Frank said. "He'd need to show a passport at the border. By the time he gets there, customs agents will have a stop notice on Nicolas Zurik. He's smart enough to know that."

"Okay," Claudia said. "A train to Chicago leaves at nine AM."

"That might do it." Frank set his plate aside. "Can you find out if he booked a ticket?"

"I will call them," Tonto said, and took out his cellphone.

He glanced at Claudia who gave him a look: *Don't mess with Tonto.*

Aloud, she said, "Feeling better now that you've eaten?"

"Yes. But I'll feel better when we find Zurik."

His cellphone chimed. Nadine calling. Aware that Tonto was watching him, he answered. "What's up? Is everything okay?"

"Yes," Nadine said. "Nora's here. She's happy to see Danny, but she's asking for you. I know you're busy—"

"Not that busy. Be there in ten minutes." He ended the call and said to Claudia, "I need the keys to the car."

Claudia took them out of her purse and handed them over.

Tonto frowned. "Where are you going?"

"To give a very frightened little girl a hug," he said, and left the room.

———

When he tapped on the door at the Midtown Hotel, Nadine called in a stern voice, "Who is it"

Pleased that Nadine wasn't going to let anyone near Danny and Nora, he said, "Frank."

A short black woman with milk-chocolate skin, a pretty face and a big smile opened the door. "Thanks for coming, Frank. I know you're busy."

"You're the one who deserves the thanks. For staying with Danny and Nora."

"I've got two kids of my own," she said. "I feel so bad for Danny. He said his dad was murdered a few days ago. Is that true?" Gazing at him, concern evident in her large brown eyes.

"Yes, unfortunately. In New Orleans."

Nadine shook her head. "The poor kid. Nora, too. She's a sweetheart. Can't imagine what I'd do if some lowlife took one of my kids. Come in and sit down."

Nora saw him and came running. "Detective Frank!"

He scooped her up and gave her a hug. Forget rules and regulations and lawsuits. Nora needed someone to comfort her.

She burrowed her face in his neck, clinging to him. He patted her back and said, "I'm really happy to see you, Nora."

"I was scared," she whispered.

"You had every right to be scared. Let's sit down so we can talk."

He set her down on the couch and sat beside her. Clutching his hand, Nora said, "Mr. Zurik is a bad man. He scared me."

"What did he do?"

"He scared Mommy too. When he came in our room. And then Mrs. Zurik took me out to her car. But I didn't want to leave Mommy." Her eyes filled with tears.

"It's okay, Nora. You're safe now. No one's going to hurt you."

"Will you stay and protect us?" Nora asked, gazing up at him.

"I'll stay for a while. Then I need to go back to work, but Nadine will protect you. She wouldn't even let me in the room until I gave her the password."

Nora gazed at him, wide-eyed. "What's the password?"

He held a finger to his lips. "Frank. But don't tell anyone."

Nora smiled and nodded her head.

"Nadine's a great detective and she's a great mom too, so she knows what little girls need."

"She helped me wash my hair," Nora said. "It was all icky."

"So were your clothes," Nadine said. "But we got some clean ones, from your pretty pink suitcase."

"My shirt was icky too. Mrs. Zurik tried to make me take some medicine, but I wouldn't."

"What kind of medicine?" Frank said, sickened by the idea. The heartlessness continued. Kill the mother, poison the daughter?

"The kind Mom gives me when I have a cold and I'm coughing. But I don't have a cold and I wasn't coughing, so I spit it out."

"Good for you. You're a very brave girl."

"Mr. Zurik told her to give it to me."

No surprise there. "When did that happen?"

"When I was in the back seat of her car. They thought I couldn't hear them, but I could. He told Mrs. Zurik to take me to her father's house and I started screaming, Where's Mommy!!"

Nora's eyes filled with tears again.

"Don't worry," he said. "You're safe here."

Knowing perfectly well that wasn't the reason she was crying. Nora wanted her mother. To distract her, he said, "Where's your brother? Danny was very worried about you. Last night when we talked on the phone, he made me promise to find you."

"Danny's taking a shower," Nadine said.

"Mommy's not here," Nora said solemnly. "Nadine says she's in Heaven with Daddy now."

Frank took a moment, then said, "Mommy's very proud of you for being such a brave girl and so is Daddy." Explaining death to young kids was never easy. A painful task that had fallen to Nadine. Frank didn't believe in Heaven and ten years from now Nora might not either.

But right now she was a little girl who needed to feel like she was still connected with Mommy and Daddy.

"What's up?" Danny said, standing in the bedroom doorway, dressed in jeans and a T-shirt, his hair still wet from the shower.

"Hi, Danny. Come sit with us,"Frank said.

Nadine rose from the couch and said, "I'll get us some bottled water."

Danny slowly approached the couch, his eyes somber. "Thanks for finding Nora, Detective Frank."

"Well, I wasn't the one who found her. The Tennessee state police did, but now she's safe here with you and Nadine. That's the important thing."

"Did you find Mr. Zurik?"

"Not yet, but we will," he said, evaluating Danny's demeanor. Angry and hurt and confused.

"He killed Mom," Danny said. "Why would he do that?"

The dreaded question. "I'm not sure. Life is complicated sometimes."

Sooner or later Danny would find out his father had been gambling on NBA games, including games he officiated. A painful revelation.

Not something Danny needed to know right now.

"But he and Dad were friends!" Danny said, his eyes glazed with tears.

"It seemed like they were," Frank said, "but sometimes ..." Searching for words to answer a question that had no answer.

Why did Dad's friend kill my mother?

242

"You and Nicky were friends," he said, "but you probably had a few disagreements, right?"

"Yes, but Nicky didn't ..." Danny glanced at Nora and clamped his lips together.

"How about some dinner?" Frank said. "We'll order takeout and have it delivered. What shall we order?"

"Pizza," Nora said. "I like cheese pizza."

Blinking back tears, Danny said, "I don't care. I'm not hungry."

Nadine came back with three bottled waters, concern for Danny evident in her eyes.

"I bet Nadine is hungry," Frank said. "What shall we get? My treat."

"I could use some dinner right about now," Nadine said. "There's an Italian place not far from here. You can get pizza and salads, pasta if you want it, and they deliver."

"Perfect. I'll let you call in the order."

While Nadine stepped into the bedroom, Frank unscrewed the top of a bottled water and gave it to Nora. "Have some water while Nadine orders dinner."

Danny sat down beside him and said, "Where's Nicky?"

"I don't know," Frank said. He'd been too worried about Nora to think about it. "He wasn't in the car with his mother."

"What if he's with his father?" Danny said, anxiously clenching his hands, white-knuckled. "Will the cops arrest him?"

Frank considered how to answer. As he'd suspected, after talking to Nora, Danny had put two and two together. Nora had been in Martina's car when the cops rescued her. Clearly, she'd told Danny that Nicolas had been in the room where their mother was murdered.

Nora hadn't mentioned seeing Nicky, but that didn't mean he wasn't in Memphis. Obviously, he wasn't with his mother. No way to know if he was with his father or not, though Frank doubted that he was.

"Nobody's going to arrest him, Danny. I'll make some calls and find out where he is."

Nadine came back in the room and said, "Dinner's all set, should be here in thirty minutes."

"Excellent." He gave Nora a hug and kissed her cheek. "I have to go to work now, but Nadine will be here to keep you safe."

"I wish you could stay and have pizza with us." Gazing at him. Big blue eyes. No smile.

"Me too, but I can't." Frank took out a card, gave it to Danny and said, "I know you've got a lot on your mind right now, Danny. A lot of questions, and I don't have the answers for you right now. My cellphone number's on the card. Call me if you feel like talking, okay?"

"Okay," Danny said, looking less anxious, but still in a world of hurt, trying to make sense of this nightmare. Trying to figure out why his best friend's father murdered his mother.

"Walk me to the door," he said to Nadine.

When they reached the door, he took out his wallet and gave her two twenties. "That should cover dinner."

"More than enough," Nadine said. "Too much, in fact."

"Not nearly enough for what you've done for these kids. If you ever need anything—it doesn't matter when, next week, next month, next year—call me and I will make it happen."

"Thank you." Nadine smiled. "You've got kids too, I can tell by the way you talked to Nora."

"A daughter. She's much older than Nora, but you know how it is." Frank smiled. "She'll always be my little girl."

"Same here. Mine are grown up now too, but you never stop worrying about them." Nadine set her jaw and said firmly, "This Zurik lowlife is an evil man, Frank. Find the bastard and put him away."

"Don't worry, I intend to," he said.

Two minutes later he got in the rental car and called Vobitch.

"What's up, Frank. You find the motherfucker?"

"Not yet, but I will."

"We're still searching Zurik's house and his office. I checked his credit cards. No recent activity, but he might have others that we don't know about."

"Let's hope not. Listen, with everything that's been going on, I totally forgot about Nicolas Junior, Zurik's twelve-year-old son. He wasn't at the house?"

"No. Tony's been watching the place. If he'd seen the kid leave, he would have told me."

"We need to find out where he is. Check with his school and see if he was there today."

"Will do," Vobitch said. "Go get the motherfucker."

Frank ended the call, thinking *Get the motherfucker and make him pay.*

But where the hell was Nicky?

CHAPTER 40

DAY 12 TUESDAY OCTOBER 21, 2014 – 3:05 AM

Shrouded in darkness, Nicolas knelt behind the Honda Accord. All quiet on the third level of the parking garage. It had taken him twenty minutes to get here. To minimize exposure of the Louisiana plate on his BMW, especially to cops, he'd driven through a maze of side streets, deserted at this hour, to reach the ten-story Hotel Marriott on the corner of a main street.

Using the screwdriver on his Swiss Army knife, he removed a screw on the Tennessee license plate. It would be easy enough to steal a car. But if he hot-wired a car, he couldn't turn it off. Worse, the owner might report it stolen. He didn't want a Memphis cop stopping him.

Sweating in the muggy air, he got started on the last screw. Stopped.

Listened. A distant sound, faint but coming closer.

Beside the Honda, his black BMW purred quietly, no lights showing, backed against the wall, nose out. He put down the screwdriver, took out his Beretta and screwed the suppressor onto the barrel.

A buzzing noise came closer. It sounded like a golf cart.

But golf carts didn't zip around hotel parking structures.

He crept to the trunk of the BMW and waited by the tailpipe. Peeked over the trunk.

A small security vehicle with a security guard inside, coming this way.

He held his breath, his finger on the trigger. He didn't want to shoot the man. That would bring more problems, but ...

Seconds later, the security vehicle passed his BMW, then the Honda and kept going.

He set the Beretta on the cement, crawled to the Honda and removed the last screw on the license plate. Took the plate, grabbed the Beretta and got in the BMW. He had intended to steal another plate, but he'd worry about that later.

Better to leave now.

He pulled out of the space and drove in the opposite direction from the security vehicle. Hands sweaty on the wheel, he took the nearest exit ramp. Hoping the security guard didn't see him, he quickly drove down the ramp, slowing only to negotiate the U-turns.

Two minutes later he left the garage. He drove around the hotel, a massive structure that catered to tourists who came to Memphis for the music or to visit the Elvis mansion. But he was no tourist. He had urgent business to complete.

Behind the hotel, he parked twenty yards from an enormous dumpster, ten feet tall and eight feet wide. Tourists generated a lot of garbage.

No security cameras in this area, and the halogen lights on tall poles were too far away to penetrate the darkness near the dumpster. He grabbed the Tennessee plate and his Swiss Army knife, got out of the BMW, removed the Louisiana plate and replaced it with the stolen plate.

Paused a moment and listened, alert for any sounds. Hearing none, he popped the trunk and took out Jackie's laptop, then Richie's. With a laptop in each hand, he strode to the dumpster.

The front cover was open, a gaping maw that emitted a horrible stench.

His neck prickled. A scuffling sound. Homeless people often foraged in dumpsters late at night. He set the laptops on the ground, retrieved his Beretta from the car and crept closer.

More sounds from the darkness beside the dumpster.

He crouched and sprang around the corner. Two big rats stared at him, their eyes red in the darkness, and scurried away.

Real rats, not scumbag informants like Richie.

Hurrying now, he put his Beretta in the BMW, retrieved the Louisiana plate and threw it in the dumpster. Picked up the laptops, heaved one into the dumpster, then the other. By this time tomorrow, they would be buried under tons of rubbish at the city dump.

Now for his next task. He jumped in the BMW and drove along the main drag. Three blocks from the Marriott, he passed a 24-hour Shell station with a convenience store. He turned onto the next side street, pulled to the curb, put on his Cardinals baseball cap and returned to the Shell station.

No cars at the pumps, bright lights in the store but no customers that he could see. He parked at Pump One, hid the Beretta under the seat and went inside.

The place stank of burnt coffee and microwaved food. He scanned the ceiling. No security cameras. Turning his face away from the sleepy-eyed clerk behind the counter, he drawled, "Gonna pick up some grub 'fore I pump my gas."

He walked down an aisle with cereal, canned tuna and soup. Took three one-liter bottles of water off a low shelf. Grabbed a foil-wrapped sandwich out of a refrigerated cooler.

The next aisle held automotive items—quarts of oil, jugs of antifreeze and wiper fluid. Beyond them, he selected a box of 30-gallon trash bags. A rack in the corner held sweatshirts and hoodies. He found an extra-large hoodie, gray with MEMPHIS in maroon letters on the front.

He draped it over his arm, carried the other items to the register and said, "Long drive to Texas. Add twenty bucks for gas on Pump One."

The clerk grunted and rang up his order, not looking at him, putting the items in plastic bags. "Including the gas, your total comes to forty-nine dollars and fifty cents."

Nicolas gave him two twenties and a ten. "Thanks. I don't need a receipt."

Outside at the pumps, he tossed the plastic bags in the BMW, pumped his gas and left.

Ten minutes later he was at his motel. He drove around back. No lights in any rooms and no other cars, but he backed the BMW against the fence anyway, nose out for a fast getaway.

He took the plastic bags up to his room, locked the door and dumped his purchases on the bed. Unwrapped the sandwich, took a big bite, chewed and swallowed. It was bland and tasteless. Turkey, mayo and lettuce on a bun, but he needed energy.

He opened the box of heavy-duty trash-bags, unrolled one and put it on the bed. He ate another bite of the sandwich, went to the luggage rack and lugged his canvas duffle to the bed. The cash he'd taken from his office had to weigh at least twenty pounds.

He transferred half the cash into the trash bag—a hundred fifty thousand dollars in hundreds—and hefted the duffle. Excellent. Ten pounds lighter. He'd leave the rest in the trunk of his car until he was ready to board the train.

The clock on the bedside table clicked over to 4:00 AM.

Five hours from now Nicky would be at O'Hare Airport in Chicago, but Nicolas wouldn't arrive until many hours later.

Picturing his beloved son's face, he tried to reassure himself. He'd told Nicky what to do. Nicky was smart. Resourceful beyond his years. Eager to have an adventure with his father. Nicky would be fine.

Nicolas methodically finished the turkey sandwich, balled up the foil and stuffed it into another trash bag. When he left the hotel, he would put all his trash in the dumpster. Leave no evidence.

Satisfied with his plan, he drank some bottled water. Now it was 4:05 AM.

Take a quick power nap, drive to the train station and find an emergency escape route.

Never go into a place without knowing how to get out of it.

———

5:00 AM – Memphis

Frank woke from a deep sleep an instant before his cellphone rang. Like he'd been expecting it. He rolled over, groped for his cellphone on the bedside table, and answered. "Renzi."

Detective Larry Jones spoke into his ear. "A motel clerk called in a tip on the BMW, but the guy that rented the room has the wrong name, Anthony Hart, and I got no time to check it out."

Fully alert now, Frank said, "Thanks for telling me. I'll check it out." He ended the call and rang Claudia. She answered right away.

"You got something, Frank?" Like she was wide awake.

"Maybe. Jones just called and said a motel clerk might have seen the BMW. I need the car keys."

"I'll go with you. Meet you at the car in ten minutes."

"Don't tell Tonto."

"Don't worry, I won't."

Frank splashed cold water on his face, put on an old pair of jeans, frayed at the cuffs, the top of his black running suit, and holstered his SIG under his navy windbreaker. He went down to the lobby, poured black coffee into two large cups, covered them with lids and went outside. The rising sun was an orange-red glow in the east. No rain, but already the air was humid.

Claudia burst out the hotel door, wearing a loose black T-shirt over baggy bluejeans. She unlocked the car and got behind the wheel. Frank got in the shotgun seat and put the coffee containers in the cup holders. "Is that your undercover outfit?"

"Always be prepared." She thrust her iPad at him. "Thanks for the coffee. Tell me where to go."

Ten minutes later, they reached their destination, a low-budget motel used by men who needed a cheap place to stay on their way to somewhere else. The lobby was as drab as the exterior and smelled funky. A twenty-something kid in a University of Memphis T-shirt smiled and said, "Help you?"

"Frank Renzi, NOPD. You called in a tip about a black BMW?"

"Yeah." Alert now and eager to talk. "When I come on duty at midnight, I drive around back to make sure everything's okay. Noticed it parked against the fence and remembered seeing it on TV. But it's not here anymore."

Frank took out the photo of Nicolas. "Is this the owner?"

"Uhm, I don't think so. The guy that checked was wearing horn-rim glasses and a St. Louis Cardinals baseball cap. His name is Anthony Hart. Said he's a big Cardinals fan."

Frank flicked a glance at Claudia, then said, "Show us the room."

The kid frowned. "He hasn't checked out yet."

"What's your name?" Claudia said.

"Ronnie. But I'm not the manager—"

"Police business," Claudia said. "Show us the room. You won't get in trouble."

Ronnie didn't look happy, but he took a set of key cards off a rack behind him and came around the counter. "The stairs are outside. Follow me."

They walked around to the back and followed him upstairs to the second floor. Frank took out his SIG.

The kid saw it and freaked. "Jesus Mary and Joseph! I don't want—"

"Quiet," Frank hissed. "Take us to the room and give us the key to open it."

Halfway down a concrete walkway Ronnie stopped at a yellow door.

"What's the setup?" Frank asked. "Where's the bed? On the right or the left?"

"On the right," Ronnie said.

Claudia took the key and said to Frank, "I'll open the door, you go in." She stuck the key card in the slot and pulled it out.

Frank burst inside, crouched low, gripping his SIG in both hands. The drapes were shut so the light was dim, but he could see no one was there. The bed neatly made. No luggage. No clothes hanging in the closet.

He walked past the TV to the bathroom. Nothing on the vanity. No trash in the wastebasket. No dirty towels.

Claudia holstered her Glock, came closer and said, "He's gone."

"I don't give a damn what he was wearing," Frank said. "It was Nicolas."

"Want to ask Memphis PD to fingerprint the room? Look for hairs and fibers?"

"No. We'll tell Ronnie not to rent the room for a few days."

Standing outside the door, Ronnie was watching them, calmer now that they'd holstered their weapons.

"Thanks for your help," Claudia said. "We need you to keep this room vacant for a few days."

"We can do that," Ronnie said, eager to please now. "What did the guy do?"

"Sorry," Frank said. "We can't talk about it. Thanks for your help."

Disappointed that the lead had gotten them nowhere, they returned to the rental car. "He knows we're after his BMW," Claudia said as she got behind the wheel. "What if he rented a different car?"

"Or stole one," Frank said. "Let's ask Memphis PD to check recent reports of stolen cars or carjackings. Let them do the legwork. We need to focus on the train station. At least we know Zurik's got a credit card with another name."

"Anthony Hart," Claudia said. "Maybe he used it to buy a train ticket. When we get back to the hotel, I'll get on my phone and find out."

CHAPTER 41

DAY 12 TUESDAY OCTOBER 21, 2014 – 5:45 AM

On the way to the train station Nicolas took care to stay within the speed limit. He hadn't seen anyone following him, hadn't seen any Memphis cops either. At this hour they were probably sitting in their squad cars beside a coffee shop, eating breakfast.

A huge billboard beside the station said: **COMING SOON!** Below it was an artist's rendering of a new train station. Construction was already underway. Opposite the parking garage were several bulldozers, backhoes and dump trucks piled high with recently excavated earth.

They'd be hard at work today. On TV this morning, a local weatherman had predicted a fine day, sunny with temperatures in the sixties.

At the garage entrance, he took a ticket from the machine. The gate swung up and he drove up the ramp. No guard at the entrance, but a security guard was driving around the second level. Not that he was worried.

The cops were looking for a man with black hair, not a bald guy in a gray hoodie. Last night he'd cut his hair, left a Mohawk on top, and shaved the sides of head so no hair showed under his hat. His old cargo jeans still fit.

A legacy from his years in New York. Back then, homeless had been his preferred disguise. Embarrassed by their own riches, New Yorkers avoided homeless people. He never made eye contact with them, typical behavior for the homeless, unless they were panhandling.

Security cameras inside the train station would pick him up, but he was wearing horn-rimmed spectacles, and none of his hair showed below his cap. His own mum could walk past him and not realize it.

If she were still alive, which she wasn't.

He parked the BMW on Level 2, went downstairs and used the garage entrance to the station. Along the way he passed a sign that said Loading Dock, a possible route for an emergency escape. He'd check it out before he returned to his car. Continuing down the hall, he entered the station.

A barrage of sound greeted him. Men, women and children milling about, dressed in shorts and sandals, chattering about their trip. Others sat in chairs perusing tourist brochures, extolling the delights of Memphis, especially Elvis and Graceland.

He went to the departure board. The train to Chicago was on time, departure at 9 AM from Track 3 downstairs. A vague sense of dread hit him.

Martina attributed his occasional fits of temper to Russian moodiness. She didn't know he was a wanted man. Hunted by Frank Renzi for sure, soon to be hunted by Martina's father.

Martina's loyalty would go up in smoke when she figured out that he had abandoned her.

Escaping his pursuers required constant vigilance. He walked the perimeter of the lobby, up one side and down the other, looking for places his enemies might hide to ambush him. Old habits die hard.

No one survived a life like his without taking precautions.

Using his well-honed observational skills, he spotted several security guards. No sign of his enemies.

Near the stairs that went down to the tracks, he stopped outside the Memphis Cafe. From inside the cafe he would have a clear view of the front entrance, sixty yards away. Perfect.

He returned to the hall that led to the parking structure.

Halfway there, he turned left at the sign for the loading dock. He passed one door—Utility Closet—then another—Employees Only—and came to an exit door. A large red sign said Loading Dock.

Cautiously, he pushed open the solid-metal door and looked around.

Seeing no one, he stepped outside. A raised cement platform extended twenty yards to his right, high enough to allow delivery vehicles to offload their wares. Best off all, the alley for the vehicles extended to the main street.

Satisfied that he'd found his escape route, he returned to the BMW, put on mirrored sunglasses, paid cash at the exit and drove out of the garage.

Across the street, station workers were coming and going from a large muddy parking lot. A sign said Employees Only, but he drove into the lot and parked between two large SUVs facing the parking garage and the back entrance to the station. The perfect vantage point.

His thoughts turned to Nicky. By now he was in Chicago.

He took out his cellphone and texted Nicky.

My train departs on time. Busy just now. See you soon! XO

Moments later he got a reply.

No problem! Already at O'Hare. See you soon. XO

His eyes misted with tears. Would he see his beloved son in Chicago?

Sooner or later the law of averages was bound to catch up to him. He had managed to survive several deadly encounters.

But sooner or later something would go wrong and it would end his life.

Or put him in jail, which amounted to the same thing.

———

7:25 AM – Memphis

Edgy and hyper-alert, Frank gnawed his thumbnail, riding shotgun beside Claudia. Anthony Hart didn't have a ticket for the 9 AM train to Chicago, but Frank was certain Nicolas Zurik would be on it.

Ahead of them, driving an FBI BU-car, Tonto took a ticket out of a dispenser and drove up a ramp into the station garage. Claudia took a ticket, followed Tonto and parked beside his car on Level 2.

"Murphy called me an hour ago," she said. "To remind me that Tonto is in charge."

Annoyed, Frank said, "This could be a clusterfuck. Zurik won't go down without a fight, and Tonto's ready to take him, dead or alive."

When he got out of the car, Tonto opened the BU-car trunk, held out a Kevlar vest and said, "We're about the same size so I got two large vests. Mediums for Roger and Claudia."

Frank said nothing and set the vest on the hood of the rental car. Took off his windbreaker and put the vest on over his black T-shirt.

Beside the other car, Roger was strapping on his vest. He looked over and said, "Better safe than sorry."

"How's your marksmanship?" Frank said. "Been to the gun range lately?"

Roger smiled at him. "Passed the shooting test last week. Scored 899 out of a thousand."

Impressed, Frank said, "Excellent. You can back up Tonto. I'm sticking with Claudia."

Strapping on a vest, Claudia said, "I'd rather avoid any shooting."

"We will do what we must," Tonto said, zipping a black windbreaker over his vest. "Now we will go down and take a look at the station."

"No. Let's check the front entrance first," Frank said. "He might have taken a taxi."

Tonto's mouth quirked but he didn't say anything. They rode the elevator down to ground level. Frank got out first and trotted toward the street, annoyed by the vest, which restricted his movements, already sweating, his windbreaker trapping body heat.

Construction noise hit him when he reached the street, two huge backhoes raking up earth, emitting clouds of dust as they dropped it into dump trucks.

Claudia caught up to him and said, "This construction doesn't help. He could steal a helmet, put on an orange vest and look like a worker."

"Let's check the station." Frank pushed through the doors into the lobby and stopped. Forty or fifty people were strolling around, drinking coffee from go-cups, some with small children. Anxiety prickled his neck.

He shook his head at Claudia, "This is bad. Get into a firefight with Zurik, we'll kill ten people."

They went back to the entrance just as Tonto and Roger opened the doors.

"Come outside," Claudia said. "The station is full of civilians. We need to plan this."

They went around the corner to a smoking area and stood in the shade of the building. "There are four of us," Tonto said, "only one of him. And we have his picture."

"I'm the only one who's seen him," Frank said. "By now he could look completely different, put on sunglasses and a hat, you won't see much of his face."

"How big is he?" Roger asked.

"My height, but heavier. Could be wearing a suit, could be wearing shorts and a T-shirt."

"We will box him in," Tonto said. "Take him down fast."

Exasperated, Frank said, "We'll never get near him. Look at us. No luggage, bulked out in vests, all of us wearing windbreakers. We'll stick out like Darth Vader."

Tonto frowned at him. "Murphy wants us—"

"Fuck Murphy! He's not my boss and neither are you. Stay here with Roger. Claudia and I will go in together, buy hats and a gym bag, act like we're happily married tourists. Then we'll scout the lobby and figure out where we can set up to wait for him."

"I like it," Roger said. "Tonto and I can go in and buy some outfits so we look like tourists." He grinned at Tonto and said, "We can pose as the bi-racial gay couple."

Clearly annoyed, Tonto said to Claudia, "All right, but hurry. We wait here."

Frank took her arm and they followed other passengers into the station. To their left, halfway down a ten-foot ticket counter, two female clerks behind Plexiglas windows were selling tickets.

On the wall to their right, red digits on a huge board showed train departures and arrivals. Leading Claudia to the board, he put his arm around her and said, "Where would you like to go, Honey-Bunny?"

She gave him a look. "Frank. I saw *Pulp Fiction* so I'm not gonna be Honey-Bunny. She died in the end." Gesturing at the display, she said, "The train to Chicago departs at 9AM on Track 3."

"I'm willing to bet Zurik is already here. Let's hit that souvenir shop."

They went in the store, which sold Elvis paraphernalia, posters, jackets and T-shirts. "Get a big straw hat," Frank said, "something touristy. And a gym bag if you can find one."

In the men's hat section, he chose a straw panama hat with a black band and a wide brim. Most of the jackets were too flashy, decorated with sequins or photos of Elvis and his toothy smile. He went to a rack of King Creole Baracuta jackets with zippers in front, found an XL and looked around for Claudia.

Wearing a straw hat with a wide floppy brim, carrying a large gym bag, she came over to him and drawled, "Y'all look mighty handsome in that hat, Sweetie."

Frank laughed. "Careful. People will think we're in love. Wait a sec while I try on this jacket." He took off his windbreaker, handed it to Claudia and shrugged into the King Creole jacket.

"How do I look, Sweetie?"

"Looks good to me. Nothing dangerous showing." Meaning his SIG.

"Great. Let's get out of here. Unless you want to buy an Elvis jacket."

"I'll be fine in my rain jacket. Tonto's not known for his patience."

They paid and returned to the lobby, wearing their purchases. "We need to stroll the lobby," Frank said. "Find someplace for us to wait."

"Okay, but let's be quick. It's already eight o'clock."

The lobby was as long as a football field and just as wide, shops, bars and restaurants on both sides. At the far end below a broad archway, a flight of stairs went down to the tracks. Beside the stairs were two elevators. Beyond the elevators, a long corridor went to the parking garage.

A nearby cafe sold coffee and pastries. Claudia pointed at a Hudson News on the opposite corner with tables outside. "If we sit there, we can see the entrance and the stairs to the tracks."

"Good choice," he said.

When they went back outside, Tonto was pacing back and forth impatiently.

Roger smiled when he saw their hats and said, jiving them, "What a cute couple."

"Yeah, yeah," Claudia said. "Get out your cellphones, I'm gonna set up a conference call."

A minute later, all their phones started ringing. When they answered, the ringing stopped. "Put the phones in your pockets but leave them on," she said. "Report in if you see anything suspicious."

"Claudia and I will cover the left side," Frank said. "You two cover the right side. Zurik could be hiding anywhere. Watch his hands. We know he's armed."

"Keep your phones on," Claudia said.

And your weapons holstered, Frank thought.

Or a lot of innocent people might windup dead.

––––

In the employee parking lot, Nicolas sat in the BMW, across from the parking garage, watching. A few station employees rode bicycles to work and secured them to metal stanchions with padlocks. Others parked cheap sedans and dented SUVs and hurried into the station.

He was hungry, but food would have to wait. He put on the gray tweed newsboy cap he'd bought in New York years ago. The over-sized cap rested on his ears and covered most of his forehead.

He'd taken everything with him when he left the motel, but hadn't turned in the room key. Always leave a bolthole for emergencies.

His suitcase was locked in the trunk. His credit cards, fake IDs, and half his cash were in his duffle on the passenger seat. With his weapons.

A husky black man in a Memphis Grizzles ball cap came out the rear entrance of the station and stood near the garage, conversing with another man, surveying the area as they talked. Then the Grizzles fan walked away toward the front entrance. His partner kept looking around, a short white man in a windbreaker. What was under the windbreaker?

Nicolas wiped sweaty hands on his pants. Was this an ambush?

On full alert now, he waited.

Ten minutes later the Grizzles fan came back and conferred with his partner, nervously looking around for whatever they were seeking.

Nicolas Zurik, no doubt in his mind.

He reached in his pocket and touched his good luck charm, a gift from Yvette. Last year when he opened the box and saw the miniature ivory white knight, he was stunned. Which pleased Yvette enormously. He took it out of his pocket and turned it over in his hand.

What was Yvette was doing now? Pleasing one of her clients?

If only he was with her. If only he could lose himself in a frantic orgy and forget how many things could go wrong.

Would he have good luck today?

He returned the white knight to his pocket. You make your own luck.

He checked the time. 8:30. By now Nicky was probably eating breakfast at O'Hare.

Nicolas checked his gear. The Beretta in a shoulder holster under his left arm. A four-inch combat knife sheathed in the small of his back. The .22 caliber revolver strapped to his right ankle. Extra magazines in the pockets sewn into both legs of his cargo jeans.

In case his enemies ambushed him.

Time to go in the station.

Either he would see Nicky in Chicago or he would be dead.

CHAPTER 42

DAY 12 TUESDAY OCTOBER 21, 2014 – 8:45 AM

Tense and alert, certain Zurik was already in the station, Frank studied the lobby, conscious of the time ticking by. *Tick, tick, tick.*

Like a bomb ready to explode.

Like Zurik would explode if they tried to take him down.

Seated beside him at a table outside Hudson News, Claudia adjusted the brim of her straw hat, pretending to read a newspaper, her eyes focused on the lobby. Hunting for Zurik.

Frank adjusted the SIG under his Elvis jacket and wiped sweat off his face. Hyped with nervous energy, neck clenched, acid burning his gut, soaked with sweat under the Kevlar vest.

Across from them on the other side of the lobby, Tonto stood outside a restaurant in a buckskin cowboy hat, looked like John Wayne in a black wind-breaker. Beyond him, Roger had on a sweatshirt with an Elvis postage stamp on the front, no hat, leaning against the wall, watching the station entrance.

Tonto spoke to a woman in a blue dress who shook her head and hurried away. Frank said to Claudia, "He's showing Zurik's mug shot, might as well flash a sign saying he's a cop. Zurik sees him, he'll bolt."

Claudia got on her cellphone and said, "Forget the picture, Tonto. Just look for him."

"He's not in the Memphis Cafe on your side of the lobby," Tonto said. "From here I can see through the windows. I have been watching customers come and go."

Frank got on his cellphone and said, "His train leaves in ten minutes. He'll go down to the track soon. Watch for him and stay out of sight."

"He might not be here," Tonto said. "We cannot be sure that he will take this nine o'clock train to Chicago."

"He's here," Frank snarled and put his phone on the table.

An older woman sitting in an easy chair near their table said anxiously, "What's going on?"

"Waiting for somebody," Frank said.

The woman looked at him, looked at Claudia, picked up her shopping bag and walked away.

"Christ, we're spooking people," he said.

Claudia's head jerked up, her eyes focused on the entrance.

"God dammit!" she said. "No, no, no!"

———

Inside the Memphis Cafe, Nicolas perched on a stool by the window, the newsboy cap tugged low to conceal half of his face. He'd been sitting here twenty minutes, nursing a bottled water, watching the lobby.

Seated at a table behind him, four jocks in University of Memphis T-shirts were eating donuts, joking and laughing.

A distraction, but he tuned it out and focused on the lobby.

Moments later three men burst through front entrance and jogged down the center of the lobby. One was the husky black man in the Grizzles cap.

No Grizzles cap now. No uniform either, but he had a gun in his hand. Three cops running his way. Gunning for him.

He exploded off the seat, the Beretta in his hand.

The Memphis jocks dove under their table. Nicolas slung his duffle bag over one shoulder and ran to the door. Two customers scrambled out of his way. A heartbeat later he was out the door.

He shot a woman who got in his way and she went down. He shot the man who stopped to help her and saw a tall man in a cowboy hat aim a gun at him. He snapped off a shot and Cowboy Hat went down. Beyond Cowboy Hat, a light-skinned black man took out a gun.

Christ, how many were there?

Nicolas shot at him, but at the same instant a woman ran in front of the gun-man. The slug hit her and blood sprayed onto the black man's face.

Then he was running and shooting. Two more men went down.

Panic erupted in the lobby, people screaming and running.

An armed security guard came at him. Nicolas shot at him and missed, the man reeling away. He shot him in the back.

Now the lobby was in chaos, men, women and children screaming and running in all directions. But chaos was his friend.

Get to the loading dock and get out of here.

———

Tonto lay on his stomach, his head turned to the side, his lips pulled back in a grimace. Kneeling beside him, Frank saw a hole the width of a pencil in his neck, near his jaw.

Glassy-eyed, Tonto looked at him and said, "Shot." His eyes drifted away.

Going into shock, Frank thought. "Stay with me," he said, and rolled Tonto onto his side. The exit wound was pumping blood. *Artery.* He'd seen arterial wounds before. Situation critical. He took off his Elvis jacket and pressed it against the wound as hard as he could.

Tonto groaned, said again, "Shot." And began to cough, blood pulsing from his mouth.

"I need help over here," Frank yelled. "Help me! Medic!!"

But the lobby was bedlam, shots fired, panicked travelers shrieking as they ran away or ducked into stores.

Time crawled by like a slo-mo horror movie in vivid color, bleeding people on the floor, the pop-pop-pop of gunshots. Two uniformed Memphis cops cut over to the side of the lobby, chasing Zurik.

Zurik was racing toward the stairway to the train tracks, but Frank had no shot at him, not with a dozen civilians in the line of fire.

An older black woman knelt beside him, said "Nurse," and examined the wound. "Artery," she said quietly. "You did what you could. Nothing to do until the EMTs get here."

"Can you get him an ambulance?" he said. "He needs immediate attention. No worries, the shooter's gone."

"Are you a cop?" Fear evident in her dark eyes. She'd seen his SIG.

"Yes. The victim's an FBI agent. Get him an ambulance."

As the nurse ran toward the front entrance, Frank saw Roger kneeling beside a woman with a bloody face, looking around wildly for help.

"Roger!" he yelled. "Tonto's wounded!"

Roger ran over, his face spattered with blood, and said, "Jesus Christ, this is a fucking disaster."

"Stay with Tonto," he said. "Press my Elvis jacket against his neck wound. I'm going after Zurik."

"Where's Claudia?"

"Don't know," he said and took off running.

He saw Zurik charge past the stairway down to the tracks and zig left into the hall that went to the parking garage. Frank ran after him.

Near the elevators an older woman sat on the floor, her face pasty white. The man with her said, "Help me! My wife's having a heart attack!"

"Ambulances are coming," Frank said, hoping this was true. If they didn't get here soon, Tonto would bleed out.

He sprinted into the hallway, the SIG in his hands. Thirty yards ahead of him, Zurik turned and raised his gun.

Frank dropped to the floor and rolled left.

Zurik shot at him, the sound reverberating off the walls. The shot missed. Frank scrambled to his feet and charged after Zurik.

Out of nowhere, a man in a worker's uniform appeared, raised a handgun and shot at Zurik. Missed. Turned and looked at Frank.

He dove to the floor, shouting, "No! Police! Police!"

And then Claudia was there, screaming at the worker, "FBI! Drop the gun!" She slapped the man's head with her Glock and he went down.

Claudia ran after Zurik, gripping her Glock in both hands.

Zurik turned and shot at her, a wild shot that missed.

Claudia got off one shot, then another. Zurik stumbled, kept going and turned down a hallway to the left.

"Claudia," Frank shouted. "Let him go. Big problems in the lobby."

She trotted back to him, panting and out of breath.

"Zurik shot Tonto," he said. "Neck wound, through and through."

"Jesus," she said. "How bad?"

"Bad. Clipped an artery. Roger's with him."

―――――

Nicolas burst through the door onto the loading dock. Burning pain seared his butt, worse pain in his hip. Ten feet away, a man in a UPS uniform unloading his truck looked at him. "Who are you? You're not supposed to be out here."

Three strides and he took the man down.

"Get the fuck off me!" the man screamed.

Nicolas slammed his nose, his fist a sledgehammer. Blood spurted from the man's nose. Another sledgehammer blow and his eyes rolled up in his head. He took out his buck knife, thrust the blade between two ribs into his heart, took his wallet and left him on the loading dock.

Do what you have to do. Get to his car and get out before the cops cordoned off the street. Gritting his teeth, he limped to the street. No cops, but off to his right, he saw squad cars, ambulances, emergency workers and uniformed cops.

A painful sprint got him to the BMW. His left buttock felt weird, hot as fire but numb. No time to worry about that now. He got in the car, drove out of the employee parking lot onto the main street and kept going as fast as he dared.

Fear jolted his heart into a jagged rhythm. Sirens behind him.

A cop car with flashing lights and whooping sirens blew by, then another.

He gripped the wheel to keep his hands from shaking. You could plan everything down to the last detail and still die. The train station had been crawling with cops, waiting to arrest him.

He turned down a side street into a residential area, turned again. Drove past two rundown houses and stopped beside a vacant lot.

He got out of the car, pulled down his cargo jeans and examined his throbbing hip. A two-inch gash, wet with blood. An inch to the right and it would have hit his spinal cord, paralyzing him.

A fate worse than death.

Gripping the front fender, he puked his guts out in the gutter.

He had killed people before, more than a few in fact. He had felt no remorse. They meant nothing to him.

But today, he was the one who might have died.

He got in the BMW and rinsed his mouth with bottled water to get rid of the taste of vomit. His underarms reeked, a putrid odor, like the carcass of a dead rat in an ally. The rancid odor of fear.

He had to vanish or he was a dead man.

Renzi had been in the train station with a colleague, a short dark haired woman, waiting for him.

Renzi was smarter than he thought.

But not smarter than the chess master.

————

"Where'd you go when the shooting started?" Frank said.

"Down the stairway to the tracks," Claudia said as they hurried back to the lobby. "Waited at the first landing, but when he didn't show, I came upstairs and saw you chase him down the hall."

"And saved me from the asshole worker," he said as they entered the lobby.

The odor of gunfire and violence lingered in the air. Bloody footprints on the floor, wounded people moaning. Shell casings and bandage packaging scattered around pools of blood. Cops and hospital workers aiding the wounded.

No injured kids that Frank could see. Adults were bigger targets.

Miraculously, the gym bag with his windbreaker was still beside the table outside Hudson News. He slung it over his shoulder and they kept going. They passed a older black man leaning against a wall with a doctor in green scrubs working on him.

Tonto was gone, presumably in an ambulance headed to a hospital.

But Roger, his face speckled with blood, was standing beside Detective Jones, getting an earful. "... not taking the blame for this mess," Jones said. "You should have waited. We got a SWAT team outside."

"We didn't set this off," Frank said. "If you and your Memphis cop hadn't come charging in here, waving guns—"

"I don't want to hear it," Jones snapped, glaring at him.

"Zurik saw you and started shooting. If you'd let us take him, it would be over and we'd have him in custody."

"This isn't your jurisdiction, Renzi."

Frank said to Roger, "Did you fire your weapon?"

"No. Too many people."

"Neither did I," Claudia said. "Not in the station. Never had a clean shot."

Frank said to Jones, "When your crime scene techs finish processing the station lobby, they won't find any shell casings from our weapons."

He took Roger's arm and walked him away from Jones.

"I'm going back to the garage," Claudia said. "Even if Zurik is gone, I might find something."

"Be careful," Frank called as she ran off.

Worried about HIV, he took a small bottle of sterilizer out of the gym bag, gave it to Roger and said, "Use this to clean your hands."

Roger looked at his hands, streaked with the woman's blood. "Yeah. Thanks for reminding me."

Two minutes later Claudia came back from the garage and said, "I think I hit him. A blood trail goes down a side corridor, but no sign of Zurik. They closed the station, so cars are streaming out of the garage."

"The bastard got away again," Frank said.

"For now," Claudia said. "But I talked to a Memphis PD dispatcher. He said they have traffic cameras at the major intersections, might be able to track the BMW that way."

"Worth a shot," he said. "Let's get in the rental car, see if we can find him."

Ten minutes later they left the garage, Frank riding shotgun, Claudia driving. In the back seat, Roger seemed dazed, no doubt having realized the woman had taken a bullet meant for him.

"It was fuckin bedlam in there," Roger said, his milk chocolate complexion pasty gray. "Like that ambush scene in *Platoon*."

Eyeing the blood and brain matter on Roger's shirt, Frank said, "You need to lie down."

"No, I'm okay." But the glazed look remained in Roger's eyes.

"No you're not, you're in shock. You need to chill out for a while." To Claudia he said, "Drive him back to the hotel. Only take two minutes to drop him there."

"Okay," Roger said. "But only for a little while. Then I'll pick up the BU-car and go to the hospital to see how Tonto's doing."

They dropped Roger at the hotel and Claudia drove back to the main street to search for Zurik.

"Roger looked pretty shaky," she said.

"He should. I've been there, done that."

She glanced over. "Really?"

"You got an hour, I could tell you about it." Recalling his encounter at the Deer Island cemetery last year with a man who'd tried to kill him.

They were rolling down the main drag, Claudia barely slowing at red lights, honking the horn at other drivers. Her cellphone rang.

She answered, listened a moment, put her phone in the center console and said, "They tracked the BMW going north, but the cameras only cover the busiest intersections. If he turns into a side street, we'll lose him."

"No doubt in my mind he was getting on that train to Chicago," Frank said. "That's where he's headed. He saw me so he knows we're after him. The Memphis cops screwed up our chances at the station. We need to grab him now."

"Let's hope he doesn't spot the traffic cameras."

Frank clenched his jaw. "If he gets out of Memphis, we're fucked."

CHAPTER 43

After twenty minutes with no sightings of Zurik's BMW on the traffic cams, Claudia drove back to their hotel. Hot, sweaty and frustrated, Frank took a shower, put on fresh clothes and sat in his room watching the carnage on a local TV channel, talking to Kelly on his cellphone.

"It's all over the national news," Kelly said. "You're lucky to be alive."

He decided not to tell her about Tonto. "We tracked Zurik's BMW on traffic cameras for a while, but lost him. By now he could be anywhere."

"What about the Memphis cops? Aren't they looking for him?"

"They're the ones that screwed up the take-down, came running in the station with guns drawn, Zurik saw them and started shooting."

"Did he see you?" Kelly asked.

"Yes." He wasn't going to lie to her. No need to mention Zurik shot at him and missed. "Claudia chased him, thinks she might have winged him. Can you call Vobitch and update him?"

"He won't be thrilled about the news coverage."

"He'll be happy if we catch Zurik."

"I'll be happy if Zurik doesn't kill you."

"Kelly, we've got two heartbroken kids grieving for their parents. I'm gonna get the bastard and make him pay."

No response from Kelly. After a short silence, she said, "When I caught the first newsflash, I called Nadine and warned her not to let the kids watch any news. She putting on a movie for them."

"How are they doing?"

"Not too bad, considering. Looking forward to seeing their grandparents. I gave the Rosensteins the address of their hotel. Nadine's done enough already, doesn't need to drag them to the airport."

"Good thinking. Gotta go, Kelly. Talk to you later."

"Frank. Don't go after Zurik by yourself. He's a killer."

"Don't worry, I won't." He ended the call, took two iced-coffees to Claudia's room and knocked.

She opened the door dressed in a T-shirt and cargo pants, toweling her hair.

"The local channels are running Zurik's DL photo," he said, stepping into the room. "And the picture of the BMW."

"Fine, but they ran the BMW photo last night. He must have seen it on TV in his motel room."

"Which gave him time to steal a license plate and put it on the BMW."

Claudia draped the towel on a chair and combed her short dark hair with her fingers. "I need to call Roger and see how Tonto's doing."

"Good idea." He gestured at a container on the table beside his SIG. "I got you an iced coffee."

"Thanks." She sat at the table, dialed a number and put it on speaker.

Roger answered and said, "I'm at the hospital, Claudia. Where are you?"

"At the hotel with Frank. How's Tonto?"

"Still in surgery, condition critical. I talked to a nurse on the surgical floor. She said he lost a lot of blood and his blood pressure's very low. I'm worried he won't make it."

"Call me after he comes out of surgery," Claudia said.

"I'll call you after I talk to the surgeon. He knows I'm waiting to hear how it went."

Claudia ended the call and drank some iced coffee, staring into space. "Pretty scary. Your number comes up and you're dead. I've been in a few shootouts but nothing like the one at the train station."

"A Kevlar vest only protects your torso," Frank said. "All those bullets flying around, Tonto took one in the neck. Think positive. He's a tough guy." He drank some iced coffee. "One report on a local channel said FBI agents are in Memphis, looking for the man believed responsible for the train station shooting."

Claudia's face flushed bright red. "Sonofa*bitch*! The Memphis cops leaked it on purpose. Detective Jones, probably."

"That'd be my guess, but fuck the MPD. Let's go get Zurik."

Her cellphone rang. She checked the ID. "Just what I need. Murphy. "

She answered the call and put it on speaker.

"What the fuck is this, Claudia? My best agent is down there in a hospital in critical condition. I sent you a helicopter so you could arrest a suspect in a New Orleans murder case, but you let him get away. Now I've got to clean up your mess and placate the Memphis PD Superintendent—"

Claudia ended the call and said, "Fuck you, asshole."

"I'll second that. Murphy wants to grab the glory, blames it on you when things go wrong."

"Let me call my friendly dispatcher, see if I can get him to tell me what MPD is doing." She dialed a number, no speaker phone this time.

"Hi Sam, it's Claudia. We talked a little while ago. What's MPD doing to find the shooter?" Claudia listened a moment and smiled. "Fantastic. Thanks, Sam."

Frank waved a hand to get her attention. "Ask him to check the incident log for reports about a stolen plate."

Claudia nodded. "Sam, can you check the incident log for recent reports about a stolen license plate?" She listened, then said, "Great, thanks."

She ended the call and said, "He's too busy to check the log right now, said he'd call me back. But MPD already set up a manhunt. The command post is in the parking lot of a Rite Aid pharmacy on ...." Claudia smiled. "Ready for this? Elvis Presley Lane."

"I can hardly wait. Will there be guitars and blue suede shoes?"

"Let's hope it's not *Heartbreak Hotel.*"

Frank strapped on his SIG. "Let's go find out what MPD is doing."

———

Locked inside the restroom at a Publix supermarket, Nicolas pulled down his cargo pants and undershorts. Craning his neck, he studied the wound in the mirror above the sink. Not life threatening, but painful, a deep three-inch gash on his buttock, bleeding heavily. Judging by the fierce pain in his hip, the slug had grazed his hip bone.

He wet some paper towels and wiped blood off the gash. More blood instantly appeared, staining his fingers. He threw the bloody towels in the trash and opened the package of diapers he'd bought. He pressed one against the wound to absorb the blood, wincing at the pain.

From a plastic shopping bag, he took out a roll of packing tape and taped the diaper to his skin. His hip throbbed, an unceasing ache.

Exhausted, he tried to think, but memory flashes distracted him. Shots coming at him in the station. The Memphis cops chasing him.

Renzi was chasing him too. The NOPD cop with the implacable eyes. Too bad he didn't kill the bastard. He'd shot at him but missed. Then a woman with short dark hair started shooting at him. Missed him once, but her second shot didn't. Not a crippling injury but it slowed him down.

Who was she? Not a civilian. She knew how to shoot.

Was she another NOPD cop? An FBI agent?

If the feds got him, he was dead. That wasn't going to happen.

Riding a train to Chicago wasn't going to happen either, and forget flying. Cops would swarm the airport and the bus station. Even if he managed to get to Canada, border control agents would check his fake passport. He couldn't risk having an agent take him to a room for a strip search. Once his clothes were off, it would be obvious that he'd been shot.

But Nicky was waiting for him in Chicago.

Depending on him to be there.

He had to drive to Chicago.

He washed his hands with soap and water, took a bottle of extra-strength pain reliever out of the plastic bag and dry-swallowed three capsules. Scooped water in his mouth to wash them down and leaned against the sink.

He was utterly alone. Problems stacking up like dominoes and no one to help him. Alexei was his only friend, the only person he could trust after Papa died.

But Alexei was too far away. He needed help now.

If he didn't unlock the restroom door soon, someone might call the manager.

If he didn't tend his wound properly, it would get infected.

If he didn't ditch the BMW, the cops would find him. Checkmate.

He had to find another car.

———

10:30 AM

When Frank and Claudia got to the Rite Aid, two MPD squad cars, big SUVs with push bars front and rear and light bars on their roofs, sat in the middle of the parking lot. Four officers armed with rifles and handguns stood beside them. The command post, a long white van with MPD decals, stood alongside a wire-mesh fence.

Claudia parked the rental car in a space near the exit. "No FBI badge," Frank said. "We know how territorial Jones is. The MPD commander won't want an FBI agent messing with their manhunt. Let me handle this."

They hustled over to the command post. A woman stood outside, clearly in charge, wearing an MPD dress-blue uniform and a name tag. Lieutenant Donna Small, but she wasn't small, she was six feet tall and frowning at them.

Frank showed his NOPD badge, introduced himself and gestured at Claudia. "My colleague and I were in the station during the shooting."

"You got anything for me?" Small asked, grim-faced.

"We think he's wounded," Claudia said.

Frank said, "We have experience taking down armed suspects."

"You have vests?"

"Yes. In the car."

"Okay. We can use all the help we can get." Small jerked her thumb at the command vehicle and said, "Larry will tell you where to go."

They went inside and Larry showed them a large map broken down into six smaller squares. Pointing at one he said, "You cover this one. We got units covering the others. Its mostly residential, working class families. We told our officers to look for homes with vehicles outside and ask the residents if they've seen any suspicious vehicles in the area today."

"We're looking for a black BMW," Frank said.

"We know that," Larry said. "With a Louisiana plate."

Frank glanced at Claudia, then said, "How do we communicate?"

"I don't have any extra comm packs, but I've got a radio handset you can use. Lieutenant Small asks for a Sit-Rep every so often. Report in immediately if you find anything."

"Great," Frank said. "Give us two in case we have to split up."

They went back to the car and took a moment to figure out the handsets.

Then Roger called.

Claudia put her cellphone on speaker and said, "How's Tonto?"

"Good news," Roger said. "He's out of surgery, in stable condition. The surgeon seems optimistic."

"Great!" Frank said.

"Wonderful news," Claudia said. "How are you doing?"

"I'm fine," Roger said. "Where are you? I want in on the action."

Frank gave him the Rite Aid address. "Call us when you get there and we'll give you our location so we can meet and talk privately."

Following Claudia's iPad map to their assigned area, they slowly drove down the first street. "Looks like most people are at work," Claudia said.

"Or inside," Frank said, "watching the station massacre on TV."

They passed a few vehicles parked outside houses, but they didn't stop to question any residents. They had to capture Zurik and get the Richie tape before MPD found him.

————

Searching for a car to steal, Nicolas drifted down a street with shabby-looking houses, no lawns in front, just gravel and dead grass. Along the way he'd passed a Toyota dealership. Plenty of cars outside, but he couldn't steal one in broad daylight with salesmen around.

He passed a few Ford pickups and older-model sedans, but there were people outside, offloading groceries or tinkering with their cars. He kept going, up one street and down another. The neighborhood was quiet. No traffic to speak of, no kids outside, nobody walking dogs.

Halfway down one block, he passed a green one-story house with an attached two car garage. The garage door was open, one bay empty, an older model Ford Taurus in the other. No lights visible in the house. Perfect. Hot-wire the Taurus, ditch the BMW and get on the highway fast.

At the end of the block he did a U-turn. Never make a move until you evaluate the risks. Danger lurked everywhere. Especially now.

He cruised past the green house again. No lights visible. The garage door open. The maroon Taurus waiting to be stolen.

He drove around the block and parked in front of a white house midway down the street. No cars in front, no lights inside. He took the Beretta out of his duffle, put in a fresh magazine, shoved it in the pocket of his cargo jeans and got out of the BMW.

Pain burned his butt like a raging wildfire. Maybe he'd break into the green house, take more pain meds and rest a bit before he left in the Taurus.

He slung the duffle over one shoulder and gritted his teeth. Forcing himself not to limp, he strode up the driveway like he belonged there, continued past the white house and studied the backyard.

No trees, no shrubs, just weedy grass that needed mowing. Beyond it, the backyard of the green house was dotted with well-trimmed shrubs and oak trees, the lawn recently mowed.

Fighting the pain, Nicolas limped across the yard, eased around a shrub at the corner of the house and entered the garage. It smelled like motor oil, cans of 10W40 lined up on a shelf beyond the hood of the Ford Taurus.

He set his duffle on the cement floor and opened the driver's door.

"Whatchyou doin with my car?" A deep male voice.

He whirled, the Beretta in his hand. "Freeze motherfucker or I'll kill you!"

The man jerked back in surprise. An elderly black man with gray hair, standing in the doorway to the house five feet away.

"Hands up or I'll shoot."

"No need to yell at me. Not gonna fight you." Gazing at him, expressionless.

"Where are the keys to the car?"

"In the kitchen. You want the car, take it."

Nicolas aimed the Beretta at the man's heart.

"Back up. One stupid move and you're dead."

CHAPTER 44

"What if he already stole a car and split?" Frank said, scanning cars as Claudia slowly drove along the street.

"He had to ditch the BMW somewhere," she said. "I saw blood in the hall near the station garage. Maybe he's too injured to drive. Maybe he's hiding in a vacant house somewhere."

"We need to find him pronto and get the tape Richie made. He killed Jackie to get it."

Many of the homes they passed had no lawn, the front yard used for parking their vehicles. Run-down houses, decades-old, their exteriors faded, bleached by the merciless sun.

His handset buzzed and Lieutenant Small said, "Give me your Sit-Reps. Unit One, go."

After Unit Five finished, Frank spoke into his handset, relieved that none of the other units had seen the BMW or Zurik. "Unit Six, nothing to report so far, still searching our grid. Out."

Claudia cruised down another street and said, "In this neighborhood a BMW would stick out like a Coco Chanel dress in a Dollar Store."

Frank nodded. All he'd seen so far were older sedans and pickup trucks. The houses all looked the same, one-story cottages with attached garages. Their only distinguishing feature: different colored siding, white mostly, a few faded greens and blues.

His cellphone rang. He answered and Roger said, "I just passed the Rite Aid. Looks like they're mobilizing a SWAT team."

"Damn!" He gave Roger their location and said to Claudia, "Park at the end of the block. Roger's meeting us. He saw a SWAT team mobilizing in the Rite Aid lot."

Five minutes later Roger pulled up behind them in the BU-car. He got out and trotted to their car, wearing a fresh polo shirt, no blood on his face. "See anything promising?"

"No," Frank said. "I don't like the sound of the SWAT team. Zurik knows he's wanted for multiple murders, won't give up without a fight. We need to find him before the Memphis cops do."

Claudia said, "We're wearing vests, Roger. Put one on and follow us in the BU-car."

Frank gave him the other handset and said, "Don't worry about the Sit-Reps. I'll do it."

Roger put on a vest and followed them.

Three sets of eyes looking for Zurik's BMW.

Claudia's cellphone rang. She answered, listened a minute and ended the call. "My friendly dispatcher says a guest at the Marriott Hotel reported his plate stolen this morning." Claudia looked over and smiled. "A Tennessee plate. He gave me the plate number."

———

Nicolas backed the old man into a small kitchen with a drop-leaf table set against one wall. Cramped but neat and tidy, smelling of cinnamon and Lemon Pledge. "Who else is here?"

"Ain't nobody here but me."

"There better not be. If you're lying, I'll shoot you." He looked in the living room adjacent to the kitchen and saw no one. "Show me how to put the garage door down."

"Can't. It's broke. Waitin' on a guy to fix it."

Gesturing with the Beretta, he said, "Show me."

In the garage the old man pointed to an electronic opener beside the door, two orange buttons, UP and DOWN. Wires ran up the wall, across the ceiling, and down to the door's motor.

"You put the door down, it won't go up again," the old man said.

Nicolas pressed the DOWN button. With an ominous grinding noise, the door came halfway down and stopped. Damn! Another problem. But the door was made of wood. If he had to, he'd back the Taurus through it.

He herded the old man back to the kitchen and sat him down in a chair. Took two zip-ties out of his duffle and said, "Put your hands behind the chair."

"I ain't goin' nowheres, no need to—"

"Shut up! Put your hands behind your back."

The man did as he was told. Nicolas fastened his wrists together with plastic zip-ties.

He went down the hall and checked the bathroom. Empty. Continued to the end of the hall. Two bedrooms on either side, also empty, pink décor on the left, dark blue on the right.

The old man was thinner than he was but almost as tall. He might find a shirt that fit him. He went in the blue bedroom.

In the bureau, he found a large sweatshirt and tossed it on the bed. In the closet, he found a jean jacket that might fit and saw a broad-brimmed sunhat on a shelf. He put the jacket and the hat on the bed and limped back to the kitchen.

"Who sleeps in the pink bedroom?"

"My daughter. She ain't here, she's at work."

"Where are the car keys?"

"Top drawer to the right of the sink," the old man said, watching him, his dark eyes wary.

He opened the drawer and took out the keys to the Taurus.

A shrill noise startled him. The telephone on the wall beside him. He held the receiver to his ear but didn't speak.

A male voice said, "This is a robo-alert from the Memphis Police Department. Be on the lookout for a black BMW and a white male in his forties, wearing cargo jeans and a newsboy hat. This man is armed and dangerous. If you see him, call 911 immediately."

Nicolas replaced the receiver. Damn it to bloody hell! Now every person in Memphis would be looking for him. Would this day ever end?

Papa had taught him to see many moves ahead and anticipate his opponent's moves. *If your King is threatened, the best thing to do is attack.*

But he couldn't. Wounded and vulnerable, he could only play defense.

Deadly in chess and in life.

"You the guy shot them folks in the train station?" the old man said. "I saw it on TV."

Alarmed, Nicolas limped into the living room and flinched. Opposite a three-cushion sofa, a muted television displayed the bloody carnage at the station. He upped the volume.

A somber black woman gazed into the camera and said, "We've just learned that six people died at the train station. Two dozen others are wounded. Memphis police are searching for the gunman, a white man in his forties, and the vehicle he may be driving."

The numbers surprised him. Six people dead? Two dozen wounded?

A photo of his black BMW appeared on the screen. Then his picture.

Fear rippled through his body. His picture on TV! A hunted man. Trapped in Memphis. Alone and injured, agonizing pain in his hip.

Exhausted, hungry and desperate for sleep.

But he couldn't sleep. He couldn't even lie down and rest.

He had to remain vigilant. He muted the TV and limped into the kitchen.

"You're bleeding," the old man said, nodding his head at drops of blood on the kitchen floor. "Best take care of that. There's bandages in the bathroom, and antibiotic ointment."

He opened the refrigerator, looked inside and took out two bottles of water. Opened one and gulped half the contents. Opened the other bottle and said, "Want some water?"

"Yes, but I can't hold it with my hands tied."

And I'm not going to untie them.

He held the bottle to the man's mouth. "Drink up. I'm going to use your bathroom. Don't do anything stupid while I'm in there."

The man took three swallows and turned his head away.

Nicolas put the bottled waters on the table and headed for the bathroom to tend his wounds.

Luther Martin Kingman watched the man limp down the hall. Didn't fool him none, giving him a drink of water. The muthafucka would as soon shoot him as not. He had to get him out the house before Delight came home for lunch.

His beautiful daughter, the light of his life.

Her momma's too, until Maybelle got the cancer that put her in the grave. Four years ago Delight found out her no-good husband was fooling around, ditched him and asked Luther to move in with her.

Smart and ambitious, Delight worked her ass off at a community college for two years to get a degree in dental technology.

Luther stayed home with his grandson—Luther Junior, but everybody called him LJ—happy to have company now that Maybelle was gone. LJ called him Pops, loved helping him vacuum the house and mow the lawn.

Delight worked at a dentist's office, cleaned Luther's teeth every four months so they gleamed like those toothpaste ads on TV. Once in a while she called if she wasn't busy, but not today.

When the phone rang a while ago, the man with the gun picked it up, listened for a bit and hung up the phone, not looking happy.

Might have been a mistake, asking if he was the one shot those poor folks at the train station. The man had gone in the living room, came back with a big frown on his face.

Every Sunday he and Delight took LJ to the New Hope Baptist Church, listened to the preacher speak about God. Luther was a God-fearing man, but right now he was more afraid of the man with the gun.

And what he might do with it.

He thought about LJ downstairs in his bedroom. No TV down there so LJ couldn't see the bloody mess at the train station. Five years old, cute as a button and twice as smart. Not in first grade yet, already knew how to read, Delight reading to him at bedtime every night.

Luther looked at the clock on the wall above the gate-leg table, bright red with silver hands, so Delight could see it while she ate breakfast 'fore she went to work. So she'd be punctual.

Delight loved using big words. Not *on time*. *Punctual.*

Now it was 11:35. Thirty minutes from now Delight would be here. Leave the dental office at noon, the office only five minutes away.

Sometimes the good Lord helped folks.

Other times the good Lord expected folks to help themselves.

Luther was already thinking on a plan. LJ knew when it was time for lunch.

Also knew his mother was punctual, liable to come upstairs any minute.

No way was he gonna let the muthafucka hurt his grandson.

———

In bathroom, Nicolas pulled down his cargo jeans and underwear. The diaper he'd taped over the wound was leaking blood. Knowing it would hurt, he ripped off the tape, biting his lip so he wouldn't scream. Inflamed red skin surrounded the three-inch gash. He ran hot water over a clean facecloth and wiped blood off the wound. Using the tube of antibiotic ointment he'd found in the medicine cabinet, he smeared what was left over the gash.

An image flashed in his mind, Papa, in the morgue when the London cops made him identify him. One shot in the forehead, two in the chest, eyes closed, lips pulled back. Death had not come instantly. There had been pain.

Now he was facing his own mortality.

What would happen to his beloved son? Nicky. Alone in Chicago.

Would he ever see him again?

Unwilling to contemplate this, he covered the wound with the bandages he'd found and taped them to his skin with surgical tape. He pulled up his underwear and cargo jeans. Took three pain pills and washed them down with a handful of water. Picked up the Beretta and left the bathroom.

When he stepped into the hall, the old man called, "Find everything you needed?"

He tried not to limp as he entered the kitchen. "Yes. Thank you."

"Got leftover mac and cheese in the refrigerator," the old man said. "My daughter made it for dinner last night. Help yourself. Heat it in the microwave, it's mighty tasty."

Nicolas opened the refrigerator, saw a ceramic bowl and took it out. Put it in the microwave and reheated it for thirty seconds. "You want more water?"

The old man shook his head. "Not now, maybe later."

His hip throbbed relentlessly as he limped into the living room with the bowl and sank onto the three-cushion sofa.

On the TV screen, news helicopter footage showed a number of police cars and ambulances outside the train station. Then video clips appeared, taken on cellphones by people who'd been there, jerky footage but clear enough to see what was happening.

Shoveling macaroni into his mouth, he watched to see if his face was visible. It wasn't, not with the newsboy cap pulled down over his forehead.

But Renzi was, wearing an Elvis jacket and a grim look.

He knew that look. A predator seeking its prey.

Then scene shifted to the newswoman who said, "We just got word that a SWAT team is mobilizing in connection with the train station massacre."

A SWAT team. He had to get out of here.

But the pain was worse now, a vicious buzz-saw raking his hip, and his head felt fuzzy, too fuzzy to drive. Maybe he'd rest for a few minutes.

He set the empty bowl on the coffee table and leaned back against the sofa.

He was tired. So tired.

CHAPTER 45

Another round of Sit-Reps, no reports of a black BMW, Lieutenant Donna Small increasingly testy. Multiple casualties at the train station, Frank figured she'd catch hell if her troops didn't find the shooter.

He was glad the other units hadn't spotted the BMW, but he hadn't either.

They'd been searching their grid for more than a hour, no sign of Zurik or his black BMW.

Claudia eased around a corner and started down another street. Frank saw a black BMW up ahead, parked in front of a white cottage.

"That's it!" he said. "It's got a Tennessee plate."

"I see it," Claudia said. "But I can't tell if he's in it."

"Slow down and do a drive-by. I'll call Roger." He got on his cellphone, called Roger and said, "Zurik's BMW is up ahead. Pull over and wait while Claudia and I do a drive-by to see if he's in the car. Be ready."

"Don't worry," Roger said grimly. "I'm ready."

"If he's not in the car, we'll drive around the block and look for any suspicious activity. You stay here and watch the BMW."

Claudia slowed to a crawl as they drew closer. Juiced with adrenaline, Frank took out his SIG, alert for any movement as they crept past the BMW.

No one was inside.

Claudia stopped in front of the white cottage. "No vehicles outside."

Frank peered down the driveway. "The backyard abuts the backyard of the cottage behind it. Drive around and check the street parallel to this one."

Claudia circled the block to the next street over and drifted past homes along the tree-lined street.

Agitated, Frank said, "Look! That garage door is halfway up and there's a car inside."

"The drapes are shut on the front windows, but I can see lights inside near the garage."

"We need to get a closer look. Let's go back and talk to Roger."

They circled back and stopped beside Roger in the BU-car. Frank rolled down his window and said, "We think Zurik might be in the cottage behind this one. Park your car behind the BMW and get in ours so we can make a plan."

When Roger got in the back seat of their car, Claudia said, "There's a car in the garage attached to the green cottage behind this one, but we can't just storm the house. Other people might be in danger."

"He might have killed them already," Frank said.

Claudia took out her Glock. "I'll go check it out. Run through the backyard and look in the windows to see who's in the house."

"You want backup?" Frank said. "If Zurik sees you, he might start shooting."

"No. Be back as soon as I know something." Claudia got out and trotted up the driveway.

Frank got out of the car and adjusted his windbreaker over the Kevlar vest, already sweltering in the heat. Holding a Glock-9, Roger gestured at the garage attached to the white cottage. "Let's wait behind the garage. If Zurik starts shooting, we'll be closer."

Three minutes later Claudia was back. "Good news, bad news. No sign of Zurik, but an older black man is in the kitchen, sitting in a chair with his arms behind his back, zip-ties on his wrists."

"Zurik's in there," Frank said. "Left his BMW here, figured he'd steal the car."

"Shall we call it in to Lieutenant Small?" Claudia said.

"Hell no!" he said. "They fucked us over at the station. We need to grab Zurik now. He took the evidence Jackie had with her. We need to get it before the Memphis cops do."

"Okay," Claudia said, "but wait until I call the town hall to get the census data for the green cottage. That will tell us who's in there. Might not just be the old man."

———

Luther Martin Kingman sat very still, focused on his grandson. No sense trying to bust the ties on his wrists, best to use his mind. Not quite lunchtime but he'd give it a shot.

He closed his eyes and commenced speaking in his mind, used his wheedle voice like when he wanted LJ to do something for him.

And he surely did want the boy to do something.

You getting hungry, LJ? Got summa that honey-ham you like, gonna make you the best sandwich you ever had. Spread sweet pickle relish on the bread, throw on some slices of honey-ham, maybe add a slice of Swiss cheese.

He paused a moment. Sometime it took several minutes to get the boy's attention and he might not have several minutes, the muthafucka asleep in the living room now, could wake up any minute.

Focused on LJ, he spoke more words in his mind.

Last time I checked there's chocolate chip ice cream left in that carton your mamma bought at the grocery store. Forget those dang books you be reading and come upstairs and see me!

Luther cocked his head and listened. No footsteps on the stairs. But LJ might not have put on his sneakers, might be barefoot.

He waited a moment. Still nothing. Gathered himself.

Spoke stern words in his mind. *Goddammit, LJ, put down the book you reading and get yo ass up here 'fore I come down there and give you what-for!*

Watching the door to the basement.

Lord be praised! The door opened a crack

LJ's face appeared. Saw his Granddaddy tied to a chair, his eyes went wide, his mouth opened ...

Luther shook his head violently, rolled his lips together.

The boy got the message right quick, shut his mouth.

Luther motioned with his head. *C'mon over here.* Flapped his lips together. *Be quiet.*

LJ, his daughter's only child and the apple of Luther's eye, tiptoed toward him, barefoot. Whispered in his ear, "Why you tied to the chair, Pops?"

"Bad man done it," Luther whispered. "Quiet. He sleeping on the sofa." Jerked his head at the living room. "Climb up on the counter, git me one-a-them knives in the butcher block."

Quick as a wink, LJ hoisted himself up on the counter, like he did when he woke up early and wanted his Fruit Loops *right now*!

Luther jerked his head at the knives. LJ slid sideways on his knees, stared at the knives and pulled out the biggest one. Luther smiled. Five years old, the boy already knew bigger was better.

Also knew enough to ease off the counter quietly, not jump off and land with a thump. Came over and whispered, "Want me cut you loose, Pops?"

"Fast as you can," Luther whispered.

The boy commenced sawing at the plastic ties the muthafucka had fastened around his wrists, careful not to saw his wrists by mistake.

Took hardly any time at all. Luther smiled at his grandson, stretched his arms above his head to get the kinks out and whispered, "Remember what I showed you in the drawer on the table beside my bed?"

LJ nodded, his eyes solemn.

"Go git it for me. Quiet as a mouse."

The boy scampered down the hall lickety-split and disappeared. Came back and handed him the snub-nosed .22 caliber revolver. Luther tucked it inside his work shirt and whispered, "Good work, LJ. Here's what I want you to do. Take that knife downstairs to your bedroom and lock the door."

"He gonna hurt you, Pops? I'll stay here and protect you."

Luther's throat clogged up and he couldn't speak. At last he said, "Don't you worry 'bout that, LJ. Go downstairs to your room, lock the door and don't open it till I tell you."

LJ kissed his cheek and tiptoed to the cellar door. Gave him a forlorn look and disappeared. And forgot to close the door.

Luther put his hands behind the chair like he was still tied up, praying the muthafucka wouldn't come in the kitchen, notice the basement door was open and go looking for a reason why.

Lord be praised!

LJ came back and shut the door, the good Lord answering his prayers.

———

Nicolas woke with a start. Were those voices?

Or voices in his mind, playing tricks on him.

Nerves jangling, he straightened up on the sofa and leaned forward so he could look in the kitchen. The old man sat in the chair, not looking at him, the house quiet as a tomb. False alarm.

But the picture on the TV screen was no false alarm. The photograph on his driver's license. Damn it to hell! Everyone within a hundred miles of Memphis was looking for him.

With an angry motion, he flicked the remote and the TV faded to black.

He was a hunted man, like that TV show. *Paladin: Have Gun, Will Travel.*

He had a gun, but he couldn't travel. His head throbbing, burning pain in hip, a festering wound in his butt, possibly infected, soon to be an abscess without medical attention. That wouldn't happen anytime soon.

Hospitals had television sets. And security guards.

His eyes fell upon a magazine on the coffee table. A smiling family on the cover of *Family Circle,* two parents with a little girl and a dark-haired boy about Nicky's age.

A terrible empty feeling grew inside him, worse than the pain from his wounds. Nicky was alone in Chicago.

He'd been looking forward to spending time with him. Telling him stories about growing up in London with Papa. Teaching him to play chess, explaining the intricacies of the game, teaching him to speak Russian like a Muscovite.

A desperate yearning to hear his son's voice seized him.

But hearing Nicky's voice would rip him apart. Render him unable to speak. He took out his cellphone and composed a text.

Call my friend now. He will help you. XO

Blinking back tears, he hit Send.

Quickly composed another text.

Help Nicky. Farewell my faithful friend. XO

He hit Send and deleted both numbers. Removed the Sim card and shoved it under the seat cushion beside him.

Sooner or later the cops would find it, but by then it wouldn't matter.

He would be dead.

But not without a fight.

He took out the Beretta and set it on the coffee table.

CHAPTER 46

Frank was ready to explode. Waiting. He hated waiting.

Waiting was dangerous. All it would take was one phone call. Someone sees the news about the train station massacre on TV, wonders why three strange cars are parked on their street, dials 9-11 and a squad of MPD cruisers arrive in two minutes flat. With a SWAT team.

Standing five feet away from him behind the white cottage, Claudia held a cellphone to her ear, waiting for a clerk at city hall to tell her who lived in the green cottage at 4334 Primrose Lane.

Frank was waiting for Roger to come back from a recon mission on the green cottage, his mind working overtime, formulating a plan.

Roger burst around the side of the green house and raced across the back-yard. Panting, he said to Frank, "He's in there! I saw him!"

Claudia put her cellphone away and said, "Did you see anyone else?"

"No," Roger said, "but I saw Zurik sitting on a couch in the living room. His weapon's on the coffee table. Might be a Beretta, but I'm not positive."

"What about the other rooms?" Claudia said.

"All the blinds are shut," Roger said. "Curtains on the front windows are too, but I managed to peek through a gap where they weren't closed tight."

"Three people live there," Claudia said. "Luther Kingman, age 59, likely the man tied up in the kitchen. Delight Kingman, age 32, likely his daughter, and Luther Junior, age five."

"We need to move now," Frank said. "I'm not giving Lieutenant Small an-other Sit-Rep."

"Wait," Claudia said. "What about the grandfather?"

"Fuck waiting! Here's the plan. Roger parks the BU-car sideways across the driveway. Claudia stands behind the BU-car with the bullhorn. I'm hiding be-side the garage. Claudia yells at Zurik to come out. Hopefully this lures him to the front window. I go in the garage, shoot out the back tires of the Toyota, make him think he's surrounded and get into the house."

"What if the woman and the kid are in there?" Claudia said.

Exasperated, Frank said. "Roger, go get the BU-car. Now."

Roger turned and dashed around the corner to the street.

Claudia clamped her lips together, silently fuming.

"Claudia, I'll get the old man out if I can, but if we don't go in, Zurik will kill him and steal the car. He'll kill anyone who gets in his way. All it takes is one bullet."

Not from Zurik's gun, a slug from his SIG.

This time Zurik wasn't getting away.

Get the bastard in his sights and shoot him.

———

Luther watched the minute hand click forward on the big red clock. 11:53. Twelve minutes from now Delight would come home and park in the driveway, expecting to eat lunch. Might see the garage door half open and wonder about it. No telling what she'd do when she came in the door and saw him tied up.

Not that he was really tied up. Had to keep his arms behind his back in case the muthafucka in the living room looked in the kitchen.

His arms were mighty tired though, about ready to cramp up. He flexed his fingers to get the blood flowing. Leaned sideways and checked the living room. Made sure the man wasn't looking his way. Stretched his arm over his head.

Touched the revolver hidden under his work shirt.

If Delight saw the man with the gun she would freak out, thinking LJ might be hurt. Anyone threatened LJ, Delight was a tigress protecting her cub.

Question was, what would the man with the gun do?

Luther thought on it. He could scream to get Delight's attention. Tell her LJ was downstairs, safe in his room. But that would take a few seconds and he might not have a few seconds.

Maybe he'd just shoot the man and hope the good Lord would forgive him for taking a life. Something he'd never imagined he'd ever do.

But a man had to protect his family.

The minute hand clicked forward. Now it was 11:54.

Eleven minutes until Delight walked in the door.

Then he heard a mechanical-sounding voice, say, "Come out with your hands up, Nicolas. We know you're in there. The house is surrounded."

Lord be praised! The police were here! But that didn't mean he was safe.

The man with the gun might decide to shoot it out with the cops. And here he'd be in the middle of it, bullets flying around.

What if LJ heard the shots and took it into his head to come upstairs?

Luther lowered his right arm and unbuttoned his shirt. Reached inside and wrapped his hand around the butt of the revolver.

Any shooting started, he'd be ready.

———

Nicolas jolted upright on the sofa. Was that cops yelling at him?

Not quite awake, he shook his head, his brain sluggish. Leaning forward, he used both hands to lift himself off the sofa. Excruciating pain shot through his butt and hip, prodding him fully alert.

Cops were outside the house! His worst nightmare.

He grabbed the Beretta and crept to the front window. Parted the curtain slightly. A black SUV was parked sideways at the end of the driveway. Standing behind the hood, a woman with dark hair held a bullhorn in her hand.

Telling him the house was surrounded.

The woman with Renzi at the station. The woman who'd shot him.

The light-skinned black man beside her looked familiar, holding a handgun with both hands like he knew how to use it.

Not Memphis cops. Frank Renzi and his colleagues. Where was Renzi?

He backed away from the window, gritting his teeth against the pain.

All the feel-good philosophers said money didn't bring happiness. Maybe not, but money got you other things.

A good education, better food, the best doctors.

Most of all, money bought you time and freedom and peace of mind.

None of which he had right now. Badly injured and alone. Nicky far away.

After Papa died, he had vowed to detach himself from others.

Trust no one and protect himself. Until Nicky was born, and he once again understood how important family ties were.

Just as world-class athletes took hours to warm up for a big event, chess Grand-masters prepared carefully before facing an opponent. Weighing alternatives, making decisions. No room for fear or doubt.

Above all, never look weak.

Russians hate weak like the stink of rotting fish. Papa's words.

His BMW was only a block away. Take the important items in his duffle with him and ditch the rest. If he could make it past the black man and the woman who'd shot him at the station, he still might survive.

As long as Renzi didn't ambush him.

Two gunshots shattered his plan. Not outside, in the garage.

Renzi was in the garage!

Soon he would be inside the house.

This he could not allow.

Gripping the Beretta in both hands, Nicolas went in the kitchen.

———

Frank crouched beside the Taurus, his back flat against the wall opposite the kitchen door, his ears still ringing. Before he shot out the back tires, he'd crept around the car to the door and peeked through the window in the top half.

The grandfather was in the kitchen, tied up but alive. No one else in sight. No sign of Zurik. But the door to the kitchen was locked. If he broke the window, Zurik might charge into the kitchen and shoot the old man.

Too risky. He had to get Zurik out of the house.

Claudia had set up a three-way call so they could communicate. Holding the SIG in one hand, he eased his Smartphone out of his pocket with the other and said softly, "No visual on Zurik. The grandfather's okay, still tied up in the kitchen. No one else that I could see."

"After I yelled at him with the bullhorn, the curtains moved on the front window," Claudia said. "He saw me and Roger for sure."

"I got no shot if he comes in the kitchen," Frank said. "The civilian's in my line of fire."

"How about we shoot out the front window?" Roger said. "Force his hand, make him think his best escape route is through the garage."

Frank thought about it. "Too dangerous. He might kill the old man, and we don't know if there are other hostages are in there. We need to keep him out of the kitchen. Claudia, get on the bullhorn again and tell him to come out the front door and surrender."

He put the cellphone in his pocket and waited.

Heard Claudia on the bullhorn. *The house is surrounded, Nicolas. Put down the gun and come out the front door with your hands up.*

He waited twenty seconds, hoping Claudia would tell him Zurik was out of the house. She didn't.

He got on his cellphone. "Maybe I can talk to him. Break the window in the door and—"

"Watch out!" a voice shouted. "He's got a gun!"

CHAPTER 47

"Shut up!" Nicolas said, standing in the doorway to the kitchen, the Beretta in his hand.

The old man gave him a venomous look, his dark eyes full of fury.

Flattening his back against the kitchen wall, Nicolas sidestepped to the garage door. Looked through the window. No one visible from this angle, but he was certain Renzi was in the garage.

He released the deadbolt. Whipped open the door and ducked back.

No shots fired at him. Renzi, playing possum.

He eased his head around the doorjamb for a quick look around the garage. He saw no one, but that didn't mean Renzi wasn't out there.

"Let the old man go. Take me instead."

He knew that voice. Renzi, the man who'd thwarted his getaway plan.

Calling Jackie in the Memphis hotel.

Sending cops after Martina to rescue Nora.

Lying in wait for him at the train station.

Tracking his car somehow, and finding it.

Pent up rage and anger exploded inside him.

He stepped into the doorway and shot out the front window of the Taurus. An explosion of glass showered across the front seat.

His next shot spewed glass out the window on the far side.

He ducked back and stood beside the door, ignoring the pain in his hip.

Focused on one thing. Annihilate Renzi.

His extra ammo was in the trunk of the BMW, but he'd come to the house with a fully loaded Beretta.

Fifteen .40 caliber rounds. Thirteen left.

Plenty to kill Renzi.

———

The car window above him exploded, raining glass down upon him. Frank brushed tiny cubes of glass off his hair. A few of them slid down his neck into his shirt.

Silence for several seconds. Then, "Frank! Are you okay?"

Claudia's voice on his Smartphone.

"Yes," he said. "But Zurik's in the kitchen. He opened the door to the garage and shot out the front windows of the Taurus. The old man is still tied up in the kitchen. You two stay put while I distract Zurik. Get him talking, maybe I can lure him into the garage."

"Stop hiding, Renzi! Stand up and face me like a man."

He took a deep breath, filling his lungs with air, knowing it could be the last breath he'd take. But he had no intention of letting Nicolas kill him.

Nicolas Zurik was an ego-driven man who considered himself above the law, ordering people killed if they got in his way. The three men in the High Roller Club. Then the shooter he'd paid to kill them.

When he found out Jackie had the tape Richie had made implicating Nicolas in the betting scheme, ruthless to the core, he'd murdered her in cold blood.

But sometimes egotistical killers made mistakes. Their biggest weakness? They couldn't resist talking about how smart they were.

Frank set his Smartphone to videotape mode, upped the volume and slipped it onto the hood of the Taurus. "Why'd you kill Jackie?"

"She lied to me. The New Jersey feds sent Richie a subpoena. She said she didn't have it."

"How did you know about the subpoena? Did Richie tell you?"

"No, but he should have. If he'd told me, none this would have happened. My so-called friend was all set to rat me out to the feds in Atlantic City. I couldn't let that happen."

So you paid someone kill him. "Why would he testify against you?"

"He was giving me tips on NBA games. Richie acted like he was squeaky clean, but he was making big bucks. His pal Benny was laying bets for him. Richie knew when to blow the whistle near the end of games, to make sure his team covered the spread."

Frank thought about what Claudia had told him. Some sports bettors made millions of dollars. And Zurik was getting tips from the ref who was officiating the games.

"You were making big bucks too, right? Betting on games. But how would the feds know that?"

"Richie double-crossed me. He taped one of our conversations at the golf club. Suckered me into asking him for tips, kept saying my name, so he could cut a deal with the feds. After all I did for him. Got him into the golf club, drove his kid to school. He knew it would ruin my life, but Richie didn't care. It was all about him."

No, it was all about you, Nicolas.

"Where's the tape?"

Silence. Too much silence, Nicolas thinking things over now.

Frank scooted alongside the car, knelt beside a flat tire and looked across the trunk at the door. "Put down the gun and come in the garage with your hands over your head."

Zurik stepped into the doorway, his face pale and sweaty, his eyes full of fury, raised the Beretta ....

Frank dove to the cement.

Blam. A slug blew past him and slammed into the garage wall.

He crawled forward to the front passenger door. Rose to his knees, SIG in one hand, the other braced against the car door. Peeked through the car window.

Blam. Another slug ripped into the garage wall.

———

Nicolas gathered his hatred for Renzi into a tight ball of anger. The self-righteous cop with the holier-than-thou attitude. Acting as though he'd never killed anyone, when he'd killed plenty.

After Renzi came to his office, he'd looked him up on the NOPD website. Homicide Detective Frank Renzi. First with Boston PD, then with NOPD in New Orleans. Cited in several officer-involved shootings over the years.

A film of sweat slicked his face and beads of sweat trickled down his back like an army of bugs. A desperate craving swept over him.

He wanted a cigarette, a nicotine rush to sooth him, the way it did when he shared a Gauloise Blonde with Yvette during their trysts.

If only he was with her, stroking her gamine face, feeling the warmth of her naked body pressed against his.

If only he wasn't so tired, his head feverish, his legs weak and shaky.

If only he had the energy to keep shooting at Renzi and kill the bastard.

But the pain had sapped his energy. His hope of escape was wishful thinking.

He stepped into the doorway, the Beretta in his hand. "Go ahead and shoot me, Renzi."

"No, drop the gun and put your hands behind your head."

"You don't have the balls to kill me. You're a wuss, like Richie."

He saw Renzi's eyes focus on something behind him. Had his reflexes been quicker, he might have saved himself, but his reaction time was too slow.

A bullet ripped into his lower back on the left side.

How could that be? He tried to make sense of it. Renzi was in the garage.

The old man was tied to the chair.

The other cops were outside in front of the house.

Staggering sideways, he gripped the kitchen counter with one hand, barely able to stand, the pain radiating upward from his back.

He tried to raise the Beretta and shoot Renzi. He'd kill the fucker!

But his arms were leaden, his hands trembling.

Nicky. He would never see his beloved son again.

But Alexei would take care of him.

A loud bang. Another slug hit him. Searing pain in his neck left him gasping for breath, the pain excruciating now. He fell to the floor. Tried to think but his mind wouldn't cooperate, slowing like a subway car coasting into a station.

His mouth filled with a coppery liquid. Blood.

Time slowed to a standstill. Agonizing moments of terror.

Unable to move, his body paralyzed.

His body convulsed. His legs hitched and jerked, his feet drumming a tattoo on the floor.

———

Shocked, Frank stared at the old man. All along he'd thought the grandfather was tied up, his hands trussed behind his back.

But he wasn't, and he had a gun.

Zurik lay on his back in the kitchen, utterly still, his eyes staring unseeing at the ceiling. Crimson blood spilled from his mouth onto the floor.

When Frank stepped into the kitchen, the gray-haired grandfather placed a snub-nosed .22 caliber revolver on the table and said, "You gonna arrest me?"

Fighting the urge to laugh, he said, "Arrest you? Hell, no. You deserve a medal."

"Frank! Talk to me!" Claudia's frantic voice on his Smartphone in the garage.

He ran to the garage, grabbed it off the hood of the Taurus and said, "Zurik is dead. I'm fine and so is Mr. Kingman. Roger, run back to Zurik's BMW and get everything in the trunk. Break in if you have to."

"On it," Roger said.

"Claudia," he said, "don't call it in until I bring Zurik's duffle bag out to you. Put it in the BU-car."

"Okay, but I hear sirens. Someone might have called MPD already."

Frank went back in the kitchen and said, "I'll bring Mr. Kingman out the front door right away." He closed the phone and put it in his pocket.

Kingman frowned. "Delight be home in two minutes. I gotta go get my grandson."

Stunned, Frank said, "He's *here*?"

"In the basement. He's the one cut me loose." Kingman went to a door in the hall, opened it and called, "LJ, get on up here. It's safe now."

Footsteps on the stairs. A little boy burst through the door and jumped into his grandfather's arms. Kingman patted his back and said, "It's okay, LJ. The bad man's dead."

Turning so the boy couldn't see the bloody carnage, he said to Frank, "The man's bag is in the living room."

Frank took his arm and led him past the pool of blood into the living room. Zurik's duffle was on the sofa. His cellphone was on the table. He grabbed the duffle bag and the cellphone and hustled the grandfather out the door.

Claudia ran up to them. "Mr. Kingman, are you and the boy all right?"

"Mighty fine now that we're outta the house."

"They both deserve a medal," Frank said. He gave the duffle and cellphone to Claudia and said, "Put them in the BU-car before MPD gets here. We'll check them later at the hotel."

A white Toyota screeched to a halt in front of the house.

"Momma!" the boy screamed, kicking his feet. "Momma's here."

A slender black woman jumped out of the Toyota and ran toward them, screaming, "What happened?" Mr. Kingman set the boy down and his mother swept him into her arms.

The sirens were louder now, maybe a block away.

"Claudia," Frank said, "put Zurik's stuff in the car and call this in so we're on record reporting it."

Claudia ran to the BU-car, opened the trunk, slung the duffle and cellphone inside and slammed it shut.

Frank turned to Luther Kingman and said, "You were very brave. The man's a killer. Wanted for murders in New Orleans and London."

"Shot them folks at the station, too. I couldn't let him hurt my grandson. Or my daughter. She comes home every day to eat lunch with us. Never thought I'd kill a person, but—"

Frank squeezed his shoulder. "You did the right thing. Don't let anybody tell you different. You had to protect your family." He took out his card, gave it to Kingman and said, "You need someone to back you up, call me and I'll set them straight."

Kingman looked at it and held out his hand. "Nice to meet you Detective Renzi."

Frank smiled and shook his hand. "Glad to meet you, Luther. Call me Frank."

Then three MPD cruisers arrived, sirens screaming, followed by a SWAT team in an armored vehicle.

———

Two squads of MPD officers entered the cottage at 4334 Primrose Lane. Beside the BU-car, Claudia was talking to Delight and her son.

Frank stood on the front lawn with Roger. "What was in the BMW?"

"Plenty," Roger said. "A trash bag full of cash and extra ammo, and a laptop. I didn't waste time looking at it, just put it in the trunk of Claudia's rental car."

"I didn't have time to check Zurik's duffle bag either. Claudia barely had time to sling it in the BU-car trunk before the cops got here."

"We can check it out at the hotel," Roger said. "No one's the wiser."

"Exactly. Possession is nine-tenths of the law." He saw Luther frown and shake his head at the MPD officer questioning him.

Frank hurried over to them and said to the officer. "I don't want any misconceptions about what happened here. A dangerous criminal invaded this man's house with a gun and threatened to kill him. Isn't that right, Mr. Kingman?"

Luther nodded. "He surely did."

The MPD officer frowned at Frank. "And you are?"

"NOPD Homicide Detective Frank Renzi," he said and flashed his ID badge. "I was in the garage. The killer was shooting at me. If it wasn't for Mr. Kingman, I'd be dead." He gestured at Luther's grandson. "See that cute little boy over there? He's five years old and he was in the basement. Mr. Kingman was defending his family."

The officer looked over at the boy. "Okay. I didn't know that."

"Mr. Kingman will tell you what happened. I think he deserves a medal of commendation from you folks." Frank took out his card and gave it to the MPD officer. "If you have any questions, call me. I'll be writing a full report for the NOPD Superintendent."

The officer took the card and said grudgingly, "Thanks for the clarification."

Frank nodded and said to Luther, "You have any problems, give me a call."

Luther smiled, his eyes crinkling at the corners. "Thank you. And thank you for distracting the man with the gun. Seemed like he was hellbent on killing you. I'm mighty glad he didn't."

CHAPTER 48

TWO WEEKS LATER

TUESDAY NOVEMBER 4, 2014 – 5:45 PM

Frank opened the cover of the gas grill on Kelly's back porch. He'd been here since Saturday. Four days off, courtesy of Vobitch. Last Friday he'd given Vobitch his written report on the events in Memphis.

The High Roller case was closed. The shooter was dead and so was the man who'd hired him. The body of Nicolas Zurik, aka Nicolas Kozlovich, remained in the Memphis morgue, unclaimed.

Yesterday Claudia Cohen had called him and said her contact at the Chicago FBI office had identified the shooter. Ten days ago, his wife had gone to the Russian Embassy in London and gave embassy officials a copy of their marriage certificate and their wedding photograph, taken six months earlier. Five weeks ago her Russian-born husband, Sasha Yukovich, age 23, had flown to America. Katerina feared he was dead.

"Another London connection," Frank said.

"Exactly," Claudia said. "We know Zurik was involved with a Russian gang in London years ago. Maybe he still had friends over there."

"Did you get a copy of the photograph?"

"Yes. Not a great copy, but it's definitely the shooter."

"What about Katerina? Did the Russians tell her he's dead?"

"I doubt that she had anything to do with the High Roller Club murders," Claudia said, "and officials at the Russian Embassy likely don't even know about it. Maybe your NOPD boss can contact them."

Frank thanked her, called Vobitch and recapped what Claudia had just told him. "Katerina won't be happy to find out her husband was murdered in the Orleans Parish Prison."

"The girl didn't know what she was getting into," Vobitch had said. "No way I'm calling the Russian Embassy in London. I'll tell the Super, see what he wants to do. At least we got Big Dawgg. Maybe Katerina can sue him for civil damages. Denial of conjugal benefits or some fucking thing."

Frank brushed Teriyaki sauce over the salmon fillets and closed the cover, thinking: *Throw a rock in a pond, no telling where the ripples wind up.*

Big Dawgg was in the OPP lockup, complaining about the food. No more chitlins for Big Dawgg. The OPP Sheriff had identified one of the prisoners who'd beaten Sasha Yukovich to death. The DA convinced him to cop a plea. Facing a Murder One charge, the prisoner said Big Dawgg ordered the hit. The prisoner agreed to testify at Big Dawgg's trial, and the DA put him into the Witness Protection Program so Big Dawgg's gang couldn't whack him.

Frank raised the lid on the grill and checked the salmon fillets. Perfect. He put them on a platter and carried it into the kitchen.

"Good timing," Kelly said. "I just put the sweet potatoes on the table."

He poured two glasses of wine and they dug into the grilled salmon Teriyaki. After a while, Frank said, "Danny called me on Saturday."

"How does he like living with his grandparents in Crown Heights?"

"I didn't ask. I was happy he called me, didn't want to rock the boat. He said he'd made friends with some kids at school and he liked his teachers. Also said he tried out for basketball and made the JV team. He didn't mention his mother. Or Nicky."

"What a sad situation," Kelly said. "Just as well he doesn't know about Nicky. Or Martina."

Martina Zurik was in a federal prison near Memphis, awaiting trial for kidnapping, accessory to Jackie's murder and several other charges. Attorney Boris Mosgov argued for bail, but the judge denied it, saying she was a flight risk. Martina kept asking to see Nicky. Her father, Pavel Volkovich, had visited her twice, demanding that she be allowed to see her son.

Who was nowhere to be found.

The search of Zurik's house had yielded a photo of Nicky, so Frank gave it to the media, asking if anyone had seen him. Two days later the manager of a New Orleans limo service called him. One of his drivers had recognized Nicky from the photo. The manager said Anthony Hill had called on October twentieth, the day before the Memphis shootout, and hired a limo to drive his nephew from Ponchatoula to O'Hare Airport in Chicago. He paid with a credit card and asked the driver to pick the boy up at a pizza shop in Ponchatoula.

The name got Frank's attention. Anthony Hill was the name on one of the credit cards in Zurik's duffle. Frank interviewed the driver, who said the kid was polite and slept part of the way. When they got to O'Hare, the boy said he knew where to meet his father, no need to come in with him.

The last known sighting of Nicky. None of the manifests for flights departing O'Hare that day or any day that week had his name on them.

Dead end. Nicky was gone.

"Did you talk to Nora?" Kelly said.

"Yes. She misses her mom, but she loves being in first grade. Leah got her into a private school for girls in Crown Heights. Nora said she didn't have to make up any work because she already knew how to read. Then she asked me to come up and see her. So we could go for a walk."

Kelly raised an eyebrow. "Are you going to visit them?"

"I might. I'm flying to Philly next week to spend some time with Maureen—"

"And check out the new boyfriend," Kelly said, smiling mischievously.

"That too. But it's an easy drive from Philly to Crown Heights. After I talked to Nora, Jackie's father got on the line and practically ordered me to come up there, said he'd put me up in a hotel and they'd love to meet me."

Kelly burst out laughing. "Same old Jack, ordering people around. But give him credit for taking the kids. It would be great if you could see them."

Frank sipped some wine, feeling the weight of responsibility. Before Jackie left for Memphis, she'd mailed a copy of the subpoena and a thumb drive to her lawyer. Frank listened to the tape Richie made for Danny and Nora, telling them how much he loved them and how ashamed he was for letting them down, gambling on games he officiated.

A whole new side of Richie, one he hadn't expected. And the main reason why he felt obligated to go to Crown Heights. He wanted to play the tape for Jack and Leah and let them decide when Danny and Nora should hear it.

He took a news clipping out of his briefcase and put it on the table. "At least something good came out of Memphis."

"What a great picture!" Kelly exclaimed. "Luther and his grandson, right?"

"Yes. His daughter sent it to me. That's her standing beside the Memphis mayor and the police chief. Luther and LJ are holding the check they gave them. A three thousand dollar reward for capturing a dangerous criminal."

"They must be happy about that."

"Not happy about what they went through to get it. Luther called and asked me not to tell anyone LJ got the gun for him." Frank smiled. "Said his daughter might kill him if she knew he asked LJ to get it for him. In his statement to Memphis PD, Luther said after LJ cut off the ties on his wrists, Luther told him to go downstairs and hide. So I rewrote that part of my report."

"So LJ's still a hero," Kelly said.

"Yes. LJ and Luther are quite a pair. I told Luther he probably saved my life. I had no shot at Zurik because Luther was behind him, in the line of fire."

"And Zurik kept shooting at you," Kelly said. "You're lucky to be alive."

Frank traced a finger down her cheek. "You worry too much. Forget Zurik. Let's go to bed and celebrate my survival."

———

1:30 PM – London

Alexei watched the boy study the chessboard. He looked so much like his father. Not just the black hair and stubborn jaw, his attitude. Single-minded focus and the will to win.

He still couldn't believe Nicolas was gone. His friend's last text had left him in tears. No casual bye-bye, no ciao. Just, farewell my faithful friend.

The utter finality of it.

An hour later he'd boarded a flight to O'Hare Airport. He met Nicky in their designated meeting spot outside a MacDonald's. Nicky was stoic, not crying but clearly devastated, a lost look in his eyes. Alexei embraced him and took him behind a nearby Departures board for privacy.

There, he gave Nicky a British passport. A legitimate one, borrowed from a friend with a son who looked enough like Nicky to get him through customs. "Act like I'm your father. Your name is Alex North and I am Donald North. Do you have any American currency?"

"Yes. Dad gave me two thousand dollars, but I spent some of it. There's eighteen hundred left."

"Give it to me. I will use it to buy our plane tickets."

The boy frowned. "Why?"

"You will not be needing American dollars for a long time." Alexei smiled. "Do not worry. Many years ago your father trusted me enough to give me access to his foreign bank accounts. You shall have all of it, every penny. No need for you to work for a long time."

Nicky gave him the money, albeit reluctantly. "Where are we going?"

"Toronto. After we pass through customs, I will buy tickets from a different airline and we will fly to London."

Their journey had gone smoothly, but other problems remained.

Urgent problems.

Nicky moved his white bishop and leaned back in his chair, confident of his move. When Alexei toppled his own king, Nicky frowned and said, "What? You concede so soon?"

"We'll play again tomorrow. I must go to work and we need to talk."

Alexei no longer worked for the Russian gang, other than the faux documents he still made for them, his specialty. His current business involved computer cleaning services, essential for those with clandestine business dealings.

But he still had friends in the gang.

One had told him a powerful man in New York City was looking for Nicky. Martina's father. Two weeks in London and Nicky had not once mentioned his mother. Was this normal?

Alexei made sure his own mother, now almost eighty, was well cared for in her dacha near Moscow. Twice a year he flew there to visit her. Perhaps it was best not to mention Martina. Or her father.

"You need to disappear for a while," he said, "Your new name will be Thomas White."

"No! I want my name to be Vladimir. Like my grandfather."

After a moment, Alexei said, "Okay. Your name will be Thomas V. White. The middle initial stands for Vladimir, to honor your ancestor who was born in Moscow. After I create your new documents, I will enroll you in a boarding school near London so you can continue your education."

"A school with a chess club?" Nicky asked.

"Yes, and I'm sure you will beat all your opponents. Your American accent will not allow you to pass as British, so I will create a US passport for you. The American company that employs your father sent him to London to work at the British branch of their company. That is your cover story."

For the first time, Nicky smiled. "Does that mean I'm an operative now?"

"Yes," he said, thinking *Why not if this makes him happy.*

"Tell me the man's name again. The detective who stalked my father and murdered him."

"Homicide Detective Frank Renzi."

"Someday I will kill this man."

The statement sent chills down his neck. So reminiscent of the words Nicolas Kozlovich had uttered many years ago after his father was assassinated.

I will find these men and kill them.

Less than two years later, Nicolas had made good on his vow.

Now his son sat across the chessboard from him. The same intensity, the same stubborn jaw and single-minded focus.

And the same will to win. Only twelve years old, but sure of himself, his dark eyes glittering with anger.

Someday I will kill this man.

Alexei had no doubt of it.

THE END

ABOUT THE AUTHOR

In her travels, Susan Fleet has worn many hats: trumpeter, college professor and music historian. While teaching at Brown University and Berklee College of Music, she discovered her dark side and began killing people. Fictionally, of course! In 2001 she moved to New Orleans, the setting for her award-winning crime thrillers featuring NOPD Homicide Detective Frank Renzi.

Susan now divides her time between Boston and the Big Easy. Although she still plays her trumpet every day, she spends most of her time dreaming up new ways to terrify and enthrall her readers.

The Premier Book Awards named her first novel, *Absolution,* Best Mystery-Suspense-Thriller of 2009. Feathered Quill Book Awards named *Natalie's Revenge* Best Mystery-Thriller of 2014.

Read more about Susan on her website: http://www.susanfleet.com

Susan says . . . If you're a Frank Renzi fan and would like an email about my next Frank Renzi crime thriller, please sign up at http://eepurl.com/ExkX9 I promise never to share your email.

And if you enjoyed *Foulshot*, I would greatly appreciate it if you'd post a review on the Amazon site where you purchased it. We authors depend upon reader reviews to spread the word about our books, and I would love to know what you thought of it!

Crime fiction by Susan Fleet

ABSOLUTION
DIVA
NATALIE'S REVENGE
JACKPOT
NATALIE'S ART
MISSING
NATALIE'S DILEMMA
SNIPER
PAYBACK
FOULSHOT

Praise for Susan Fleet's non-fiction

Women Who Dared: Maud Powell and Edna White

At a time when most women stayed home to raise children, violinist Maud Powell and trumpeter Edna White traveled the world, thrilling millions with their performances.

"Susan Fleet is an expert on female musicians who deserve wider recognition in the history of jazz and classical music." — Matt Morrell, Jazz at WGBH, Boston, MA

"Fleet's heroines were successful, artistic performers, attracting and enriching broad audiences." — Howard Mandel, music critic, *Billboard*

"Getting to know Edna White [inspired] Susan to learn about other talented yet forgotten women instrumentalists. This book will add to the important history of female musicians." -- Grady Harp, Vine Reviewer, Amazon

True Crime: Tales of Murder and Mayhem

DARK DEEDS: Serial killers, stalkers and domestic homicides
DARK DEEDS: Volume 2

"Well researched and well written. The inner world of these killers is vividly and psychologically portrayed." – Arthur Smukler, MD, psychiatrist

"Well researched true crime shorts. While many were familiar to me as an avid true crime fan, even the ones I knew about were written in a fresh and informative manner." – Amazon reader

ACKNOWLEDGMENTS

First, I confess that I'm a big NBA basketball fan and like Frank Renzi, I root for the Boston Celtics. However, the NBA referee in *Foulshot* is a fictional character, as are all the others.

Similarly, the High Roller Club is my invention and does not exist, but the Memphis train station does. To research my ending, I went to Memphis, stayed at a hotel on Elvis Presley Boulevard, and drove past the train station. However, the shops inside and the violent events that take place there are the product of my imagination.

In case you're wondering, while I was there, I visited Graceland, preserved as a tribute to Elvis Presley and his family. All visitors wore masks and we kept our distance, indicated by blue-suede shoe prints on the floor, when we toured the mansion and the grounds.

To research sports gamblers, betting terms and the history of sports betting, I consulted the book. *The Odds: One Season, Three Gamblers, and the Death of Their Las Vegas* by Chad Millman (2001).

Many thanks to my beta readers, who prefer to remain anonymous. Their insightful comments on early drafts were extremely helpful. My deepest thanks go to John Amaral, who proofread the manuscript and offered suggestions that greatly enhanced the book. His technical expertise and his knowledge of firearms, ammunition and weapons terminology were invaluable.

Heartfelt thanks to the NOPD homicide detective who listened to the premise of my story and answered my questions about police procedures. However, the events and actions in *Foulshot* are fictional. In some instances I have taken a certain amount of dramatic license. Any errors or inaccuracies are mine alone.

And finally, a huge thank-you to all my readers! Without your continued support, my work would be in vain. I get comments about my books from readers all over the world. I love reading them and always answer them, so feel free to send me an email: susan@susanfleet.com

www.ingramcontent.com/pod-product-compliance
Lightning Source LLC
Chambersburg PA
CBHW060855250626

47159CB00008B/2752